The Secret of the Storm Country

Grace Miller White

The Secret of the Storm Country

The present edition is a reproduction of previous publication of this classic work. Minor typographical errors may have been corrected without note, however, for an authentic reading experience the spelling, punctuation, and capitalization have been retained from the original text.

ISBN: 978-1-64799-252-1

CHAPTER I
THE SQUATTER FOLK

The lazy warmth of a May afternoon, the spring following Orn Skinner's release from Auburn Prison, was reflected in the attitudes of three men lounging on the shore in front of "Satisfied" Longman's shack. At their feet, the waters of Cayuga Lake dimpled under the rays of the western sun. Like a strip of burnished silver, the inlet wound its way through the swamp from the elevators and railroad stations near the foot of south hill. Across the lake rose the precipitous slopes of East Hill, tapestried in green, etched here and there by stretches of winding white road, and crowned by the buildings on the campus of Cornell University. Stretched from the foot of State Street on either side of the Lehigh Valley track lay the Silent City, its northern end spreading several miles up the west shore of the Lake. Its inhabitants were canalers, fishermen and hunters, uneducated, rough and superstitious. They built their little huts in the simplest manner out of packing boxes and rough lumber and roofed them with pieces of tin and sheet iron. Squatters they were appropriately named, because they paid no attention to land titles, but stuck their shacks wherever fancy indicated or convenience dictated. The people of the Silent City slept by day and went very quietly about their work under the cover of darkness, for the game laws compelled the fishermen to pull their nets at night, and the farmers' chickens were more easily caught, his fruit more easily picked when the sun was warming China.

Summers, their lives were comparatively free from hardships. Fish were plentiful and easy to take; the squatter women picked flowers and berries in the woods and sold them in the city and the men worked occasionally, as the fit struck them. But the winters were bitter and cruel. The countryside, buried deep in snow, made travel difficult. When the mercury shrank timidly into the bulb and fierce winds howled down the lake, the Silent City seemed, indeed, the Storm Country.

"I were up to the Graves' place yesterday, helpin' Professor Young," said Jake Brewer, the youngest and most active of the three men.

"Never had no use fer that duffer, Dominie Graves, myself," answered Longman. The speaker turned a serious face to the third member of the party. "Ner you nuther, eh, Orn?"

Orn Skinner was an enormous man, some six and a half feet tall. Two great humps on his shoulders accentuated the breadth and thickness of his chest while they tended to conceal the length of his arms. A few months before he'd been in the death house at Auburn. Through the efforts of Deforrest Young, the dean of the Law College at Cornell, he'd been pardoned and sent home.

The gigantic squatter removed his pipe from his mouth and smoothed the thready white beard, straggling over his chin.

"Nope, I hated 'im," he muttered. "He done me dirt 'nough. If it hadn't been fer Tess an' Lawyer Young, he'd a hung me sure."

1

"Ye didn't git the deed to yer shack land afore he died, did ye, Orn?" interrupted "Satisfied" Longman. "Tessibel told ma the preacher promised it to ye."

A moody expression settled in Skinner's eyes. "So he did promise it," he explained. "He writ Tess a letter. He said as how he were sorry for his meanness an' would give me the deed. But he didn't!"

A shrill voice calling his name brought "Satisfied" Longman to his feet, and he hobbled away toward the shack.

"'Pears like 'Satisfied' ain't got much strength any more," said Skinner. "He ain't been worth much of anythin' sence I got back."

"Him an' Ma Longman've failed a lot sence Myry an' Ezry died," agreed Jake. "An' no wonder! Them two didn't amount to much to my way o' thinkin', but their pa an' ma set considerable store by 'em ... Ben Letts were a bad 'un, too. It used to make me plumb ugly to see 'im botherin' Tess when ye was shet up, Orn, an' him all the time the daddy of Myry's brat."

"Yep, Ben were bad," agreed Skinner. "I were sure he done the shootin', but 'tweren't till Ezry swore he saw 'im that the lawyer could prove I didn't do it. But Tess says Myry loved Ben. Women air queer critters, ain't they?"

"Myry sure was," assented Brewer, thoughtfully. "In spite of Ezry's tellin' her, Ben'd most drowned him, an' done the killin' they was goin' to hang you fer, up she gits an' takes the brat an' goes off with Ben. It were the worst storm of the year. No wonder him, Myry an' their brat all was drowned."

Longman, coming out of the shack, overheard the last remark. The other two fell silent. After he'd sat down again, he dissipated their embarrassment by saying,

"But Tess says Myry air happy now 'cause she air got Ben. Fer myself, I dunno, though. But, if Myry air satisfied, me an' ma air satisfied, too."

The other two nodded in solemn sympathy. After a moment, Jake took out his pipe and filled it. Holding the lighted match above the bowl, he glanced at Skinner.

"Where air Tess?" he asked.

"She air up to Young's. He air learnin' her book stuff, an' his sister air helpin' the brat sing. It air astonishin' how the brat takes to it. Jest like a duck to water."

"Tess air awful smart," sighed Longman, "an' she air awful good, too. She sings fer ma 'most every day. I heard her only yesterday, somethin' 'bout New Jerusylem. Ma loves Tessibel's singin'."

Then, for perhaps the space of three minutes, they lapsed into silence. At length, Jake Brewer spoke,

"Be ye goin' to let her marry the Student Graves, Orn?" he asked.

"I dunno," Skinner muttered, "but I know this much, I don't like high born pups like him hangin' 'round my girl. 'Tain't fittin' an' I told Tess so!"

Orn knocked the ashes out of his pipe and rose slowly.

"Guess I'll be moseyin' 'long, pals," he smiled. "The brat'll be back 'fore long."

"Wait a minute, Orn," Longman broke in. "Ma's got some pork an'

2

beans she wants to send up to Mother Moll. She thought, mebbe, Tess'd take 'em to 'er."

"Sure, 'Satisfied,' I'll take 'em home an' the brat'll take 'em up the ravine next time she goes to the professor's."

"Mother Moll were the only one of us all," Jake told Skinner, while Longman was in the shack, "what stood by Tess. She allers says Tess air a goin' to surprise us all. She says as how the brat'll be rich an' have a fine home. I dunno—but old Moll do tell the future right good when she looks in the pot."

"She told the brat I were comin' home from Auburn," added Skinner, "when it looked certain I were goin' to hang."

Longman came out of the shack with a pan in his hands.

"Yep," he corroborated. "An' she told ma years ago she'd lose her brats in a storm. Old Moll air a wise woman, all right."

The dish of beans in his hand, the Bible-backed fisherman directed his steps toward his own home, some distance away beyond the ragged rocks.

The old squatter walked slowly. His health had broken in prison and his strength seemed hardly sufficient to move the big body. The path, an outcropping ledge of the precipitous cliff, was very narrow because of the unusually high level of the water in the lake. Picking his way slowly, he considered reminiscently the events which had almost destroyed him.

He recalled the long years of monotonous existence in the shack, the hard nights pulling the nets and the varied scrapes Tess had tumbled into. Then, suddenly, came the shooting of the game keeper, his own arrest, trial and conviction. The white glare of hateful publicity had been thrown, without warning, upon him and his motherless brat. He'd been torn away from his quiet haunts at the lake side and shut up in the narrow confines of a fetid cell. The enforced separation from his daughter, at the critical period between girl and womanhood, had left her alone in the shanty and exposed her to countless perils and hardships. Unmitigated calamities, especially the long imprisonment, they had seemed at the time, but the event proved otherwise.

Friends had arisen and helped him establish his innocence and win his pardon. The responsibilities thrown upon the squatter girl had been met with love and courage and had disciplined her high temper and awakened her ambition. The dirt and disorder that had formerly obtained in the shack had disappeared. Her housewifely arts had transformed the hut into a comfortable home, rough to be sure, small and inadequate, but immaculate and satisfactory.

The shanty stood on a little point of land projecting into the lake. Huge weeping willows shrouded it from the sun in summer. They mourned and murmured of the past, when the breezes of morning and evening stirred their whispering leaves. Their bare limbs thrashed and pounded the tin roof when the storm winds tore down the lake. In front and to one side, Tessibel's new privet hedge shone a dark, dusky green, and the flower beds were beginning to show orderly life through the blackish mold. The shack itself was rather more pretentious than most of the squatter shanties. It had two rooms and was thoroughly battened against the storms.

3

Coming into the path, Orn met his daughter and went with her to the house.

The greatest change the year had brought was in the girl herself. She had ripened into the early maturity common to the squatter woman. She was no longer the red-haired tatterdemalion who had romped over the rocks and quarreled with the boys of the Silent City. Her tom-boy days, amid the ceaseless struggles against the hardships of the Storm Country, gave to her slender body strength and lent to it poise and grace. Bright brown eyes lighted by loving intelligence illumined her face, tanned by sun and wind, but very sweet and winsome, especially when the curving red lips melted into a smile. A profusion of burnished red curls, falling about her shoulders almost to her hips, completed the vivid picture. Tess of the Storm Country, the animate expression of the joy and beauty of the lake side in spring, was the boast of the Silent City.

Late that same night, Tessibel lay asleep in the front room of the shanty. Four miles to the south, Ithaca, too, slept,—the wholesome sleep of a small country town, while Cayuga Lake gleamed and glistened in the moonlight, as if fairies were tumbling it with powdered fingers. Above both town and span of water, Cornell University loomed darkly on the hill, the natural skyline sharply cut by its towers and spires.

An unusual sound awakened her. She lifted her lids and glanced about drowsily, then propped herself on one elbow. Her sleep-laden eyes fell upon the white light slanting across the rough shanty floor. Suddenly, like a dark ghost, a shadow darted into it—the shadow of a human head.

At the first glimpse at it, Tessibel looked cautiously toward the window, and there, as in a frame, was a face—a man's face. Tess dropped on her pillow. For possibly two minutes, she lay quietly waiting, while the shadow moved curiously to and fro on the floor. Twice the head disappeared, and as suddenly returned, poised a moment, then, like an image moving across a screen, was gone. Instantly Tess sat straight up in bed. Perhaps one of the squatters needed her. She crept to the floor, yawning, tiptoed to the door, and unbarred it. Without pausing to cover her feet, she stepped outside, the fresh scent of May blossoms sweeping sweet to her nostrils. The warm night-wind, full of elusive odors, brushed her face like thready cobwebs, that broke at her touch, only to caress her anew.

Midnight held no fear for Tessibel, for she loved every living creature, those traveling by day being no dearer than those flying by night. She felt no deeper thrills for the bright-winged birds singing in the sun than for yonder owl who screeched at her, now, from the weeping willow tree.

After picking her way to the front of the shanty, she made a tour of the house and encircled the mud cellar, calling softly the while. No one appeared; no voice, either of friend or stranger, answered the persuasive importunity of Tessibel. But, after she was again in the doorway, she heard north of the shanty the crackling of twigs as if some stealthy animal were crawling over them. If there were an intruder, he'd gone, and the girl, satisfied, went back into the house and once more lay down to sleep.

4

When she woke again, Daddy Skinner was moving softly near the stove, kindling the fire, and Tessibel lay in languid silence. She watched him yearningly until he felt her gaze and looked at her. His twisted smile of greeting brought an exclamation of love from the girl. All the inhabitants of the Silent City knew this crippled old man could play on the emotions of his lovely young daughter as the morning sun plays upon the sensibilities of the lark. How she adored him, in spite of his great humps and his now hobbling legs!

Soon, her father went to the lake for a pail of water, and she sprang from the cot and dressed hastily.

CHAPTER II
THE COMING OF ANDY BISHOP

Later in the forenoon, when Tessibel returned home from an errand to Kennedys', she found Daddy Skinner on the bench at the side of the shanty, one horny hand clutching the bowl of a pipe in which the ashes were dead. It took but one sharp glance from the red-brown eyes for Tess to note that his face was white, almost grey; she saw, too, with a quiver of loving sympathy, that his lower lip hung away from his dark teeth as though he suffered. She sprang toward him, and dropped to her knees, at his side.

"Daddy Skinner!" she exclaimed. "Daddy Skinner, ye're sick! Ye're sick, darlin'!... Tell me, Daddy, what air the matter? Tell Tessibel."

She laid her hand tenderly on his chest. His heart was beating a heavy tattoo against the blue gingham shirt.

"Ye hurt here?" she queried breathlessly.

The pipe dropped to the soft sand, and Skinner's crooked fingers fell upon the profusion of red curls. Then he slowly tilted up her face.

"Yep, I hurt in there!" he muttered brokenly.

And as ashen and more ashen grew the wrinkled old countenance, Tessibel cried out sharply in protest.

"Why, Daddy, what d'ye mean by yer heart's hurtin' ye?... What do ye mean, Daddy?... I thought the doctor'd fixed yer heart so it wouldn't pain ye no more."

The man considered the appealing young face an instant.

"I want to talk to ye about somethin'," said he, presently, "and I know ye'll never tell anythin' Daddy tells ye."

With a little shake of her head that set the tawny curls a-tremble, Tessibel squatted back on her feet.

5

"'Course I won't tell nobody, but if ye've got a pain in yer heart, daddy, the doctor—"

"I don't need no doctor, brat. I jest—jest got to talk to ye, that air all."

A slender girlish figure cuddled between Daddy Skinner's knees, and warm young lips met his. Never had Tess seen him look just that way, not even when he had been taken from her to prison. The expression on his face was hopeless, forlornly hopeless, and to wait until he began to speak took all the patience the eager girl-soul could muster.

"Brat, dear," he sighed at length, "I ain't needin' to tell ye again what I went through in Auburn, hev I?"

Brown eyes, frightened and fascinated, sought and found the faded greys.

"'Course not, Daddy Skinner! But what fer air ye talkin' about Auburn Prison?... Ye promised me, Daddy, ye'd forgit all about them days, an' now what're ye rememberin' 'em fer?"

Skinner's face blanched, and drops of sweat formed in the spaces behind his ears and trickled in little streams down his neck.

"I got to remember 'em, child," he groaned.

"What fer I want to know? Ye'd best make a hustle an' tell me or, in a minute, I'll be gettin' awful mad."

The pleading, sorrowful face belied the threat, and a pair of red lips touched Skinner's hand between almost every word.

"Do ye bring to mind my tellin' ye about any of the fellers up there, Tessibel?" came at length from the man's shaking lips.

Tess stroked his arm lovingly.

"Sure, Daddy, I remember 'bout lots of 'em, an' how good they be, an' how kind, an' how none of 'em be guilty."

"Ye bet none of 'em be guilty," muttered Daddy Skinner. "Nobody air ever guilty who gets in jail.... Folks be mostly guilty that air out o' prison to my mind."

"That air true, Daddy Skinner," she assented, smiling. "Sure it air true, but it ain't no good reason fer you to be yappin' 'bout Auburn, air it?... Now git that look out of yer eyes, an' tell Tessibel what air troublin' ye!"

But Daddy Skinner's grave old face still kept its set expression. The haunted look, born in his eyes in the Ithaca Jail, had returned after all these happy months. Tess was frantic with apprehension and dread.

"Ye know well's ye're born, Daddy, nobody can hurt ye," she told him strenuously. "Ye've got Tessibel, and ye've got—" She was about to say, "Frederick," but substituted, "Professor Young."

The girl lovingly slipped her fingers over her father's heavy hand and drew it from her curls.

"Ye're goin' to peel it off to me now, ain't ye?" she coaxed.

"Let's go inside the shanty," said the fisherman, in a thick voice.

With the door closed and barred, the father and daughter sat for some time in troubled silence.

"I asked if ye remembered some of my pals in Auburn Prison, an' ye said ye did, didn't ye, Tessibel?" asked Skinner, suddenly.

6

Tess gave an impatient twist of her shoulders.

"An' I told ye I did, Daddy," she replied. "'Course I do. I ain't never forgot nobody who were good to you, honey."

"An' ye're pretty well satisfied, ain't ye, brat, most of 'em there air innercent?"

"Ye bet, Daddy darlin', I air that!"

"Well, what if one of them men who were good to yer old father'd come an' ask ye to do somethin' for 'im?"

With an upward movement of her head, Tessibel scrambled to her feet.

"Why, I'd help 'im!" she cried in one short, quick breath. "I'd help 'im; 'course I would."

"An' ye'd always keep it a secret?"

"Keep what a secret?"

Daddy Skinner's face grew furtive with fear.

"Why—well now, s'posin' Andy Bishop—ye remember Andy, the little man I told ye about, the weenty, little dwarf who squatted near Glenwood?"

Tess nodded, and the fisherman went on, hesitant.

"He—were accused—of murderin'—"

"Waldstricker—Ebenezer Waldstricker's father?" interjected Tess. "Sure, I remember!" Her eyes widened in anxiety. "Andy were sent up there fer all his life, weren't he? An' weren't he the one Sandy Letts swore agin?... 'Satisfied' Longman says Waldstricker give Sandy money for tellin' the jury what he did."

"Like as not," answered Skinner. "Anyhow, Bishop were there fer life! He air been there five years a innercent man.... My God, Auburn fer five years!"

The last four words were wailed forth, the look of hopeless horror deepening in his old eyes. Then he threw back his shoulders and spoke directly to Tess.

"Well, what if he skipped out o' jail, an' what if he'd come here an' say, 'Kid, 'cause what I done fer yer dad, now you do somethin' fer me!'"

Tess was trembling with excitement as she stood before her father. The generosity of her loving nature instinctively responded to his apparent need. She was instantly eager to show her love and loyalty.

"I'd do it, Daddy!" she exploded. "I'd do it quick!"

"But what if—if—if—if—it made ye lots of trouble an'—an'—mebbe some of yer friends—if they found it out—wouldn't think 'twere right?"

A queer, obstinate expression lived a moment in the girl's eyes. Then she smiled.

"I ain't got no friends who'd say it were wrong to help somebody what'd helped my darlin' old daddy."

Skinner bent his heavy brows in a troubled frown over stern eyes.

"But ye couldn't tell yer friends about it, kid," he cautioned.

A mist shone around the girl's thick lashes.

"Daddy, ye know I never blat things I hadn't ought to.... Slide yer arms 'round yer brat's neck, look 'er straight in the eye, an' tell 'er 'bout Andy; an' if she can help, she sure will."

A noise in the vicinity of the cot gave Tessibel an involuntary start. She turned her head slowly and saw two feet protruding from under her bed. Clinging to Daddy Skinner, she watched, with widening lids, a dwarfed figure crawl slowly into full view, and Tess found herself staring into a pair of beautiful, boyish, blue eyes.

A slow smile broke over the dwarf's face.

"Yer brat's the right sort, Orn," he cried, in the sweetest tenor voice Tess ever heard. "Ye don't need to make her promise no more.... Her word air good's God's law."

"So it air, Andy," replied Orn. "Tessibel, this air my friend, Andy Bishop, an' he were a good pal, as good as any man ever had."

For one single, tensely-strung moment, Tessibel contemplated the ugly little figure and the upraised, appealing face. Then as a sudden sense of protection spurred her to immediate action, she sent back a welcoming smile. Two or three quick steps took her to the dwarf's side.

"I air going' to help ye, Andy," she announced brokenly. "Ye was in prison fer life, wasn't ye, huh?"

"Yep, an'—an' I broke out, kid.... An' I ain't able to tell how I done it."

"Oh, never mind that!" soothed Tessibel. "Ye was lookin' in the window last night, wasn't ye?"

The dwarf rolled his eyes at the squatter, then back to the girl.

"Yep, that were me, but I didn't do no murder, brat; that air the main thing an' Sandy Letts lied when he told the jury I done it."

"He said as how ye gunned Ebenezer Waldstricker's father, eh?" Tess interrupted. "Eb air the richest man in Ithaca, an' him an' his sister air been to Europe, but they come back early in the spring. I see 'em every Sunday at Hayt's when I go there to sing. He air goin' to marry Mr. Young's sister, Helen, an' he air gittin' some pink peach when he gets her, ye can bet on that."

"But he'll get me by my neck if he can," lamented the dwarf, in despair. "Waldstricker air a mean duffer—a mighty mean duffer."

"He air awful religious," reflected Tess, soberly. "I s'posed he were awful good."

The dwarf made a gesture of disgust with his hand.

"Well, good or bad, I never killed his daddy," he returned. "I saw Owen Bennett when he done it, but him an' Sandy socked it off on me. I got life an' Owen got ten years.... There ain't no makin' him own up he done it, air there, Orn?"

"Nope," mumbled the fisherman. "Most men won't take life sentence by confessin' when by keepin' still they c'n git off with ten years."

"Mr. Waldstricker air a awful big, handsome lookin' man," asserted Tess, thoughtfully. "Folks says he air good to the poor, too. He air the biggest, fattest, elegantest elder in our church."

Andy flipped his fingers in the air and summed up what he thought of the last statement in five words.

"Shucks! That fer the church," mocked he.

"It air just like Sandy Letts to lie about ye," remarked Tess, changing the subject abruptly. "There ain't a hatefuller man in the Silent City 'n him. He makes a pile of money, though.... Once last fall he dragged the lake fer two students an' got a thousand apiece fer handin' 'em over to their folks, dead."

"He'd git five thousand fer handin' me over to Waldstricker, alive," replied Andy, solemnly. "I wouldn't a gone up if 't 'adn't been fer him. He can lie faster'n a horse can trot."

Heaving a deep sigh, Orn turned to his daughter.

"What we goin' to do with my pal, Tess?" he asked. "He's got to keep out of sight of folks.... Eb Waldstricker's five thousand bucks fer gettin' 'im back to Auburn will be settin' men like Sandy flyin' all over the state."

The dwarf shivered from the top of his head to the soles of his feet.

"I don't want 'em to git me," he whimpered disconsolately. "Ye won't let 'em git me, will ye, Orn?... Will ye, kid?"

Tess cheered the dwarf's despairing mood by a reassuring smile and confident nods of the shining curls.

"Nope," she promptly promised.

And, "Nope," repeated Orn, grimly. "Git back under the bed, now, old man. Any minute Sandy might be comin' in. Ye can't depend on that squatter. He'd steal the pennies off'n his dead mammy's eyes."

As was her habit when thinking, Tess threaded her fingers through several red curls, while her eyes followed Andy Bishop crawling feet first under her cot.

"I bet ye didn't do nothin' wicked, ye poor little shaver," she remarked.

"Bet I didn't do no Waldstricker murder," answered the dwarf.

"I know where I can hide 'im," she then said, with a satisfied smile. "I'll fix up the garret fer 'im. 'Tain't very big, but no one but me ever goes up there. You, there, under the bed, ye ain't 'fraid of bats or owls, air ye?"

"Nope," came forth a sweet voice. "I ain't 'fraid of nothin' nor nobody but Ed Waldstricker and Sandy Letts."

Tess giggled in glee.

"Well, they nuther one of 'em gits in my garret if I see 'em first," said she, "an' the owls air as tame as cats, an' 'll be company when ye're lonely nights. Deacon air the speckled one an' he loves every inch of Daddy an' me. If ye're good to 'im, he'll love you, too, Andy." Turning to her father, "The person what'll help Andy air Professor Young, I bet."

Daddy Skinner's face fell perceptibly, and two long lines marked off the sides of his nose.

"Who's he?" came from under the bed in a stifled breath.

"He air a awful nice man," explained Tess. "He lives in Graves' old place on the hill, an' he learns me new things out of books every day.... His sister's teachin' me to sew, too. I told ye she air goin' to marry—"

"Tessibel," interrupted Skinner, gravely fearful. "Ye said jest now Waldstricker were a goin' to marry Young's sister. That makes them two families kinda like one. Ye bet Young'd stand by his sister's man.... See?... Besides that, Young air a lawyer, an' if ye tell 'im about Andy, it'll sure be 'is duty to pinch 'im an' put 'im back where he were."

"He helped you once, Daddy!" the girl rebuked him.

"But I were in jail all the time, don't ye see the difference, brat?... Till

9

'twere proved Ben Letts done the murder, I were kept in jail, too, an' they'll put Andy back if ye say anythin' to Young 'bout it."

"They sure will," came the dwarf's sobbing tones.

Tessibel sighed.

"Well, us uns'll have to keep our clacks shut 'bout 'is bein' here, then," she acquiesced, "an'—an'—Andy'll have to keep in the garret till the man in Auburn coughs up, that air all, huh?... He can come down sometimes when it air a rainin' hard or dark nights when there ain't nobody around, an'—an'—darlin', ye can offen chat with 'im when I air outside watchin' fer folks.... Now, can't ye, Daddy?"

The young speaker went close to her father, smiling. She wanted to chase that hunted look from his eyes, to make him feel a little more secure about his prison friend.

"Please don't be lookin' like that, sweety," she pleaded. "Ye're just like ye was goin' dead.... I tell ye nobody'll hurt the poor little feller in the garret.... I'll see to that.... I'll fix it up all comfy fer 'im."

With this idea of future protection for the little man, Tessibel began to reconstruct the shanty. Dark curtains were hung at the square little windows, for it was quite a daily occurrence for Sandy Letts to peek through them before entering the door. Tessibel didn't wish to shut out the sunshine and moonbeams, but then there was Andy Bishop to think of, and Andy already had a warmer place in the squatter girl's heart than even the sun or moon. Tessibel was beginning to love him, not only because he'd been a friend to Daddy, but on his own account, because he was a soul in torment and needed her.

It took quite three hours to arrange the garret for the dwarf's occupancy. There were many pieces of fishing tackle to be sorted and hung in the kitchen rafters. The nuts that had been spread out on the floor to dry, now had to be gathered in sacks and stored in the mud cellar. The cobwebs must come down, and a cotton tick filled with new, fresh straw to be put in the garret. It was about three o'clock when Tessibel ushered the little man up the ladder and displayed the clean attic.

"'Tain't high 'nough fer me to stand up in," she told him, "but ye'll get along all right, an' I air goin' to fix ye somethin' so ye can see to read.... Can ye read?"

"Sure, I can read." Andy's voice rang with pride. "My ma, she's dead now, she learned me how, she did!"

"Then I'll get ye lots of books," replied Tess, "an' ye'd best always keep hid less'n I let ye down, 'cause Sandy might catch onto yer bein' here. Waldstricker's money'll set loose a lot of sneaks like him lookin' fer ye!"

Late that afternoon the dwarf ate his first meal in the garret, and Tessibel and Orn Skinner ate theirs at the table, but the conversation of the father and daughter intermingled now and then with a soft statement or a question from above, and there was happiness in the Skinner hut.

As soon as they finished supper, Tess went to the foot of the ladder and called softly.

"I air goin' to tell ye somethin', Andy,—ye listenin'?"

"Yep, brat. Sure, I air listenin'."

"I air a goin' somewheres to find out somethin'," announced the girl mysteriously. "Mebbe when I get back I'll tell ye what ye'll like to hear.... Ye'll stay hid, won't ye?"

"Sure so," agreed Andy.

After bending to kiss her father affectionately, the girl said to him,

"Now, Daddy, I air goin' out a little while, an' you two be awful careful how loud ye talk.... Somebody might hear ye!"

And for a short moment after the girl had gone there was silence in the shack. Then a prolonged sigh drifted from the garret.

"My God, Orn, but she air a fine young thing fer ye to be fatherin', huh? Ain't she?"

Andy's voice, though but little more than a whisper, expressed his wonder and admiration.

"God's best," muttered Orn, and once more they lapsed into the companionable silence of good friends.

CHAPTER III
TESSIBEL MEETS WALDSTRICKER

The shanty door closed behind Tessibel, and her hand still on the knob, she hesitated a moment before starting for Mother Moll's. The girl had kept her promise of the year before, for every week she had caught and cleaned a mess of fish and carried them up the ravine to the woman's shanty. But today, Tess wanted to consult the seeress about Andy. She believed implicitly in the fortune-pot. Hadn't the old, old hag told her, long ago, when Daddy Skinner was in prison, that the state couldn't hurt him, and other things, too?

Turning into the lane up the hill, she met Sandy Letts carrying his drag and a great coil of rope.

"Hello, kid," he greeted her. "How air yer Daddy?"

He eased his load to the ground and straightened up, slowly stretched his mighty arms, and shrugged the stiffness out of his powerful shoulders. Sandy and his burden filled most of the path.

Tess, desiring to avoid contact with him, stopped a few paces away.

"Daddy ain't so well these days, Sandy," she answered. "His heart hurts 'im."

"Ain't that too bad?" the man sympathized. "But, then, brat, yer daddy ain't so young as he were once. Reckon he air not long fer this world. When

11

yer Daddy croaks, what'll you do, Tess? Ye'll need a home. Ye ought to be gettin' a man."

The squatter'd stepped forward directly in front of her while he was urging his suit.

"My daddy ain't old an' he ain't goin' to die, uther," flared Tess, an angry light in her brown eyes. Oh, how she loathed and hated this fellow who blocked her way! "You shan't say such things about my daddy! I don't want any man but 'im." Noting his unshaven cheeks, loose hanging lips, the lips and his large irregular teeth discolored with tobacco, the girl drew back with a gesture of instinctive repulsion. "I wouldn't take you anyway."

Instead of answering her, the squatter placed his great hands upon her shoulders, and holding her thus at arm's length, looked down at her. Her straight young figure, glowing face, and flaming eyes under the ruddy aureole of her hair made a picture of grace, beauty and passion that would have fascinated a more fastidious observer than Sandy Letts.

"God, girl, but ye air a beauty!" he cried, enraptured.

Tessibel's struggles to get away from the grip of the heavy hands aroused the evil passions of the man's nature into insistent activity.

"Here, brat, give yer man a kiss," he commanded, and at the words, his hands slipped from her shoulders, and his strong arms began to close around her body. His face was so close she had to force her hand in between his lips and hers. Then she made a desperate struggle. Rearing the red head backward, she succeeded only in freeing herself partially.

"You let me go, you Sandy!" she cried out sharply. "I'll tell my Daddy on you. Let me go!"

Then she went at him, kicking his shins with her feet, poking him with her knees, and gouging his eyes and digging his face with her nails. As well might Sandy try to make love to a cornered wildcat. He threw her from him, and Tess, springing up, uninjured, raced up the hill. Sandy's words, broken by fierce oaths, overtook her,

"You just wait! I'll tame ye yet, ye devilish brat, ye!"

At the top of the lane, Tess stopped to get breath. The familiar sounds of the early summer evening assailed her ears. The narrow lake shone in the clear light of the dying day like a broad strip of silver set in the bosom of the hills. Her eyes rejoiced in its calm beauty, and a feeling of peace and security grew in her thought.

Tess was about to cross the ravine when a step behind her caused her to turn. Ebenezer Waldstricker, riding whip in hand, was coming toward her. At his unexpected appearance, the blood fled from her face, leaving her quite pale and trembling. This was the man who was seeking Andy Bishop as at one time Dominie Graves had sought her father. How lordly he seemed, looking down upon her unsmilingly from his great height. Arrogantly he surveyed her from head to foot.

"You're the little church singer, aren't you?" he questioned after a while.

Tess noticed with fascination that one corner of his mouth curled up as if smiling, while the other was rigidly drawn down. She'd never seen an expression just like that before.

"Yep," she murmured, dropping her lids.

"Where are you going?" asked the man, tersely.

Tess glanced about. She wanted to turn and run, anywhere to escape from the brilliant dark eyes and the unmatched lips.

"I were goin' to see Mother Moll," she stammered, slowly. "She lives over there in the gully." She hesitated, pointing to Moll's shack. "Sometimes she reads out of the fortune-pot fer me."

Waldstricker glanced first at the little hut, then back at Tess.

"You don't mean you have faith in witchcraft?" he ejaculated, incredulously. "Why, girl, that's positively against the Bible commandments."

"Air it? Well I swan!" She nodded her head as though digesting a new idea. "Anyway, Mother Moll always tells me the truth. She can see things comin' years and years."

Waldstricker contemplated the grave young face for an instant, noting involuntarily the abundance and beauty of the wind-blown hair. He turned about on the path.

"I shall go with you," he said.

Her desire to forbid the proposed visit, struggling with her awe of the powerful man at her side, confused her. She couldn't think clearly. She twisted her fingers into her red curls.

"I'd ruther ye wouldn't," she explained. "Ma Moll hates strangers worser'n she does the old nick!"

Waldstricker ignored the girl's speech except that the frown deepened on his brow.

"Nevertheless I'm going," he returned, sternly. "I can't realize that God-fearing men and women have such iniquity among them. Come on; I'll go with you!"

Tess would gladly have deferred her visit until another day, and returned home, but she feared he'd follow her there. Here was a man of whom she was heartily afraid, and as she dared not defy him, she obediently walked across the gully bridge, and hurried along the path.

Then she paused, looking at Mother Moll's shack, snuggled in a jut in the ravine. It was quite close now. Tess knew the witch was at home, for a thin line of smoke drifted zig-zag from the toppling chimney.

She looked back and found Waldstricker eyeing her. She noted both corners of his lips were down now.

"I came from Ithaca purposely to see you and your father," said he.

Tess was so startled she took two sudden steps backward.

"My daddy ain't very well!" she exclaimed, nervously. "He don't like strange folks comin' around, Daddy don't."

Waldstricker shrugged his shoulders indifferently.

"However, I must see him," he responded.

Tessibel felt a surging anger against this man. He had the same imperious bearing she remembered in Dominie Graves.

"What fer? What d'ye want to see Daddy fer?" Her voice was compelling.

13

"About a matter that may make him a lot of money," the man explained, pompously. "When may I come?"

She considered a moment before replying. This put a different face on the matter.

"Could ye come tomorrow?" she demanded finally.

"Yes, at two, then. Tell your father, please."

"All right," muttered Tess.

Waldstricker's whip cut a cluster of wild flowers and nipped clean the stems of their upraised heads.

"Oh!" cried Tess, sharply, hurt to the quick.

As if reading her thoughts, he retorted, "A flower hasn't a soul, so what does it matter?"

Tess turned tear-dimmed eyes from him to Mother Moll's shack. Shocked at his brutality, his arrogant cruelty to the flowers she cherished so tenderly left her dumb. That his statement was false, she knew. To her the flowers expressed Love's sweetness and beauty, but she couldn't explain her faith to this haughty, dictatorial millionaire at her side.

She was all of a tremble as she mounted the narrow shanty steps.

An aged voice croaked, "Come in," in response to her knock. Before pulling the latch string, Tessibel paused and said to Waldstricker,

"Wait a minute! I'll go first, an' tell Mother Moll you're here."

She crossed the threshold and saw the old woman swaying to and fro in a wooden rocker.

"It air Tessibel, Mother Moll," she said gently. "I want to see what's in the pot."

Mother Moll smiled a withered, joyous smile.

"Come in, my pretty," she clacked. "Yer Moll's allers glad to see yer shinin' eyes. Come in, my love."

Tess advanced into the kitchen.

"That duffer Waldstricker's come along with me," she told her in a low tone.

The old woman struggled to her feet with the aid of her cane. Her watery eyes glared at the tall man in the doorway, and he as angrily stared back at her. The woman hobbled two steps forward.

"If ye've come for me to tell ye somethin', it won't be nothin' very pleasant," she growled at him. "Git me the pot, brat, dear!"

Tessibel went to the grate and lifted the iron kettle from the fire. It was steaming hot, and she brought it over, placing it at the woman's feet.

"Set down," the hag commanded Waldstricker. "I'll tell ye what's doin' in the pot, an' then git out! I hate ye!"

Waldstricker, with the peculiar down twist of his mouth, glanced darkly at Tessibel, but the girl's unresponsive, serious face turned his attention again to the witch.

"You're a wicked old woman," he said grimly. "The county should care for such as you."

But Mother Moll did not catch his words. She was crooning over the pot inarticulately. The seams in the skin around her eyes netted together, almost

14

closing the flaming red lids. Through the narrow slits she was following the steam as it rose and disappeared in the air. Then slowly her finger began to trace shadow outlines in and about the pot.

"Mister, I see ye crowin' like a barnyard cock," she croaked, "and ye think ye're awful smart and awful rich. An' so ye be, but some day—" She stopped, sank back, then looked again into the steaming kettle. "I see a wee leetle man like this—" She raised the cane beside her, and Waldstricker, startled, leaned nearer the ragged grey head. "I see ye huntin' the leetle man— like a dog hunts a rat."

"Yes, yes!" from Waldstricker, "and what else, woman?"

Lowering her stick again to the floor, Mother Moll rested her weight upon its crooked handle and for a time muttered over the pot with raven hoarseness.

"Ye think ye're smart, but ye ain't as smart as ye think ye air. The leetle man sets on yer head—"

The hag paused, cracked forth a gurgling scream, then proceeded. "He sets on yer head and lays on yer heart, an' with all yer money, ye can't find 'im."

"I will!" gritted Waldstricker through his teeth, now, in spite of himself, intensely interested in the old woman's revelations.

"Ye won't," rapped out the seeress. "Not till it air too late. I see—I see—" Lifting one hand, the bony old finger made rapid gyrations above the pot.

"What do you see?" burst forth the man impatiently.

"Hair," cried Mother Moll, swaying nearer him, "hair stranglin' yer throat till ye can't speak, curls weavin' round yer neck like a hangman's rope."

Waldstricker glanced backward at the squatter girl. She stood in rigid silence, listening intently. Her hair, copper-colored in the light from the window at her side, framed in its shining curls a face rapt and absorbed. Waldstricker leaned forward again, the better to see the rising steam wraiths.

"I see all ye love best sufferin'." Letting the cane fall clattering to the floor, Mother Moll continued, doubled-fists outstretched to the man before her. "I see the shadow of shame gathering about ye, I see a girl—a little girl— yer sister—holdin' out her hands pleadin' to some other man—" Again the aged voice trailed into that chattering laugh. "An' I air seein' somethin' else." The old woman rubbed the palms of her horny hands together and pitched forward on her toes. She lifted her shaking, wizened face and thrust it so near the man that he drew back with a rough ejaculation. Then smiling a wide, toothless smile, she laid her finger on her lips. Drawing it away again, she mumbled.

"Hair stranglin' 'em both, same as you, long curls like snakes stranglin' all of ye. God! what hair!"

Waldstricker, with flashing eyes, suddenly got to his feet.

"Come out of here," he ordered Tess, roughly. "That hateful hag! The hateful wicked old woman!"

A wild, exultant yell left Mother Moll's lips.

"Yep, get out o' here!" she shrieked. "Get out quick, both of ye! Yer lives'll twine like this, an' this, an' this." Tensely she locked together her bony

15

fingers. "An' hair'll strangle ye, wretched man, an' may ye never breathe a fine breath after it touches yer proud throat!"

Moved by a kind of superstitious horror of the prophecies of the old witch, Waldstricker pushed her roughly aside, seized Tess by the arm and dragged her out of the house. On the path he let her go and stood transfixed, as though the length and abundance of the red curls, falling in disordered confusion to her hips, fascinated him. Then he lifted his great shoulders, and a tense breath slipped through his teeth.

"What an awful old woman!" he flung out disgusted. "If there's any power in law or money, I'll root her out of that shanty as I will the rest of her tribe."

Tess was thoroughly frightened. His ruthless roughness hurt her and his threats against Mother Moll and the squatters terrified her. Would he try and root Daddy Skinner and herself from their shanty? No, he couldn't! He couldn't! Neither would his long, powerful hands place their grip upon the life of the dwarf. Mother Moll had said so, and she believed—oh, how she believed it!

Waldstricker started to speak again, but unable to bear longer the cruel corner-curl of his lips, Tess of the Storm Country turned and fled swift-footed away toward the lake. The man watched the flying figure bounding along toward the span of blue water. Then with another flip of his whip, which struck the heads from the flower stems, he wheeled about and walked swiftly up the hill.

CHAPTER IV
TESS AND FREDERICK

Tessibel left Waldstricker with but one idea buzzing in her active brain; to reach Daddy Skinner—to tell him all that had just happened. She fled around the mud cellar and opened the door with swift-coming breath. When she entered the kitchen, her father was seated on her cot. He raised his eyes and greeted her.

"Daddy," panted the girl, closing the door, "I jest seen Waldstricker an' he air a comin' down here tomorrow. I don't know what he wants, but Andy mustn't come out of the garret, not fer anythin'. An', Daddy!" She paused with a sudden sob, "He says he air a goin' to root Mother Moll off'n her place. But don't let 'im turn us out of our shanty, will ye, Daddy?"

16

"Nope," answered Skinner, grimly. "I ain't held it all these years to let it go now fer a duffer like him."

"An', Daddy dear," blurted Tess, "Mother Moll told old Waldstricker's fortune out of the pot, an' she says as how he ain't never goin' to git Andy back to Auburn till it air too late, even if he uses up all the money he air got. What d'ye think o' that?"

A little groan came from the garret. It no sooner fell on Tessibel's ears than she scurried, nimble-footed, up the ladder. Poking her head through the hole in the ceiling, she peered around. It was very dark, and even straining her eyes, she could see nothing.

"Andy!" she whispered. "Andy, dear!"

"I air here, kid," murmured the dwarf from a dark corner.

"Don't be worrin'," encouraged Tess, softly. "I air begun to love ye, Andy, an' you bet nobody durst touch ye. Whatever ye hear, be mum. Daddy and me'll take care of ye, an' God will too."

Later she left the shanty in deep thought, and by the time she had wended her way to the ragged rocks to meet Frederick Graves, she had uttered many tense little prayers for the suffering dwarf in her attic.

These rocks were a bower of delight to the sentimental girl. It was here in the gloom that in every expression of nature Tess heard Frederick's voice; his clear tones came swiftly on the wings of the wind, in the sonorous clap of the chimes as they spread their chant over the lake.

She was now seated on a broad, grey rock-slab, bending slightly forward, listening for her lover's step.

"Frederick!" she breathed in delight as a tall form loomed from the shadowy path.

In another moment she felt herself gathered into strong arms, and for a while the boy and girl were silent in their mutual happiness. The lakeside was quiet except for the sound of the tumbling waves and the intermittent rumble of a train on the tracks above.

Now and then, far back in the forest, an owl whoo-whooed in croaking tones, and in a nearby tree a family of baby birds twittered continuously in their sleep.

All the daisies in the meadows, all the nodding buttercups in the fields, seemed to be blossoming in Tessibel's heart at one time. She was in Frederick's arms, and the whole world could offer her nothing more.

"Tessibel, my little love," began Frederick, between caresses, "you remember what I begged you to consent to early in the spring?"

Tess made a movement to sit up.

"Ye mean—?" she stammered, confused.

Frederick drew her close.

"I want you to marry me right away," he murmured, entreatingly.

The words were whispered in passionate sighing out of the darkness into her ear. Tess drew back a little.

"Right away?" she repeated, gulping. "What do ye mean by right away, darlin'?... Now?"

Again strong arms evidenced strong affection.

"Yes—now," answered Frederick, earnestly. "You must! You must!... I can't be happy unless you do—Oh, Tessibel! Won't you, Tess?"

Never had anything thrilled her as his halting insistence.

"An' Daddy Skinner—air he to know?" she stammered, chokingly.

"No, no!"

"An'—yer mother?"

"Well, not—not quite yet, dear."

Two slender hands covered a scarlet face, and tears trickled between tense fingers.

"Then I can't!" Tess caught her breath in a sob. "I jest can't! Oh, why couldn't Daddy know—an' yer mother, too?"

Frederick strained her against his breast.

"Because they can't—not yet," he whispered. "Not a soul must know. Just you and I, darling. It'll be all right, dear, and I need you more and more—every day."

The deepening tones in his voice frightened, while they thrilled her. She pressed him back to look into his eyes, but even through the growing gloom she could see the blue-veined lids were closed.

"Frederick," she murmured, drawing her face backward. "Frederick, let me tell ye somethin'. Everybody had ought to know when a girl gets married. Oh, they ought to know, so they ought. Daddy Skinner an' yer mother, too."

Then of a sudden she was attacked by a strange tugging in her own heart. She tried to free herself from his arms, but her resistance only made him the more determined to bend her to his wish. She had always been submissive, and he'd worshiped her for her womanly acquiescence to his will. Trembling fingers forced her face upward and hot lips sought and found hers. She shivered under the strong masculine pressure.

"Now listen to me, my love," he continued between fierce kisses. "Come with me tomorrow night, and we'll get married and—and—"

Tess was trying heroically to hold to the principle she knew was right, even though her heart directed otherwise.

"Not less'n I tell Daddy," she breathed back.

Her low denial served only to lock Frederick's arms more tightly around her.

"You've got to come and you mustn't tell him, either," he urged. "You mustn't!"

Succeeding at last in releasing herself, Tessibel sighed. She wanted to be firm with him, to impress lovingly upon him her reason for refusing him; but when he reached forth and folded her again in his arms, that fine firmness gave way. She burst into wild weeping, holding him close as he held her, trying through broken sobs to tell him what was burdening her heart.

"It air like this, dear," she wailed, dismally. "Oh, I want to marry ye more'n anything, but I've never deceived Daddy a bit in all my life. I never done nothin' less'n I told 'im, and, Oh, I want to tell him, Frederick! I do want to tell 'im!"

Frederick hadn't anticipated this resistance on Tessibel's part.

"Tess," he said, almost angrily, "I wouldn't ask you to do anything

18

wrong." Then softening, he pleaded accusingly, "You don't love me well enough to be my wife."

"It'd be wicked," whispered Tess, falteringly.

"It would be right!" cried Frederick, in quick contradiction. "Tess, you will, you will!"

The red curls shook slowly a mute negation.

"I don't believe you love me at all," groaned Frederick. Then taking a long breath, "You want me to be unhappy, I know you do."

She lay limply in his arms while through the sensitive, honest mind raced all the objections against his desire. There were his powerful friends—his college—his—

"Yer mother—don't want ye to marry me," she cried, suffering.

"I know it," returned Frederick, promptly. "Still a man can't always please his mother. Why, darling, what kind of a world would this be if mothers picked out their sons' wives? A poor place! I can tell you."

"But yer mother air awful good and loves ye just like Daddy loves me," argued Tessibel, "an' when ye don't do right, everything goes wrong. If Daddy Skinner ain't to know—"

"Nor anybody else," cut in the boy, growing moody after his sharp retort. "I won't have any one know about it. Tessibel, I want this more than anything else in the world. I love you—I love you, and you love me. Then why not? You do love me, don't you?"

"That air why—I do what—ye want me to, I s'pose."

And as the halting words fell from her lips, the student crushed her to him.

"I want you, dear," he breathed warm in her ear, "and it won't have to be a secret over a year, not much over a year, darling, and I'll——I'll——Oh! You will, Tessibel? You will?"

"Frederick!" she acquiesced, weakly. "Oh, Frederick darlin'!"

And for some time after her sudden consent, they sat on the rocks close in spirit—close in thrilling nearness. Perhaps twenty minutes later, Tess drew from the boy's arms.

"Daddy air callin' me," she said, softly.

And she went back to the shanty with the words, "I'm goin' to be married tomorrow," ringing in her heart.

CHAPTER V

A GOSSIP WITH "SATISFIED"

The next day, directly after the midday meal, Tessibel went to see Mrs. Longman, whose triple tragedy had made the woman an invalid, with broken nerves and useless hands. Every few days since the drowning of Myra Longman and Ben Letts and the baby, the squatter girl had carried to the sick woman some little offering to gladden her lonely existence. As Tess walked along the rocks, the image of Frederick Graves persistently pervaded her thoughts. Before the going down of another sun he would be her husband. Of course, just now she couldn't leave Daddy Skinner and Andy Bishop, but by the time Frederick had a home ready, Andy would be free from the charge of murder, and Daddy would live with them.

Tess never paused on the rocks between her home and the Longman shanty that she did not think of Myra, and thinking of Myra brought the vision of Teola Graves. A lonely little heart twist followed for the dead baby who had been born in her hut. This day she did not hesitate as long as usual. She must return quickly to Daddy Skinner and help keep guard over Andy Bishop. Waldstricker was coming at two o'clock!

Rounding the lake point, on which stood the hut of her squatter friends, she spied "Satisfied" seated on the bench near the doorway. Tess waved her hand, and the old fisherman signaled in return.

"Ma thought ye'd be comin' soon, brat," was Longman's greeting.

"I air brung her some salt-risin' bread," Tess announced, sitting down beside the fisherman.

Longman moved his pipe to one corner of his mouth.

"It air good o' ye, Tess," he thanked her, puffing. "Me an' ma air lonesome—me an' ma air."

Tessibel touched him with affectionate assurance.

"I love ye, an' Mammy Longman, too," she smiled. "I air glad to bring somethin' when I can."

For a few moments they sat quietly, the man smoking his pipe. Then he slowly knocked the ashes from its bowl, giving it a final rap in the hollow of his hand.

"Every day me an' ma miss Myry an' Ezry more," said he, stolidly. "Us uns just plumb lately made up our minds both them kids was too good to live, but us uns'd be awful satisfied to know if they air happy."

Tessibel brightened. She flashed a radiant smile at the sad-faced man.

"Sure, they be happy!" she ejaculated. "Everybody air happy in Heaven; Ben Letts air a singin' 'round the throne jest the same's the rest of 'em air."

In open disbelief Longman slowly shook his head.

"Myry never could sing—Myry couldn't," he answered, moodily, and his voice sank on the last two words.

Tess knew that, too, for she had heard the young mother try many times to quiet the brat with the uneven, discordant tones of her voice; but she knew, too, the great difference between Heaven and earth. She gazed out over the lake dreamily.

"But ye see, 'Satisfied' darlin'—" she began.

"An' once, when Ben were soused," interrupted Longman, hoarsely, "I heard 'im singin', 'Did ye ever go into an Irishman's shanty?' It were more like a frog croakin' than a man singin'."

"But folks don't never get soused in Heaven," Tessibel imparted, reverently, "an' they got a mess o' angels up there—" She looked upward, a solemn expression on her young face—"angels what Jesus keeps jest to learn folks how to sing. The brat's singin' too, as much as a little kid can, 'Satisfied'."

She edged a little nearer and slipped an arm around the fisherman's shoulders.

"It air just like this, honey, down here there air such a lot of work jest to get fish an' beans. Up in Heaven they don't do nothin' but dance around the throne an' sing all day. So everybody's got to learn how or he wouldn't have nothin' to do."

"Well, I swan!" ejaculated "Satisfied," smiling wryly. "Will ye tell ma about it like ye did me, Tessie? Ma air been worryin' fearin' Myry weren't comf'table."

Tess bobbed her curly head.

"I'll tell 'er in a minute," she assured him; "but, 'Satisfied,' I were a goin' to ask ye somethin'."

Longman nodded.

"An' I were goin' to ask you somethin' too, brat," he said. "How air the singin' goin' in church?"

Tessibel sparkled like the morning dew.

"Oh, it air goin' fine, 'Satisfied.' I love it more'n more. Miss Young helps me with my songs an' she's learnin' me to sew, too. Why, I git my five dollars every Sunday jest as reg'lar as Sunday comes. I ain't never knew how far a fiver could go afore. We won't be needin' nothin' this winter, Daddy and me won't, dear."

She gave a delicious giggle to which Longman added a chuckle.

"That air good, brat," he replied. "There ain't nothin' like home comfort in this world."

"An' ye see, 'Satisfied,' I ain't lettin' my Daddy fish much now, only 'nough fer us an' fer Professor Young an' Ma Moll.... Daddy ain't very well."

"He air gettin' old," sighed Longman, taking up his pipe.

"No, he ain't," contradicted Tessibel, quickly. "He air got somethin' the matter with 'is heart. Mr. Young had a doctor fer him, an' he says he mustn't work. Now I got my singin' he don't have to.... Why, 'Satisfied,' I air savin' 'nough money to get a new bed an' a overcoat for Daddy. A bran new overcoat, too! Nothin' second-hand, ye bet! He ain't goin' to git no cold this winter, bless 'im!"

Longman allowed one of his thin arms to fall around the straight young figure.

"That air nice, Tessie," he returned admiringly. "Ye be a pert brat, you be!"

Tess paused a moment or two.

"'Satisfied,'" she hesitated, going back mentally to her former unspoken query, "do ye know the Waldstrickers?"

Longman nodded.

"I knowed the old man who was murdered—young Eb's father. Made some stir in town when he got shot!"

"Eb's been home quite a while now," observed Tess thoughtfully.

Longman's head and shoulders moved several times in affirmation.

"So ma read out'n the paper," he then said, "an' Bishop's lit out from the coop, too, ain't he?... Funny how he done it!... Bigger men'n him stay there all their days.... They'll find 'im, though, them prison folks will, poor little duffer!"

Tess caught the sympathy in the squatter's voice.

"I air hopin' they don't," she sighed quickly.

An inquisitive, almost furtive expression shot into the fisherman's face.

"When ye goin' to git married, Tess?" he hesitated.

Tessibel shook her red curls, flushing.

"Oh, I ain't knowin' jest the time yet," she parried. "Ye know, 'Satisfied,'—"

"Don't ye ever see much of the student nowadays, eh?" the squatter cut in.

Because of its sudden palpitation, Tess laid her hand over her heart. Oh, if she could only tell her old friend that that very night she'd belong to Frederick forever! Passion leapt alive into her eyes, and her cheeks flushed.

"I air a lovin' him, 'Satisfied,'" she murmured.

Longman made a nervous movement with one hand and shook his head.

"Tess, I been goin' to tell ye somethin' fer a long time," he stammered, almost inaudibly. "Ye won't git miffed with a old friend, will ye?"

"Sure not, 'Satisfied'," asserted Tess, gently.

"It air 'bout Student Graves," explained Longman.

A glint of gold flashed from under her lowered lids and a slow, deep scarlet ran in waves upward from her chin.

"What 'bout the student?" she demanded, dropping again to the bench and placing the basket at her feet.

The squatter looked down. It was hard to say what he must with the young face so confidently questioning.

"He air a goin' round with a nuther girl," he barked presently. "I been hearin' an' so air ma—"

Tessibel rose, startled, and once more took up the basket. Some gossiping tongue had been reviling her dear one.

"It air a big lie, 'Satisfied'," she uttered breathlessly. "I don't want to hear nothin' against 'im uther. What tongue told ye that only wanted to make ye feel sad fer me." She paused, then turned, but whirled back. "When ye love a person an' love 'im hard, lies told about 'im don't set well. Ye know they don't, Daddy Longman."

"Sure, I know it," replied the squatter, in quick-spoken sympathy. "Only ma and me thought as how ye ought to know the things we heard."

Tess was standing rigid, gazing stormily defiant into the weather-beaten old face. Wasn't she going to be married to the student that night! And how many, many times Frederick had told her he loved but her; that no other woman could ever take her place!

"I ain't goin' to believe it, if the hull hellish world tells me so," she flashed forth tempestuously. "Now I air goin' to give the bread to Mammy Longman, 'Satisfied'."

Longman stayed her with a word.

"Ye ain't mad at me, brat, be ye?"

Tess stretched forth impetuous fingers.

"Nope, only I love the student, that air all! An', 'Satisfied,' I air a cussed brat to be swearin' when Frederick says as how it air wicked. I keep forgettin' when I git mad."

The squatter sighed, making a quick shake of his head and several weird clicks with his tongue. Moodily he watched the bounding youthful figure until it disappeared through the shanty doorway. Fully ten minutes passed before Tess reappeared.

"Ma were satisfied with the bread, eh, brat?" asked Longman, in a cuddling tone. "Ain't she likin' it, honey?"

Tessibel choked suddenly. There was something in the quavering tones of the old fisherman, of the lonely, bereaved old man, that saddened her loving heart. She went to him and touched him impulsively.

"Yep, she liked it, 'Satisfied'," she murmured, "an' I told 'er all about the singin' in Heaven. She hadn't thought Ben Letts might be there with Myry an' the brat.... Most folks ain't knowin' how awful long the forgivin' arm of Jesus air."

And kissing the old squatter once more, Tessibel started homeward.

CHAPTER VI
WALDSTRICKER MAKES A PROPOSAL

While Tess was making her call at Longman's, Helen Young was entertaining her fiance, Ebenezer Waldstricker.

"I shall never be satisfied until Bishop is back in Auburn, Helen," said he, snipping the end from a long cigar.

The girl held up her needle and deftly shot the thread through the eye of it.

"He's sure to be, dear," she soothed. "Here's Deforrest!" She hesitated, laid down her work and stood up.

Professor Young shook hands with Waldstricker as his sister went to his side smilingly.

"Ebenezer wants me to go down to Skinner's with him," she explained. "Won't you come along, too, Forrie?"

The lawyer threw an interrogative glance at the churchman.

"Certainly," he answered. "Why? Anything particular?"

The question was asked of Waldstricker, who lifted his shoulder with a long breath.

"Yes," he replied. "I've a little plan to get hold of Bishop! I'm certain sooner or later he'll land back here among his own people. If I can whet their appetites with money, they'll turn him over the moment he appears."

"No doubt," observed Young. "But the Skinners—What have the Skinners to do with him?"

Waldstricker thought a moment, inhaling the smoke the while.

"The girl, Tessibel, who sings at church might be of great assistance to me," he said presently.

"How?" interjected Deforrest.

"Why, she goes among the squatters daily and would be likely to know if Bishop sneaked into any of their huts. If I can interest her in the reward— I've an idea she'll be of service to me."

"Perhaps," responded Young, in a meditative manner.

Waldstricker looked at Helen smilingly. "I think I started to give you an account of what happened yesterday," he said. "Did I tell you I came to see you, dear?"

Helen sat down and resumed her work.

"Yes, Ebenezer, but I was out!" she smilingly nodded. "I'm so sorry. If I'd known, I wouldn't have gone to town!"

"It didn't matter at all." Then he laughed, coloring a little. "Of course, I always hate missing you."

A loving look passed between the two, and Waldstricker proceeded, "But as long as I was here, I thought I'd speak to Skinner. On the way down the hill I met his daughter coming up. Rather startling personality, that girl! But she's woefully ignorant!"

"She hasn't had much chance, poor little thing," excused Helen. "She really has a beautiful voice, though."

"So I've noticed on Sundays."

"And she studies every minute," Professor Young thrust in, "and is so eager to learn; she's advanced amazingly!" He laughed in a reminiscent manner.

"One day," he proceeded, much amused, "she ran up the hill after me. I didn't notice her until she was at my side, all out of breath. 'Well, some little girl's been running,' I said."

"I want to learn things," she panted.

"Then I asked, 'What things?' and she answered, 'Oh, all about readin' and writin' and the things big rich folks know. If I had books, I'd learn 'em too.' ... Naturally I bought the books."

"Naturally," laughed Waldstricker.

"Well, I stopped to ask where she was going and if her father was at home. Then she told me that she was on her way to a seeress, Mother Moll, she called her, wasn't it?"

"Yes," assented Young, nodding his head. "The old woman lives on the north side of the gully."

Waldstricker bent forward and pursued. "I went into the hut with the

24

girl." He stopped and his lip took an upward curve. "The old hag tells fortunes from a pot, a steaming pot full of boiling water, I think."

Here he turned suddenly on Deforrest. "That's got to stop, Young. It's against the Bible, prophesying and the like."

"She's really a harmless old thing, though," replied the lawyer sententiously, "and every squatter on Cayuga Lake loves her. Believe me, Eb, she's absolutely harmless."

"Not harmless if she's disobeying God's law," contradicted Waldstricker, seriously. "Isn't there some way by which she can be turned out of the shack?"

Deforrest shook his head. "Not that I know of as long as she holds her squatter rights. Her people take care of her, and she tells their fortunes to pay for food." He broke off the explanation, only to take it up again, "No, there isn't any way to oust her. Frederick Graves' father tried to get the Skinners off, but failed."

"Oh, I didn't know," observed Waldstricker. "I must have been away at the time." He drew out his watch and looked at it. "Shall we go on down, Helen? It's a little early. I told the girl I'd come at two, but a half an hour doesn't matter.... I can't rest until I get hold of that dwarf."

During the interval in which Helen went for her garden hat, Waldstricker said to Deforrest,

"I may need you, Young, in this Bishop case. I'm privileged to call upon you, of course?"

"I'll do anything I can, Ebenezer," agreed Young.

So it happened that when Tess rounded the mud cellar, she glanced up the hill and saw the three making their way leisurely toward the lake. She gave one bound and literally hurled herself through the shanty door into the kitchen.

"Walderstricker air comin!" she hissed through her teeth in quivering excitement. "Scoot under the tick, Andy! An', Daddy, get on my cot, an' don't say no word less'n they ask ye something face to face.... Let me do the talkin'."

She had no more than settled her father on the cot and heard the last of the dwarf's burrowing in the attic when a long shadow fell across the threshold. Stepping forward, she met Deforrest Young, who held out his hand to her.

She greeted her friend with a dubious smile, and taking his hand, bowed awkwardly to his sister. In her confusion she ignored Waldstricker entirely. Their presence in the squatter's hut was so portentous and the time for the preparations to receive them so short, Tessibel's wits almost deserted her.

"Come in, all of ye," she stammered, at last, and stepped backward across the uneven kitchen floor toward the cot at the further side of the room.

Then she placed chairs for them, and when all were seated, settled herself on the floor near Daddy Skinner, and shaking her curls back from her face, looked with grave brown eyes from one to the other of the ominous group.

"I'm very glad to see you, Tessibel," said Helen graciously.

"I air awful glad to see you, too, Ma'am," returned Tess, still embarrassed.

Miss Young smiled toward Ebenezer, then back at the girl.

"You remember Mr. Waldstricker, don't you, Tess, dear?"

Tessibel allowed her gaze to rest on the elder. Of course she remembered him. What did he desire of Daddy Skinner? That was all she wanted to know.

"Yep," she answered, more calmly. "I remember 'im, sure I do! He—"

Waldstricker interrupted her with a quick interrogation.

"We had a little meeting yesterday, didn't we, Miss Tessibel? You didn't wait for me to tell you what I wanted." He delivered this most affably, and Tess counted him very handsome, indeed, when both corners of his mouth went up, but she knew that other trick of those lips. Not knowing how to explain her flight, she kept silent. Deforrest noted the shadow that clouded the lovely face and ascribed it to embarrassment. Thinking to put her at her ease, he asked,

"Have you been studying today, my dear?"

"Well I guess I have!" The girl sent him a radiant, grateful smile. "I studies every day, an' air learnin' my Daddy a lot of things now, ain't I, Daddy?" She looked backward at the man on the cot as she asked the last question.

"Yep," affirmed Skinner, faintly.

"Daddy air sick," she explained. "You'll be excusin' 'im if he don't talk. I'll do all the gabbin' if ye don't mind."

Tessibel had regained her self-control. She knew that Waldstricker's presence meant danger to her loved ones, Daddy and Andy Bishop. In their defense, eager to hinder him, her quick thought sought his purpose in coming to the shack. Could it be about Mother Moll, she wondered. She would ask him. Looking up at Waldstricker, she addressed him timidly,

"I hope, sir, ye ain't mad at Mother Moll any more?"

Waldstricker, intent upon his idea of interesting her in the search for his father's murderer, waived her question aside. He would attend to the witch and her fantastic mummeries later.

"Never mind the old woman now," he began pompously. "I came here today on purpose to see you about another matter."

Why, yesterday he had said he wanted to talk to Daddy; now today he wanted to speak to her. She sat up a little straighter, each shoulder carrying its load of red curls, the ends of which lay in a bronze tangle.

"I'd do anything I could," she answered shyly, a lovely red dyeing her face.

"I knew you would! Mr. Young has told me how anxious you are to learn and to improve your condition.... Isn't that so?"

Tess nodded, looking from the speaker to Deforrest, who threw her his ever-ready smile. Her gaze returned to the churchman and he continued,

"Now, I've a plan which, if it succeeds, will give you lots of money! You could do almost anything you'd want to then."

Tess didn't move, only stared back at the handsome, swarthy face incredulously.

"I couldn't earn much," she ventured, gulping. "I get five bucks every Sunday fer singin' at the church, but—"

"Oh, I don't mean a few dollars," Waldstricker told her. "I was talking about a lot—thousands."

Daddy Skinner straightened out on the cot and Tess tried to swallow, but couldn't. She knew now that he referred to the reward for Andy.

"Lordy massy!" she got out at last, huskily.

Deforrest Young coughed, and Waldstricker's hand went quickly to his face.

"I'll explain about it," he said, "and then you can decide if you wish to do it."

"All right," replied Tess, leaning her chin on her hand. "Gowan an' blat it out."

"I suppose you know my good old father was murdered," the visitor asked her after a slight period of silence on his part.

Andy and what he had told her about the brawl in the saloon raced through Tessibel's mind.

"I heard 'bout it," she replied, nodding.

"And you've heard, too, probably, the man who murdered him escaped from Auburn a little while ago?"

Tess wanted to say "No," but she feared a long explanation would follow which might trouble Daddy and the wee man in the garret, so she acquiesced by bowing her head. "I guess he were the man Daddy were talkin' 'bout, weren't he, Daddy?"

She turned toward her father, but his red lids were closed, and he was breathing heavily.

"Daddy goes to sleep awful easy!" she excused to all three. Then she told Waldstricker, "Yep, Daddy said the man broke out o' jail."

The man she spoke to looked keenly at her.

"The officers feel pretty sure he'll make his way down the lake side," he explained, "eventually landing among his own people."

A flash of the brown eyes and a quick stiffening of the supple body under the red curls expressed the girl's resentment at the slur implied in the speaker's statement.

"Among us squatters, I s'pose ye mean?" demanded Tess, belligerently.

"Yes," nodded the elder, with a contemptuous smile at the angry young face.

Tess hated that tone in people's voices when they talked about squatters.

"And I was wondering if you wouldn't like to earn the reward offered for Bishop's capture," Waldstricker finished abruptly.

Tessibel's foresight had discounted the effect of this announcement. To save Andy, she must deceive Waldstricker and persuade him to leave the search of the Silent City in her hands. Her brown eyes were bright with her purpose; she smiled slowly up at him showing every white tooth.

"You bet I would!" she exclaimed, shaking her curls as she tossed her head. "How much air it, huh?"

"Five thousand dollars," replied Waldstricker.

"Jeedy!" gasped Tess. "That air a pile of money. I bet I earn it!.... What'd ye bet?"

She turned impetuously to Deforrest Young, and he laughed.

"I hope you may!" was all he said.

Tess was all eagerness now, her cheeks flaming and her eyes dancing.

"But I wouldn't know the man if I seen 'im in any of the squatter's huts, huh?"

She flung this at Waldstricker, more of a question than a statement.

"He's a dwarf," he answered immediately, "and very small—like this. Sandy Letts knows him and is looking for him, too."

At his statement, Tessibel's quick imagination pictured Sandy's brutal face and greedy eyes, and for a moment her flaming courage almost faltered.

"If a dwarf sneaks down here," she observed with a sweep of her hand toward the door, "I'd get 'im easy. I know everybody."

"But would I have to halve up with Sandy, eh?" she continued, as though struck with a new thought.

"Not unless Sandy helped you find him," Ebenezer replied genially. "You could do as you pleased about that."

"Oh, Sandy couldn't help me, not a bit," Tess argued earnestly. "Sandy ain't liked any too well 'round here."

"Well, manage it as you choose."

Waldstricker smiled at his success with the girl. "I don't care for Sandy myself," he continued. "All I want is to get Andy Bishop." His face hardened with hate as he pronounced the dwarf's name.

Tess put her hands under the curls over each shoulder and drew them together beneath her chin.

"Five thousand dollars!" she ruminated. "I'd have a bully time a spendin' it, wouldn't I?... I'd buy my Daddy a new overcoat every day fer a year, an' I'd git 'im four new beds—one fer every corner of this here kitchen, an' I'd git 'im a flannel shirt thick as a board to keep the pains from 'is bones.... Then, I'd buy me a cow an' a calf an' a horse an' a little baby pig an' a few cats an' a lot of dogs, an' I'd let all the squatter brats play in my flower garden—"

Helen broke off this chatter with an amused laugh.

"Then mebbe I'd go to school a while," Tess kept on, "an' learn myself a lot out o' books, an' after that I'd take singin' lessons an' I'd sing to everybody what asked me—Then mebbe—" She dropped back for lack of words. "I wonder if that'd take the hull of the five thousand."

Waldstricker stood up.

"You've got the right idea of spending money," he laughed. "And now, young lady, we'll leave you, and if you hear that this dwarf is in any of your friends' huts, you let me know, and I'll come right down."

"Sure," said Tess, heartily. "Ye bet I will."

Scrambling to her feet, she lifted the ruddy curls and flung them back on her shoulders. To Ebenezer, watching her, came like a haunting memory the witch's cry, "Hair, stranglin' ye—God, what hair!"

But he dismissed the suggestion easily and turned to Helen, smiling.

"Why not bring Miss Skinner to the next musicale and have her sing?... Wouldn't you like that, Tess?"

"I'd get scared stiff," gasped Tessibel, terrified.

"But, Tess, dear," Helen thrust in, "I'd teach you the songs, and—"

The girl was looking down upon her dress, her face gathering a deep red.

Miss Young divined what was going on in the girlish mind.

"And I'd help you make a new dress," she went on.

"A hull lot of money folks'd be there, eh?" Tess demanded. Oh, how afraid she always was of a crowd of those—different people!

Her words directed Waldstricker's attention to the contrast between this squatter girl in the bare shack and the fashionable folk who'd throng his spacious drawing room.

"Well, a few," he answered, "but you come along with Miss Young just the same, will you?"

Tessibel took the outstretched hand awkwardly enough and as quickly dropped it and began to fumble with her own fingers. She looked down at the floor while she traced a line on it with her toe.

"Mebbe," she replied in a very subdued voice.

She stood in the door and watched them walk slowly up the hill. Then she turned back into the kitchen.

"My God, brat!" sobbed a voice through the hole in the ceiling. "Wasn't that a nice list of beautiful things ye was goin' to buy? Oh, kid, I air bettin' Waldstricker gits me."

Tess chuckled low, as she turned her face upward.

"Andy," she said, "ye needn't be worryin' 'bout me an' Jesus handin' ye over to that old elder. Why, Him an' me air goin' to stick to you like pitch to a nigger."

She turned to go, but hearing a sigh, took four steps up the ladder and finished,

"Why, honey, Waldstricker air got as much chance a ketchin' you as a tallow dog has chasin' an asbestos cat through hell."

CHAPTER VII

WALDSTRICKER AND MOTHER MOLL

"Deforrest is so interested in the little Skinner girl," Helen Young explained to Ebenezer Waldstricker when they were alone after supper. "Ever since he helped to get her father out of Auburn, he's done all he could for her."

"He's a philanthropist at heart, I imagine," remarked Ebenezer, agreeably.

"Yes, and so good to everybody. Dear Forrie! I wish he'd meet the right woman and marry her. He'd be so happy in a home of his own. When I think of leaving him alone—"

The tender face flushed crimson, and happy eyes dropped under the man's bright gaze. He reached over and took a slender hand in his.

"But you're not sorry you're coming with me, are you, dear?" he chided gently, and Helen lifted her head with a glad cry.

"Oh, no, no, darling!... I'm the happiest woman in the world!"

"And I'll keep you so," replied Ebenezer, in earnest.

"I was thinking, though," observed Helen, after a moment, "that Deforrest might come with us if he hasn't made other arrangements."

Waldstricker contemplatively kissed each pink finger of the small hand he held, then pressed his lips to the soft palm.

"I should like very much to have him, Helen," said he. "I'm very proud of your brother, you know."

"You can't make me happier than to praise him," she smiled.

For several minutes no more was said. Then Waldstricker spoke as though thinking aloud,

"I wonder if that little Skinner girl will be of any assistance in the matter of locating Bishop?"

"Perhaps," replied Helen. "She seemed very eager to get the money! Don't you think so?"

"Yes, I think she did, but I've been wondering if she's trustworthy. Is she, Helen?"

Miss Young made a hasty affirmation.

"Yes, indeed, she's more than that!" she exclaimed. "She wouldn't deceive any one she loves for anything in the world, so Deforrest tells me."

"I sincerely hope so," sighed Ebenezer. "I've quite set my heart on her helping me. Money is no object in a matter like this."

"Of course not," murmured Helen, sympathetically.

"Letts also is doing some good work," Ebenezer continued. "He's been through nearly every hut on the Rhine."

Helen shivered. "I can't tolerate that man around," she replied. "Once in a while he comes here to see Deforrest or to sell something, and I can't get him away quickly enough."

"He's a good spy, though. That's all I want. He and the Skinner girl ought to produce that dwarf between them."

"I hope so for your sake, dear," murmured Helen.

Waldstricker took out his watch and glanced at it hurriedly.

"It's time for me to go, sweetheart," said he. "I want to get home before dark. Come as far as the lane with me—do!"

"The twilight is lovely, isn't it?" whispered the girl, when they were traversing the pear orchard.

"Made more lovely because of you," replied Waldstricker, sentimentally.

"How romantic you are tonight, dearest!" Helen laughed.

They had turned slowly up the hill, when suddenly Helen stopped and slipped her hand into Ebenezer's arm.

"There is that old woman you heard read from the fortune pot!" she exclaimed. "Let's step one side until she's passed us? She rarely lets a person go by without speaking."

Waldstricker threw up his head arrogantly.

"I'm not afraid of the hag," he replied pompously.

Together they advanced up the hill. Mother Moll, leaning on her cane, crept slowly down toward them. When her faded, nearsighted eyes caught sight of the two approaching figures, she halted in the middle of the road until they were almost upon her. She stared at Waldstricker fully fifteen seconds, while he looked steadily back at her. Then her withered lips spread wide in a sneering, cackling laugh.

"So he air aready been settin' on yer head an' layin' on yer heart, mister," she greeted him, "the leetle man like this, huh, ain't he?"

She shook her cane at the tall man and clacked at him again. Helen was conscious that at Moll's insults, Ebenezer's anger was rising by the minute. She was herself greatly moved by a kind of superstitious awe of the old woman's cryptic utterances. But seeking to avoid any further unpleasantness, she smiled in a friendly manner and asked,

"How do you do, Mother Moll?"

The hag thrust forward her face and raised one withered arm,

"I air fine, young lady," she screamed, crooking her fingers at the girl, "an' feel finer'n you can do this day, or ye'll ever with him." She pointed her cane at the scowling, dark-faced man; and slowly bobbed her head back to Helen. "Yer life'll draw out long an' terrible, till ye'll wish ye hadn't never seen 'im. He'll set up a knot hole an' drag ye livin' through it. Then he'll turn yer heart inside out an' haul ye back again."

She paused, while Waldstricker's face grew darker and darker. The frown on his brow roused Helen to action.

"Let's go on, dear," she whispered. "Don't pay any attention to her foolish talk."

"Not yet," returned Waldstricker, ominously. "Not yet!"

Moll laughed discordantly, shaking her head until the wisps of gray hair fell in strings about her face.

"He knows I ain't done tellin' ye what'll happen if ye line yer life with his'n," she croaked. "Lady, he air wicked, awful wicked, an' nothin' but misery, deep an' plentiful, air a goin' to make him any better. Every one he loves—"

Incoherently, she rambled on and the man's countenance took on an expression of such rage that Helen Young uttered a cry of dismay. She had never seen Ebenezer in one of his savage moods. Before she could draw him away, he had lifted his riding whip and a sudden twist of his arm brought it sharply down on the grandam's thin bent shoulders.

"Ebenezer!" screamed Helen, horrified.

31

"Drat ye, ye brute!" cried Moll, tottering back, "an' twice drat ye!" She swayed forward on her cane. "Ye can lick me till I die, an' 'twon't change yer own life any. It'll only add to the sufferin' ye got to go through yerself."

Waldstricker's arm went up again, but Helen grasped it frantically.

"Ebenezer, don't!... Don't strike her any more. Please!... Go home, Mother Moll.... Please go! Oh, do!"

The old woman leaned heavily on her stick, tearless sobs shaking her emaciated frame. For a space of sixty seconds her watery, faded eyes stared into Waldstricker's flashing dark ones—then she drew a long, convulsive breath.

"It air like ye to hit the awful young an' the awful old," she shrilled at him, "but, 'twon't do ye no good. Curls'll bring yer to yer knees, hair'll make yer heart bleed blood redder'n the sun, an' the leetle man'll jerk 'em tight 'bout yer throat till ye thunder out fer mercy."

"Come along," muttered Ebenezer, roughly, to Helen. "If she torments me any more, I fear I'll kill her."

His words were not so low but they caught the quick ear of the old woman.

"Kill me, yep, kill me, ye proud whelp! Go 'long; do it, ye big coward! Before ye're done with life, ye'll hate yerself worse'n uther folks hate ye."

She hobbled a little distance, reaching backward to rub her shoulders. Then she twisted completely around, facing the other two.

"Mind my word, pretty miss," she croaked in half grunt, half yelp. "Let 'im go like ye would a snake; like ye would a slimy worm a crawlin' at yer feet." Still snarling in pain, she lifted one shaking arm and pointed a crooked forefinger at Waldstricker. "She won't always stay with ye, ye skunk ye!" Then she staggered away, Helen and Ebenezer staring after her until she was lost in the gloom of the gully.

"Isn't she dreadful?" Ebenezer said, with a rueful laugh.

"She's so old," was Helen's gentle reproof. "She's not accountable for anything. Deforrest says she's very good to the other squatters."

"They're an unseemly mess." The man struck at an overhanging bough savagely. "And your brother has power enough to remove the worst of them if he wanted to. That old hag, for instance—"

"Deforrest wouldn't do it," interjected Helen.

"He may if I make it worth his while," replied Waldstricker. "But there, I was foolish to let 'er get on my nerves so. I beg your pardon, dear. My only excuse is I dislike to see the laws of God broken in such an iniquitous way. Why, I felt when I struck her the righteous indignation the Master must have felt when he drove the money changers from the temple."

Helen looked at him, startled. She was shocked at his words, as she had been terrified by his act.... A dreadful doubt darted into her mind. Was Mother Moll right? Could she be? Instantly she dismissed the suggestion, condemning herself for paying any attention to the empty vaporings of the half-witted, childish, old woman. She was sorry for Moll, of course, and grieved and hurt because Ebenezer had lost his temper and struck her. But her loving heart

32

excused him. Certainly the provocation had been great. Old Moll was unusually impertinent.

Intent to repair the momentary disloyalty of her doubt, she pressed his arm lovingly.

"There, dear, let's not speak of it again. It's over now and we'll forget all about it."

A little later, when Waldstricker was moodily riding toward Ithaca, Mother Moll's hateful prophecies repeated themselves in his mind.

CHAPTER VIII
TESSIBEL'S MARRIAGE

During the few hours after the departure of Waldstricker, Professor Young and Helen, Tessibel Skinner was preparing for her marriage. For the present she had dismissed her fear for Andy Bishop and had turned her attention to her own wonderful secret, her marriage to Frederick that evening. She went so nervously from one thing to another that when she stood fully dressed before her father, he scrutinized her inquiringly; but he confined his curiosity to the simple question,

"Goin' out, brat?"

"Yep, Daddy," admitted Tess, confused for an instant, "an' darlin', don't worry if I ain't back fer quite a little while. I air goin' to ride with Frederick." She leaned over him and cupped his bearded face with her hands, her eyes like stars, first shining, then shadowing. "Ye trust yer Tessibel, don't ye, Daddy Skinner?"

Since the first instant she'd been placed in his arms, a wee baby, the squatter had never ceased to marvel at her loveliness. An expression of adoring affection settled over his face.

"Sure, I air a trustin' ye, child," he assured her huskily, "or I wouldn't be lettin' ye run 'round wild on the rocks like ye're doin'.... Ye won't be gone too long, honey?"

"Nope," answered Tess, kissing him, "bar up, darlin', an' don't open to any knock lessen ye know who 'tis," and she ran out of the shanty and closed the door behind her.

"Fine lookin', yer girl, eh, pal?" remarked Andy, presently, from the ceiling.

"Yep," agreed Orn, morosely.

"She air got a beau, now, ain't she, old horse?"

33

The fisherman's face darkened with anger.

"Yep, an' I hate 'im like I hated his pa. But when a girl air fell in love with some feller, that air all there air to it."

"I hope he won't never hurt her," sighed the dwarf.

"He better hadn't!" mumbled Skinner.

During the silence that followed between the squatter and his prison pal, Tessibel was climbing the hill to meet Frederick. Many conflicting emotions took possession of her as she neared the summit. After tonight she would no longer be Tessibel Skinner, but Frederick's wife, and he, her husband, her own forever and forever. This night-ride would be her cherished secret until Frederick gave her permission to tell Daddy Skinner—until the whole world should know. Her mind was busy with the events of the last thirty-six hours. She was cogitating upon the happiness of her future, when she saw the waiting vehicle ahead of her, and Frederick's dark figure silhouetted in the moonlight. Faster and faster fluttered her heart, and faster and faster moved her feet. She reached the carriage without the student's realizing it.

"Frederick!" was all she had breath to say.

At the whispering of his name, the young man sprang to the ground. In another moment he had Tessibel in his arms.

"You've come!" he murmured low, kissing her. "Oh, my dearest, you're here!"

Then he lifted the slender figure into the buggy. Even in the pale light, Tessibel noticed his face gleamed white, and his eyes shone darker than usual. She sat very quiet as he gathered up the reins, and it was not until they were well on their way along the Trumansburg road that the boy turned to her. How beautiful she looked, her shoulders completely covered with dusky-dark curls and her head bowed in maidenly shyness! All his doubts as to the expediency of his act were set at rest. She was deeply essential to his happiness, to his progress. To know she was his wife, married to him, so that none could separate them, would make his absences from Tessibel much easier to bear. He had in the past feared Deforrest Young. Now that fear was being set at rest. He never had worried that Sandy Letts would win Tess any more than he had been apprehensive of Ben Letts before the drowning of the squatter. The one person he stood in awe of was his mother. Again his eyes sought the silent girl at his side. She had ever been a hallowing influence in his life, and to lose her would be worse than death. After tonight the glory in those unreadable brown eyes would ever shine for him. He threw one arm across her shoulder, and drew her closer. "My little moonlight girl!" he breathed in ecstasy, his cheek against hers. "Are you happy, my sweet?"

Tessibel couldn't have spoken if she had so desired. Her heart seemed filling her throat. Happiness hushed her voice, and gratitude to God for giving her Heaven's best prevented her expression of it.

The next twelve miles were passed in silence. And ever after, when Tessibel in imagination recalled the white road, winding its way into the hills, the quietude of the countryside, the shimmering moonlight, it seemed like nothing real. And she remembered, as in a daze, Frederick taking her in his arms after the minister had married them—how he had called her over and over his wife, his darling, and other whisperings divinely sweet.... In memory all those hours were like strangely mysterious dreams.

Daddy Skinner was waiting for Tessibel. He had sat listening for hours, mostly in silence, a deep brooding expression bending his ragged brows together in a stern frown.

From his position in the attic, Andy Bishop could see the fisherman's face. The dwarf was quick to recognize that something was wrong with his friend.

"The world air waggin' yet, Orn," he remarked soothingly.

"Sure, but 'tain't much of a world," grunted Skinner, sighing.

Andy bent his head a little farther through the hole.

"It air a lot, while we got Tess," he answered. "We got Tessibel, ain't we, pal?"

The squatter's mouth wrinkled at each corner.

"Yep, I guess we got 'er all right, but I wish to God she'd come home."

"She'll be along soon," assured Andy, with a smile.

For a few minutes they remained silent. Then Orn Skinner burst forth again,

"I ain't got as much use for that feller Tess loves as a dog has for a million fleas, an' I never liked 'is pa, uther...."

"Ye wouldn't wish she'd be lovin' Sandy Letts, even if he does make money, eh, Orn?" asked Andy.

"Thunder, no!" snorted Skinner. "I'd ruther she'd be dead 'n married to Sandy. But that ain't sayin' a honest squatter airn't better'n a high born pup.... I wish Tess loved a decent chap."

At that moment the speaker's daughter was standing alone on a small country inn porch, some miles from Trumansburg, waiting for her husband.

Frederick had gone to get the rig to take them back to the squatter settlement. There was absolute stillness, absolute calm everywhere but within herself. Her heart fluttered with new emotions, new desires, ambitions to make herself worthy of the man she'd married. Her eyes were on the sky, her soul among the stars, her own stars that had crept out one by one, each to look lovingly down upon her happiness.

What a glorious night it was! More wonderful than yesterday even! Or any of her many yesterdays! This hour, the climax of her love, had transported her through the mystery of immeasurable joy. She would never again be the old Tessibel. She was Frederick's wife! Her breath came in sudden, quick, happy sighs, for just then she heard his voice from out of the darkness. Ah, his tones, too, were deeper, richer than yesterday!

Even in the shadow, Frederick saw her distinctly as he came toward the house.

"My own little wife!" he whispered tumultuously. "How happy I am!"

"Won't ye take me home now?" murmured Tess. "It air late an' Daddy'll be worried."

"We'll start at once," promised Frederick tenderly, leading her down the steps.

Daddy Skinner heard the horse coming down the hill, heard Frederick as he said his low, "Good-night, my darling," and unbarring the door, the fisherman waited impatiently for his daughter to enter the shanty.

One glance and he stretched out his hand.

"Ye're sick, brat," he stammered. "Be ye sick, my pretty?"

Dropping her eyes, Tessibel shook her head.

"Nope, I ain't sick," she faltered. "But—but—"

She wanted to throw herself upon her father's broad shielding breast and sob out her joy. But she couldn't do that so she stood hesitantly, her lips quivering.

"I air wantin' to be hugged in yer arms, Daddy Skinner," she told him. "Tell yer brat ye love her awful much."

And according to his custom in his daughter's sentimental moments, the fisherman, after dropping the door-bar, seated himself in the wooden rocking-chair, and held out his arms.

"I were just a sayin' to Andy, I wished ye'd come home," said he. "Love ye, kid?... I love ye better'n all the world, and everythin' in it.... Well! If my pretty brat ain't cryin'.... Sandy ain't been chasin' ye, has he?"

"Mebbe she air been a fightin' with her beau," piped the dwarf, from the ceiling.

The girl's mind traveled back through the events of the evening.

"Nope, I didn't fight with 'im, Andy," she smiled through her tears.

Daddy Skinner's beard rubbed lovingly over the dishevelled curly head.

"There! There! My little 'un!" he singsonged. "I'll rock my babe a bit. Ye stayed out too late, I air a thinkin'."

Oh, to tell him everything that had happened in the past few hours. But she had promised Frederick, and Tessibel would rather have died of grief than betray her trust. She put her lips close to the fisherman's ear.

"I air lovin' the student, Daddy," she whispered. "I didn't see Sandy tonight. I jest been with Frederick."

The squatter's only answer was to press her lovingly to him and for a long time he swayed back and forth slowly. Suddenly he ceased rocking.

"Ye'd best git to bed, baby," said he. "Crawl back, Andy, and let the brat undress."

Andy's shining face disappeared with a "Good night, brat," and "Good night, old horse."

The father and daughter heard him settle himself on the straw tick, and soon all was quiet above. And later by half an hour, Tessibel was dreaming of the young husband who that day had opened a new world to her, who had led her from girlhood into the immensity of womanhood.

36

CHAPTER IX
THE MUSICALE

Tessibel, arrayed in her new dress and slippers, a roll of songs under her arm, stood in the shanty kitchen. Neither Daddy Skinner nor Andy had made any comment when she told them she had really consented to sing at the home of the dwarf's enemy. Now she craved their commendation. A little doubtful, she went to the ladder, and glanced upward. The dwarf was nowhere to be seen.

"Andy," she called softly.

"Huh?" drifted from somewhere above in the darkness.

"Crawl to the hole, dear, an' squint down at my dress."

A little scramble and a face peered down upon her,

"Ye been a cryin', Andy," said Tess, a break in her voice. "What ye been a cryin' fer, honey?"

"Seem's if Waldstricker air goin' to take ye away from my pal an' me."

Daddy Skinner gave a grunt with no articulate word in it. Tess whirled around on him and fastened her bright eyes upon her father's bent head.

"Daddy," she began tremulously, "air you an' Andy thinkin' things ye hadn't ought to of Tessibel?"

Skinner shook his head.

"Me an' Andy hates Waldstricker, that air all," he said.

Tess shrugged her shoulders.

"I ain't et up with love fer him uther," she offered in defense, "but Miss Young wanted me to—oh, daddy, why didn't you tell me I couldn't go right at first—"

"Of course, ye be goin'," broke in Daddy Skinner, "but don't ye forgit us, my pretty!"

Tess gurgled in joy. She went to her father's side and gathered the dear head into her arms.

"If that air all what air worryin' ye, then kiss yer brat," said she. "I air goin' to sing an' mebbe I'll only see Waldstricker to speak to 'im. If he says anythin' 'bout Andy—"

"What'll ye tell 'im, kid?" gasped the dwarf.

"Oh, I'll string 'im like I allers does," returned Tess. "Now you're done squallin' like a baby, look at me!"

"Ain't she swell?" enthused Andy. "Orn, have ye looked 'er over?"

"Sure," mumbled the Squatter, "an' she air finer'n silk."

Tessibel hugged her father again, fluttered a kiss from the tips of her fingers to the little man above, and repeating her usual admonition to them, not to talk aloud, she started for Young's with palpitating heart. Deforrest met her as she ascended the front porch. Smiling he took her hand. His eyes expressed his approval of the winsome face and the trim figure in the new dress.

37

"Prompt as usual," he greeted. "How beautiful you are tonight, my dear!"

The color swept to Tessibel's face in great waves. She loved everything beautiful, the roses, the violets, the blue of the sky! Even the night things were beautiful, too. Did Professor Young think her beautiful like all these wonders? She smiled, her face shining in its mantling crimson. Deforrest took her arm, leading her into the living room, where Helen stood at the table, drawing on a long white glove.

"Gaze upon your handiwork," laughed her brother. "Quite a surprise for Ebenezer and his friends, eh?"

Helen examined Tessibel from the top of her head to the tip of her pretty boots with critical, gratified eyes.

"Yes," she decided, "you're all very satisfactory, Tess." Then to her brother, "Now, let's go, dear."

When Deforrest drove his horses up the long roadway leading to the Waldstricker mansion, Tessibel noticed the house was lighted from cellar to garret, that a long line of vehicles was making its slow way to the porch. Her heart fluttered with embarrassment. As they drew up to the stone veranda, Tess reached spontaneously for Helen Young's hand.

"It seem's if I jest couldn't sing afore such a awful lot of folks," she murmured helplessly.

Helen returned the pressure of the cold fingers.

"Try to imagine you're in church," she suggested. "You won't break down, my dear, I feel quite sure."

"I—I—air goin' to try to be awful careful anyhow," replied Tess, hopefully, but she heaved a deep sigh as Deforrest Young lifted her quite into his arms and placed her on the low, broad porch-stone.

Amid a crowd of laughing people, they passed into the house, and while they were removing their wraps, Helen took the opportunity to give her little protege a few last admonitions.

"Don't forget to put the 'g's' on your 'ing's,' and remember always to say 'your' quite plainly," she whispered.

"I will," Tessibel promised.

By this time, they had entered the crowded reception hall, and the squatter girl's heart leapt into her throat when Ebenezer Waldstricker came forward to meet them. He welcomed Helen Young tenderly, taking her hands in his. Tess noticed both corners of his mouth were up.

"I'm so happy to have you here, Helen, my darling," he murmured, bending over the hands he held.

A flushed face smiled into the speaker's.

"And I'm happy to be here, too, dear." Then turning, Helen announced "Here's Miss Skinner ... Tessibel, Mr. Waldstricker."

Until then the Elder had not seemed to be aware of the girl's presence, but at the introduction he extended his hand, formally polite. When, in shy greeting, Tess lifted her eyes, one corner of his mouth drew down rigidly. She was more at ease when Deforrest Young joined them. Her welcoming smile caused that gentleman's heart to bound in delight. They made their way slowly and with difficulty down the long hall, Tessibel growing more and more conscious of the curious glances directed at them from all sides. When they reached the drawing room door, her agitation grew perceptibly, having noticed that Waldstricker was detaining Helen. Deforrest held her arm with an encouraging pressure.

"Don't be afraid, dear," he whispered in her ear. "You'll stay near sister and me the entire evening. There!" They had crossed the room and neared a row of chairs arranged against the wall. "Sit down by this open window. My sister will be here soon.... Why!—Why! childie, you mustn't tremble so!"

A mist gathered under Tessibel's lowered lids. Each moment she grew more frightened, and from the corner of her eye measured the distance between their place and the piano. Oh, how thankful she was when Miss Young took a seat beside her. Near the door she recognized Madelene Waldstricker. Across the distance Tess studied the girl a moment. How pretty her gown was!

Tessibel glanced down at her own dress; at her rounded arms shining white under the little ruffle of fine lace. Her dress was pretty, the prettiest she'd ever had, and gratitude toward the woman at her side overcame for the moment her embarrassment. Presently Waldstricker came to them with the request for a song, and Deforrest Young escorted Tess to the piano. He pitied her from the bottom of his heart, as she clutched frantically at his arm.

"You've only to be yourself and sing as you do for us, my dear," he bent to whisper, "everybody will love you then."

That magic word "Love!" It always thrilled Tess into doing her best, and she must do no less tonight for her friends' sake. She sank down quite helplessly into the chair to which Deforrest led her and watched Ebenezer escort Helen to the piano. Her muscles grew taut with fright. How she wished to be back with Daddy Skinner and Andy! But she took the song Deforrest handed her, and through a veil of embarrassment, saw his smiling face close to hers.

"Sit here," he said, in low tones. "I shall be near you."

In one melodious touch of ivory keys, Helen started the prelude and every one in the room grew silent and attentive. Then from the side of the instrument there suddenly appeared before the quiet audience a radiant vision, a girl with tawny, glittering curls hanging in a golden fire-shower about her slender figure. The unfathomable brown eyes swept over the throng a quick glance, then dropped to the sheet of music in her hand.

A spontaneous murmur of admiration fell from many lips. For an instant Helen Young's hands poised above the keyboard, then descended; and as spontaneously as a bird begins its love song to the blue, so Tessibel Skinner began to sing.

The powerful voice rose up and up in seeming unending volume,—up and up until Deforrest Young sank against the wall and locked his fingers together. How had his sister dared to risk such a song with such a child!... Then he took a long satisfied breath, for he saw the little singer sang as a lark sings, without fear or self-consciousness, without knowledge of limitation to her thrilling harmony.

When Tess ceased on a high note, held until it drifted softly to the furthermost corner of the room, a round of applause went up to the high ceiling, and Miss Young, glancing around proudly at Tess, smiled and nodded. The girl felt another song thrust into her hands. This time she was less tremulous and sent back to Deforrest Young a charming, youthful smile. Helen's fingers rippled over the keys softly for a minute or two, and once more Tess began to sing.

"That I may know the largeness of God's love, teach me the fullness of thine own," she thrilled forth.

A groan forced its way almost to Deforrest Young's lips. What a child she was! Yet she sang that song with the abandonment of passion known only to a woman. How beautifully, lithely young she looked, standing there with those flowing, shimmering curls and the tender, throbbing voice pleading to be taught the fullness of human love, that she might find the largeness of the Infinite. Turning swiftly to the window, he pressed his lips together to stifle his emotion. He could no longer bear the stab at his heart, nor risk the mist rising in his eyes. Tessibel, wholly unconscious of the stir she was making, sang on and on, her gaze on the sheet in her hand. Suddenly she raised her eyes and there near the door was Frederick Graves, his face waxen white, his dark gaze bent upon her. Close beside him stood Madelene Waldstricker. But a single instant Tess faltered in her song. Then again, passionately, insistently, and tempestuously she sang, "That I may know the largeness of God's love, teach me the fullness of thine own!"

She saw his lids droop as she carefully pronounced each beautiful word, and saw him, without a glimmer of recognition for her, turn to the girl at his side. He hadn't even welcomed her with his eyes. Never before had he failed to greet her smilingly. She chilled to the bone, nor dared look again. When the song was finished, she sat down limply. Deforrest Young, strangely stirred, took her hand.

"Sweet child," he murmured, "it was delightful! Lovely!"

At the same moment Waldstricker was bending over Helen Young.

"My dear, how ambitious you are for so young a pupil!" he laughed.

"There's nothing she can't sing," she replied, rising. "Hasn't she a wonderful range?"

"Very," replied Waldstricker, and he, too, turned to look at the squatter girl.

Tess was striving to listen to Deforrest Young, but her disturbed mind was where Frederick stood with Madelene Waldstricker. Her whole loving heart desired him to come and speak to her.

"I never heard her sing like that before," Madelene was saying to Frederick. "I believe you know her quite well, don't you?"

"I know who she is," stammered the student, flushing, "but as to saying I know her well—"

"She's very beautiful!" interjected Madelene.

Frederick lowered his head flatteringly, "Not as beautiful as another girl I know," he whispered, and Madelene dropped her eyes with a happy sigh.

40

"Let's go and speak to her," she suggested. "I feel I must, I'm the hostess, you know."

Frederick reluctantly fell into step with her, and together they crossed the room, a striking picture of entrancing youth. Tessibel's heart ached at the unusual sight. For one burning moment she wanted to scream, to spring up and do some terrible thing to the small girl walking so familiarly at her husband's side. Then she looked away miserably. She could not bear the sight, nor did she turn again until she heard a strange, rather high, girl's voice say,

"It was very lovely, Helen! Such a surprise to every one! I'm ever so grateful to you."

"Tessibel, this is Miss Waldstricker," introduced Helen.

Tess raised a scarlet face at the sound of her name.

For one moment the two girls gazed into each other's eyes. Each had in her panting heart a feeling of proprietorship for the tall, dark boy standing moodily behind Madelene. Tess knew he was there, yet did not look at him.

"You've a beautiful voice," observed Miss Waldstricker, with a shade of condescension in her manner.

Tessibel could feel the blood pulsing even to her finger tips. What did she care for compliments from Madelene Waldstricker? She wanted to hear them from Frederick! Miss Waldstricker whirled suddenly to bring him into the conversation.

"Mr. Graves.... Ah, yes, of course, you know Miss Young, and this—and this is—Miss Skinner, Mr. Graves."

Then Frederick bent over Tessibel's hand, and her fingers shook in his. She raised her eyes slowly and he was looking upon her as if she were a thing apart from him now and ever would be. A crimson wave flew to her face—a flood tide of humiliation.

"I've met Miss Skinner," she heard in a low, unfamiliar tone. "Your voice, Miss Skinner, as Miss Waldstricker says, is very beautiful."

The accent of the ice in his words caused her to withdraw her hand from his instantly. She was stung to the quick by his coldness and indifference. She could not answer him. Was this her Frederick—this the boy who had so often knelt at her feet in ardent adoration? He had gazed at her as if she'd been a stranger, had praised her singing only by repeating what another girl had said. Her head burned like fire, and her heart gave a rebellious, defiant twist. She was his wife. All the passion within her tempestuous soul raged in stout protest against his treatment of her. Couldn't—oh, he could have said—have said—just a little something! Then anger fell from her in a trice. Desolation like an ash encompassed her. Of course, she was but a squatter; Frederick was ashamed of her, ashamed he even knew her. It was just at that moment she saw her husband place Madelene's fingers on his arm and laughingly move away with her. Tess started out of her jealous agony as some one touched her arm. Deforrest Young was smiling down upon her.

"Let's go to supper," he invited.

The girl made an effort to master her confusion. Slowly she rose and took the professor's arm. The unfamiliar, embarrassing formality helped to

41

hide her anger and consternation. She found herself positively unable to eat. When had she ever been capable of taking food when her heart filled her throat? She was conscious every moment of the presence of her husband and Madelene a little farther down the table, and that Frederick's attention was wholly taken up with his companion. She had but to raise her eyes to see Madelene's face beaming with pleasure.

Suddenly the voice of a stranger roused Tessibel from her bitter meditation.

"I heard, Mr. Waldstricker, you've located Andrew Bishop. It's true, I hope."

If it hadn't been for the queer feeling in her legs, Tessibel would have stood up. Located Andy Bishop—where? Why in her shanty, of course,—up in the garret under the straw tick. If they had found him, it must have been there. When? Tonight, since she'd left home. She bent over and searched the table for Waldstricker. He was seated next to Helen Young, and his gaze was directed toward his questioner.

"Well," he replied, "that's not quite right, but we hope—" he hesitated, swept his flashing eyes to Tessibel and smiled, "we hope to have him back in Auburn soon. I have two good detectives working for me."

Taking a deep breath of relief, Tess subsided in her chair, and she was not sorry when the signal was given for the company to leave the table.

CHAPTER X
A VICTIM OF CIRCUMSTANCES

Frederick Graves had just left Tess at the shanty door. He had found it difficult to explain away his conduct on the evening of the musicale at Waldstricker's.

"It were awful," sobbed Tess, after Frederick had mollified her anger somewhat. "I wanted to die! Ye looked like some big man I didn't know 't all."

"Silly baby," laughed the student. "There were so many people there who know my mother—" He paused and kissed the upraised, tearful face passionately. "I didn't think you'd care. I supposed of course you'd understand. I'm awfully sorry you didn't. You'll forgive me, darling, won't you?"

Tess snuggled nearer him. She wanted to forget how unhappy she'd been.

"Sure, I don't care now,—such a awful lot," she sighed.

42

Later in the evening, when he came into the hall of his home in Ithaca, he was greeted by his young sister, Babe.

"Fred," she called softly, "come on up, mother wants you."

For some minutes after taking off his hat, he remained in the lower hall considering just what to say to his mother. Shaking his head dismally, he mounted the stairs and went reluctantly to the front room. He hated scenes with his mother. He hated everything about the house, hated even the thought of going back to school. He wanted to take Tess away from the lake—make a home for her—to be with her always. How dear she had grown day by day since he'd married her! His very being fired at the memory of her clinging sweetness.

When he opened his mother's bedroom door and walked self-consciously forward to turn up the light, a fretful voice from the bed halted him.

"Fred, if you're going to make the room bright, please bring the screen forward."

He dropped his hand from the gas jet.

"It doesn't matter," said he, sulkily, and he moved to the foot of the bed. "Let it stay as it is.... Babe said you wanted me."

Mrs. Graves settled her glasses on the bridge of her nose and looked at him.

"Yes! I did tell her to send you in. What's the matter? Anything?"

"No." The answer was brutal in its curtness.

"You've been with that Skinner girl again." The woman sat up in bed and exclaimed angrily. "I can tell by the way you act."

A sudden fury took possession of the student.

"Of course, I haven't been to Skinner's," he contradicted roughly. "Didn't I tell you I wouldn't go and see her any more? What do you want now?"

Relieved by his words in spite of the ugly way in which they were uttered, Mrs. Graves sank back on the pillows. "Sit down," she invited.

He was too nervous and angry willingly to grant even so small a request just then.

"I can listen as well standing here," he answered crossly.

"But I can't talk as well when you stand," insisted Mrs. Graves, peevishly. "Frederick! What's happened to you since your father died? That squatter girl's turned your head. I know it. She's completely spoiled you."

Tessibel and all her girlish sweetness came vividly across the boy's mind. It was ridiculous to blame Tess. Ah, if he were as good as Tess desired him to be, his life would be the most exemplary.

"Please leave her name out of it, will you?" he rasped rudely. "Even if I can't see her, I won't hear anything against her."

Mrs. Graves sat up in bed, throwing back wisps of gray hair, that persisted in falling over her nose.

"Oh, you won't, eh?" she shrilled loudly. "Well, now, you listen to me.... You'll hear what I please to say to you, young man. It's a good thing you don't go to Skinner's any more. It's time you were interested in a decent girl. You've got to marry sometime. It's just as easy to love a rich girl as a poor one. Why don't you propose to Madelene Waldstricker?"

"Madelene's all right, I suppose," the boy answered "but I don't want to marry her."

"You better want to," his mother rejoined tartly. "You've got to do just that very thing."

"You're crazy, Mother. I won't do it. What do you take me for, anyhow? Get that idea out of your head and keep it out."

"If your father were here, you wouldn't dare to say such things to me.... I want you to sit down, do you hear?"

Frederick dropped into a chair wearily. The time had come to tell his mother that Tessibel Skinner was his wife. After that was done, there could be no such arguments. He started to speak, but his mother interrupted him.

"Madelene Waldstricker's wild over you," she explained. "You can't deny you've shown her open attention, at the same time you've been stealing down to that Skinner girl's hut.... Oh, don't deny it any more! But Madelene doesn't know very much about that, and she has lots of money. It's your duty to Babe and me."

"I won't marry her, or anyone else," Frederick repeated.

His voice was very low but every word was distinct.

Mrs. Graves lifted her pillow, turned it over, patted, and sank back upon it.

"Why?" she demanded, searching his face with accusing eyes. "Because of that fisherman's—"

Now he would tell her; now he would explain! He coughed, took out his handkerchief and wiped his lips.

"I shouldn't think you'd say anything against Tessibel Skinner," was what he said at last, "considering what she did for us."

Mrs. Graves uttered a scream, and covered her face with her hands.

"Now throw that in my face, will you?" she cried. "Can't you let me forget my shame and disgrace? Can't you see that girl coming into my life would bring constantly before me my daughter's downfall and death?"

Her voice was tragic, and Frederick's heart always had been tender toward his mother. He saw as vividly as if it had happened but yesterday Teola dying in the church. It had been such a dreadful experience for all of them. Frederick had never doubted for one moment that that terrible ordeal had been the cause of his father's death. He went quickly forward and slipped one arm about her shoulders.

"I'm sorry, mater," he murmured. "There, forgive me!—There!—Don't cry!... Now don't get nervous—the doctor said you mustn't cry."

Mrs. Graves shivered in the strong arms.

"I've reason enough to cry," she whimpered brokenly. "You won't do anything to help me, and you're the one who should."

"I'll go to work," he said eagerly. He sat down on the edge of the bed. "I'm tired of college anyway!"

"Go to work!" echoed his mother. "What could you do? You wouldn't

44

get ten dollars a week. Nor anything like it. You haven't any profession, and what is there in Ithaca to do anyway?... Oh, if your father'd only lived!"

She broke into a fresh burst of tears.

"Hush, please, dear," said Frederick, smoothing back the grey hair. "Go on and tell me what you want. There, see, now, I'm listening."

Mrs. Graves used her handkerchief vigorously.

"I said I wanted you to marry Madelene Waldstricker," she responded in ruffled tones. "You've but to ask her, and she'll jump. Babe says she talks of you all the time, and is frightfully jealous of you."

A fair, lovely face, glorious glistening brown eyes, and shrouding red curls passed between Frederick's vision and his mother's face, and he groaned.

"Don't! I said not to talk of Tess."

"But I can't help it," snapped Mrs. Graves. "I've got to tell you about Madelene, haven't I? You must ask her now.... She's staying here tonight."

Frederick withdrew his arms from under his mother and dropped his face hopelessly into his hands.

"Oh, God, help me!" he groaned between his fingers. "I can't do that, Mother! I can't!"

A tender hand went out slowly and touched him. He lifted his face with a sharp gesture and grasped his mother's fingers in his.

"Don't ask me to do that, oh, don't, darling mater, don't!" he moaned. "Anything else—I'd do anything else."

The feminine fingers closed over the masculine ones.

"I must ask you, my son," insisted Mrs. Graves, gently. "It's the only hope I have.... I've kept so many things from you, but now I'll tell you why. The lake place is mortgaged to Ebenezer Waldstricker for more than it's worth, and I've borrowed a lot of money from him and from Madelene."

Frederick's hands fell from his face.

"Good God! My God!" he exclaimed hoarsely. "Why didn't you tell me before?"

"I couldn't—I couldn't, Fred, but now you see why you must do this for all our sakes. I haven't any money at all only what they let me have. Babe and I won't have any place to go if you don't help. Oh, Fred, you will think of it, dear, you will?"

The boy got up feeling as if something worse than death had happened to him. He saw no way out.

"Yes, I'll think of it," he temporized.

Mrs. Graves sank deeper into her pillow and closed her eyes with a long sigh. Frederick said no more, but turned quickly and went out of the room.

He staggered downstairs like a drunken man. He ought to have told his mother he was married to Tessibel Skinner. He couldn't marry any other woman!... How could he, when he was already married—married to the sweetest girl in the world? Oh, to get away somewhere to think quietly! To get something to stop the throbbing in his head! This new horror facing him was more than he could bear. He'd go back now and tell his mother he was married to Tess.... No, he'd wait until morning! He opened the library door and stepped in, crossed the room slowly and drew down the curtain. Turning,

45

he saw a girl rise from the divan. Madelene Waldstricker reached out two rounded arms with an impatient gesture.

"Ah, you've come," she said, smiling into his eyes.

Frederick gazed at the small girlish figure curiously. The new interest in her awakened by the talk he'd just had with his mother, contended with the image of Tess in his mind—radiant, loving, splendid Tess.

He walked to the table and feigned interest in a book.

"I've been with my mother," he said hesitatingly.

"Yes, I know," asserted Madelene, coming to his side, "and she's awfully ill, isn't she?"

"More nervous than anything," replied the boy, impatiently.

"The doctor told your sister and me this afternoon she must have perfect rest if she ever recovers," explained Madelene. "He says she ought to be in a good health resort.... I wish I could help her."

"She tells me you have," blurted Frederick.

"But not so much as I'd like to," Madelene assured him softly.

There was deep sympathy in her voice, and Frederick looked at her critically. This small brown girl had taken on new significance to him. She had come into his life suddenly as a large part of it, that deadening financial part that tied him hand and foot and made him feel like a galley slave. But he could never marry her, never! He belonged to Tessibel Skinner by all the rights of Heaven and earth. He studied the eager girl again—for so long a time that she dropped her lids, blushing. Truly, Tess and Madelene formed a strange contrast—his bride with the red gold of her curls and eyes holding him a willing captive, and this bright-eyed, brown-skinned, little creature, before him with that eloquent, calling appeal of money for his mother.

Never before had he thought any one could for any reason whatever come between him and Tessibel Skinner. He did not concede it now in its fullness, but Madelene was looking pleadingly into his face and had spoken of his mother with tender sympathy. He suddenly reached out and took her hand. He would tell her of his young wife. He would take her into his confidence right then, and all would be well for them both—and for Tess.

"Listen, Madelene," the boy said earnestly. "I have something to say to you."

At the touch of his fingers, Madelene went white and swayed toward him. Her head fell forward on his chest, and his arms closed around her, as if to keep her from falling. Of a sudden, a flushed face was lifted to his, and a smile flashed around a rosy mouth.

"Oh, I'm so happy, oh, so happy!" whispered pursed lips.

And Madelene sighed as she dropped her head against him once more. For the moment Frederick's mind went blank, but the girl's voice drew him back.

"Oh, I was afraid you loved that girl who sings in the church," she was saying. "I've heard so often you did. I just couldn't bear the thought of it, Frederick. Your mother and Babe kept telling me you didn't, but I suppose I was a little jealous."

She laughed and snuggled nearer him. But a short hour before another girl, the girl he adored, his wife, had been in the same tender position. He was so dazed that for the moment he could not find words for an answer. Then slowly he led her forward to the divan.

"I want to talk to you," he ventured hesitatingly.

"Oh, I love to hear you talk," Madelene babbled with joy.

Frederick flushed. He'd have to tell her of his marriage with Tessibel before she really admitted anything that would afterwards make her sorry.

"What I've got to tell you is very serious," he said at length. "You'll listen to me, Madelene?"

Five small fingers touched his lips.

"Nothing is serious now," came the interruption, "not now that I know you love me. It's all I want in the world to make me supremely happy," and she sighed.

Frederick shuddered. Why, he hadn't told her he loved her! He was as far from loving her at that moment as the very stranger on the street.

"But it's something you must know," he thrust in desperately.

"I know what it is," averred the girl smiling. "I know all about it.... It's just money, that horrid old money your mother borrowed of brother and me.... But what does money matter? I've lots of it, bunches of it, and more than enough for us all, and so has Ebenezer."

Frederick shook himself impatiently. She must listen while he explained the impossibility of their ever being anything to each other.

"I couldn't take—"

"I'm not asking you to take anything but me," laughed the girl. "Just me, see? There, dearest! Now don't talk of anything disagreeable tonight. I just want to be happy."

And like a contented, purring kitten, she once more settled herself against him. Somehow Frederick couldn't tell her of Tessibel just then. The right moment had come and gone. In the morning he would! By the light of the day it would be easier. Then he would explain everything to her and his mother.

"Put your arms around me," whispered Madelene.

Thrusting Tessibel from his mind, he drew the little figure close into his arms.

"Kiss me," she breathed, and two hours later, when Frederick Graves shut his bedroom door, he had promised to marry Madelene Waldstricker.

CHAPTER XI
FREDERICK INTIMIDATED

Confused and angry with himself and Madelene, Frederick crossed the room slowly.

What an awful mess! Married to Tessibel and engaged to marry

47

Madelene! His mother sick and head over heels in debt to the Waldstrickers! The situation was becoming more complicated by the hour. He sat down by the open window to think. The simple thing, and what he really wanted to do, was to announce his marriage and let himself and the others take the consequences. He didn't intend to 'give up Tess, and for a few minutes his memory was alive with all the suffering of his brave young wife during the past two years. What she had done for his sister Teola made him shudder with grief. There was no other woman in the world like Tess, and the sweetness of his intimate experiences since his marriage touched him to tears.

"I won't give her up," he groaned aloud, "whatever happens, I'll stand by Tess. She's worth all the rest—I love her better than life itself. In the morning I'll tell mother and Madelene the truth."

But no sooner had he reached this conclusion, than the many embarrassing consequences his confession entailed presented themselves. He could hear his mother's querulous complaints. She hated Tess, blaming the little squatter girl for the trouble which had made her an invalid and taken her husband from her. Would he be compelled to choose between his affection for his mother and his love for Tess? No, surely not that!

Yet there was Madelene! How could he face her, after all that had happened. He bitterly regretted his weakness in permitting the girl to avow her love for him, in engaging himself to her.

And worst of all, that harrowing debt! He groaned at the thought of it.

Madelene had told him, "Your mother won't have to worry any more, dear. We can send her away for a nice, long rest, and when Professor Young's lease is up, we'll fix the lake place for a summer home."

"If I could marry Madelene," he thought, "the debts—"

He got up, lighted a cigarette, his fingers shaking so he almost dropped the match. He couldn't marry Madelene!

Yet to acknowledge his relation to the squatter girl meant a certain and final break with the Waldstrickers, the financial ruin of himself and his mother.

Even at that cost, he must do it. Tessibel was his wife, his dear little wife. He had promised to make a home for her. But how? Could they get along at all, and what would he do with her impossible father? As his mother had said, he had no ability to earn anything. Bitter tears of discouragement filled his eyes.

Suddenly, a thought found its way into his brain and seemed to clear the situation completely.

"If I could explain it to Tess," he whispered, "and she would consent, everything would be easy. I know she'd help me!"

Again and again, and from many different angles, the argument repeated itself.

He lay wakeful in bed, his mind a confused jumble of diversified thoughts, in which his mother, then Tess, and again the Waldstrickers demanded his attention and sought to influence him. Worn out, at length he fell into a troubled sleep.

He was late in rising the next morning. When he finally went into his mother's room, he found Madelene seated by the invalid's side, holding her hand. Frederick knew by the expression on their faces, that the girl had confided to his mother the agreement made in the drawing room the evening before. Smiling a little uncertainly, he crossed the room.

"Good morning, mater! Good morning, Madelene!" said he.

Madelene smiled shyly, stood up and moved a little away. Frederick bent over his mother, who kissed him and murmured, "I'm so pleased and happy."

He straightened up and took Madelene's outstretched hand, very much inclined to tell them both then how impossible it was for him to carry out his engagement. But his mother, ostentatiously turning on her pillow, cried laughingly.

"Don't mind me, children, dear!... Kiss your sweetheart, if you want to, Frederick!"

Snuggling to his side, Madelene threw her arms around his neck, and whispered,

"You do love me, dear, don't you?"

Smiling into her eyes, he kissed her.

"Of course I do," he lied promptly. "Don't you know it, little girl?"

After breakfast, Mrs. Graves summoned them to her room again. Relieved of her pressing anxieties, and excited by the sudden fruition of her cherished plans, she looked and acted much better. She talked gaily to the young people of their future, laughed at the girl's blushes, and chaffed her son about his coming responsibilities.

"Frederick," she suddenly said more soberly. "I think you should go right away now and see Ebenezer, and ask him properly for Madelene's hand."

Feeling that such a course would commit him irrevocably, the boy hesitated.

"Don't be afraid, Fred dear," Madelene broke in. "I know Eb likes you, and," blushingly, "I think he will not be much surprised, either."

If he could only summon courage enough to tell Madelene before they met her brother! Perhaps if he could get the girl alone he might.

"Come along with me," he said spontaneously. "We'll go together."

"Then wait until I get my hat," and she danced away, the happiest girl in Ithaca.

On the way down the street, although he responded with dutiful tenderness to his companion's conversation, his mind was busy with the same old question: What should he do about Tess? If he could tell Madelene, or perhaps it would be easier to make Ebenezer understand his position.

But before he came to a decision, they met Mr. Waldstricker coming out of the First National Bank on Tioga Street. He looked very prosperous, very powerful, as he stood smilingly waiting for them.

"We were just coming to see you, Eb," said Madelene, blushing. "Frederick—well, we both wanted to speak to you."

"All right, little girl," Waldstricker said pleasantly. "If it is something special, we can go to the office; or perhaps you can tell me here."

Hoping to gain courage by further respite Frederick suggested,

"We'd better go to the office, I think."

But Madelene was too full of her new happiness to brook any more delay.

"Oh, you men!" she exclaimed. "Don't be so formal and business-like!" She took hold of one of her brother's hands, while she held Frederick possessively by the arm. "We came to make an announcement and receive your congratulations, and I want them now."

"So that's it?" chuckled her brother, smiling into her shining eyes. "Well, I am pleased! And I do congratulate you both, heartily. Fred, run into the office in about an hour, I want to talk to you."

Frederick brightened.

"And I want to talk to you," he answered.

He swung to Madelene's side, drew a long breath and made a quick resolution that before long he would make his confession to Ebenezer.

At the appointed time, Frederick entered Waldstricker's office. He'd resolved to make a clean breast of his marriage to Tess. But without giving him a chance to say anything more than "Hello, Ebenezer," that gentleman began,

"Glad to see you! Sit down.... So you think you want to join my family, do you? I suppose you know you're asking a great deal, when you haven't any money or any profession, either. But then, my sister's fond of you, and that means a lot. Fortunately, she has enough money so that you need not worry about that. The question is, can you make her happy?"

He paused. Frederick fingered his hat, let it slide to the floor, and picked it up before answering.

"Mr. Waldstricker, I think ... I want first ... I can't ... You see...." He wanted desperately to tell the powerful man at the table that he couldn't marry his sister, but somehow the words wouldn't come.

The older man thought he knew the cause of the young man's hesitation.

"There, there, my boy!" he laughed, pleased at his own insight. "Don't try to explain anything. I know it's been hard for you. Frederick," he continued more soberly, "as you know, I'm Madelene's only near relative. Her mother has been dead many years, and since father ... was killed, she has only me left. I want her to be happy, ... to have everything that makes life worth while. She's chosen you, and I feel sure she's wise in her choice." He stood up, his great height towering above the boy, who also rose. Ebenezer thrust forth his hand and took Frederick's. "I'm giving her to you," he went on. "Make her happy and there's nothing I won't do for you."

Of course Frederick couldn't just then tell this man, who trusted him, that he was already married to a squatter girl. Perhaps later—yes, later he would. He hung his head in shame and the elder man, again mistaking the emotion, ascribed it to diffidence.

"Mr. Waldstricker," began Frederick, "you were so kind to my mother and so was Madelene. I'm not fit to marry your sister."

"Pshaw, boy, you're too modest!" Waldstricker laughed good-naturedly. "If she's satisfied, that's all there is to it."

50

Turning back to the desk, he seated himself.

"Sit down again, Fred," he continued. "Have you planned to get married immediately?"

Frederick shuddered. It seemed as if a great gulf were opening under his feet and he were about to be swallowed up.

"Well, we hadn't considered that," he hesitated embarrassedly. "Probably not for two years yet, until I get through college."

Here was a ray of hope. Lots of things could happen in two years.

"Nonsense!" was Waldstricker's prompt rejoinder. "Why should you bother with college? You'd better get married right along and go to Europe for your honeymoon. Then when you come back, take your place in my business and help me. I need some smart young fellow, and there's no sense in wasting your time at college. It isn't as though you had your own way to make."

Frederick sought to make objections to these plans, but Waldstricker impatiently got to his feet and stood looking down at the boy in the chair.

"It's settled then, isn't it? Say no more about it," he said with finality. "Run along and hunt up Madelene and tell her what I've said."

In parting, Waldstricker shook hands with Frederick, and placing his hand on the boy's shoulder said with genuine emotion in his voice, "Make her happy, my boy, and there's nothing in the world too good for you."

Frederick went into the sunshine, his head in a whirl. Waldstricker's promises unfolded visions of ease and success surpassing in splendor his wildest dreams. He had not meant to betray Tessibel nor to deceive Madelene. Yet since these things were forced upon him, he would see what he could do, but he took a long, deep breath when he thought of how difficult it would be to explain his action to Tessibel.

CHAPTER XII
MAKING READY FOR THE WARDEN

The next day, while Frederick was studying over the problems relating to his engagement to Madelene Waldstricker, Tessibel Skinner was sitting with Helen Young on the veranda of the latter's home. The young squatter girl was receiving a lesson in sewing.

"It air goin' to be pretty, ain't it?" she asked, holding up a blue chambray dress.

"Yes, very," replied Helen. "You're doing nicely. I'm very proud of you, dear!"

A shadow crept into Tessibel's eyes.

"I'll be a missin' ye awful after—after—"

"But you may come as often as you like to—our—home after we're married," said Helen, affectionately. "Mr. Waldstricker will soon grow fond of you, too, and the distance is only a little over a mile, short cut."

"But you'll be so rich," sighed Tess, "an' mebbe'll be awful busy."

"Never too busy to see my friends," Helen smiled. "There! Now you've been sewing an hour.... Let me hear you read.... By the way, I meant to tell you last night's paper said they're trailing the man who killed Mr. Waldstricker's father down here. The offer of five thousand dollars' reward is stirring a lot of men to hunt for him."

"I thought as how they'd lost 'im, sure," remarked Tess, inwardly quaking.

She forced her voice to say this in a tone as nearly natural as possible.

"Yes, I think the paper says they did lose track of him," replied Helen, "but they've suddenly found his trail again.... He must be somewhere near here. A deputy warden by the name of Burnett is coming to Ithaca.... Mr. Waldstricker will be very much pleased if they find him."

Tessibel's questioning gaze prompted Helen to proceed.

"The paper says, too, the men up there in Auburn are pretty sure he's somewhere among his own people."

A scarlet wave dyed Tessibel's face, and then receded. Her eyes drew down a little at the corners.

"Ye mean 'mong the squatters, don't ye?" she queried sharply. "Squatters air jest as good as any one else, Miss Young."

"Well, now, dear, I didn't mean they weren't," Helen laughed pleasantly; "and I'm sure if they're all like you, Tessibel, they're very nice indeed."

The memory of Teola Graves, the small, sickly baby, and the sudden death of Minister Graves passed through Tessibel's mind. The promise to her of the deed to the land on which their shanty stood was also in that procession of ghosts belonging to the past.

"Daddy and me was goin' to own our hut ground," she confided thoughtfully, "but—but—the dominie died afore we got it—so we air squatters yet jest the same as the rest. Squatters be awful nice folks! Most of 'em air better'n me."

"Well, anyway," took up Helen, wishing to keep off dangerous ground, "the paper says the warden's going to start from the head of Cayuga Lake and search every house and cabin until he—"

Tessibel rose to her feet unsteadily. In her vivid imagination she saw the strong arm of the law reach out from Auburn Prison and drag from her care and protection the wee, twisted little man chanting over the verses and prayers she'd taught him.

"I ain't a goin' to read today,—I got to go now," she gulped. "Good bye, Miss Young."

Daddy Skinner unbarred the door when he heard Tessibel call his name. At the sight of his young daughter's agitated face, the fisherman slid into his chair, beckoning her to a place on his knee.

"What air doin', Tess?" he questioned swiftly. "Ye're as white as bleached starch."

Tess placed her finger on her lips, glancing in the direction of the garret. Getting up, she barred the door and crept back to her father's side.

"Burnett air a scootin' down here after Andy," she murmured, too low for the dwarf to hear. "Miss Young says it air in the paper. I got to tell the poor little feller now so he won't die o' fright when the warden comes."

She went to the ladder and looked up through the hole. Then she set one foot on the lower rung and began to sing softly,

"Rescue the Perishin';
Care for the Dyin'."

And on and on she sang, in throbbing melody, to the end of the hymn. Tess had long ago discovered the fear-dissipating qualities of "Rescue the Perishin'." A long happy sigh in the attic told her the dwarf had enjoyed her song.

"Andy," she called in a low tone, "come down an' set beside the cot. I has to talk to ye."

Andy needed no second invitation. His legs were stiff but his heart full of good cheer, as he scrambled down the ladder with the Bible in his hand. Crawling across the floor, he propped his bent little body against the cot, and looked inquiringly at Daddy Skinner, and Daddy Skinner stared moodily back at him.

"Andy," Tess began, squatting beside him. "Ye remember how slick Daddy Skinner hopped out o' jail an' right back to me?"

Andy bobbed his head.

"Yep, I remember, brat," he responded. "I were glad fer him, but I sure were sorry fer myself when he left Auburn."

"An' I were that happy I nearly died," replied Tess, musingly. "Well, I air goin' to show ye a verse in the Bible what hauled 'im smack out o' prison." Tess took up the holy book and opened it. "There! now read it.... Right where my finger air! See?"

For several seconds Andy studied the words under Tessibel's pointing finger, and Daddy Skinner evinced his interest by bending nearer in a questioning attitude.

"If ye have faith as a grain of mustard seed," Andy spelled haltingly, and then glanced up, mystified. "Why, it air talkin' about movin' mountains.... Ain't it, Tess?"

"Sure!" agreed Tess, displaying her white teeth in smiling affirmation. "See?"

Andy shook his head.

"No, I don't see, brat," he replied. "I ain't wantin' to move no mountains, I ain't."

Tess flung back her curls impatiently.

"Oh, Andy, yer head air all bone. Now look at me."

Misty, eager eyes were raised to the girl's.

53

"Can't ye see, Andy dear," she proceeded solemnly, "it air harder to get a mountain out of yer way than 'tis to stay out of prison."

"Mebbe 'tis," conceded Andy, brightening. "I never thought of it like that."

"But ye must begin thinkin' quick," ordered Tess. "Now every minute of the day ye air to say over an' over verses I show ye. And the man who helps folks move mountains'll keep ye right in this shack.... I air thinkin' that'd suit ye some, huh?"

Andy looked at her meltingly.

"I'd ruther be here than any place in the hull world," he murmured in reverent humility.

"Then," avowed Tess, "I air a goin'—Oh, Andy, I got to tell ye somethin', honey, an' I—"

"What?" gasped Andy, faintly.

Tess paused an instant.

"Burnett's pell-mellin' down from Auburn after ye," she blurted. "I just heard it at Young's."

Andy's face blanched to the hue of death. He had been so satisfied—so secure in the little garret under the protection of his friends, and now he would have to go back after all.

"Burnett?" he repeated almost inaudibly. "Burnett's comin' after me?"

Tess reached out and touched him.

"But he ain't knowing ye air here," she asserted hastily. "An' he ain't a goin' to know it uther. An' I tell ye, Andy, if ye'll learn yerself that verse 'bout the mustard seed, it'll keep ye here."

"I'll learn it, brat," promised Andy, but he seemed as if turned to stone.

"But what be we goin' to do, kid?" asked Skinner, a look of helplessness wrinkling his face.

"I dunno," replied Tess, with her hand still on the dwarf's arm.

And that was true, too! Tessibel didn't know just at that moment what she could do to save Andy from the officers, but of one thing she was certain; that beyond where the birds flew, and above the fast-moving clouds, and over all and under all, was an arm and a love upon which she had leaned and trusted, and they had never failed her. With this thought deepening the red-brown eyes, she turned and looked first at her Bible-backed father and then at the little dwarf.

"There air one thing ye both got to do," she instructed them. "Ye got to stop yer worryin' an' ye got to stop bein' 'fraid."

Andy's jaw dropped.

"Stop bein' 'fraid!" he muttered. "Stop bein' 'fraid! God, Tessibel, ye don't know what it means to allers be in the shadow of the prison, you don't."

"Oh, yep I do," interposed Tess, blandly, "'course I do. Weren't Daddy Skinner there? An' Daddy never'd got out in this world if it hadn't been for a helpin' hand; the same'll help you, Andy."

"She's talkin' of Professor Young," grunted Orn, glancing at the dwarf.

Tess turned to her parent impatiently.

54

"I ain't nuther talkin' about Professor Young, Daddy. I ain't goin' to tell him Andy's here 't all! I'll tell you both who I mean right now."

The men leaned forward, the dwarf's head shooting out like a turtle's.

"Who d'ye mean?" he entreated brokenly.

The color mantled Tessibel's brow and swept in rich waves over the lovely, earnest face.

"Jesus," she breathed radiantly, flashing her eyes from one to the other. "Jesus jest air a dotin' on ye, Andy, ye poor little dub ye! He allers dotes on folks in trouble."

"Shucks!" grunted Andy, and "Holy thunderin' Moses!" fell from Daddy Skinner.

Tessibel stood up, an angry glint in her eyes.

"Ye can say, 'Shucks!' if ye want to, Andy, 'cause you don't know nothin'; but, Daddy Skinner, you ought to be ashamed of yerself. Why, he's the man what got ye out of jail! I couldn't a done nothin', an' Professor Young couldn't a done nothin' uther if Jesus hadn't helped him. An' now ye're saying, 'Holy thunderin' Moses,' just's if ye didn't believe it."

The fisherman drew a shaking hand across his shaggy chin whiskers.

"I s'pose I do believe it, brat," he groaned, "but it air all so kind a mysterious like, an' Young, ye know—Young fought like the devil to git me back home."

"I know he did, Daddy," affirmed the girl, "but can't ye see ye'd a gone to the rope if—"

A shrill cry broke from the dwarf, interrupting Tessibel's explanation. Those ominous words recalled his own terror of Auburn Prison. Tears gathered thick in his eyes and ran down his cheeks. The sight of the little man's misery so affected Tessibel that she wound one arm about his neck.

"Andy, darlin'," she comforted, "don't blubber like that. Don't I say! There, put yer head on Tessibel's shoulder! I air a goin' to mother ye a bit."

She took up her skirt, wiped away the dwarf's fast-falling tears, and then her own.

"Now ye mustn't snivel," she faltered, trying to be courageous. "Why, if ye keep it up, I don't know what Daddy an' me'll do. Listen, Andy, listen to Tess."

Placing a slender finger under his chin, Tess drew the wry face up until his tearful eyes were directed into hers.

"Andy," she imparted, "there ain't a deputy in this hull world can get ye, an' don't ye be worryin' 'bout it. Jesus'd butt in an' help ye afore the man could get his nippers on ye. He'll fix it so they can't get ye, I bet."

And of a truth, Tessibel knew whereof she spoke.

"But Burnett'll be here most any time, now," shivered the little man, his chest rising and falling with emotion, "an' I tell ye, Tess—" Here he straightened up, his eyes glistening. "I tell ye, once let 'im git after a house he thinks a feller air in an' he'd turn it topsy-turvy, tissel end up. Why, Burnett can smell a man from prison a mile. I know him, I do! Hain't I seen,—and you have too, Orn,—many a poor cuss get away just like I did, mebbe over the

55

river, mebbe a hundred miles or two, or he might even git in another state, but Burnett'll haul him back by his neck, jest the same."

Andy wilted at the end of his long speech like a hothouse plant in the frost.

"But he ain't a goin' to git you, Andy dear," Tess interposed, hugging the bent little figure. "Me an' Daddy loves ye, an' we'll hide ye, we will. Be glad ye're little, honey. If ye was big, it'd be harder to sneak ye out of sight."

"I don't see where ye're goin' to hide 'im, Tess?" remarked Skinner, making the statement a question by the rising inflection in his voice. "It air jest like Andy says, if Burnett gits on 'is scent, he'll find 'im all right, all right, an' five thousand dollars'd spur any man on to hunt 'im down."

The squatter girl smiled in sudden decision.

"They won't find 'im where I put 'im," said she, decisively.

"Tell us about it, brat," urged her father, wistfully.

Tess thought a minute, and hummed a minute.

"He air goin' to get put in my straw tick! That air where ye're goin', Andy," she explained presently. "An' I air got to be awful sick an' git in bed an' stay there. I don't know anything else to do! Oh dear! I can't look sick to save my life, can I?"

She got up and went to the glass and considered minutely her own rosy reflection. After contemplating it for some time, she came back and sat down, leaning a dimpled chin on the palm of one hand.

"I guess as how I don't need to be sick anywhere inside me," she decided. Then a smile smoothed away the slight pucker on her brow. "I know! I could hurt my foot, couldn't I? I guess as how that air best.... I'll hurt my foot.... Mebbe I'll sprain my ankle. I dunno yet, but I'll be a bed all right, an' I'll have Deacon with me. I bet when that warden sees me spread on that cot an' a owl starin' at 'im, he won't even think o' askin' me to git up."

The dwarf uttered a weird cry in chorus with a groan from the squatter.

"What'll ye do, if he tries to take ye offen the bed?" Orn questioned.

Tess tossed the profusion of curls over her shoulder, and her smile showed two rows of white teeth.

"I'll grin at him first, like this," she laughed, "an' if that don't do no good, I'll sing at 'im. I air bettin' he won't touch me then. But if he goes to haul me off, I'll holler an' make such a fuss I bet he'll be glad to let me alone."

With this statement, Tessibel rose and finished, "Get off'n that bed, Daddy. I air goin' to begin rippin' the tick now. If them deputies be comin' down the lake, us uns got to be ready.... It's only straw, ye know, Andy, an' awful soft. I'll fix yer head so it'll hang out a little. Then ye can breathe."

Before the shadow of the willow trees went to sleep in their soft earth bed late that afternoon, Tessibel had fitted the dwarf into the space she had made vacant in her straw tick. At the top of the springs, which consisted of taut ropes, she made a comfortable pillow for the little man's head. And then they waited, the hearts of the two men heavy with bitter fear, and the heart of the girl vibrant with faith that all would be well with her friend.

CHAPTER XIII
SANDY PROPOSES TO TESS

Andy Bishop was stretched out in the middle of Tessibel's straw tick, while the girl measured her length on the cot to assure her father that the dwarf would be fully concealed from prying eyes.

"Does he seem all hid, Daddy Skinner?" queried she.

The squatter walked to the head of the cot and peered from all points of vantage.

"He sure air, kid," he chuckled. "I can't see nothin' but a row of red curls a mile long. Andy'll git back in the garret all right if Burnett don't pull you off'n that bed."

"He won't do that," said Tess. "Jesus'll see I stay on it, I bet."

"There's some un a comin' now," hissed Skinner between his teeth, startled. Tess had no more than cuddled under the blanket when a loud knock resounded throughout the shanty. Daddy Skinner lifted the bar and opened the door, his large form filling the narrow door-frame. At the sight of Sandy Letts' smiling face, he stepped back, relieved.

"God, Sandy," he grinned, "ye might as well kill a man as scare him to death. Come in an' set."

Lysander stepped into the kitchen, and his eyes fell upon Tess.

"What air the matter with the brat?" he asked, looking from Orn to the girl lying there so languidly.

"She air kind a hurt—" began the fisherman.

"My foot air all packed up in a rag," interjected Tess. "I air always doin' something to myself. The next time I come jumpin' down the lane, I hope I won't be hurtin' my ankle."

She smiled wanly at Sandy, and he grinned back at her.

"If I knowed ye was sick, Tess, I'd a brought ye some candy," said he, good-naturedly.

"Candy ain't good for a girl's teeth," sighed Tess. "Don't never bother 'bout bringin' it, Sandy."

"A pound or two won't hurt ye," asserted Letts. "An' when I likes a girl, I allers bring 'er sweets. I say kid, ye do look awful pretty, layin' there with your curls all stretched out that way. Now, my cousin Ben, he wanted to marry ye, too, but he never liked yer hair; I love it."

"Daddy were jest a sayin'," put in Tess, with a fleeting glance at her father, "that it air mighty good for my curls to get spread out like this. Wasn't you, Daddy?"

Daddy Skinner stared at her, and her warm, glowing smile gave strength to the old man's heart. Without waiting for his reply, Tess turned to Letts.

"Where ye been, Sandy, an' what ye been doin'?" she asked, simulating an interest she did not feel.

Lysander, pleased at the attention, thrust his thumbs into the

57

armholes of his vest and spread out all his fingers, giving a little important twist to each.

"I been down to Riker's a searchin' their shack fer Andy Bishop," bragged he, "an' now I air goin' to Longman's."

A little groan fell from Tessibel's lips.

"I air ashamed of ye, Sandy," she said slowly. "Longmans wouldn't have no murderer in their hut.... They be awful good folks.... Ye know they be, Sandy."

"Sure I know it, Tessie, but I've said as how I air goin' to search all the squatters' huts an' I air goin' to do it, I can tell ye that."

Tess smiled at him wistfully, pleadingly.

"I'd hate ye all my life, Sandy Letts," she vowed, winking one eye at the burly squatter, "if ye'd come in my house and butt 'round. Course ye can do it if ye want to, but I'd never speak to ye again in the hull world."

Sandy threw back his head and guffawed.

"I wouldn't do nothin' like that to you, pretty kid," he answered with pride in his tones, "'cause I know if ye had that dwarf in this hut ye'd pass him up to me quick.... Five thousand ain't to be got off'n every bush these days. I air after that Waldstricker reward, an' I air goin' to get it!"

Tess spread a little wider a few of the dusky, shining curls.

"It's a lot o' money," she said thoughtfully.

Letts hitched his chair nearer the cot and bent over eagerly.

"Sure it air, Tessie," he said, "an' I air here today a purpose to tell ye somethin'. I want you an' yer pa to listen wise to me fer a minute. I air goin' to git that there five thousand an' I air goin' to marry you."

Tess started to speak, but Lysander stopped her with a wag of his head and a wave of his hand.

"I said for ye to listen," he cried brusquely. "Ye ain't havin' offers like mine every day, miss, an' yer Daddy won't never have no chances like I air givin' 'im. I said listen, an' here air what I say.

"It won't be more'n a week afore I hand that dwarf over to the warden. Burnett air comin' down from Auburn. He air almost here by this time. Then when I git the money, I air a goin' to put yer Daddy in a nice place where he'll get rid of 'is rheumatiz, an' after that I air goin' to fix my shack up with a lot of new stuff, an' ye can have the choosin' of it, brat, an' there air my word, by God."

Sandy gazed from father to daughter with a broad smile. He had delivered his speech in pompous pride, his voice rising higher and louder with each word.

"What do ye say, Orn?" he demanded.

Skinner looked at Tess out of the corner of his eye. He could see her lips moving ever so slightly, and he knew she was murmuring a prayer for the little man in the straw. His own eyes felt stinging tears around their lids.

"Ye'll have to settle it with the brat," said he at length, wiping his lips with the back of his hand. "I've allers said 's how if Tess wanted to git married, I wouldn't say nothin' 'gainst it, as long as she got a good man."

"An' I air that," Sandy affirmed positively. "'Course I been in jail more'n

58

fifty times, an' mebbe I'll git in fifty times more, but that don't do a man no harm as I knows of. I'd allers leave a little money home for my fambly."

He threw his bold, black eyes upon the little figure in the bed, and the girl dropped her lids.

"How about it, Tessie?" he wheedled in low tones.

Tess wriggled. She didn't know just what answer to give. She wanted to keep the big squatter good-natured, yet desired that he should go away. She was sorry for the little man beneath her.

Prompted by instinct, she turned her solemn brown eyes upon Letts.

"I'll say this to ye, Sandy," she began. "If ye'll let me alone, an' not be tryin' always to kiss me—"

Lysander cracked his knee with one large fist.

"I ain't never got a kiss from ye yet, brat," he chuckled.

"'Course not," she responded; "but 'tain't because ye ain't fit fer one, now air it, Sandy?"

"No, ye can bet on that," laughed the man, "an' I got marks on my shins to this day you put on 'em the last time I tried it. But I like to see ye fight, brat, I swear I do.... Now, how about gettin' married to me, huh?"

Tessibel contemplated the heavy face a moment. She was going to drive a hard bargain with Lysander if she had to drive any at all.

"Ben used to make me awful mad teasin' for kisses," she exclaimed. "I told him an' I air tellin' you, Sandy, I ain't goin' to give any man my kisses less'n I marry him."

Letts puffed out his chest and struck it with a loud resounding whack.

"I air glad of that," he grinned. "It sounds good to me, you bet. I don't want no other man palaverin' over my woman. I got—"

"An' you been makin' me mad lately, too, Sandy," Tess interrupted, "what with runnin' after me an' makin' me fight to keep my own kisses, I don't have no peace. Now, I'll tell ye what I'll do. You get busy an' find Andy Bishop, an' git that five thousand, then ye come here again an' ask me what ye just did, an' ye see what I say to ye. Eh? How'd that suit ye?"

A scarlet flush rushed over Lett's swarthy skin.

"But ye got to promise me ye won't ever try fer no more kisses, till I git married to ye, Sandy," Tess continued. "You said what you wanted; now, I've said somethin', an' I mean it too."

Letts shifted one large boot along a crack in the floor. He was thinking deeply.

"That's pretty tough on a feller when he air lovin' a girl the way I love you, brat," he said after a while.

"But ye got to promise what I want ye to, Sandy, or mebbe I'll git married to some 'un else."

"Ye'd better not, kid," he muttered darkly, "if ye don't want to git yerself an' the other fellow into trouble."

"Then ye'd best promise 'bout the kisses," returned Tess, decidedly.

"I'd kiss ye now fer a two cent piece," he undertoned passionately, but Daddy Skinner had his hand on the other man's arm before he could move toward the cot.

"I wouldn't do nothin' like that, Sandy," he said, ominously. "No man don't kiss my brat less'n she air wantin' his kisses. Tessibel said as how when ye git Bishop an' the five thousand, ye can come back.... Today, she ain't feelin' well, an' I air goin' to ask ye to go along home, or wherever ye were pointed fer when ye stopped 'ere."

Then Daddy Skinner opened the door.

"The leaves won't be fallin' from the trees, brat," he flung back sulkily, "afore I come fer ye, an' don't forget it!"

Daddy Skinner closed the door and dropped the bar after his departed guest, and there was silence in the shanty until the sound of Lysander's footsteps faded away.

Then Tess crawled off the dwarf and stood up.

"Landy," she groaned, "wouldn't that crack yer ribs! Now I got to be prayin' to beat the band every minute to keep Andy in the garret an' to save me from bein' married to the hatefullest old squatter devil in the hull world."

CHAPTER XIV
THE WARDEN'S COMING

At ten o'clock in the morning, the day after Andy Bishop was fitted into Tessibel's straw tick, a covered runabout wound its way along the lower boulevard running to Glenwood. Two men were seated in it, solemn, dark-browed men, with dull eyes and heavy faces. The man holding the reins was heavy set, square shouldered, and more sternly visaged than his companion. Some one had said of Howard Burnett, that the Powers, in setting him up, had used steel cables for his muscles and iron for his bones; and surely there was a grim grip to his jaw that presaged evil to those opposing him.

"Devilish queer," he muttered, after a long silence, "how that little dwarf ever disappeared the way he has, isn't it, Todd?"

"Not so strange after all," protested Todd. "Andy Bishop could crawl into a rabbit hole and still give the rabbit room to sleep."

"That's true, too, but you'd think his deformity would prevent his getting very far.... Now wouldn't you?"

"Well, I don't know about that, either." The speaker struck a match under the lapel of his coat, and cupping the tiny flame in his hand, held it up to the dead cigar in his mouth, and added between puffs, "Human nature's a funny thing!... Now Andy's got a kind a pleasin' way with him ... even if he is deformed, ... and he's got a peach of a voice. Why, he speaks as soft as a woman.... I wouldn't want him to ask me to do anything I was set against if I didn't want to do it."

"Rotten rubbish!" spat out Burnett. "I don't give a tinker's damn about his voice. It's up to me to run the dwarf to earth, and I'm goin' to do it."

After a very long silence, Todd turned to Burnett.

"But what does get me is why the five thousand Waldstricker's put up, ain't been bait to catch Bishop before this," he said ruminatively.

"Well, it hain't, that's evident," growled Burnett, setting his teeth.

As a rabbit lifts its head, frightened at unusual sights and sounds, so Jake Brewer lifted a startled face as Howard Burnett pulled up his horse suddenly at the squatter's side. The warden stopped the man's progress by lifting his hand.

"Say, you, wait a minute there," he added to his imperative gesture.

Jake paused, curious and attentive.

"Haven't seen a dwarf, anywhere, named Bishop, have you?" Burnett shot forth, leaning toward Brewer.

The squatter shook his head. "There be some Bishops round here," he retorted surlily, "but there ain't no dwarf as I know of by that name."

"Where's the road leadin' down to that row of shacks by the lake?" demanded Burnett. "Ain't there a lot of squatters living there?"

Brewer assented by a wag of his head.

"No end of 'em," said he, "but there ain't no very easy way gettin' down with a horse.... Still, mebbe ye could.... Might tie yer wagon an' walk down."

"Who're you?" shouted the warden, gruffly.

Jake cringed as if the questioner had struck him.

"Jake Brewer," was the unsteady response.

"What's your business?"

"I ain't got no real business," replied the other apologetically. "I fishes an' hunts an' things like that."

"A squatter—eh?"

"Yep, I air a squatter all right," Jake admitted, "but I air a decent man, an' allers been decent. I don't do nothin' I hadn't ought to."

"Who's sayin' you do?" snapped Burnett. "Now, I want to ask you a few questions. I'm from Auburn Prison, and if you lie to me, I'll put you where the dogs won't bite you.... Do you get me?"

Jake's jaw dropped, but he stood still, and looked at the officer anxiously.

"Yep, I get ye," he returned submissively, "an' I ain't a goin' to lie to ye nuther.... What do ye want?"

Burnett's fierce eyes bent a compelling glance on the man in the road.

"How many squatters 're living down by the lake?" he demanded harshly.

Brewer thought a minute.

"I calc'late mebbe there air fifty, mebbe a hundred," he answered. "I ain't never counted 'em, mister."

Jake moved on a little, but the warden stopped him peremptorily.

"Any jail birds down there?" he thrust at him.

Brewer made a negative gesture.

"Not's I know of," he stammered.

"Ain't nobody down there been in jail? Anybody ever been to Auburn?"

Jake's crooked fingers mounted from his hair line to the back of his skull, lifting the soft cap partly from his head. Then he scratched his chin thoughtfully.

"Well, there ain't no guilty man down there," he said, at last. "There air Orn Skinner—"

Burnett gave an exultant cry.

"My God, I'd forgotten he came from this part of the country! So Skinner's here among this set of squatters, eh? What luck! I'll bet—"

"Ye won't find no dwarf in Skinner's shanty," expostulated Brewer with conviction.

"That's up to me to find out!" growled the warden. "Where does Skinner live? Near here?"

Brewer's fingers directed south.

"First turn to the left, 'bout a mile ahead," he pointed out. "Skinner's shack air close to the lake. A hedge and lots of flowers air growin' 'round it."

Burnett tightened his lines, chirruped to the horse, and drove on, the squatter staring open-mouthed after him.

The summer sun bathed the hillside and warmed the Skinner shanty. Tessibel's hedge lifted its green head upward as if to catch the golden rays. The flower beds rimmed the hut like a bewildering, gorgeous rainbow. Everything belonging to Tess seemed at absolute peace with itself and the world.

Orn Skinner, his head sunken between the two humps on his shoulders, was lazily whittling a stick when the sound of a horse's hoofs in the lane near Young's barn arrested his attention. It was the one sound the squatter expected that day, yet dreaded. Furtively, he leaned back near the partly open door.

"Some 'un's coming, Tess," he warned.

Evidently, the fisherman did not expect an answer, for he straightened up once more and proceeded to whittle. The pitter-patter of the trotting horse, and the clatter of the wheels upon the flinty road, broke rudely upon the familiar little noises of the quiet summer morning. One sidewise glance satisfied Orn that the men in the vehicle were from Auburn prison. He stopped whittling but a moment when Burnett drew up.

"Hello, Orn," called the officer, stentorian-voiced.

"Hello," and the squatter made a polite salute with his stick.

Burnett tossed the reins to the man at his side and climbed to the ground, advancing toward the fisherman.

"This your hut, Skinner?" he interrogated.

Orn Skinner's tongue clove to the roof of his mouth. He endeavored to speak, but apprehension and dread had apparently paralyzed his vocal organs. He hadn't fully realized until that moment how desperate the venture to which he had committed himself and Tess. Between Andy Bishop and this formidable giant from Auburn was but the brave little daughter inside the hut. Would she be able to carry through the hazardous task she'd undertaken?

"You remember me, don't you, Skinner?"

It took several seconds before the fisherman could clear his throat enough to speak.

"Yep," he succeeded at length in muttering. "I remember ye all right.... Ye air Burnett from Auburn, ain't ye?... What do ye want around here?"

Suddenly there came to the powerful officer a wild desire to throttle the heavy-headed squatter. He had a feeling that this man knew more than he could be forced to tell, perhaps.

"Better hold a civil tongue in your head, old fellow," he threatened, "if you know what's best for you."

Orn lifted one great shoulder.

"Ye ain't got nothin' on me, Burnett," he snarled defiantly, "but I know ye wouldn't be comin' 'round here if ye didn't have somethin' to come fer."

The warden shoved his grim face so close to the speaker's that he drew back, intimidated.

"Sure, I come for something," snorted Burnett, viciously.

"Then peel it off," answered Skinner, deep in his throat. "I air listenin'."

He was bending so far back now that his shaggy head rested against the shanty boards. Burnett was piercing him with a strange, mesmeric gaze.

"Where's Andy Bishop?" boomed like thunder from the warden.

That name, though he knew his questioner's errand, so suddenly falling on Orn's ears, congealed his blood and knotted his muscles with fear.

"Andy Bishop?" he echoed irresolutely. "Andy Bishop? Who air Andy Bishop?"

Burnett lifted a huge fist, but dropped it again. The time hadn't arrived to punch from Skinner the knowledge he wanted. Later, perhaps—

"Now none of that, Skinner," he barked savagely. "None of that, you hump-backed brute. You know perfectly well who I mean, and you know where the dwarf is, and we want him and we want him quick.... He made his getaway from Auburn.... Now give him up, see?"

Second by second, and minute by minute, Orn Skinner was gathering his courage and strength. All through his life he had been used to brutal officials like Burnett; so swallowing hard, he raised his great gray head and looked straight into the other's dark face.

"If ye mean that little dwarf who were up to Auburn when I were there, I don't know nothin' about him," he said. "I ain't never heard he come from this end of the lake."

The warden's fist knotted once more.

"You're a liar, Skinner," he scraped from his throat. "Now look here! I know confounded well you know where he is. If you don't want me to hand you trouble by the bushel, you'd better cough up that little dwarf. Get me? Eh?"

The fingers holding the broad-bladed knife sank to the fisherman's knee, and for a moment the stick Orn had been cutting poised in the air. Then a slow, broad smile showed his discolored teeth.

"It air the truth I been tellin' you," he declared deliberately. "I don't know nothin' about Bishop, an' I don't want to know nothin'…. Ye ain't got anything on me, Burnett. I air a livin' here peaceful with my kid."

"Well, I'm goin' to search your shanty, anyhow," Burnett growled menacingly, his under jaw sticking out like a bull dog's.

"Well, search it, I ain't carin'," consented Orn. "But my kid air sick in there, an' I don't want ye to scare her."

Without waiting for further parley, Burnett, like an enraged lion, bounded to the shanty threshold and one long stride took him well on his way across the kitchen. Suddenly he stopped, staring straight ahead of him, as if some shining spectre from another world had appeared in his path.

CHAPTER XV
THE SEARCH

Burnett wiped his hand across his eyes to efface the vision which so unexpectedly impeded his official progress. It was the sight of a girl, nestled on a cot, and over the pillow upon which her head rested was strewn in a wild, magnificent disarray, a profusion of tawny curls, such as he never had seen. For a moment the corpulent deputy from Auburn, the terror of all the criminals in the country around, forgot his delegated obligation to the state. Tessibel Skinner's two slender arms huddled a small, speckled hoot owl; and as in a dream, Burnett noted the girl's red lips touched the bird affectionately in a hasty little caress. Another thing he noted was the unflinching and prolonged questioning glance with which the red-brown eyes met his. Tess couldn't speak a word at first, now that she was actually face to face with the man after Andy. He was even sterner than she had imagined he would be.

Quite gravely she considered his big frame from head to foot, took hasty account of the firm setting of his jaw, and the deep, clean-cut lines from his eyes to his chin. Then, she smiled a rare, enchanting smile, the deepening dimples around the red moist lips suffusing the deputy warden with a warm, welcoming glow.

"I heard ye talkin' to Daddy, mister," she said, gulping. "I air awful glad ye came in to see me too. I'd a been hurt if ye'd gone without my gettin' a peep at ye."

During each infinitesimal space of time, Burnett stood in the sunshine of Tessibel's smile, his austere churlishness was slipping from him like a loosened garment. As if forced by an unseen hand, he took one step nearer her.

"Set down, sir," invited Tess, clutching the owl with one hand, and making an elaborate sweep with the other. "That air Daddy's chair—ye air awful handsome and big, but the chair'll hold ye all right."

Burnett caught his breath and sank into the indicated seat. He'd intended to turn that shanty over from top to bottom, to rip it almost to the ground. But the sight of the red-headed sprite on the cot fondling a woodland owl, and the effect of her smile upon the beating of his heart, dissolved his rage and stayed his action.

"Well, I'll be damned!" was all he said, and Tess smiled again. She didn't mind if he swore. The one thing she desired was to get rid of him as soon as possible. She was conscious of the gyrations of Andy Bishop curled in the straw under her slender body, and she knew her curls were shrouding a face distorted with anxiety.

"Are you sick, kid?" questioned Burnett, when he could draw a natural breath.

"Well, ye see," acknowledged Tess, "I ain't 'xactly sick, but I got my ankle all packed up. Sometimes girls hurt their ankles an' they have to put a rag 'round 'em."

Tessibel was very careful not to say she'd hurt hers in this explanation to Burnett's question.

"An' then ye see, sir," she pursued, "if ye turn yer foot over an' can't walk, ye have to go to bed a spell, huh?"

"Well, I should say so!" asseverated Burnett, mustering the manner he always used with ladies. "Say, by George, I didn't know Orn Skinner had a pretty kid like you."

"My, didn't ye?" gurgled Tess, with shy lids drooping and her color mounting. "I thought everybody in the hull world knew I were Daddy's brat. He air had me fer ever so long. I been growed up for a lot of years." She shifted the owl in her arms. "This owl air named Deacon.... Want to pet 'im a minute, huh?"

The warden threw back his head and roared. He felt as if he'd been hung up for days by the thumbs—that this girl had mercifully cut the ropes and let him down once more to peace and happiness.

"No, thanks, I'll let you keep your pet," he laughed good-humoredly. "Queer play fellow for a girl, that's my opinion."

After a few more compliments, through which Tessibel flirted her way into the big man's regard, the officer rose to his feet.

"Little lady, I came here for a specific reason," he announced. Unquenchable mischief shone upon him from smiling, enquiring eyes.

"Oh," giggled Tess, "anyway, I air awful glad ye come."

The grim lips of the deputy curled upward again. Tess adored his mouth twisted at the corners like that.

"I might as well get it over first as last," ventured Burnett. "But I'm more'n anxious you shouldn't be mad at me. The fact is we've traced a man down from Auburn—"

Tessibel interrupted him, startled; at least she acted so.

"From Auburn!" she gasped.

"Yes, ma'am, a murderer! Andy Bishop. Little man like this," the warden explained, measuring a short space from the floor. "By some means or other he wriggled his way out of prison—"

Tessibel's lips trembled and she turned her eyes away. Old memories rushed over her, memories of the cold winter when she'd been alone in the shack.

"An' ye thought 'cause Daddy'd been up there once, the man must a run right straight here, huh?" she accused, with a sob in her voice.

"Well, I'll admit till I saw you I thought—I thought, but now—," a negative gesture with his hand finished his answer.

Tessibel turned withering, tear-wet eyes on her visitor.

"I 'spose ye air thinkin' my Daddy even had something to do with his flyin' the coop?" she flared up. "Air that it?"

"No! No! I didn't think that 'at all," the under-warden made haste to deny. "I just couldn't think that about your father."

Tessibel dimpled, suddenly glowing like a vivid poppy.

"Thank ye," she whispered, wiping away the tears. "Why! My Daddy wouldn't do nothin' bad for anythin' in the world. He's the best old Daddy livin'."

"Of course he is," vouched the warden, placatingly, "but what I want to know is would you mind, or would it hurt your feelings—The fact is, I came to search this house."

Tess had expected this, and without demurring, flashed forth,

"Ye mean ye want to go 'round it, don't ye, lookin' in all the corners an' places; air that it, sir?"

Burnett acknowledged this by a nod.

"Sure, search it if ye want to, I don't mind. Ye'll 'scuse me not gettin' up, won't ye? There ain't much to search, but ye can go in the garret if ye want to. It air only a cubby hole; even the weest man in the hull world couldn't stand up in it."

Andy stirred perceptibly beneath her.

"Then there air Daddy's room," Tess continued, "an' this room air the kitchen an' the dinin' room an' the parlor, an' all the other rooms.... An'—an' it air my room, too."

"My God, but you're a cute kid!" he chuckled.

Tessibel's laugh rang out deliciously fresh and free, and Burnett caught it up and sent it back in one loud guffaw. Then the girl lifted one of her curls and spread it out to its extreme length. Tess had been born possessing all the arts of her sex, and used them effectively, upon an occasion like this.

"I wish my ankle wasn't wrapped up," she smiled hospitably. "I'd show ye 'round the shanty myself. Ye noticed the hedge when ye come in, didn't ye? Well—I planted that an' all the flowers—and this owl belongs to me an' I keep 'im in the garret,—an'—I almost got a dog once, but not quite! Job Kennedy owns 'im, an his name air Pete, but he likes to live here better'n he does to Job's." Tess gasped for breath and flushed rosily. "But I air keepin' ye, sir," she excused, "an I mustn't do that. You go on and look in Daddy Skinner's room an'—then ye go up in the garret, an' then ye can look behind the chairs an' behind the stove, an' ye can look under the bed—"

She paused dramatically and held up a warning finger.

"Please don't scare none of my bats nor my uther owls in the garret. They be awful nice bats an' awful nice owls too! Ye wouldn't hurt 'em, would ye, mister?"

"I won't do anything you don't want me to, kid," the infatuated man promised. "Honest, I won't search the house if you say not."

"Oh, sure, search it," insisted Tess. "Then ye'll be pretty sure there ain't nobody hidin' 'round."

Burnett walked toward Daddy Skinner's room.

"I wouldn't mind havin' a daughter like you," he vowed, looking back. "I got two nice boys to home, but I tell you a man misses a lot in the world, if he doesn't have a girl. Why, kiddie, I've had a better time in the past five minutes than I've had in the past five years." He paused, his hand on the latch of the door into Daddy Skinner's room.

Tessibel gurgled and giggled, and giggled and gurgled, as if she hadn't a care in the world although she felt a paralyzing pain in her heart for the dwarf beneath her. Then she threw a mischievous glance into the man's face and offered,

"While ye air searchin' the shanty, I'll sing to ye, huh?"

"Now, can ye sing?" interrogated Burnett, smilingly.

"Oh, Golly, sir, I been singin' since I weren't no bigger'n this owl," replied Tess. "I'll begin now."

She knew Andy must be numb with fright and the weight of her body, and remembered how many times when he had been kept in the garret long periods together, while people were coming and going, and danger ran high, she had sung to him—it had soothed his pains, allayed his agony.

So as Burnett disappeared from sight into the little back room, Tessibel began to sing the old, but ever newly encouraging song,

"Rescue the Perishin';
Care for the Dyin'."

And in the fleeting moment during which the officer from Auburn was searching Daddy's room, her hand went backward quickly and reassuring fingers touched the dwarf's face concealed by her curls, and still she sang,

"Rescue the Perishin';
Care for the Dyin'."

Then Tess felt Andy's body relax and heard the faintest possible sigh.

When Burnett came forth unsuccessful but cheerful, her fingers were toying with her curls, and she broke off her song, question him with her eyes.

"There ain't a soul in there," laughed the man. "I might a'known Bishop wasn't around here; in fact, I did know it the minute I looked at you, kid. Now, just as a matter of law and order, I'll take a peep in the garret and under the bed, and then I'm done ... Say, you got some voice, ain't you, kid?"

"It can holler good and loud," grinned Tess.

"And you're some religious, I bet, according to the hymn you've been singin'," went on the warden. "Now ain't you?"

Tess sobered instantly. She was always very careful not to be irreverent about sacred things.

"You can bet your boots, I air some awful religious," she acquiesced earnestly. "I've knowed about God and Jesus ever so long."

"That's nice," responded Burnett, becoming grave in his turn.

Oh, would he never go! Would he never finish?

When Burnett walked toward the ladder, she sighed dolefully.

"Does your foot hurt you, kid?" he asked, glancing over his shoulder.

"Nope," faltered Tess. "I guess I were a thinkin' what'd happen to the little man when ye get 'im."

The warden was trying the strength of the ladder.

"Oh, I'll hike him back up state quicker'n scat when I get my fingers on 'im," said he, his head disappearing in the hole in the ceiling.

In less than thirty seconds he was down again and had taken a squint under the bed.

"There isn't any dwarf under there either," he said, amusement in his tones. He stretched forth his hand, reaching down to the girl on the cot.

"Now, don't hold nothing against me, kiddie, for comin' here, will ye? Just shake hands with a feller and say it's all right, eh?"

Tessibel lifted the owl high in the air and opened her fingers. There was a small ghostly flutter and in another instant Deacon had disappeared into the garret.

She gave the warden both her hands, and for the little minute Burnett stood by the bed holding them in his and assuring her of his good will. Tessibel sent up a prayer of thanksgiving. Her little Andy, Daddy Skinner's friend, was saved!

When Burnett reached the door, he looked back at her. The girl's lips were parted in a brilliant, farewell smile. He whirled about and came toward her again.

"Kid," he said huskily, "I'm a hard-headed old cuss, harder'n brass tacks. I been made so by just such men as Andy Bishop—" He paused, and during his short hesitation, pregnant with meaning, Tessibel kept her eyes on him. "I was wonderin', little one," he finished, shame-faced, "when you say your prayers, if you'd pipe one for me. I need it, so help me God, I do."

In another moment he was at the door, and in response to the hasty glance he sent her, Tess flung him a misty, loving smile.

"Sure, sir, sure I will," she called, "an' thank ye for bein' so kind."

Burnett strode out; Tessibel rolled off the dwarf's body to one side of the cot, and Andy gave an audible grunt.

"I air gee-danged glad that air over," sighed Tess. And as she lay very still, the warden's hearty voice came floating to her.

"That's a mighty fine girl you got, Skinner."

Tess also heard her father's husky reply. "Bet yer life, she air.... Good day to ye, sir."

Shortly after, the anxious listeners in the shanty heard the click of the

68

horse's shoes and the rumble of the departing wheels on the stones amid the wagon's creaking complaints against the steepness of the hill.

CHAPTER XVI
TESSIBEL'S SECRET

Tessibel Skinner had been married to Frederick Graves for six long weeks: She had become somewhat accustomed to the deception practiced on Daddy Skinner, and Frederick was constantly allaying her fears and misgivings by telling her that she belonged to him now; that she was his darling, his joy, the better part of his life. Many times he assured her between kisses that it wouldn't be necessary to keep the marriage secret long. Each day, each hour, each minute, the girl-wife basked in the thought of her young husband's love. She unfolded the hidden beauties of her nature to him as spontaneously as the opening flower responds to the genial warmth of the rising sun.

Early one morning Tessibel arose, a new light shining in her eyes. Because Daddy Skinner was still abed, she started to the shore for water. It was a glad, shining, diamond-studded earth that greeted the view of the expectant girl; there was wonderful stillness everywhere, and for some minutes she stood contemplating the scene before her. South from the Hog Hole to the northern curve at Lansing, the lake was dappled, its surface broken here and there by little capfuls of breeze, which dimpled in the light, while the smooth spots reflected the blazing glory of the morning sun. The leaves of the weeping willow tree swept the rapt, upraised face, and Tess drew down about her head and shoulders one of the thickest branches. These century-old trees were really a vital part of her life—old loves to Tessibel, loves that had kept watch over her since the day of her birth in the shanty.

A brilliant flame flooded her face.... Frederick stood with her in spirit nearness. What she would tell him that evening would be whispered so low that not even the nesting birds could hear. She imagined the tenderness with which he'd clasp her in his arms, and thrilled, visualizing the darkening of his eyes. Tessibel was painting pictures—her exalted soul running the gamut of joy.

What a wonder-world it was! What a glad, peaceful, new day, her first real day of living—the beginning of life itself; Frederick's life and her life! Now, of course, he would tell his mother they were married—would take her to Daddy Skinner, and—and—She could plan no farther just then. Her whole being was God-lifted. Even the waves lapping at her feet seemed to speak the language of a world to come.

She dipped the pail into the lake slowly, filling it with water. Then with a last sweeping glance over the golden-tinted waves, she returned to the shanty. Daddy Skinner by this time was seated in his chair, his grey face wearing an expression of misery.

"Ye air sicker this morning, honey, huh?" asked Tess anxiously, lifting the pail to the table.

"Yep, brat, awful sick, but mebbe I'll feel better after a while."

"Yer coffee'll be ready quicker'n scat, dear," said the girl. "Flop on my bed an' stretch out a minute. Tessibel'll get her daddy's breakfast."

Five minutes later she had fried the fish and made the coffee.

"I air goin' to give Daddy his eatin's first, Andy," she called up through the hole in the ceiling.

"All right; sure, do, kid," assented the dwarf.

Daddy Skinner gradually felt better, and during the morning Tessibel's youthful spirits rose by leaps and bounds. All through the day she warbled out her happiness, lovingly bantering the two crippled men. Thus the minutes crept on to eventide, to that hour on the ragged rocks with Frederick.

She left the shanty early, that she might commune undisturbed for a time with her dear wild world. Through the gloaming the dull sound of the cow bells came distinctly from Kennedy's farm. The roosters were crowing a last good-night to the sun. The monstrous shadows of the great forest trees were going to sleep in the earth for another night. While the daylight was fading, the girl sat relaxed against the rocks, her unfathomable eyes contemplating the purple-spanned lake. She had drifted into a reverie ... blissfully dreaming, with Frederick the foremost figure of her dreams. The solemn descent of night ever signified the mystery of his love to her. Now, from the fullness of her unalloyed joy, she glanced up at the sky and blessed the whole world. In imagination she deciphered the words the stars were forming. Stretched from pole to pole, they lettered the heavens with the wonders of infinitude. In a diadem of gold, "God is love" was written; from the unsearchable north to the south where in their turn the slender rimming clouds sent it on to the world beyond. "God is love," whispered the swaying trees, and "God is love" came softly to the ear of the sensitive girl, as an echo is flung back from the rocks and is sent home to its maker.

And even as Tess dreamed, the passion stars in their invisible courses bent toward her. Impulsively she lifted her arms upward toward those twinkling participants of her secret, emblems of the immeasurable glory of her love for Frederick. By a simple turn, she could see the tree of her old-time fancies, the familiar figure in the tall pine, with swaying, majestic head and beckoning arms.

At that moment, she perceived Frederick making his way along the ragged rocks. She could hear her heart's blood pulsing madly, striking at her wrists, throbbing at her temples, making a race the length of her quivering body. Now, she could see him plainly in the dim light, and a smile deepened the dimple at each corner of her mouth. An indefinable shyness kept her from running to him to tell her glad tidings. But what made him walk so slowly and with hanging head? It wasn't like Frederick. Something unusual had happened or he would not lag so in coming to her.

She was even more mystified at the peculiarity of his greeting. With nerves as tautly drawn as fiddle strings, she remained very still. In his own time he would tell her all about it. She lifted her arms, but Frederick, unheeding, sank to the rocks beside her. She laid her hand on his, expressing her love to him by the simple contact.

"Don't!" he said shortly. He drew away from the caressing fingers impatiently. "I've come to tell you something."

"Well, here I air," answered Tess, quietly.

There was an exquisite tenderness in the young voice. In the white light of the early evening Tessibel could see Frederick's brows fiercely drawn together. Probably his mother was worse and that accounted for the change in him. She became instantly all devotion.

"Air ye goin' to tell me about it, honey?" she entreated softly. "It'll make ye feel better.... Tell Tessibel."

He turned away, and moved nervously until his shoulders were fitted into a rock cavity; then, he dropped his head back with a prolonged sigh. It was even more difficult than he had imagined.

"Of course I needn't tell you ... that I love you, need I, Tess?" he stammered, after a while.

He could not assure her too many times of his affection. She leaned against him, adoring, wrapped in the delight of his love as a water lily is wrapped in its green sepals.

"I know it, dearest!" she murmured, much moved. "Ye tell me that every day. But what else air ye—"

"You'll forgive me, and not be ... too unhappy?" Frederick interrupted her anxiously.

Unhappy, while her whole being was transfused with ecstasy! Unhappy, when his life and hers intermingled in one glad, glorious song of inseparable unity! There never could be a diminution of her joy. Frederick loved her! That was enough.

"There ain't nothin' I wouldn't forgive," she vowed, misty-eyed.

"But, Tess, I feel as though you won't forgive me this," sighed Frederick. "But if you'll promise me—"

"I do—I will," she interjected, sitting up. "Why, of course, I'd forgive ye anything."

Frederick dared not look at her. Even in the twilight he could feel her eyes searching his face for an explanation.

"I need you to help me, Tessibel," he said at length.

Help him! Hadn't she ever been ready to help him? He had but to ask her. She dropped her head against his arm again.

"Tell Tessibel," she urged, smiling.

One slender, girlish arm slipped lovingly about him. A set of small fingers took his cold hand in a firm grasp.

"Tess loves ye, dear," came soothingly. "Now tell 'er, an' then ye'll be happier."

Shame rose rampant in the boy's breast.

"I can't do it," he muttered under his breath.

But he knew all the time he would. The events of yesterday, culminating with Waldstricker's brilliant offer, closed every other path. He groaned, catching his lips tensely between his teeth. Some one had to suffer, but the sacrifice must not touch his mother nor estrange the Waldstrickers. That Madelene would be wronged by his action gave him little concern. But at that moment to hurt the girl at his side; oh, how he hated the bitter necessity! Conscious of the despicable part he was playing, but having really decided, he drew himself from the girl's arms. To gain a little more time, he thrust his fingers several times through his damp hair.

"Tess," he hesitated, "you've promised you'd never tell about our being married."

An encouraging touch turned the boy's twitching face to hers.

"An' I ain't never goin' to till ye let me," she asserted soothingly. "Ye ain't lettin' that worry ye, darlin', eh?"

She encouraged him to answer by the tender cadence on the end of her question.

"No, no, Tess!" Then desperately, "Oh, in God's name, how am I ever going to get it out?"

Tessibel became suddenly terror-stricken. It must be something very serious to force from him such language in such heart-rending tones. She shivered nervously.

"You mustn't think for a moment, Tess," the boy burst forth, with renewed courage, "that I don't love you! I shall love you always, always."

"Always," echoed Tess, reassured. If Frederick loved her, nothing else mattered. Perhaps his mother was—Her thought snapped in two at an ejaculation from Frederick.

"And what I do is because—well, because—I must," he stammered. "You understand that, don't you, sweetheart?"

"Sure," agreed Tess, puzzled.

"And nothing will ever be changed between you and me—"

"Nothin' can ever hurt us, Frederick," she interrupted quickly.

And Tess believed this to be the eternal truth. Faith the size of a grain of mustard seed had piloted her through severe storms. Since Daddy Skinner had been restored to her, that faith had grown to the size of the mountain itself.

"I won't let it," went on the student, swiftly. "Neither must you. You must trust me—you must believe! No, don't put your arms around my neck till I've finished!... And then, oh, my little girl, I shan't let you out of my arms, ever! ever!"

Greatly moved, he suddenly reached forth and drew her unresistingly to him, smothering her hair, her eyes with kisses, clinging to her, as if he would never, never let her go.

Her heart beat wildly against his.... And she loved him more than all the world, and loved God more because of him.

But he released her almost immediately, and Tessibel sank back, sighing. She was no longer nervously eager to divulge her secret. She waited almost mechanically, as one waits for an advancing joy—as a hungry man watches abundant preparation for the appeasing of his hunger. Hearing him groan, she turned troubled eyes up to his.

"Daddy always says for to tell bad things quick!"

But this only served to call forth another deep breath of misery. After a lapse of what seemed ages to the waiting girl, Frederick gathered courage, and began,

"Tess, I've told you how very ill my mother is, haven't I?"

"Yes, an' I air awful sorry, dearie," she murmured.

The compassion he aroused subdued her voice to a whisper.

"And she's asked me to do something for her and I've—got to do it, Tessibel," faltered Frederick.

"Sure ye have," Tess agreed.

"I didn't decide to do it, honey,"—Frederick was avoiding the vital part—"until I saw how I could not let it make any difference to us. It won't make any difference, dear heart!"

And Tess, already living in some distant day with full heart and full arms, breathed.

"No, darlin', no difference to us.... 'Course not!"

"Oh, I'm glad, so glad to hear you say that!" said Frederick, relief in his voice. "It won't be so dreadful, my sweet, if you trust me. And it won't be long—perhaps a year, perhaps two years—"

Tessibel's muscles grew suddenly rigid.

"Years, ye say?" she repeated, stupefied. "What years? Why years?"

The resigned and submissive Tess changed instantly to an intense, resolute woman, with compelling, fear-clouded eyes. Frederick, alarmed, hastened to explain.

"You remember Madelene Waldstricker, don't you?"

Did she remember Madelene Waldstricker? Would she ever forget that one night when he had treated her, his own wife, as though she were a stranger?

"Sure, I remember 'er," she admitted, flushing. "What about 'er?"

Before replying, Frederick snatched her hand and kissed it.

"My mother.... Oh, Tessibel, it'll be all right—" He paused, then finished despairingly, "My mother wants me to marry her!"

Tess caught the picture his words suggested; then recoiled as if death in monstrous guise had appeared before her, open-armed. Incredulous horror leapt alive in her eyes. He had said, "My mother wants me to marry Madelene Waldstricker." But even though his mother had demanded it, he couldn't! He wouldn't.... But he'd said he must!

Tess clenched her hands until the nails pressed into the flesh of her palms. Her throat refused to yield a speaking voice, but something screamed aloud within her as if a giant hand had clutched and torn her soul.

73

"But ye air married to me," she got out at last, piteously.

Frederick put his arms about her.

"I know it, girlie dear!... I'm not denying that, but no one knows it but us, just you and me, and I'm afraid ... I've got to do ... this ... Mother ..."

"Oh, God, no!" shuddered Tess.

Oh, he couldn't mean to desert her now when she needed him so—needed him more than she had even in those days when the shadow of the hateful rope hung over her beloved father; even when Teola's child had been thrust upon her, and Ben Letts had daily menaced her desolate life.

She was still for so long a time Frederick feared she'd fainted.

"Tess!" he spoke sharply.

"What?"

But it didn't sound like Tessibel's voice answering.

"Will you hear me out, dearest?" he pleaded. "Oh, won't you listen to me?"

Surely she was listening intently. He had never spoken when she had not given loving heed, if she were within the sound of his voice. Frederick attempted to raise her face to his, but with a pathetic little word of protest, she slipped from his arms, and fell face downward to the rocks. The tortured boy would rather have had her scream, strike at him, anything, than sink into that accusing, forlorn prostration!

"Tessibel! Tess!" he cried. "Whatever I do can't separate you and me. It can't! I swear not to let it!"

He stooped and drew her gently to a sitting posture.

"No, I won't let it!" he reiterated excitedly. "I won't! No other woman could ever take your place. Can't you see, Tessibel? Can't you understand what I'm telling you?"

"Nope," whispered Tess. "I ain't able to understand. Oh—" She lifted a white, twitching face. "Oh, don't go 'way an' leave me! Not now—not just yet!"

"But you said," he entreated, "you've always said, honey, you'd stand by me, and you will, won't you? This is the only way you can help. You will, dear, please!"

"I 'spose I air got to," she stammered, shivering. "Course I do everything ye want me to. But—but—tell me ... why."

"It's just like this," Frederick explained reluctantly. "My mother needs—money. She's got to have it. She's already borrowed a lot of Waldstricker and ... even our lake place is mortgaged to him. His sister loves me—"

The speaker felt the slender body recoil as from a blow.

"Tess!" he cried, "I don't love her. Oh, can't I get you to understand anything? If you tremble that way, you'll drive me mad. I'm only going to marry her.... Well, to pay the money, that's all."

He cut and clipped the words as though he hated them, yet finished his explanation determinedly. As keenly as a darting flame, it burned into Tessibel's soul.

"Tell me ... more," she breathed dizzily.

"It'll only mean you and I will be apart for a little while, Tess," stated Frederick. "When I get back home, I'm coming straight to you, and—"

74

"She air lovin' ye, ye said?" interrupted Tess, huskily.

"But I don't love her, Tess!... I love only you!... You know that, sweetheart!... You hear me, darling?"

"Yep, I hear," whispered the girl.

Frederick settled back against the rocks, drawing her into his arms.

"My father," he proceeded more calmly, "left us without any money. I suppose I didn't realize how hard it's been for mother. She's only just told me she'd mortgaged the lake place to Waldstricker and had borrowed money from him. In a way I've been awfully selfish.... I've only thought of you, dear."

Of course, now she couldn't tell him that intimate secret! If he knew, he couldn't, he just couldn't do the thing his mother demanded; and she had promised to help him. He had said it was the only way she could be of any service, and her great love rose up and demanded the sacrifice. Tess scarcely recognized her own voice when she next spoke.

"Did ye tell Madelene—I mean Miss Waldstricker—ye'd marry her?" she asked.

"Well ... yes," stammered Frederick.

"And ye—ye—ye kissed 'er?... Oh, say ye didn't kiss 'er!... Ye didn't, did ye?"

It was a plea to which Frederick would have given worlds to truthfuly answer, "No." But his conscience, evidently sensitive in small matters, compelled an almost inaudible, "Yes."

Raging jealousy, unendurable pain, arose within her.

"But ye couldn't—be married—to 'er, Frederick. It ain't possible, it ain't!"

"I know I'm married to you," the boy assured her, swiftly. "I'd only be married to her in the eyes of the world!"

The eyes of the world, the world through which she had so far walked with proudly lifted head! Her dearly cherished love seemed to be tumbling in ignominious ruins, and that very love had left her defenseless. No one would ever know he belonged to her; that she belonged to him. She would have to creep with bowed head in assumed shame and disgrace even among the squatters.

"I'll die," she shivered, thinking of the coming spring.

His burning kisses stung her lips, through which his words tumbled one over the other.

"You can't!... You shan't die!... Tess, you shan't! I'm only going away for a little while.... You're mine, Tess, do you hear?... You've got to live and love me always! You're mine! Oh, my love! Don't cry like that!..."

The crushing strength of his arms hurt her. Suddenly another picture shot across her brain, like a searing rocket. She clung to his arm as if she feared that minute would snatch him from her. Then suppliantly she lifted not only her face, but also her hands.

"Oh, she won't be like I air been to ye—like—like—"

Frederick heard the anguish in the agonized, girlish voice.

"Not like—not like I air been to ye, darlin'. Oh, God, not that!" she cried again.

She waited in panting suspense for a fierce denial. Then she struggled frantically in his embrace. All that was alive within her—all the super-vitalized part of her soul—seemed scorched by the picture his significant silence had painted.

"Let me go!" she demanded.

Frederick tightened his arms about her.

"Not yet, not yet! Stay here, rest here, my sweet."

But again seeing that image of the small woman in her place, Tess struggled and freed herself.

"I air goin' to Daddy now," she whispered. "An' you can go home too, please."

But he caught her again to his breast.

"You belong to me!" he cried intensely. "I won't go!—I'm going to stay, Tessibel! I will—I will stay!"

Tess wrenched herself free.

"Ye c'n come again," she promised. "Some other time afore—"

Frederick caught her broken sentence and finished it.

"Yes, yes, Tessibel," he exclaimed. "I'll come back soon, very soon!"

"Sure, soon," quivered Tess, swaying, "go on, please!"

She flung up her hands, crying low in suppressed agony, as Frederick whirled from her and walked rapidly away. He had not taken ten steps before he was moved to go back, to take her again in his arms, but thinking over all that had happened, of how hard it had been to flounder through his explanation, he shut his teeth and went on.

With super-hearing, Tess listened until the sound of his footsteps died in the lane.

He had gone—Frederick—her husband! Gone to another woman! No, that couldn't be! He was hers always and forever. She sank down on the rocks—on the dear, ragged rocks, where she had watched for him and prayed for him, where life had been at its highest and best.

She tried to recall all he had said. Oh, yes, he was coming back. What did he mean by coming back? When? She dully wondered if it would be tomorrow, or the day after, or the day after that. Three days, perhaps, three long, interminable days to think of him and to long for him. Could she live three days? She sprang to her feet. She must see him again—now—this minute; hear him unsay that awful thing. Why, he couldn't belong to Madelene Waldstricker! Like a deer, Tess sped along the rocks in the direction of the lane. A night bird brushed a slender wing against her curls as he shot by her. To him she paid no heed save to swerve a little.

Wildly, twice, three times she cried, "Frederick!"

An owl hooted a mocking response from the willow tree nearby.

"Frederick! Frederick!" rang through the night, out over the lake, unanswered. He was gone! The realization of this brought the girl crouching, shivering to the shore, where her feet were lapped by the incoming waves. And there she lay, until as in a dream, a bewildered dream, she heard Daddy Skinner's voice calling her. By a supreme effort she gathered her senses together.

"I air comin', Daddy."

She stumbled through the night back to the shanty, her secret locked in her breast.

CHAPTER XVII
TESSIBEL'S PRAYER

For four lingering days, hour after hour, Tess of the Storm Country waited for Frederick. He had promised to return, and so each day when her household duties were completed, she hastened to the ragged rocks at the edge of the forest. But her eager hope passed into sick apprehension as the lingering twilights of successive evenings deepened into the darkness of night and he did not come. Tess grew paler and more dejected, so that even Daddy Skinner's fading sight remarked it.

"Ain't feelin' quite pert, be ye, brat?" he inquired.

Tessibel started nervously.... It was habitual now if any one spoke to her quickly.

"I ain't sick, daddy," she assured him. "I guess it air the hot day makin' me tired."

"Nuff to bake the hair off a cast iron pup," observed Andy, from the garret hole.

"I'll bet it air some warm up there, pal," sympathized Orn.

"Ye bet yer neck," agreed Andy cheerfully.

Then Tessibel hopefully started for the rocks in search of the sunshine which had left her life with Frederick four days before.

Deforrest Young, too, had noticed the change in his little friend ... had observed her extreme nervousness and unusual shyness when she recited her lessons. Today, moreover, she had not appeared at all. Late that afternoon he called at the Skinner home to find the reason.

Daddy Skinner occupied his customary seat on the bench in front of the shack, watching with listless, dull eyes the restless waves. He greeted the professor with his twisted smile, as the latter called to him from the lane.

"Where's Tessibel?" asked Young, after they had remarked upon the weather and the health of themselves and their friends.

"Well, I don't know just where she air gone," replied Orn, "but seems to me's if she went off toward the rocks. Shall I call her, eh?"

"No, no! I'll go look for her," answered the professor.

He found her sitting pensively on the rocks, her hand resting on the head of Kennedy's brindle bulldog, and in the moment he stood there gazing at the girl, he felt unaccountably saddened.

When Tess became conscious of his presence, she gave him a shadowy, fleeting smile, which vanished almost before it had fully appeared. Her eyes were heavy and dim with unshed tears, and she was as pale as the mist clouds that drifted slowly across the sky and away over the eastern hills. Perhaps it was the melancholy of that smile appealing to his deep love that made Professor Young hurry toward her, holding out his hands.

Pete greeted him with a welcoming whine, wagging his whole body, in default of the tail he had lost.

"Your father said you were here, child," Young said in a low voice. "May I sit down?"

Tess acquiesced by a nod of her head, and he settled himself comfortably on the rock. Crouching down on the other side of her, Pete put his head in the girl's lap. Her hands rested upon his broad back, while the man played with him, pulling and poking his heavy jowls and hanging lips, and the dog uttered delighted growls at the attention.

"I'm afraid my little girl hasn't been quite well of late," Young began presently.

The red-brown eyes fell and a flushed, lovely face bent beneath a shower of bronze curls.

"Has she?" he queried again, with tender sympathy.

Lower and lower bent the auburn head until the man could no longer see the troubled face.

"I knew there was something wrong with my little pupil," said he softly. "Now tell me about it."

"I can't," whispered Tessibel. "I ain't able."

Oh, if she only could! At that moment it seemed that all of her troubles would take wing if this thoughtful, solemn-eyed friend shared the burden of her heart. When she lifted her face again and repeated, "I can't tell," Deforrest Young placed his fingers under her chin and kept his eyes steadily upon her until the transparent lids drooped and the long lashes rested on her cheeks.

"Is it something you'll tell me some time?" he asked.

Tessibel shuddered, and made no reply, although there was a slight negative shake of her head.

"Then I'll ask you another question, Tess dear," insisted Young. "Isn't there something I can do to help you?"

Tessibel shook her head, a violent blush suffusing her face. Tears gathered thickly in the brown eyes. To see her thus was agony.... His great love sought to share and bear her suffering, yet he could not force her confidence.

"I'm going to exact one promise from you," he continued, much moved.

"I'll be awful glad to promise what I can," she murmured humbly.

"Then it's this." Compassion for her abject misery was expressed in the very tones of his deep voice. "If at any time in the future you need me ... for anything, no matter what, will you—will you come to me and tell me? Will you let me help you?"

Impetuous appreciation of his sincerity caused Tess to touch his arm.

"Nobody were ever so good to me in all the world," she said brokenly.

Never had Deforrest Young so keenly desired the right to care for her as he did then. The impulse to take her in his arms, to tell her, as he had once, that he loved her, almost unnerved him; but he could not. Tess seemed of late to have grown away from him, to be no longer the light-hearted child she had been, even in that dark time when her father was in prison.

"You haven't promised me yet, Tessibel," he insisted seriously.

"I promise ... sure!" said Tess, swallowing hard.

In the silence that followed, Pete, as though conscious that all was not well with his adored mistress, rose on his haunches, and tried to kiss her face. The dog's sympathy was sweet. She wanted Frederick so badly! Oh, she thought, if she dared ask Deforrest. She would! She could not bear another night of this uncertainty, this suspense.

"I air wishin' to ask ye somethin'," she stammered. "Don't tell anybody, will ye?"

"Certainly not," declared Young, quickly.

"Do ye—do ye happen to know where—the student Graves air—today?"

Young considered the long curls falling over each shoulder and the anxious eyes. She was staring fixedly at him. Was the student somehow connected with her present distress? Frederick's marked attention of late to Madelene Waldstricker was, he supposed, generally known. He had not seen him with Tess for a long time. He had concluded the young man's interest in the squatter girl had passed. Was it possible that Tess still cared for him?

"Well, that's hard to tell," he told her presently, looking out over the lake. "But if they've had good luck, I suppose the young people are quite well on their way to Paris by now. The ceremony, one of those hasty affairs, was performed yesterday. They took the night train to New York."

Tessibel's breath caught in her throat.... The heavens seemed to tumble into the lake.... An awful booming sounded in her ears. She grew limp, sick at heart, ... dizzy, but she made no outcry, only, unconscious of its pain, bit her lip until it bled. The hope she had nursed, that he would not do this awful thing was lost.

Pete stirred uneasily. Restrained by Tessibel's hand on his head, he laid down again making whining noises in his throat, inarticulate expressions of his love for the suffering girl.

"Didn't you know he was going to marry Miss Waldstricker?" asked Young.

"Yep,—I knew," whispered Tess, when she could breathe, "but—tell me—about it."

"There's not much to tell," explained the Professor, reluctant to distress her. "It seems the young lady didn't want a large wedding and did want to start abroad immediately, so they had a private affair—no one present but the relatives."

Tess made an effort to control herself.

"Graves won't go back to college any more," went on Young. "He's going

79

into business with his brother-in-law, Mr. Waldstricker. I understand when they return from abroad they will live with my sister the rest of the winter."

There was no response from the drooping little figure at his side.

Tess was thinking of the winter without Frederick. She sickened as she pictured him away off in that foreign land. It seemed he must be at the very end of the world. It bewildered her to think of his being with another woman than herself. She could not think of them as married—He was her husband. She was silent so long that Young spoke to her softly. "Shall I take you home, my dear?"

Numb and dazed, she sat dumbly enduring the hurt.

"Nope, I air goin' to stay here awhile." 'Twas only a trembling breath that wafted the man his answer.

Young hesitated. Then rising he walked away along the rocks, leaving Tess and the brindle dog amid the falling shadows.

Spent with emotion, the squatter girl heard the retreating footsteps of her friend die away in the twilight. Then she pushed the dog gently from her lap and laid herself down upon the rocks and pillowed her aching head upon his body.

Gradually the tender melancholy of the dying day touched her mood with subtle sympathy and soothed her troubled spirit. Rapt in rueful revery, she followed mechanically the flight of a flock of birds. Like swift shadows flitting over the water, they dipped and winged upward and away, out of her vision.

Frederick had gone from her life almost as completely and as suddenly as those birds had disappeared from her sight. How mercilessly short had been her days of happiness, those days threaded and inter-threaded with her husband's love.

The sun had set and the purples and reds were fading from the fleecy clouds in the eastern sky. The gloaming grew in caressing cadences up from the limpid lake to the ragged rocks. The night winds blew gently down the hill side, the swaying leaves were whispering "hush, hush," and the surface of the lake, shimmering in the mellow light of the rising moon, was flecked here and there into silvery sparkles. The airs of evening fluttered the ringlets upon her forehead and enveloped her hot body in cooling comfort. Responsive to the quiet beauty about her, the turmoil of her thoughts subsided. The sharp anguish which had at first stunned her was becoming but a dull ache, permitting her to think connectedly.

This place and this hour held the most vital associations of her young life. Here in the gathering gloom, Frederick had wooed and won her, and had spent with her many of the too few hours of her wedded bliss. Upon such another evening, she had made him the promises that had led to her only deceptions of Daddy Skinner, and here, four short days ago, her husband had murdered her joy.

Reflecting upon her plight, its hopelessness well nigh overwhelmed her. Through the utter desolation of her life rang the haunting, words of the Cantata she'd heard sung last Eastertide in the Big Ithaca Church.

"Oh, was there ever loneliness like this?"

80

Over and over the melody repeated itself, insistently recalling the Master's agony in the garden, and lifting her thoughts slowly upward away from herself to His ultimate triumph and glory.

Betrayed and deserted by the man that loved her, she fixed her attention instinctively upon the Divine Love "with whom is no variableness, neither shadow of turning" and sought courage from the words of Him "who spake as never man spake." His command, "Love your enemies, do good to them that hate you and pray for them which despitefully use you," came to her tortured heart, a healing inspiration.

Immediately she got to her feet. The dog, tired of the enforced inactivity, jumped up and ran to and fro on the rocks, barking. She had given her husband up to another woman—he had said it was all she could do for him. But she loved him and her love rejoiced in giving. Pete, puzzled that the girl did not join him in his play as usual, came back and stood in front of her and looked up into her face. She turned to the old pine tree, her familiar friend, and extended her arms to the God of her exalted faith.

"Goddy, dear, goodest Goddy," she prayed, "bless my Frederick wherever he air—an'—help Tessibel to die—in—in the spring."

CHAPTER XVIII
A LETTER

A great deal had happened during the three weeks Frederick had been gone. Helen Young had married Ebenezer Waldstricker, and they had been away now nearly two weeks on their honeymoon. Deforrest Young, too, had spent most of the time out of Ithaca. Tessibel Skinner heard from him frequently, and through his good letters, she had been able to keep up her studies.

One Monday morning while Tess was doing the simple chores around the shack, she had the door open to admit the vagrant breezes of the summer day. Andy, as his custom was on such occasions, lay quietly upon the attic floor, secure from the observation of any chance passer-by. Stepping to the door to shake her dust rag, Tess saw Jake Brewer coming up the path.

"Hello, Jake," she called, a little loudly to warn Andy, "how air ye?"

"Pretty tol'able, thank ye, Tess," Brewer answered politely, "how air you, and how's yer pa?"

"Daddy's pretty bad this mornin'," she told him, a reluctant smile appearing for a moment at the corners of her mouth.

81

"Pshaw! Tessie, ye don't tell me. It air the heat, ain't it? But Tess, I air got somethin' for you," he sniggered. "Bet ye can't guess what it air."

"Sure, I can't, Jake." The girl tried to match his cheerful manner.

She wished she might greet her squatter friends as of yore, but her heart was sad and lay stonelike in her breast. Of late, Jake had been very kind, running many errands for her. Daddy Skinner was a favorite with the inhabitants of the Silent City, and now that he was so ill, all the other squatters did what they could for his sorrowing daughter.

"Come in, Jake," invited Tess. "Mebbe Daddy'd like to see ye.... He ain't up yet.... Wait a minute.... I'll ask 'im!"

Jake stayed her with a chuckle and a beckoning motion of his forefinger.

"First I'll give ye what I brung ye, Tess," he said, while he fumbled in his pocket. "Here! Look! It air a letter with a big ship up in the corner of it.... Ain't it cute?"

Tessibel held out a trembling hand for the square envelope Brewer proffered her. How many times within the past weeks had she visualized a ship as it took its rapid way to the other side of the world! How many times had she seen her husband with Madelene Waldstricker on that pictured steamer! Now here it was before her very eyes, more stately even than her mind had portrayed it. She stared at the letter, her face going very white.

"Ye don't seem to be tickled, brat," said the squatter, grinning.

"I air, though, Jake," she replied, "awful tickled.... Come on in an' see Daddy!"

She slipped the letter into her pocket and led the way to the back room. She bent over the bed and roused her father.

"Jake air here to see ye, Daddy," she said. "Sit down, Jake! He can't talk very loud, but ye can see he air awful glad to have ye here.... Daddy dear, Jake Brewer air tryin' to shake hands with ye."

Orn's great hand lifted slowly.

"Glad to see ye, Jake," he mumbled. "I ain't the best this mornin'!"

"Ye'll get better with the goin' of the warm weather," consoled Jake. "These days be hot now for the wellest of us."

"Yep," murmured Daddy Skinner, drowsily.

Tessibel left the two men alone, and went back to the kitchen. Her throat was filled with longing, her lips drawn a little closer together. She sat down near the door, looking out upon the lake. She dared not open the letter then, not until Jake had gone and Daddy was asleep.

Brewer came out quietly, his cheerful manner subdued somewhat.

Tess got to her feet. She tried to smile, but the serious expression on the squatter's face brought her quickly to his side.

"Jake," she murmured, quick-breathed, "ye think he air awful sick, eh?"

Brewer shifted his gaze out through the door. The sight of the girl's pleading face hurt him.

"He ain't real pert; that air a fact," was his reply.

"We air doin' everythin' we can think of," Tess told him. "Mr. Young's doctor comes awful often, an' he says Daddy air got heart trouble."

"He do seem to have a hard time breathin'," answered Jake, trying to be cheerful; "but if I was you, Tessie, I wouldn't worry. He'll be gettin' well. He air stronger'n a horse."

Tess wanted to believe her father was better. She couldn't allow her mind to take any other view of it.

"He air always been right rugged," she said, nodding, "an' if his heart'd only stop beatin' so hard—" She hesitated and touched Brewer's arm. "Thank ye fer bringin' my letter," she interrupted herself irrelevantly.

"That air all right, Tess," smiled Brewer. "Ye see when I go to the Postoffice fer our mail, I ask fer your'n an' fer Longman's, an' I most allers get some fer one or t'other.... Nice day, eh, ain't it?"

"Yep," affirmed Tess, dully. She bade the fisherman good-bye and stood watching him take his way along the lakeside until he had disappeared.

When she turned she caught sight of Andy's glistening eyes looking at her.

"Jake air a good feller, ain't he, brat?" he asked.

Tess came directly under the ceiling hole.

"Yep, he sure air," she answered. "Andy, I air a feelin' so bad today. Will ye listen for Daddy if I go out a spell?"

"Course I will, go long," he urged. "Close the door when ye go out. I'll keep my ears open."

Tess walked slowly along the lake shore path, her head drooping wearily. She knew the letter in her pocket was from Frederick. To have opened it even before Andy's loving eyes, or in the presence of any other person, would have been, in her opinion, a desecration.

Against the high gray shoulder of a ragged rock, she sat down pensively. It was here she and Frederick had spent so many happy hours and, now, alone, she had come to read his letter. She took it slowly from her pocket, studied the picture of the ship in the corner, and whispered over and over the name under it. It seemed almost impossible to tear it open. What had he told her? She pressed the envelope to her lips. Her darling's hands had touched it, his fingers had written her name upon it. Ripping it slowly along the edge, she took out the contents, and there fluttered to the rock a yellow backed bill. Tess picked it up and examined it carefully. Frederick had sent her some money. Tess laid it down again and placed a small stone upon it. Then she took up the letter.

For a few seconds her eyes misted so profusely she could not read. She dashed the back of her hand across her lids, choking down hard sobs that rose insistently. When she could control her emotions enough to read, she fixed her eyes upon the first words: "My own darling:"

Crunching the paper between her fingers, she dropped her head and wept wildly for several minutes. She wanted Frederick then as she had never wanted a soul in all the living world.

"I am here alone in the writing room," Tess read on, wiping her eyes. "Oh, Tessibel, when I think of you there without me, I go almost mad! What I've done seems the very worst thing in the world, and it grows worse as the hours go by. Forgive me, my darling. I dared not come back after that night; I was afraid some one would see me and tell my mother or some of the Waldstrickers. Tessibel, if I could only jump into the sea and get back to you, I should be the happiest fellow in the world. I love you more and more, and I'm perfectly miserable without you."

Her fingers on her lips, and her eyes on the letter, Tess wept softly. Oh, how she loved him, too, her husband.

"I won't stay away very long, my dearest," the letter continued. "I'm coming back to you and shall never leave you again. I'm sending you some money which I want you to use, and I'll send more very soon. This will make you comfortable for a little while."

Tess picked up the bill and looked at it once more. Then she put it down again and went on reading the letter.

"I shall always love you better than any one else in the world, Tessibel ... when I return we shall be together most of the time. I shall, I hope, get over my fear of Ebenezer Waldstricker. I'm studying in my mind a way to make it possible for us to have a home together, of which no one shall know. Believe that I love you ... always and always, my darling.

Your
Frederick."

Tess lifted her head with a long-drawn sigh. But there was something more to read, a line or two tacked on the end of the letter.

"P. S. My darling, I want you to burn this! I fear some one might get hold of it.

F."

After reading over and over the letter, until she had almost learned it by heart, she went back to the shanty, to do as Frederick had bidden her. Kissing the pages again and again and weeping softly so as not to disturb Andy, Tess burned the letter.

That night when Daddy Skinner was sleeping, his laboring breath heard plainly through the shanty, a red-brown head bent over the kitchen table. Around the flickering light fluttered the summer moths, and once in a while one of Tessibel's beloved night things dashed in at the window, took a zig-zag course about the lamp, and flew out again into the shadowy weeping willows. A long, sobbing sigh from the girl brought the dwarf's eager face to the hole in the ceiling.

"Air ye sick, brat?" he whispered.

Tess lifted her eyes from the table.

"Nope, Andy, I were thinkin', that's all," she answered, low-toned.

And perhaps fifteen minutes later, when she had written a name on several envelopes and had torn them up in seeming disapproval, Andy ventured again.

"Ye act awful sad, brat dear. Can't ye tell me about it?"

Tessibel rose to her feet, the gleam of the night light radiating upon the red-brown of her eyes. She swallowed the lump in her throat before she could speak.

"I air a little sad, Andy dear," she murmured.

"What were ye doin', honey?" asked the dwarf.

Without answering at that moment, Tess took up the envelope she'd sealed. Two steps took her to the mantel, where she placed the letter against the clock, standing a minute to gaze at it. The next instant she explained to the little man leaning above her.

"I were writin' a little, Andy, darlin'."

Then she went softly into Daddy Skinner's room and closed the door.

CHAPTER XIX
ITS ANSWER

While Tessibel Skinner, lonely and despondent, was grieving in the squatter country, Frederick Graves arrived in Paris with his young wife. There had been for him but few hours since that last evening upon the ragged rocks, during which Tessibel's face had not haunted him, the brown eyes, sometimes smiling, more frequently shadowed with tears. Impotent remorse possessed his days and filled his wakeful nights with anguish. At such times when life seemed intolerable, the thought of the comfort he had supplied for his mother and sister was balm to his troubled soul.

He regretted, too, that he had not gone to the squatter settlement to see Tess again before his marriage to Madelene. He had thought, then, that the sight of her pleading pain would be more than he could bear. He had already vowed to himself over and over with clenched teeth that he would stay but a short time away from America. He must see Tess. He did not worry over her keeping the secret of their clandestine marriage ... he had implicit confidence in her promise.

Madelene's keen enjoyment in displaying the many sights, already familiar to her, bored him to distraction, and they had been in France but a few days before she discovered his indifference to the wonders which seemed of such importance to her. On the way over she had noticed his spells of abstraction. She had seen how quickly the shadows descended upon her husband's face when it was in repose. With an intuition characteristically feminine, she concluded rightly that Frederick's interest was not in her, that his attention was really concentrated upon something quite apart from his wife and their honeymoon. She determined to find out the reason.

One morning, breakfasting in their charming room, Madelene started a bright conversation, which Frederick met with but a chilly response.

85

"What's the matter with you, Fred?" she demanded curiously. "You haven't spoken a pleasant word for two days."

A faint smile sketched itself about the corners of Frederick's lips.

"Aren't you stretching that a little, my dear?" he evaded half-playfully.

"Well, perhaps a wee bit," laughed Madelene, ruefully. "But honestly, dear, you look as if you'd lost your last friend instead of being on your— honeymoon."

She sprang up, rounded the table and perched daintily on the arm of his chair.

"I do want to make you happy, darling," she urged. "What's the trouble?"

Frederick made a slightly impatient gesture with one shoulder.

"I'm happy enough, Madelene! But it's this beastly weather! I suppose that's the reason I feel so lackadaisical. If you don't mind, I don't believe I'll go out today."

Madelene uttered a little cry of disappointment.

"Now, I am vexed!" she pouted prettily.

"Oh, then I'll go with you, of course," Frederick hastily cut in. "It doesn't make any difference to me."

The young wife felt an impulse to anger.

"But it ought to make a difference, Fred dear," she pointed out to him. "Why, you make me feel so small ... so insignificant.... I don't want to drag you about if you don't want to go."

Absorbed in his self-centered meditations his wife's sightseeing excursions seemed to him a perfect nuisance.

"I didn't mean to hurt you, dear," he apologized hurriedly.

Madelene got up and went to the window and gazed down upon the street.

"I know what we'll do," she stated, dancing back to the table. "Let's go to some quiet, cool place for a week or two. I hate Paris in the hot weather, anyway. And it'll be fun to be by ourselves ... and we'll have long walks.... Would you like that?"

The dark wave of blood surging into Frederick's temples made her look curiously at him. Why should he be embarrassed at such a suggestion?

"As you please, my dear," he interrupted her thought.

Madelene sighed. He did look ill. It might be the hot weather, but he had such a strange, detached manner most of the time ... as if he were far away ... or she was. Her mind was busy with the problem. She could not eat.

Frederick, too, was but toying with his breakfast. He was wondering just what Madelene was planning to do in the country. It would be even harder for him there than in the city. With Tessibel's face always between them, he could not make a lover's love to her anywhere.

An hour or so later, while Frederick had gone to smoke under the trees, his wife stood critically studying her reflection in the glass ... with but few misgivings. She was pretty, surely so, and very rich! What more could a man want? In the coolness of the country, Frederick would be better. He would lose his moroseness and give his undivided attention to her. She would make all the arrangements for the change without disturbing him. He should not be bothered a little bit; and Madelene grew quite happy again with the thought of having Frederick all to herself in some romantic country spot.

She summoned her maid, and for a while with the aid of the hotel officials, she sought for a place near Paris, yet far enough away to escape its harassing heat and noises. By night Madelene had decided upon a farm near the village of Epernon.

"We can get in to the city to shop, Marie," she told her maid. "But Mr. Graves simply can't stand the hot weather in town."

"He does look sick and worried, ma'am, doesn't he?" agreed the maid.

Twenty-four hours later Frederick and Madelene were settled in a pretty villa nestled at the edge of the forest. Nature in its noblest expression surrounded them. At the going down of the sun, Madelene stood beside her husband on the porch, and pressed her cheek fondly against his shoulder.

"It's so beautiful, isn't it, dear?" she whispered coaxingly.

Out of his wife's words and the gentle gloaming, came a deadly sense of loneliness. A shiver shook Frederick from head to foot. His only answer was an ejaculated affirmative in a hoarse voice. The weird sighing of the trees took him back to Ithaca, back to the ragged rocks ... to Tessibel. For a moment he was so agonized that tears stung his lids to a deep hurt.

If in noisy Paris he had been carried in spirit to the squatter country, where a girl stood and gazed at him with red-brown eyes, how much more did she haunt him in the quiet spot where the leaves sang the same old tunes they sang in her world, where the wind played among them as it did in the Silent City! Now and then from yonder clump of trees a bird twittered; an owl screeched from the tall tree at the right, and farther on a brook chanted its purling song like Tessibel's brook under the mudcellar. Oh, his dear little girl! His Tess of the Storm Country! If in those olden days he had desired her, now that desire was a hundred times more poignant. In all his willful life he had never suffered like this. Tess with her clinging arms, her sweet, winning ways! He sighed a deep, long sigh. Yet soon he would hear something from her. He had written her, ... had sent her money for the necessities of her simple life ... his heart throbbed at the thought of a letter from her.

Madelene's conversation he had not heard, and it was not until she spoke directly to him that he remembered her presence.

"Don't you think so, Fred?" she was asking.

He heaved another sigh as he left Ithaca and came back to France after that flight of fancy.

"Don't I think what? I really didn't hear what you said, Madelene," he admitted guiltily.

Madelene experienced a hot flash of indignation.

"Do you mean to say you've allowed me to talk all this time and you haven't heard a word I've said?" she demanded in a thin, rasping voice.

"I'm sorry," murmured Frederick. "Pardon."

Then the girl lapsed into a sulky silence, and Frederick, too sick at heart, too indifferent to her likes and dislikes to care, did not encourage her to repeat what she had said.

It was perhaps a week later when young Mrs. Graves felt her first real jealousy. In the happiness of her hasty marriage, she had almost forgotten the story told her by the gossips of Ithaca. It was only when her husband's eyes were encircled and darkened by a far-away expression that Tess entered her mind. But even then, after a glance in the mirror, she dismissed the little singer contemptuously.

One morning just before breakfast, they were standing under the trees. On Frederick's face was that dreary look of discontent. Madelene contemplated him steadily. She had watched and studied, but had not yet solved the problem that occupied her mind. Was the squatter girl the obstacle? she wondered. It didn't seem possible. Frederick was so fastidious. Why, the girl could scarcely speak a word of good English! But it would do no harm to make sure. She decided to speak to her husband of Tessibel Skinner. But how?

Frederick owed her some consideration, and Madelene deeply desired he should be more attentive to her. Suddenly she laughed aloud. Frederick turned, the cloud partially lifting from his eyes.

"A happy thought, I dare say?" he inquired.

"Not very," answered Madelene flippantly. "I was wondering how long it would take that Skinner girl to earn enough money to pay for a trip like this."

Had a bomb gone off in his face, Frederick couldn't have been more appalled. His brows drew together in a dark frown; his face grew livid and tensely lined. Madelene noted the effect of her words. Her suspicion was confirmed,—the problem solved! It was the squatter girl who stood between her and her husband!

"I forbid you," said Frederick in a low, angry voice, "ever to mention that name again."

Then he whirled about and walked away through the trees. In alarm, Madelene sped after him.

"Frederick!" she implored. "I'm awfully sorry I said that.... I didn't mean to hurt you."

He shook her from his arm.

"Very well," he replied savagely, "but just please don't speak of her again."

Tears blinded the girl's vision.... An enraged feeling rose in her heart. Never in all her spoiled life had any one spoken to her in such a way. If Ebenezer had been there, Frederick would never have dared!

By this time, having stood mute for several seconds, she was thoroughly indignant. This was her first real conflict with Frederick, and she began to feel ill as well as incensed.

"It's dreadfully disagreeable of you to get angry over a little thing like that," she said impetuously. "One would think you loved that girl and not me. I was told lots of times you were crazy about her, but of course,—"

She hesitated now. She wanted to say cruel things about the squatter girl back in Ithaca, but she dared not. She was overwrought with anger, but her husband's threatening face forced her to silence.

"Are you determined to keep harping on a subject I wish to forget?" His words carried an ominous meaning, which quickened her already awakened jealousy. Determined to probe the matter to the bottom she demanded.

"Why should you wish to forget her? Does she disturb your memory as much as that?"

"Perhaps," replied Frederick gloomily.

He saw the danger involved in the discussion and curbed his tongue. Then he left her and walked quickly into the house. Madelene followed, angry and rebellious, and found him seated at the table, white-faced, with the morning mail unnoticed before him. Still enraged, she glanced over the letters indifferently.

"They're all for me with the exception of one," she said sulkily, "and it's an Ithaca letter.... May I open it?"

Frederick took it from her and looked at the envelope. His name was staring back at him as if every cramped letter were an accusing eye, and the writing was in the hand of Tessibel Skinner! He studied it a minute....

"You have mail of your own to read, my dear," he said quite kindly. "Let's have breakfast."

When during the morning Frederick found a moment to himself, he took from his pocket the letter that had been searing through his clothing to his heart. Gazing upon it, he shook as if he had the ague. Trembling hands held it up to the light. Several times he turned it over. What had Tess written to him? Had she told him, as he had her, that she loved him better than all the rest of the world? He uttered a desperate ejaculation and stretched out his arms. If he could have spanned the world that separated them, he would have dragged her to him by the terrible force of his desire. Again he turned the letter over.

Something kept him from ripping it open. He longed to delay the happiness of reading it, and while he waited, he lifted it to his lips and passionately kissed the crude writing. It ran up hill a little, but that only made him smile and love it the more. It brought memories of past joys, memories of Tessibel's endeavor to learn. Poor little child! Suddenly he slipped the paper knife into the envelope and slowly dragged it across the top.... Then he inserted his fingers and pulled out—the bill he had sent her. In a sudden passion he looked frantically into the empty envelope.... Nothing!... Absolute emptiness!

The money fluttered from his hand to the floor, where it lay like a sentient thing, staring back as if mocking him. He stood half-blindly gazing upon it. When he looked more closely, he stooped and picked it up. There written across its yellow back was the one little line,

"Darlin', I air a prayin' for you every day. Tessibel."

In a storm of remorse, he collapsed to the floor with his face in his hands.

CHAPTER XX
MADELENE COMPLAINS TO EBENEZER

"Read that letter; then you'll see why I'm angry," said Ebenezer Waldstricker to Helen one morning after he had frowningly perused a letter from Madelene. "Her last two have had a touch of this thing in them, too. If I find—"

He stopped because his wife had dropped her eyes and begun to read.

"Dear Eb:—

"Your letters have come along one after another, but they haven't made me feel happier. I do dislike to act as if I were telling tales; but I'm so miserable, and you're the only one in the world I can call on in my distress. You will forgive me, I know, dear Ebenezer. We've been here now such a long time, that I really feel as if we ought to come home, but I simply dread it more and more I think of it.

"You can't imagine how doleful Fred is, and I know it's the Skinner girl who's causing it."

Helen uttered an anxious exclamation. She knew her husband's dislike of the squatters. Her quick glance at his face called from his stern lips the cold question.

"Have you finished?"

"No."

"Then do!" he snarled, opening and closing his hands impatiently.

"You may ask me what proof I have," Helen read on, a slight pucker between her brows, "and I will say this: Fred has two or three times called me by her name, nearly dying of embarrassment when I asked him to account for it. Then once in his sleep he called out quite sharply, 'Tessibel!' He flies into all kinds of rages when I ask him questions about her. He won't admit he's ever cared anything for her—"

Helen looked up again and paused momentarily.

"Well, Ebenezer, he used to like Tessibel!"

Waldstricker waved his hand angrily.

"What's past is past!" he roared. "And now he's got to treat my sister decently, or I'll know the reason why.... The young pup! Why, here I've given him the chance of his life!... But finish the letter!"

Helen sighed as she again allowed her eyes to rest on the page in her hand.

"But I feel sure his interest in her isn't because of what she did for his sister," Madelene's letter continued. "Will you take some pains to find out all you can for me, Eb dear? It might be well for you to see her yourself, and perhaps you could make her admit something. I don't want you to worry about me, though. If I can make Fred act like a human being, I'll be happy enough. Tell Helen I shall bring her a lot of pretties from Paris, and will be awfully glad to see you both. Love to all.

Madelene."

"P. S. Perhaps you can make that girl tell you whether she's had a letter from Fred or not, and make her give it to you if you can. I think he's written her, but he says not."

"I'm very sorry about it," Helen murmured. She laid the letter on the table and looked across at the dark-faced man opposite, "but really I don't think Tess cares for him at all now. Deforrest has repeatedly said she never speaks of him, and that as far as he can make out, she has quite forgotten him."

"I'll make it my business to find out," muttered Waldstricker. "If I discover she has any hold on that young—"

"They may just've been romantic," excused Helen. "Why don't you ask Deforrest to find out for you?"

Ebenezer shook his head.

"I'm going down first myself," said he.

Helen rose and went to her husband's side. Her eyes were misty with unshed tears. She so desired Ebenezer to be himself again. She felt a little rebellious when she considered Madelene's turning her peaceful home into such a turmoil.

"You won't be stern with her, dear?" she pleaded.

"I'll treat her as she deserves," snapped Waldstricker.... "If Deforrest weren't so stubborn and hadn't rented Graves' place for the next four years, I'd do my best to oust the Skinners from that property.... One thing is certain, the old witch has got to go."

Helen sighed, exasperated. Her husband's face was crimson and the cords in his neck as rigid as taut ropes.

"Ebenezer dear, why will you get yourself into such a state of excitement over a set of people who'll never come into your life at all?" she begged of him.

There was gentle reproof in her tones. Ebenezer glanced at her sharply.

"Never come into my life at all!" he repeated. "Does this look as if they never came into my life, eh?" He leaned over and tapped Madelene's letter. "Am I going to see my sister—"

"Madelene is probably mistaken," interjected Helen, hopefully.

"It'll be better for the squatter girl if she is," answered Ebenezer, whirling and going out.

Now it happened that Tessibel was standing outside the cottage clipping her hedge when she heard the sound of horses' hoofs coming down the lane. She stepped to the shanty door, gave the sound which warned Andy of a stranger's approach, and was back again when Waldstricker's great black horse came in sight. Opposite her, he drew his steed to a standstill and bowed curtly. Tess had never seen his lips so sternly set, not even when he had dragged her from Mother Moll's hut. She made no move to go to him.

"I came to speak to you, Miss Skinner," he called. "Come here?"

Then Tessibel went a few steps nearer, without laying down her shears. Looking up into his face, she asked,

"What do ye want, Mr. Waldstricker?"

It was hard for Waldstricker to tell just what he did want when that pair of red-brown eyes were gazing at him.

"I think I'll dismount," he said suddenly.

Throwing one leg over the broad back of the horse, he slipped to the ground. The bridle over his arm, he walked toward the girl until she was standing but a step away.

"You haven't any news of Bishop for me, I suppose?" he asked.

Tess grew suddenly intuitive. Immediately she knew he had not come to ask her about Andy. She shook her head, her tongue cleaving to the roof of her mouth.

"Have you done anything to locate him?" persisted Waldstricker.

He was feeling his way to bring in the other matter, and looking more closely at the girl, he reluctantly admitted to himself she was beautiful.

"My daddy's been awful sick," said Tess quickly. "I ain't much time to do anything but take care of 'im an' sing in the church."

Waldstricker was not interested in the sick squatter, so he gave no sign of sympathy. Rather, he wanted to come to the crucial point immediately, but Tess was so unapproachable that he remained quiet a few embarrassing moments to think of the right thing to say.

"You must be a little lonely now Mr. Graves is married," he stated presently.

Tessibel grew deathly pale, and took one backward step. Had he come to talk of Frederick? Had he found out the secret she had kept religiously so many weeks?

"Mr. Graves?" she repeated, and then again in almost a whisper, "Mr. Graves?"

It was the first time in ever so long she'd pronounced that loved name aloud.

"Yes," said Waldstricker, darkly, "and I came down today to see the letters you've received from him."

Tess lifted her head and looked him straight in the eyes. Did he know she had had that one precious letter? Who'd told him about it? But she couldn't give it to him,—it was burned. Neither would she admit receiving it.

"What letters?" she asked, when she could speak.

"Those Mr. Graves sent you from France!" responded Waldstricker, in very decided tones.

Tess thought quickly. Frederick had told her he was afraid of Waldstricker. So was she! He was the man who had been instrumental in taking her husband away from her. She felt a cold rage growing into active life within her. How dared he come here.

She was looking at him so steadily that the powerful churchman lowered his eyes, and for a moment pretended to be arranging the horse's bridle. Then, he centered his bold, black eyes upon her until her nerves tingled.

"I wish to see what he's written you," he repeated, this time rather lamely.

"I ain't got any letters," Tess told him.

92

"Haven't you received any from him?" demanded Waldstricker.

The girl shook her head so decidedly that her curls vibrated to the very ends. It was as though every bit of her loving body would shield the dear one way off in France from this compelling, mesmeric man.

Waldstricker felt she was not telling the truth. He grew enraged, the blood flying purple to his face.

"I said I wanted you to give them to me," he repeated emphatically, going nearer her.

"An' I says as how I didn't have none," evaded Tess, growing angrier by the minute. "An' if I did, I wouldn't give 'em to you. 'Tain't none of yer business if I get letters, I'll have ye know!" She took several backward steps toward the shanty. Her rising temper stirred up the impudence she used in her conflicts with the rude fishermen. "Jump on yer horse an' trot home," she finished tauntingly.

Waldstricker's mingled surprise and anger showed in his exclamation. What an impertinent little huzzy she was! In his heart he believed Madelene was right, but the defiant squatter girl baffled him. He would go home more than ever satisfied Tess Skinner was keeping from him something about his young brother-in-law. He mounted his horse, his muscles working with rage.

"I'll make you confess sooner or later," he muttered ominously, "or I'll know the reason why."

"Scoot!" was all Tess said, and she waved her hand and snapped the pruning shears together derisively.

Waldstricker whirled his horse up the lane, and striking the animal with a spur, bounded away.

CHAPTER XXI
THE END OF THE HONEYMOON

Helen Waldstricker walked nervously up and down the library. Many times during the past hour she had gone to the window and stared out into the night. It was almost impossible to read or work with her mind in such a state of perturbation. Every sound caused her to lay aside her book. She was waiting for Ebenezer to return from the station with Madelene and Frederick.

Helen dreaded the home-coming of the newly married pair. Ebenezer was all upset over the letters his sister had written him from abroad, and as Deforrest was obliged to be away so much, she had spent many hours of mental worry by herself.

The sound of a carriage took her into the hall, where she stood until Ebenezer threw open the door.

The first sight of her young sister-in-law showed Mrs. Waldstricker that the girl was not at all contented and happy. Madelene's face was pale, but not more so than Frederick's. Ebenezer looked like a thunder cloud. Helen, with her usual tact and sweetness greeted the young people in a sisterly manner.

"I'm so glad to have you both back," she purred, kissing first one, then the other. "Now, dear,"—to Madelene, "come along up with me and get off your wraps and then we'll have dinner."

The two women went upstairs together in silence, and it was not until Helen had closed the door and Madelene had removed her wraps that Mrs. Graves turned upon her brother's wife.

"I suppose you noticed from Ebbie's letters that I've been awfully unhappy?"

"Yes," admitted Helen, "but I was in hopes it had passed over."

"It's worse now than it was before," answered Madelene, "I'm perfectly certain he doesn't care for me—"

"Then why did he marry you?" interrupted Helen.

"For my money! That's why!"

Helen's answering ejaculation brought a short, bitter laugh from the girl.

"Oh, no, dear," protested Mrs. Waldstricker. "You must be mistaken. I'm positive, he's an honorable young man."

Madelene flung herself impatiently into a chair.

"Sit down," she said. "Don't stand up!... Oh, I'm so tired! It seems years since we left France. And Fred's been like a death's house all the time. I can't for the life of me see why he should act the way he does. Why, Helen, he goes days without as much as ever starting to speak to me. If he talks at all, I simply have to drag the words from him."

"That's dreadful," sympathized Helen, "but perhaps he isn't well, dear. Why don't you get him to see a doctor?"

Madelene shrugged her shoulders disdainfully.

"It's not a doctor he wants, it's that Skinner girl, I can see that plainly enough."

Helen dropped on the arm of the girl's chair and slipped her arm around her neck.

"Well, now you're home," she soothed. "Ebenezer'll help you if he can, and I know Deforrest will. I'm perfectly certain though, Tessibel Skinner would do nothing to make Frederick swerve from his loyalty to you."

"Do you know whether Eb went down there to see her?" asked the girl, wearily.

"I think he did. He asked Tess for Frederick's letters, but she said she hadn't received any from him. And really, I don't believe she did, for she tells everything to Deforrest and she'd tell him that, I'm sure."

Madelene shook her head incredulously.

"I feel perfectly positive he wrote her," she asserted.

"Well, perhaps!—" said Helen.

Then they were silent a few moments.

"I suppose you haven't guessed something I have to tell you," stammered Helen, presently.

Madelene turned her eyes upon her sister-in-law. Then she smiled.

"Helen, dearest, aren't you glad about it?"

Helen blushed and radiated a smile.

"Yes, very, and so is Ebenezer! We both feel as if we have much to be thankful for—and now if you were only happy—"

"Oh, Helen, I know I've upset Ebbie a whole lot,—but who else could I go to?... Do tell me when—"

"In May, dear," whispered Helen. "I wish you were as happy as I.... But there's the dinner bell. Let's go down."

When they entered the dining room, Ebenezer was standing alone, his back to the grate.

"Did you say anything to him, Eb?" demanded Madelene.

"Certainly, child, but he insists he scarcely knows her. He rehearsed the trouble his sister had before she died—"

"Oh, he's told me that, too," interjected Madelene, tartly, "but that wouldn't make him mix her name up with mine, would it, and make him get mad every time I mention her?"

"He seems to be very much incensed that any one should accuse him of caring for her," observed Ebenezer. "And Madelene—"

Helen went quickly to her sister-in-law.

"Dear," she interrupted her husband, "if I were you, I wouldn't say anything more about it to Frederick until you're certain.... Here he comes, now. Do be pleasant to him, both of you."

But in spite of Helen's good offices, the first dinner at home was anything but a happy one for the young couple.

CHAPTER XXII

THE REPUDIATION

A week after the arrival of Frederick and Madelene Graves in Ithaca, Tessibel Skinner sat sewing near the kitchen stove and talking to Andy Bishop in the shanty garret. Outside the wind gusted over the lake, the snow birds making shrill, protesting twitters against the coming blizzard.

"You ain't mournin' 'bout somethin', kiddie, be ye?" whispered the dwarf from the hole in the ceiling.

"A little," she confessed, glancing up at the dwarf, while she knotted the thread. "I air jest thinking how awful it air fer Daddy to sleep so hard. That medicine he takes must be awful strong."

"So it air, brat, but he don't suffer," comforted Andy.

"Get back, Andy," warned Tess, getting up. "Some one air walkin' in the lane."

She could hear the steps plainly, now. Whoever it was paused in front of the shack. When the knock came, she placed her sewing on the chair. With a glance at the attic, she walked forward and took down the bar. The opening door revealed Frederick Graves standing in the falling snow.

"I've come back, Tess," he breathed brokenly.

The girl staggered back speechless to the middle of the room. Dismayed eyes sought Frederick's, eloquently demanding a reason for his coming. The boy followed her swiftly in and closed the door. How ill she looked! God, could it have been his own conduct that had made Tessibel so fragile! He had promised to love and cherish her forever. The thought that he could revivify her by the very strength of his overflowing love took him forward a step. Tess looked helplessly about and retreated a little.

"Daddy's sick," she murmured.

"I'm sorry. I'm very sorry, dear.... I had to see you, Tessibel," cried Frederick, passionately. "I hurried back from abroad because of you, my darling.... Oh, Tess dear—"

Tessibel made a dissenting gesture.

"Please go away," said she, in agitation. "Go away, please."

Instead of obeying her, the boy came nearer.

"I can't go!" he answered hoarsely, running his fingers through his thick hair. "I've suffered horribly for what I've done.... Tess, don't make me suffer any more—Oh, darling, please understand—"

"I air understandin'," interrupted Tess, steadying herself. "Ye can't do nothin' now.... Won't ye please go?"

"No," replied Frederick, setting his teeth sharply. "No, I won't! I came to tell you what I want you to do."

Tessibel sank into the chair, her legs refusing to hold her up any longer. Frederick was looking down at her sorrowfully. How could he ever have left her? His excuse about his mother's needing money now seemed small and unimportant. How like a glorious golden mantle her curls encompassed her! A spasmodic desire to twine them again around his fingers gripped him. He wanted to take her in his arms, to love her, to be loved in return, as she had loved him on the ragged rocks. How beautiful she was—yet how frail and worn! It seemed as if the ice that had warped and frozen his heart to a hard, unresponsive mass, during the months with Madelene, was melting in the presence of the girl he loved. His soul had thirsted for the sight of her, his arms yearned to hold and press her close. He stood a moment undecided, then suddenly bent forward and drew her forcibly to him. Groaning deeply, he dropped his hot lips upon her neck, and Tessibel started back as if he'd stung her.

"If you look at me so cold and white, Tess," he moaned, "I shall—I'll—"

96

Then he sought for her lips and found them, kissing her stormily until she felt a keen sense of terror and physical pain. His passionate insistence carried her completely out of herself for the instant.

"Tess, Tess!" he murmured, "nothing matters now! Don't send me away from you again, sweet."

Tess lay in his arms, mute and unresponsive.

"Say one little kind word to me, Tess," he implored again, brokenly.

But Tess couldn't speak. She felt her tongue burn as if infinitesimal sparks had touched each groove upon it. She could not stay in his arms! Before the world he belonged to another woman. She pushed him away, drew herself from his embrace, and sat down again. Her action brought a fierce ejaculation from the boy's lips.

When Frederick ordered his horse that morning, Madelene had slipped her hand into his.

"May I go with you, dear?" she begged. "Do order my horse, too, won't you?"

He colored to the roots of his hair and shrugged his shoulders impatiently.

"I'd rather go by myself," he returned so curtly that Madelene bit her lips to keep back the tears.

Stung with jealousy, the young wife watched her husband ride out under the bare trees to the road beyond. Then she ordered her own horse, and dressed herself quickly.

Affairs between the young couple had reached a crucial point. Madelene's suspicions of Frederick were unusually active. She had it clearly in mind that he had gone to the Skinner hut. All the distance to the lake her face burned. She knew well enough she was doing something unpardonable, but how could she stay calmly at home when stinging jealousy goaded her to action?

She cantered past Kennedy's farm and on down the hill, her thoughts in a turmoil. If Frederick were not with the squatter girl, how happy she'd be! She hadn't formulated an excuse for Tessibel if she found her suspicions incorrect. She'd have to tell her something reasonable. Ah, she would pretend she'd come about the church singing.

Beyond and below the lake lay grey and somber, shadowed by the winter sky. The wind stung her face and tweaked her fingers through her warm gloves. Directly in front of the Young house, she reined in her horse and contemplated it. How much had happened since she had married Frederick, and Ebenezer had married Helen Young—how much to her and to him!

Frederick's conduct had destroyed her illusions about marriage. She could be supremely happy if he would treat her a little more as if she were his wife, more as the husbands of her friends treated them. She rode on again slowly until through the willow trees she saw the smoke curling upward from the chimney of the Skinner shanty. Her heart beat furiously when she slipped from her horse and tied him to a fence post. Intuitively, she felt she'd find her husband with Tessibel Skinner. She walked the rest of the way down the hill, stopped before the hut and looked it over. All without lay dressed in its winter garb, and the small house, save for the smoke, appeared uninhabited.

Then as a human sound from a tomb, came Frederick's voice. Madelene staggered back. She realized that not for one single instant had she doubted she would find her husband there. And he was there! She'd heard his voice passionately insisting something. Red fire flashed in front of her eyes.

Without thought of consequences, she flung open the door and stood on the threshold, breathless and crimson, in all her indignant wifehood. Frederick stood near the chair in which sat Tessibel. In one single moment Madelene sent an appraising glance over the girl huddled in the wooden rocker—a woman's glance, mercilessly discovering her condition. Then her blazing eyes came back to Frederick. He had not spoken at her appearance— he had only reeled backward a few steps.

"You see I followed you," said Madelene in cold, metallic tones. "I knew you were coming here when you left home."

Tessibel got up slowly, went forward, and closed the door. Once more the man she loved had brought humiliation upon her.

"He were just a goin' to go!" she whispered, and she went back and dropped into her chair.

"Oh, he was, eh?" Madelene laughed harshly. "It's very good of you to let him go. I'll give you to understand my husband—"

She made a rapid step toward Tess, whose head went up instantly. The red-brown eyes battled an instant with the blue, stopping Madelene's progress. Frederick, stung to action, reached forth and grasped his wife's arm.

"Madelene!" he exclaimed. His tone brought flashing eyes upon him.

"You think I'm going to stand tamely by and watch you come here to see her?... You both think I'm a fool, I suppose. Well, I'm not such a fool as I look!"

Defiantly, the speaker surveyed her husband up and down. "I knew very well you intended coming here. That's why I asked—you to take me today and why I—followed you. I've had hard work to make myself believe you'd leave me for—"

Her scintillating look swept again over Tess from head to foot. Her eyes drew down at the corners; so did her lips. It dawned dazedly on Tess how much Madelene looked like her brother. Then, suddenly Mrs. Graves laughed, a note of triumph riding in her tones. She faced Frederick and throwing out both hands, disdainfully, at the squatter girl huddled in the chair, cried,

"My God, look at her! If you've any eyes, you'll see ..." and turning upon Tessibel, "Were you trying to pass off on my husband a spurious—" The scorn in the contemptuous tones of the shrill voice stung like a whip lash.

The appeal gathering slowly in Tess' eyes was but a dumb response to the other woman's taunting, bitter words. She could not have spoken had her life been at stake. She crouched down in terrified shame.

Then like a flash the meaning of his wife's words rushed over the almost stupefied man! God! and he had not known! Tessibel, her new light of coming motherhood, cowered before him like a stricken thing. He sprang forward during Madelene's hesitation and grasped his wife's arm again. He was so furiously angry his tightening fingers brought a cry of pain from her.

"Hush!" he cried peremptorily. "Hush!... You're crazy!... Haven't you any heart?... You've gone mad!"

Madelene shook off his hand.

"Yes, I'm mad half crazy. And you've made me so. Ever since I married you, you've had this girl in your mind morning, noon and night.... Now I know it! Oh, what a fool I was! I—I suppose possibly the next thing we'll know you'll be claiming the—"

Frederick shook her roughly.

"I said to stop it," he gritted. "Come away this minute."

Madelene, crying now, was struggling to pull herself from Frederick's grasp.

"I want to talk to that woman before I go," she screamed in desperation. "Let me go, Fred! I will speak to her."

"You'll not if I can help it," answered Frederick. "Come out of here, I say!"

By main strength he was drawing his wife toward the door. Tess was staring at them as if they were creatures from another world.

"I'm sorry," Frederick said directly over Madelene's head to her. "Dreadfully sorry."

"Sorry!" shrieked Madelene. "Sorry for such a woman! Look what you've done to me, both of you!" She wrenched herself from the strong fingers and flung back to the squatter girl. "I want to know if my husband is the father—"

Frederick had hold of her once more. The anger in his white face was terrible to see.

"If you speak to her again," he said murderously, "I'll—I'll—"

"I suppose you'll kill me," shrilled his wife. "Well, go ahead! The only way you'll ever get her will be when I'm dead!" Then she thrust her white working face close to his. "If she won't speak, will you? You're my husband, and I find you here with this—this—.... Are you the father of her baby?"

"No," said Frederick, dropping his eyes. "No, of course not!"

Tessibel bent her head to receive the last brutal stroke he had to give. She moved but uttered no sound.

"Well, do you love her then?" demanded Madelene.

And Frederick, not daring to look at Tess, repeated, "No, of course not.... Don't be a fool!"

"Then, what do you want of him, girl?" Madelene cried hoarsely to Tessibel. "You've heard what he said."

Tess thought she was going to die. All the awful hurt which had lain dormant for so many weeks rose up with ten thousand times the vigor. It was as if Heaven had belched out flames to consume her, and she knew there was no escape from this thing that had come upon her. Frederick had not only repudiated his love for her, but his baby too. She threw back her curls with a proud gesture.

"I don't want 'im," she said straight to Madelene. "Take 'im away an' don't let 'im come here any more."

When Madelene started to speak again, Frederick shoved her from the hut into the gray day. He turned once and looked at Tess. She was just where he'd left her, her eyes brimmed with sorrow and her teeth locked tightly together.

Then the door banged shut and she was alone in the kitchen. A little later she heard as in a dream the sound of horses' hoofs retreating far up the lane. Then all the powers of darkness closed in about her, and malicious elfin voices chattered her shame in her ears. Frederick had repudiated her and his child and had gone! Tess staggered forward, and a few minutes afterward, when Andy slipped down the ladder, he found her curled up on the cot insensible, her face shrouded in red curls.

CHAPTER XXIII
THE QUARREL

When Frederick Graves closed the door of the Skinner hut, he wheeled furiously upon his young wife.

"Come home," he said gruffly. "You've done enough harm for today."

"If I've done more than you have," retorted Madelene, tartly, "then I'm some little harm maker!" Suffering intensely from jealousy, she whirled about, crying, "That's what's been the matter with you all the time we've been abroad! And I know very well Tessibel Skinner sent for you to come home."

"That's a lie," interrupted Frederick, fiercely.

Madelene paused in her ascent of the hill lane.

"What made you come down here today, then, if you didn't want to see her yourself?"

Frederick was silent. He hated scenes like this. If he spoke his real mind, he'd plunge himself into hot water at once. And he was always careful not to do that. Silence at the present moment was better than speech. Besides, his late contact with Tessibel Skinner had left him aquiver. Oh, how he loved her! Every nerve in his body called out for sight of his beloved. He would have gone back to the shack if he'd dared.

"Where did you leave your horse?" snapped Madelene, when they'd nearly reached her own.

"In the lower stable at my father's old place,—over there."

"I'll help you mount and then get my horse," said he. "Do you wish to ride on without me?"

Mrs. Graves made a dissenting gesture.

"No, of course, I don't. I want you to come with me directly. I won't let you out of my sight so near that girl. I think it's perfectly outrageous! I somehow believe you lied to me about—"

"Keep your opinions to yourself," growled Frederick. "I've no wish to hear them."

Madelene was about to put her foot into the stirrup. Instead, she stood while fresh tears gathered under her lids.

"Frederick, you're cruel and awfully ugly to me," she said plaintively. "How can you do such things after all the money I've given you?"

Frederick expressed his feeling by a cynical little laugh.

"Perhaps if you didn't throw up your confounded benevolence so often, I might show more gratitude," he snapped back.

Then he lifted her to the saddle, gave her the bridle, and walked beside her to the barn.

His thoughts were busy until, when they reached home, the silence between them was appalling. Thankful to be a few minutes by himself, the young man went away to stable the horses and his wife entered the house. Madelene found her brother sitting before the grate fire. Helen looked up and smiled at her sweetly.

"Come and get warm, dear," she said. "You've had a long ride, haven't you?... Why, what's the matter, Madelene?"

Mrs. Graves dropped into a chair.

"I'm so awfully unhappy," she cried, "and Frederick's as mean as he can be.... I hate that Skinner girl!"

Mrs. Waldstricker dropped her work into her lap.

Ebenezer looked at his sister critically.

"What's she done to you now?" he asked, without waiting for his wife to speak.

Madelene flung up an angry, flushed face.

"She's done enough! I hate her and always shall. She sent for Frederick to come down there—and he went—"

"Are you sure?" asked Mrs. Waldstricker, in a shocked voice.

"Of course I'm sure! I'm not in the habit of saying things I'm not sure of, Helen. I might have known when people told me he was in love with that squatter it was true."

Her loud, angry voice reached Frederick as he entered the room. The frown deepened on his brow. He looked at his brother-in-law for a minute. He never remembered being so angry before.

"Madelene has told a direct falsehood when she says Tessibel Skinner sent for me," he said. "She did not!"

"But I found him in her shanty, Ebenezer dear," thrust in Madelene, "and she's a wicked, little huzzy."

"Hush!" cried Frederick, white-lipped.

"I won't hush, so there!" screamed his wife. "I won't! I won't!... And, Ebenezer, she's bad, she is! She's going to have a—"

Frederick wheeled around desperately. Madelene was placing him at the extreme of his endurance. Human nature could bear no more.

"Oh, my God, such a woman!" he exclaimed.

"There, you see!" gasped Madelene. "He won't listen to a thing against her, and he's been acting as guilty as he could all the way home.... No wonder I don't believe a word he says!"

Mrs. Waldstricker picked up her work, folded it, and laid it on the table.

"But, Madelene, it's so bewildering," she exclaimed. "Tell us, dear, just what happened."

Between sobs and tears Madelene went over the trial she had passed through, and continued, "While we were abroad, I thought there was something the matter with him, and I know one day he got a letter. He wouldn't let me see it, though I begged him to. Now, I know it was from her!" The speaker flung about upon her sister-in-law. "If you could have seen her today, Helen, the shameless thing! She didn't even have the grace to say she was sorry for anything she'd done."

"She probably wasn't," monotoned Waldstricker. Then he looked directly at his wife. "I've often argued with your brother about those squatters. They're a pest to the county. Deforrest—"

"Oh, don't blame Deforrest, Ebenezer," Helen interjected agitatedly. "He's so good at heart, and he did all he could for the little Skinner girl. I know there's some mistake. I'll go down and see her tomorrow."

Waldstricker got up heavily.

"You'll do no such thing," he retorted. "Don't dare go near—her!"

Helen flushed at her husband's tone.

"But Deforrest is away," she argued timidly. "I feel I ought to do something."

Madelene went hastily to her brother's side.

"Don't let her go, Ebbie," she gasped. "It's an awful place; a little bit of a hut—"

"I've been in it many times," interrupted Helen, with dignity, "and I do feel, Ebenezer—"

"I want no argument about the matter," said Waldstricker, sternly. "If she's in the condition Madelene says she is, then her home is no place for my wife.... It's shameful, absolutely shameful!"

"But, Ebenezer, she's probably been unfortunate. Poor little child! I wish you'd—"

Waldstricker cut her plea in two with an angry gesture.

"I command you not to go there," said he, sharply.

"Very well," sighed Helen. "Of course, I'll do as you wish."

Then she got up quietly and went upstairs. Indeed, had she her way, she'd have gone to Tessibel Skinner without hesitation. She knew her brother would be grieved to his heart's core, if this awful thing had happened to the little red-headed squatter girl. But she had no choice in the matter.

Frightened, too, she wondered what Ebenezer's plans were. He was so relentless in his desire to punish sinners. Bye and bye, when she was less nervous, she'd ask him to wait until Deforrest returned before doing anything.

Her head was throbbing with excitement. Her heart, too, ached for Tessibel. She lay down on the bed and closed her eyes. Presently, she heard Ebenezer's slow tread coming upstairs. When he entered the room, she raised her lids and smiled.

"Come here, dear," she murmured.

He came directly to her side.

"What is it, my darling?" he asked tenderly.

"I feel so unhappy about the little Skinner girl," sobbed Helen.

"I'm sorry, dear, but you must not go against my wishes. As a good and obedient wife, you should realize I know best. I can't allow you to go down into that cabin."

"I won't go, dearest, but will you please promise me one thing—"

Ebenezer bent upon her a look so stern she dared not finish. "Oh, I do wish Deforrest were here!" she ended irrelevantly.

"I do, too; but as long as he is not, you must trust me to do what I think best."

He went out abruptly, and Helen Waldstricker cried herself to sleep.

CHAPTER XXIV
WALDSTRICKER INTERFERES

That evening Frederick Graves shook in his shoes when he returned home and received Waldstricker's message to meet him in the library at nine o'clock. If there was one person in the world he didn't want to see just then, it was his dictatorial brother-in-law. He stood in his room considering the situation, when he heard the grandfather's clock on the stairs slowly strike the hour of nine.

"Well, it won't help any to keep him waiting," he muttered.

Unwillingly, he walked down the stairs to the library door. Pausing, he saw Ebenezer seated at the table reading the Bible.

"Come in and sit down," greeted the latter, curtly.

"Thanks," said Frederick, taking a chair. "Mind if I smoke?"

The man thus addressed made no answer. He read a verse or two partly aloud as if to himself, then closed the book and laid it on the table.

"What's the matter between you and Madelene?" he inquired presently, fixing Frederick with a steady gaze.

"Nothing.... Nothing, that I'm to blame for. Madelene followed me to the lake and found me in Skinner's shack. That's all the row was about."

"Why were you there?" Waldstricker did not change his tone.

Frederick threw his cigarette into the smoldering grate and shrugged his shoulders impatiently.

"Can't a fellow stop in a shanty without the whole town gossiping about it?" he demanded peevishly.

"That's just it, Frederick. I don't want people talking about my sister's husband and a squatter girl," the older man explained. "I must know why you were there."

"Look at here, Eb," exclaimed the boy, "why don't you let Madelene and me fight out our own quarrels? I don't interfere with you and Helen."

"Huh! I should hope not!" growled Waldstricker. "But quarrels are not what we're talking about.... Why were you in the Skinner hut?... Are you in love with that girl?"

"God! No! Are you mad? What's the matter with everybody?"

"There's nothing the matter, my boy, only I want to warn you I won't have my sister unhappy."

"She makes herself unhappy," growled Frederick, selecting another cigarette from his case.

"I can't see any use of your going down there at all," Ebenezer went on, turning to poke the fire. "It doesn't look well after the things that happened in your family."

"That's just it," said Frederick, using the elder's words as an excuse; "our trouble makes it quite proper some one of my family should go there. The girl did enough for us, God knows."

Waldstricker gave a decided negative shake of his head.

"It's your mother's place to go, not yours. You don't want a scandal, do you?... Let her go there if any one does."

Again Frederick found an excuse.

"She can't go when she's out of Ithaca, and I took Miss Skinner a message from my mother today. If Madelene hadn't acted so abominably, I'd have told her about it."

Waldstricker looked keenly at the other man.

"I didn't notice you tried very hard to explain matters this afternoon! Now, did you?"

"I was mad," retorted Frederick, sulkily.

"May I see the message your mother sent?" came quickly from Waldstricker.

Frederick started. Evidently his brother-in-law didn't believe his story.

"If Miss Skinner'll give it to you, you can!" said he. "... I say, Eb, let Madelene and me get out of this the best way we can, won't you? Tell Maddie to behave herself and leave the Skinner girl's name out of her rages at me.... That's all I ask."

"No," thundered Ebenezer, wrathfully. "I won't have my sister in tears all the time over a squatter girl. Madelene says you received letters from her abroad."

"Well, I didn't," snapped back Frederick.

"That's past, anyhow! Now, then, I'm going to tell you something. I need a man to go to San Francisco to our office there, and as Madelene wants a change, I'm going to send you."

Frederick shuddered. Had he dared, he would have rebelled at this wholesale delivering him over, tied hand and foot, to his tempestuous young wife. If he were sent away, what would become of Tessibel? His heart turned sick with apprehension. He had had no time to explain his plans to her.

"You have no objections to going, I suppose?" Ebenezer broke in on his harassing thoughts.

"No! If Madelene's satisfied, I am," replied Frederick, flipping the ash from his cigarette.

"Then be ready to get away by, let me see, early in March," his brother-in-law announced.

Early in March, and this was but December! He had that much grace then. He could do something for Tess if the family relaxed its vigilance upon him a little.

"And there's something else," proceeded Waldstricker. "It's—it's this!"

Then he deliberately made a statement that brought a red fire into Frederick's eyes. He staggered to his feet.

"You wouldn't, you couldn't do that, Ebenezer," he groaned.

"Oh, ho!... That gets you on the raw, does it, young man?" sneered the elder, one lip-corner rising to an unusual height. "So you do care that much, eh?... A while ago you made the statement she was nothing to you."

"I want to be human," Frederick managed to get out.

"Human, eh? No, that's not it! What you want is a few other women on your staff besides your wife. But you won't as long as you're married to my sister, and I'm running things. I'll see that none of the members of my family disobey my law or God's law either."

The big man got to his feet, slipped his hands into his pocket, and stared at his white-faced, young brother-in-law.

"How does my little scheme suit you?" he demanded grimly.

"I think it perfectly devilish, by God, I do," cried Frederick.

"Oh, you do, eh? So you swear with your other faults?... Does my sister approve of that?"

"I've never asked her," snapped Frederick, "and if you're through with me, I'd like to go."

"Have a little talk with Madelene before you go to bed—and, oh, Fred—" he called after the young man hurrying up the stairs.

Frederick paused, his hand on the banister.

"By the way, I shall want your assistance in the little matter I spoke of."

CHAPTER XXV
THE SUMMONS

Jake Brewer paused in the lane opposite Skinner's home. The shanty was almost snowed in. A thin curl of smoke trailed up from the chimney and drifted among the leafless branches of the willow trees.

Brewer dropped a pair of dead rabbits to the deep snow at his side, and shifted the gun he held in his right hand to his left. Then, he fumbled in his overcoat pockets. Discovering what he wanted, he picked up the rabbits and walked through the path to the hut.

Tess took down the bar at his rap.

"Lot o' snow, Tessie," smiled Brewer. "Here, I brought ye some letters."

Tessibel took the two letters the fisherman handed her.

"They got yer name writ on 'em, brat," said he, knocking the snow from his boots against the clap boards. "That's how I knowed they was your'n."

A shadowy smile flitted over the squatter girl's face.

"Sure, they be fer me," she replied. She turned the letters over in her hands. "Thank ye, Jake, fer bringin' 'em.... Come in a minute, won't ye?"

"Sure, an' I air always glad to do somethin' fer ye, kid.... How's yer pa this mornin'?"

Brewer stepped into the hut, placed his gun and the rabbits in the corner, and spread his hands over the stove.

"He ain't so well today, Jake! Poor Daddy, he suffers somethin' awful with his heart, Daddy does.... It air rheumatism."

"Ever try eel skins, brat?" asked Brewer, sitting down. "My grandma wore a eel skin for rheumatiz for twenty-five years, an' Holy Moses, the sufferin' that woman had durin' 'em times my tongue ain't able to tell!"

Tess glanced at the letters in her hand half-heartedly.

"We've tried 'em, too, Jake," she answered. "Daddy's been wrapped in 'em night after night. But they don't seem to do no good."

"D'ye ever have Ma Moll incant over him, Tessie?"

Tessibel nodded her head.

"Yep, I give 'er three dollars for ten incants an' they didn't do no good uther." She went a step nearer Brewer. "But I air prayin' hard, Jake, every day for 'im," she confided softly.

Brewer nodded his head.

"I guess that air better'n incants any time if ye can do it, kid," he smiled.

"I guess so, too," agreed the girl. "Tell Miss Brewer I'll be to see her soon as the weather gits better."

Jake got up, scratched his head, and thought a moment.

"I might leave ye a rabbit, seein' yer daddy ain't well 'nough to do no gunnin'," said he.

"Ye're awful good, Jake," murmured Tessibel, following the man to the door. "Stop in any day."

"All right," and Jake struck out toward the rock path.

Tess closed the door and put up the bar. Andy was eyeing her from the ceiling.

"What ye got, kid?" he whispered.

Tess held up the letters.

"Two of 'em, an' this one air from Mr. Young. Shall I read it to ye, Andy?" she asked, looking up.

The little man chuckled with joy.

"I'd like to hear it," said he.

Tess drew a chair under the boyish face peering upon her, and sat down.

"Dear Tessibel," she read.

"I hoped to be home this week, but find my work won't be finished. Please keep at your books and study hard. Get the doctor any time you need him for your father. I know you're trying to be a brave little girl, and may God bless you.

Affectionately,
Deforrest Young."

Tessibel choked on the last word.

"It air awful hard to be brave, Andy," she faltered, brushing away a tear.

The dwarf made a dash at his own eyes.

"Ye got another letter," he cut in irrelevantly.

"Yep," said Tess.

After pulling forth the second sheet, she spread it out and read it through without looking up.

"Miss Tessibel Skinner:

"It is necessary for you to attend a church meeting next Wednesday afternoon at three o'clock in the chapel. Please oblige,

"SILANDER GRIGGS, Pastor."

"Anything much?" demanded the dwarf, interestedly.

"Nope, Andy, only a note askin' me to come to church tomorrow afternoon, but I jest can't go, Andy!... I can't! I ain't been fer two Sundays, now, 'cause I been feelin' so bad."

She raised her eyes full of misery to meet Andy's sympathetic gaze. How could she go after that awful scene nearly three weeks before with Madelene and Frederick? She never could face the Waldstricker family again.

"I won't never go to church, ever any more," she mourned presently.

"Mebbe not, dear," returned the dwarf, smothered in his throat. "An' the church'll be worser off'n you!"

Troubled in spirit, Tess considered the letter a few minutes.

"I s'pose they be gittin' up somethin' fer Christmas, an' I ought to go an' tell 'em I can't sing. I said as how I would over three months ago if Miss Waldstricker'd help me; but I can't.... Will ye look after Daddy while I air gone, Andy?"

"Sure," agreed the dwarf. "I'll slide under his bed an' talk the pains right out o' 'im."

"I wish the meetin' was in the mornin'," Tess sighed. "It gits dark so early, an' Mr. Young ain't home! He'd come an' git me an' bring me back if he were. It air a long walk," and she sighed again.

"Mebbe 'twon't be so cold tomorrow as it air today," cheered Andy and they lapsed into silence.

CHAPTER XXVI
THE CHURCHING

The dawning of Wednesday brought one of those drab days so frequent in the lake-country. The daylight, dim even at high noon, hardly suggested a possible sun shining anywhere. Misty sheets of stinging ice-particles drove from the northern skyline to the hill south of Ithaca.

The snow crunched sharply under Tessibel's feet as she picked her way from the shanty to the lane. Kennedy's brindle bull, leaping and barking, invited her to a frolic. The girl called the dog to her, and petted him.

"No, no, Pete, Tess ain't able to run an' play with ye any more," she told him, sadly, "but ye can go with me to Hayt's."

Nuzzling her hand, the great dog walked soberly by her side, as though he understood. Tess shivered a little as the frost-laden air bit nippingly at her ears. The winter birds between her and the lake lifted their wings and mounted against the wind, some driving in flocks, others now and then by twos and threes. Tess followed their flight through the storm.... How strong and happy they seemed!

For an instant she paused at the gate in front of Deforrest Young's empty house. The snow had drifted until the path could no longer be discerned. A little twinge of loneliness touched Tessibel's heart. Her friend would not be at the church that day.

When she came within sight of the chapel, she bent and petted Pete. She took his head between her gloved hands and looked into the lovely eyes shining out of his ugly face.

"Go home, Petey dearie," she said. "Tessibel air goin' to church. They don't let dogs in God's house, honey."

Obediently the dog turned and trotted off.

Tess opened the chapel door and stepped in. Buffeted, as she had been by the storm, she met the warmth within with a grateful little sigh.

Half-way to the stove in the middle of the room, she stopped, arrested by the unusual group beyond. Ebenezer Waldstricker stood there, surrounded by the elders of the church. In all she counted five men: the minister, Silander Griggs, and three elders. At one side sat Frederick Graves.

Puzzled and embarrassed by Frederick's presence and appearance, half-conscious of something menacing in the stern faces turned toward her, she was tempted, weary as she was, to turn back into the blizzard raging without. As she awkwardly scraped the snow from her shoes, Pastor Griggs came to her and led her to a seat near the fire.

Waldstricker gazed at her critically, but didn't bow his head. Tessibel didn't mind if people failed to speak to her, and she didn't like Waldstricker anyway. She did not look at Frederick after that first fleeting glance, but bowed her head on the pew-back in front from sheer weariness. The memory of that scene in the cabin three weeks previous recurred with renewed clearness. Madelene's insulting words, re-echoing in her ears, made her grow faint from stinging humiliation. Oh, how sorry she was she'd come to church! She could have asked Jake Brewer to bring up a note explaining that she could not take part in the Christmas doings.

The sound of moving feet told her the time had arrived for opening the meeting. If she thought at all of the absence of the female members of the church, she sought for no other reason than the steadily increasing blizzard.

One by one she heard the men take their places. Then, the pastor cleared his throat loudly and began to pray. Perfect silence save for his droning voice filled the small chapel. Tess heard him praying for the members of the congregation, for the mothers at home with their children, and as usual for all earthly sinners.

"And particularly, dear Lord," continued the deep voice, "may thy tender mercy and loving kindness visit the heart of our sinning sister here present and soften it, making her obedient to these thy servants, to whom Thou hast committed the government of thy church."

Why! What had he said? "Sinning sister ... here present." Why, they were all men but her! The pastor finished his prayer with a resounding "Amen," in which the elders joined reverently. Confused, Tessibel sat back in the pew, puzzled and frightened.

"I have before me here on my desk," Griggs announced, "a letter from Deforrest Young. In answer to a letter from the church, asking him to be with us this afternoon, he has requested that Brother Ebenezer Waldstricker be instructed to vote in his name.... I do so instruct you, Brother Waldstricker."

Ebenezer moved in his seat as if in consent.

"It's a delicate matter which we have to consider," observed the minister, looking from pale face to pale face.

Tessibel glanced at the speaker. He, too, was ashen in the dim afternoon light.

"Come to the point, please," commanded Waldstricker, curtly.

The minister bowed his head in silent prayer.

"Tessibel Skinner," he said, "I ask you to stand up."

The girl got up obediently, but sank down again, her trembling legs refused to support her. She did not, however, turn her startled brown eyes from her pastor's face.

"It is charged against you, Tessibel Skinner," he read from a paper before him, "that you have broken the laws of God and violated the discipline of this church; that you, an unmarried woman, are now pregnant. Are you guilty or not guilty?"

As the accusing voice ceased, the stern eyes of the dark-faced men, who had watched her closely during the reading, seemed to pierce her through and through, ... to lay bare her most intimate secrets.

What should she say? She wasn't unmarried, as the pastor had charged, but the rest was true. Without Frederick's consent, she couldn't explain; she couldn't deny the charge. Surely, Frederick would stand forth and defend her now. She listened intently for a sound from him. She dared not turn toward him, for fear she might break her promise by some look or word. But nothing except the storm-sounds disturbed the silence of the little church. Frederick had failed her again!

Unable alike to plead guilty or not guilty, she sat head bowed and eyes downcast before her judges.

Waldstricker broke the appalling hush.

"Speak up, girl," he ordered harshly. "You're guilty, aren't you?"

The forlorn child struggled to her feet and raised her eyes to the speaker's face.

"Oh, sirs, don't ask me 'bout it," she begged with outstretched hands. "I can't tell ye nothing 'bout it 'cept ... I air goin' to have a baby in the spring."

Waldstricker glanced significantly at the other elders who nodded in acquiescence. Then he turned to the minister, still in the pulpit.

"It is enough," he decided sternly. "She has confessed her sin."

Dropping again into the pew, Tessibel cast a quick glance toward Frederick, who stared set-faced out into the storm.

"We find, Tessibel Skinner," continued the minister, as though reciting a carefully rehearsed speech, "you have sinned grievously. Your silence convicts you. You are no longer worthy of membership in this church, of communion with Christian people. But it is not right that you should suffer alone. For your soul's welfare and in the interest of justice, I ask you the name of the man—"

Tess got up again and faced them ... disgraced and outcast might be, but she must be loyal to her promise.

"Don't ask me that, sir," she pleaded, bewildered, flinging a terrified glance toward the door. "I air goin' now, an'll never come no more, but don't ask me to say nothin', please."

She turned into the aisle as Griggs stepped from the platform. She directed an appealing glance toward him that cut the man's heart through like a knife.

"I want to go," she repeated. "Please!"

"Not yet," broke in Waldstricker, grim-jawed. "It's the duty of this church to teach you a lesson if it can."

Tess looked helplessly at the row of stern men. What did they intend to do to her? Oh, if they'd but let her go back to Daddy Skinner!

"Please let me go home to my daddy," she pleaded faintly. "I'll never come no more, but I can't—I can't talk."

Waldstricker walked toward her menacingly.

"You've got to talk," he gritted, grasping her arm. "You've simply got to answer what the pastor just asked you."

Tess flashed him a look of abhorrence. Oh, how she hated this man!... It seemed to her that he killed for the sake of killing ... tortured for the pure joy of it. She set her teeth hard on her under lip, shaking his hand from her arm.

"I won't talk!" she cried. "You let go of me! See? You touch me again an'—an'—I'll—I'll—"

She paused for some fitting threat. Would no one help her? No, not a friendly face met her searching gaze. If she could get to the door—out into the snow, under God's grey sky! But as if divining her intention, the elders gathered in an accusing squad in front of her. Frederick remained in his chair by the window, apparently oblivious to the tragedy being enacted in his presence.

"I wish ye'd let me go home to my Daddy Skinner," she prayed again.

Her curls fell in a cluster over either shoulder as she sank to her knees in the aisle.

Waldstricker whirled upon Griggs.

"Make her tell us what we must know," he insisted, "or by the God that rules this house, I'll have her sent to some place where incorrigible girls go!"

Incorrigible girls! He had said incorrigible girls of her, Tessibel Skinner, who obeyed even a glance from any one she loved. Desperately, she made a direct appeal to him.

"My daddy's near dead, Mr. Waldstricker. Please don't send me away from him, not yet—not just yet."

"Then answer what we ask of you, child," interjected the minister. "I think Brother Waldstricker has some questions to ask you."

Waldstricker drew a paper from his pocket.

"How old are you, Tessibel Skinner?" he demanded.

"Over half past sixteen," whispered the girl's white lips.

She was over half past sixteen. There was no harm in telling that. It wouldn't hurt Frederick for the church people to know her age.

"Are you a member of this church?"

Tessibel lifted her head. "Ye all know I air."

"Then answer this," shouted Eb. "Who is the man that made you unfit for decent people to speak to?"

The wobegone face hid its crimson tide in two quivering hands. The end of the shining red curls swept the floor. Frederick made no sound.

"Who is he?" insisted Waldstricker once more.

"I can't tell," moaned the girl.

"I'll make you tell," he threatened, infuriated.

"I won't!" reiterated Tess, raising her head. "I can't."

Madelene's sad, tearful face flashed through Waldstricker's mind with the suspicions she had aroused against Frederick. Like an angry horse, his nostrils lifted and sniffed the air. Fury against this girl rode in his heart.

"You needn't tell us the man's name," he taunted triumphantly. "We already know it."

Up struggled Tess to her feet and thrust back the tawny curls feverishly. If they knew, then Frederick had told them.

"And you've got to marry him," Waldstricker's hoarse voice came to her ears.

Why, she was married to him!... that long ago night. If he had told them anything, why had he not told them all? She dared not look around, but waited breathlessly.

"We've decided," Ebenezer proceeded, "that if you consent to our plans, you will suffer no further disgrace. You can go away with your husband and have your home—"

Tess grew dizzy ... this time with joy. She had been given back her husband, her Frederick! Waldstricker had used the word "home." A home with—with—His voice broke in upon her dreams brusquely, creating grotesque figures in her brain. What was he saying? She turned dilating eyes toward him.

"Lysander Letts! Lysander Letts!" Waldstricker shouted again.

The door at the side of the pulpit swung open and Sandy slouched in and came forward.

"Here's your woman," the elder continued, looking from Tess to the squatter. "Take her, and may God forgive you both for the sin you've committed."

Tess stood rigidly waiting. She didn't turn her head toward the oncoming man; rather she centered a prolonged gaze upon her persecutor. When she felt some one pause at her side, she moved away, still without speaking.

"Parson Griggs, marry the man and woman," roared Waldstricker.

Excitedly he tossed the damp hair from his forehead, his cheek muscles working involuntarily. His scheme was near its fruition. Tessibel Skinner was almost married. Already Ebenezer could see, in his mind's eye, how happy Madelene would be when he brought her the news.

The big, dark-faced squatter was standing beside the red-headed girl, and Silander Griggs was hurriedly hunting through a book for the marriage ceremony.

"Make it short," gritted Waldstricker to the minister.

Tess stood as if she had died standing, her face devoid of blood even to the lips. Misery, deep and unutterable, rested upon the white face. When she raised her eyes and saw Letts at her side, and Griggs with an open book in front of her, she wheeled away without a word.

"Marry him!" cried Waldstricker.

"No," said Tess.

"Letts, take hold of her hand," commanded the elder.

Sandy, rage working alive in his eyes, tried to obey the churchman. But the girl took another step away.

"Gimme yer hand," growled Sandy.

All he wanted was to get the squatter girl into his possession. He had

112

not forgotten the threats he had made in other days, and in another hour, he would wring from her the name he wanted.

"No," said Tess again.

"You mean you're not going to marry Mr. Letts?" asked Griggs.

Tessibel caught her breath, swayed, but shook her head.

"No, I ain't goin' to marry 'im," she answered.

Marry Sandy Letts, a man she hated! Of course she couldn't!... She was already married. She couldn't commit such a sin as that, not even if—if—She turned a little and glanced in the direction of Frederick, but dropped her eyes before they found him.

Waldstricker grew intense with suspense, and a sudden determination to test his and Madelene's suspicions came over him.

"Frederick," he cried, "come here and help us force this huzzy to marry the man who betrayed her!"

Frederick rose from his chair as though to obey, and in turning, looked squarely into the girl's eyes.

"My God, Eb, I can't!" he protested, his voice thick with horror. "Let her go, Eb! For God's sake, man, you can't marry her against her will! Let her go!"

He sank down, and rested his head on his arms upon the chair back, his shoulders shaking violently.

The minister came to Tessibel's side. He placed a pitying hand on her head, facing his elders.

"Let her go home, brethren," he entreated. "You can't make her do this thing if she refuses, and the ... business can go on without her."

"She's a wicked girl," snorted Ebenezer, with a bitter twist of his lips.

"I say to let her go," repeated Griggs.

"And I say she shall be punished," Waldstricker glared from the minister to the elders and then rested his gaze on Frederick, who was by this time sobbing in great gulps.

Pastor Griggs considered his parishioner's angry face. Griggs was young and stood in awe of some members of his flock—Waldstricker most of all, but the sight of the girl in such anguish overcame his timidity, and he cried:

"Let him that is without sin among you first cast a stone at her."

Tessibel sank sobbing to the floor, and her pastor stood by her side, hand uplifted, waiting.

Then over Ebenezer's countenance flashed a look of self-righteous fanaticism, which made large the pupils of his dark eyes and inflamed his swarthy skin deepest crimson. He strode to the stove, picked from the scuttle a ragged chunk of coal, and when he turned again, he had changed from red to white. Crazed, he took two steps toward the kneeling girl.

"I can cast the first stone," he said swiftly.

He lifted his arm and before any man could stay his hand, something whirled through the intervening space and struck the kneeling squatter girl. High pandemonium broke loose. Voices, some censorious, some approving, contended.

"I have first cast a stone at her," cried Waldstricker, above the din. "Let others follow if they dare!"

Tessibel crouched lower to the floor, a bleeding wound in her neck. She had made no outcry when the missile met and lacerated her flesh. Dully, she wondered if they intended to kill her, and for a moment a sickening dread took possession of her when she thought of Daddy and Andy. She was growing faint and dizzy, but struggled to her feet as Griggs took her arm. He led her through the Chapel aisle, pushing aside the other men. At the door, Tess caught one glimpse of Sandy Letts' dark, passionate face.

"Go home," the minister said hoarsely; "and may God forgive us all."

How Tessibel found her way home, she could never afterwards tell. Spent by the struggle with the storm, she staggered into the shanty. It took almost the last atom of her strength to close the door against the howling blizzard. Leaning against the wall, she looked up and saw Andy staring at her from the hole in ceiling, his fingers on his lips.

"It were awful cold under the bed," he told her. "Yer Daddy air asleep, so I came up here to keep warm!"

When he noticed the girl's unusual appearance, he scurried down the ladder, waddled across the kitchen, and stood in front of his friend.

"What air the matter, brat?" he quivered.

Solicitous, he helped her into a chair near the fire and took off her hat and coat. The blood from the neck wound had made crimson blotches on her white waist.

"Ye're hurt, honey," he cried, alarmed. "How'd it happen?"

"I air hurt a little," said she, faintly. "Fetch me some water, dear, an' don't—don't tell Daddy!"

"Get on the cot, kid," said he, "an' I'll put up the bar."

In another moment he was leaning over her. He brushed back the tousled hair from the girl's forehead, and pulled away the long curls seeped with blood.

"I air yer friend, brat," he whispered. "Tell me 'bout it."

Tessibel had to confide in somebody.

"I'll get a rag first an' wipe ye off," said the dwarf. "My, but ye did get a cut, didn't ye?... What did it?"

Gently he began to wash away the crimson stain from her face and neck.

"Somebody hit ye?" he demanded presently.

"Yep."

"Who?... Who dared do it?" The dwarf's face darkened with rage. "Where were the brute that done it?"

"Andy," sobbed Tess, "I air goin' to tell ye somethin'; ye may think I air awful wicked, but—but—Andy, don't tell Daddy, but in the spring I air goin' to—"

"Yep, I know, Tess," he murmured. "I heard the woman yellin' at ye the uther day way through my blankets. But 'tain't nothin' to cry over. God'll bless ye, brat, and God'll bless—it!"

Her sobbing slowly subsided, and in halting words Tess told the dwarf the story of the afternoon's dreadful experience.

"And, Andy, it were awful. Mr. Griggs wanted to let me go home, but the uther men wouldn't, an' then the minister says like Jesus did to the men who were goin' to stone the poor woman, 'Let him that ain't a sinner throw the first stone,' an' Waldstricker picked up a great hunk o' coal and hit me with it. Do ye suppose he air so awful good an' I air so awful wicked he had a right to strike me?"

"Sure he didn't, Tess," Andy comforted. "Course not!"

The willows moaned their weird song to the night, the wind shrieked in battling anger over the tin on the roof, while the snowflakes came against the window like pale eyes looking in upon the squatter girl and the dwarf on his knees beside the cot bed.

CHAPTER XXVII

DADDY SKINNER'S DEATH

It was Saturday evening, three days after Tessibel Skinner had been churched from Hayt's Chapel. The night wind called forth moaning complaints from the willow trees. The rasping of their bare limbs against the tin roof of the cottage did not disturb Daddy Skinner struggling for breath in the room below. All the familiar night-noises kept a death vigil with the squatter girl.

A sound outside made her lift her head. Kennedy's brindle bull was scratching to come in. She rose, went to the door and opened it. Pete ambled over the threshold and curled down by the stove.

"Anythin' the matter, brat?" whispered Andy.

"No, I were lettin' in the dog," explained Tess, resuming her seat beside Daddy Skinner who was stretched, dying, on her cot. She had moved him from the back room into the warm kitchen, and at that moment he was sleeping restlessly. The sight of his working face brought a quick hand to Tessibel's lips, and her white teeth set deeply into the upraised knuckles to help stifle the groans. Every trouble of her own sank into insignificance before the calamity facing her. Many times Tess had viewed death afar off, but not until the past three days had it threatened her own loved ones. In that hour she was experiencing the extremity of sorrow, and each aching nerve in her body seemed to possess a stabbing volition of its own, for again and again the torturing points stung her flesh like whips.

For three long days she had managed somehow to uphold the dear, dying father. No word had come from Deforrest Young, and Tess felt sure he had returned twenty-four hours before. Perhaps Waldstricker had robbed her of her dearest friend. Bitterly pained, the girl realized what the loss would mean to her. Yet she had no censure in her heart for Deforrest Young; indeed no bitterness for Frederick Graves; only a deep, deep gratitude to the one, and a great, overwhelming love for the other. And while thinking of what an empty void her life was becoming, Tess saw her father's head turn and his lids lift heavily.

"Daddy!" she murmured, but if he heard, he did not heed. He was gazing steadily at something over and beyond her head, and then he smiled at it. In superstitious dread, the squatter girl glanced where the faded eyes were directed. What had he seen? A face, perhaps, or the passing shade that always haunted a squatter shanty when some one was dying, but then, many times she, too, had seen faces in the rafters up there among the dry nets.

"My pretty brat," were the words that brought her startled eyes back to her father. Her throat filling with heavy sobs, she went over and kissed him stormily. The horny, stiff fingers gathered a few of her red curls and drew them slowly upward until parched lips touched them, while tears stole from under withered lids, and Tess cried out in sharp anguish.

"Daddy Skinner, I can't live without ye!" she moaned, cupping his face with her hands. "Take Tessibel with ye; take 'er, please!"

She cuddled at his side, lifted one of his heavy arms and put it around her in pleading anguish. Just then it seemed as if it would put off the approach of death if she insisted on staying within the broad grasp of Daddy Skinner's arms.

She was wiping away his tears, tenderly touching the dying face with faltering fingers.

"I saw yer ma," choked Skinner thickly, and he smiled again.

Tess turned her head, a dreadful sinking in her soul. Her mother's face, then, was what Daddy had seen away off up there among the rafters. The mother who had died so long ago had come after her dear one. Drawing one tense set of fingers backward across her cheek, Tess stood up quickly. Perhaps—perhaps—

She threw a glance at the ceiling. Daddy Skinner had seen her mother. They were going away together. If they would but take her with them! She turned unsteadily to go she knew not where, but the sound of her father's voice brought her quickly back.

"Brat," he faltered, "lean down—I want to tell ye somethin'."

Tess bent her ear close to the thick blue lips.

"I air here, Daddy! Tess air here," she mourned.

Long, laboring breaths moved the red curls hanging about the girl's rigid face.

"I said as how I air here, Daddy," she murmured again, touching him.

But Daddy Skinner was once more gazing into the dark rafters, his jaws apart, the greyness of death settling about his mouth.

"Daddy! Daddy!" screamed Tess. "Don't look like that! Don't go away— oh, Daddy, please!... Andy! Andy!"

The dwarf slipped down the ladder, and dropped at the side of the bed.

The dog roused from his nap by the stove was already there, nuzzling his tawny head against his distressed friend, while he made inarticulate sounds of sympathy in his deep throat.

"Pal Skinner!" Andy cried, white with apprehension. "Give us a word, old horse."

Placing his hand upon Pete's collar, the dwarf drew him, with a word of command, to the floor beside him.

The dying fisherman looked from his prison friend to his daughter. He lifted a limp hand, and it rested upon the girl's bowed head. The other he dropped heavily on Andy Bishop's shoulder. It was as if he were giving to them both his parting benediction. In mechanical sequence the dwarf counted the dying man's mouth open and shut five times before the struggling voice came forth.

"I were goin' to say somethin' to ye, Tess," he then gasped, moistening his lips. "Gimme a—drink—of water."

Andy held the cup while Orn drank. He struggled to swallow, belching forth hot breath.

"When I air gone, brat dear," he articulated huskily, "stay in the shanty an' take care of Andy till there ain't no more danger fer 'im. Ye'll promise me, Tess?"

She enclosed his hand in hers and held it to her lips.

"I were a wantin' to go with you and Mummy, Daddy," she sobbed. "I air always lonely in the shanty without ye—but if ye say, 'Stay with Andy,' then I stays."

"That air what I says, brat, darlin'," panted Skinner.

Then for many minutes he was lost in the terrible struggle of strong life against the grip of death. Tess wound her arms about his neck and lifted the great head to her breast. She stared at his changing face as at an advancing ghost.

He seemed to be slipping slowly into the great beyond, and she was powerless to hold him back.

How many times had Daddy Skinner spoken of dying! How many times had she heard him agree with Andy that death was better than life any day! But at those times she had beaten back the muttered words of her father and the dwarf. Ah, in those days, death had been far away, kept off by happiness unsurpassed!

"It air hard fer some folks to die," wailed the fisherman. "An' so easy fer uthers. Me—now me—Oh, God, oh, brat-love, let me go! I hurt so! I hurt awful—let me go!"

The heart of the tortured, sobbing girl seemed to be bursting from its pain and suspense. Her beloved father wanted to go away—to follow the wraith mother beckoning from the rafters. How could she open her arms and allow him to leave her alone in the shanty!

"Help me, brat-love," sighed Daddy Skinner once more. "Help yer old sick daddy!"

Help him! How could she? Hitherto Tessibel's faith had loyally responded to every demand upon her. But she couldn't help her daddy die!

She knew not how! Then, as if drawn by some invisible power, her eyes lifted, piercing the shadows among the time-dried nets. And there, for one small moment, she saw—she saw a face, a young, girlish face, infinitely sweet, smiling down upon her.

"It air the Mummy!" she cried, her voice vibrant with love. "I air goin' to help 'im, darlin'."

Buoyantly her mind gripped the old-time faith, the redoubtable faith that had opened wide Auburn Prison, that had restored to her arms this same adored father. She had helped him then—and oh, to help him now! His great cry, "God, Tessibel, let me be goin'!" rang in her ears. Her gaze was glued to his face. Terror and pain were strangling his throat until his eyes grew death-dark in the struggle. Tessibel lifted her ashen face, wildly working in entreaty. Oh, for a little faith! Faith the size of a grain of mustard seed! And Daddy Skinner would be gone to that place beyond the clouds and the blue, where suffering is not. Did he, could he, believe? Did she, could she, believe, too? Then in a blinding flash, she remembered the mysterious dawning of her own faith. Enduring sublime suffering, she bent once more and drew her father's heavy head to her breast.

"Daddy! Darlin' old, good Daddy, look at yer dear brat, an' listen to 'er."

"I air a listenin', my girl," he said between set teeth. She put her head directly in line with her father's vision.

"Look at me, Daddy," she craved tremulously, "an' listen to me. Can't ye remember how ye came back from Auburn like the innercent man ye were?"

"Yep," whispered Skinner.

"'Twere the Christ on the cross helped ye, Daddy. Ye air wishin' to go away now with my mummy, huh?"

"Yep," groaned Skinner. "God, aw kind, merciful God, let me go!"

Tess laid him gently back on the pillow. A bright light flashed into her soul. The red in her eyes turning almost to black.

"Then go, my darlin'! Go, Daddy," she moaned, rising and looking upward. "Take 'im, Mummy, little love-mummy, take 'im back to Heaven with ye."

Inspired by that smiling face in the rafters, Tessibel opened her lips and began to sing,

"Rescue the Perishin';
Care for the Dyin'."

It was a glorious strain that echoed and reechoed around and around the shanty kitchen. It gathered within its heavenly power the moaning of the wind and the haunting noises of the tin-rusted roof. Even the weeping willows, bowing their mournful heads in sympathy, could no longer be heard in their endless chant.

Strangely stirred, Pete struggled up, disregarding the dwarf's desire to detain him. He placed his forefeet on the edge of the bed, lifting his head to the girl's shoulder. Responsive to the pressure of his body, she threw her arm around him. Gravely the golden eyes of the great dog regarded his suffering master on the cot as the tender melody of the song continued to fill the shanty.

Tessibel ever afterwards remembered Daddy Skinner's eyes as for those last few moments he lay looking at her. They were kindly, tender, smiling, as he watched her lips moving in the song he'd always loved to hear her sing.

He seemed to realize that she was singing him into the very presence of the Savior of the world—into the presence of Him who was leading Tessibel Skinner and her squatter father through their garden of Gethsemane.

"Rescue the Perishin';
Care for the Dyin'."

On and on she sang, and on and on the dying man gropingly felt his way to Eternity. Sometimes he smiled at her; sometimes at the wraith in the rafters. But not for one moment did the voice of the little singer cease its insistent cry for a complete rescue.

The dwarf was silent, his shining face reflecting the peace and security of which the squatter girl sang.

"Rescue the Perishin';
Care for the Dyin'."

The beautiful voice did not falter. Suddenly the powerful lungs of the fisherman gathered in one long, last breath, and when it came forth to meet Tessibel's song, the broad shoulders dropped back, the chest receded, the smile faded from the gray eyes—and Daddy Skinner was dead.

He had died listening to those appealing, melodious words, "Rescue the Perishin'; Care for the Dyin'." That sudden collapsing change in the gaunt figure seemed to freeze the very song on Tessibel's lips. Her voice trailed to a limp wail, as if an icy hand had caught her throat. Silence succeeded silence. Even the storm seemed for an instant to still its raging roar, then Pete threw back his head and howled his grief. As his resonant cries filled the shack and mingled with the turmoil of the elements, Tess clung to the dog, staring with horrified eyes at the huge beloved form crushed and crumpled upon the cot. Death had come and gone. The mystery in the shadowy rafters had taken Daddy Skinner away.

The dwarf raised his head and looked at Tess. Slowly he leaned over and pressed his lips to Orn Skinner's brow, and as he rose, he lifted the girl's rigid arm from the tawny back and seized the dog by the collar to quiet him.

Then came one of those unthinkable, weird cries, a nightmarish cry from the girl's throat, and—as God tempereth the wind to the shorn lamb, so in Divine pity he covered Tess of the Storm Country with mental oblivion.

CHAPTER XXVIII
YOUNG DISCOVERS ANDY

During the minutes Daddy Skinner lay grappling with death, Ebenezer Waldstricker sat in his handsome drawing room with an open Bible on his knee, talking to his wife.

"I've explained to you time and time again, Helen," said he impatiently, "why I struck her and I'm not sorry I did it."

"It seems awful, though," replied his wife, reflectively.

Waldstricker frowned into the wistful face.

"Why awful when the Bible ordered me to do it? I've given you the Master's own words to verify it. Didn't he say, 'Let the man without sin first cast a stone?'"

Mrs. Waldstricker raised her eyes to her husband's face.

"But Ebenezer—"

"There's no argument, my dear," the man interrupted. "I tell you I know whereof I speak. It came to me like a flash on Wednesday in the church ... I had to show the world a man—a man without sin."

Helen stared back at him in amazement. Her husband had never before expressed himself in quite such bombastic terms, and, oh, dear, she knew he was good; but for any human being to claim to be without sin! She'd never heard of such a thing.

"But, dearest," she argued pleadingly and partly rising, "are you sure?"

"I have no doubt about it," interpolated Ebenezer, striking his chest emphatically. "As I said, I know whereof I speak."

Helen sank down again.

"I'm glad you can explain it, dear," she murmured dubiously. "It'll be easier for you to make Deforrest understand about it when he comes. He's so wrapped up in that girl.... He'll be here in a few minutes, I think, if the train's on time."

"I'll make him understand all right," answered Ebenezer.

The words had scarcely left his lips before both husband and wife heard the approach of sleigh-bells.

"He's coming now," said Mrs. Waldstricker, and she rose and started to the window.

"Sit down and don't look as if you were going to die," her husband commanded. "But perhaps you'd better go to your room while I'm explaining the thing to him."

When Deforrest Young opened the door and walked in, his face was wreathed in smiles.

"Well, hello, everybody," he cried heartily. "It's an awful night."

Ebenezer rose and extended his hand.

"So 'tis," he agreed.

Helen went forward quickly and helped slip the snow-covered coat from Deforrest's shoulders. At the same time she lifted her lips for a kiss. How she adored this brother of hers, and how anxiously she desired he should be satisfied with Ebenezer's account of the church proceedings.

"I'm lucky to be home for Sunday," remarked Deforrest. "I was afraid the case wouldn't close before day after tomorrow. But the jury came in last night, and everything was quickly closed up."

"We read about it in the paper," said his sister sympathetically. "It must have been a harrowing thing to go through."

"It certainly was! But the acquittal helped. The woman is very young and without friends, and I was glad to get it for her."

"But she's bad!" cut in Waldstricker. "Every paper said she was guilty."

"But the jury pronounced her innocent," exclaimed the lawyer, "so that puts an end to the argument!"

Ebenezer fingered the leaves of the book he held.

"I've the happenings of a week to tell you, Deforrest," he stated deliberately, as if dismissing the former subject.

Professor Young bent down and slipped off his overshoes.

"I'm awfully tired, old chap," said he. "Won't they keep till morning? I'd like a bite to eat, and then—then bed." He smiled at his sister. "How about something to eat, sis, dear?"

"Helen, go see about supper for your brother," ordered Ebenezer.

Mrs. Waldstricker, seemingly glad to escape, left the room quickly.

"Fire ahead, Eb," said Young. "I suppose I might as well hear it now as any time."

"You sent Parson Griggs a letter for me to vote in your name?"

"Of course," responded Young. "I knew Helen was interested in the Christmas festival, and I thought you'd do as well as I."

"And so I did, brother," replied Ebenezer, pompously, "and your vote turned the tide into the channel God wanted it. Some members allowed their human feelings to run away with 'em."

Ebenezer's mysterious words suddenly awakened Deforrest's interest.

"Has something out of the ordinary occurred?" he queried.

"Yes," assured Eb, "but I've attended to it all right!"

Professor Young sighed.

"That's good! There, now, I'll sit by the grate and warm up while you tell me about it."

He dropped into a large chair, and extended his feet to the cheerful blaze. Waldstricker paused before making his explanation. At length:

"We put a member out of the church last Wednesday," said he, steadily.

Deforrest Young turned completely around and stared at his brother-in-law.

"Put a member out of the church!" he repeated, thunder-struck. "Why church a member?... That is out of the ordinary, I should say. What'd he do?"

"It wasn't a man, 'twas a woman."

"Well, for God's sake!" Deforrest's voice was low, deep, and filled with disgust. "I hope you men didn't make a mess of yourselves.... What happened?... Some girl kissed her sweetheart under the pine trees?"

The elder glanced over the top of his brother-in-law's head.

"Worse than that!" said he. "Much worse than that!... We churched a Magdalene!"

It took an appreciable length of time for Young's tall figure to rise from the chair. He turned around and stood with his back to the fire.

"I didn't know we had a Magdalene in the church," he commented drily, and then more impetuously, "Oh, Lord, why don't you spit it out and not beat all around the bush telling me?"

There was something about Ebenezer's slow manner of approaching the point that made Young impatient. In the meantime his mind was rapidly running over the women in the Hayt's congregation.

Waldstricker got up, too, drawing his big frame to its full height.

"We churched—Well, the fact is,—We churched Tessibel Skinner."

When the name fell upon Deforrest Young's ears, every muscle in his body became rigid, making him taller by inches.

"Tessibel Skinner?" he repeated mechanically, as if he'd heard awry. "Did you say Tessibel Skinner?"

Waldstricker took a long breath. Deforrest was receiving the action of the church with better grace than he had anticipated.

"Yes, Tessibel Skinner!" he repeated. "She's with child."

In the awful minute after the torturing words had fallen from the other man's lips, Deforrest Young felt as if he must tear the lie from the speaker's throat. For it was a lie! God! What a lie! A lie told against Heaven's best—the best girl in all the world. Without a word, he reached for his overcoat.

"What're you going to do?" demanded Ebenezer, a little perturbed. "You needn't see her.... She's been justly dealt with."

There was no answer from the tall lawyer. Only one thing was in Deforrest Young's mind—to go to Tessibel Skinner. He gave no thought to the wild night, no care for his own fatigue and hunger. Disdaining another glance at Ebenezer, he whirled to go. Helen's pale face appearing in the doorway made him pause.

"Deforrest," she quivered. "Deforrest, dear, oh, don't go out tonight! Stay and let Ebenezer tell you about it, do please! The church has done all it could—it must be all right if the church did it, Forrie."

Then Young's wrath broke loose....

"All right? All right?" he thundered. "The church has done all it can, eh? Well, by God!" He turned a livid face from one to the other. "What a cursed outrage!"

Waldstricker cried out, horrified.

"Man, man, what are you saying!... How dare you provoke the wrath of God!... How dare you question the decision of the church! Besides, I tell you she's a Magdalene. She's been justly punished. I attended to it myself."

Then Young saw clearly that the church action had but expressed his brother-in-law's will. He knew his implacable hatred of the squatters and particularly of Tessibel. He recognized that revenge had prompted him. Pushing the protesting elder aside, he ejaculated:

"You pious hypocrite! Get out of my way," and was gone.

The bitter winter wind nipped at Young as he strode down the steps and battled his way to the stables. Waldstricker's words were pounding at his brain like a hammer. What had they done to Tess? He remembered Ebenezer had said that his vote—his own delegated vote—had turned the tide against his pretty child!

He had no mercy for the stumbling horse as he spurred down the long drive, into the public thoroughfare, and thence to the shore road. When he came opposite to his own closed, uninhabited house, he could see by straining his eyes the dusky shadow of the willow trees shrouding the Skinner home.

A glimmer of light struggled from the curtained window of the hut. With desperate haste he tied his horse to the fence post. He could scarcely stop to spread over the animal the blanket he'd brought for the purpose.

Then as he waded through the snow and rounded the mud cellar a dog's mournful howling, pierced and punctuated by a girl's shrill, heart-broken cry, fell upon his startled ears. In another minute he had flung himself against the shanty door and forced it open. Kennedy's bulldog greeted him, growling, and beyond him, stretched out upon the body of her dead father, lay Tess. Hovering over her, chattering, was Andy Bishop, the dwarf, the condemned murderer of Ebenezer Waldstricker, Sr.

CHAPTER XXIX
THE VIGIL

During Professor Young's instant of hesitation on the threshold, the wind gusted sheets of snow into the Skinner shanty. Quieting the dog by a low-spoken word, Deforrest stepped in and closed the door against the storm. The acrid smoke drawn from the stove by the back-draft, filled the room,—a choking cloud.

Andy stared at the intruder for an instant, and then turned again to the girl lying unconscious upon the body of her father.

Young's vision comprehended the whole tragedy. He pulled off his cap and gloves and shook the snow from his shoulders. Advanced to the bedside, a glance satisfied him that the squatter was dead and that Tess had fainted. He had recognized the dwarf the minute he saw him, and heartsick with apprehension, he wondered what he was doing there.

"Get up," said he. "Let me look at her."

The dwarf moved aside hesitatingly.

"Air she dead, too?" he whimpered.

"Bring me some water," commanded Young.

Andy went to the pail, dipped a portion of water into a small basin, and waddled back with it.

"Her daddy air dead," he offered. "Ye can see he air dead."

"Yes!" nodded Young, taking the dish.

He did not speak again until Tess groaned, and opened her eyes. She made a half struggle to sit up, and Young lifted her to her feet.

123

"Lean on me," he said gently.

Tess stared at him, incredulously. He had come after all! Relief crumpled her up in his arms.

"Daddy air dead," she whispered.

"Yes, dear," soothed Young. "There, lean your head on my shoulder, poor little broken baby."

His tones were so tender, so soft! They went to the heart of the stricken dwarf, and like a hurt child he burst into tears. Professor Young turned and looked at him.

"Don't do that," he said huskily. "Sit down—don't cry!"

Without moving from her position, Tess said, "Andy, Andy, dear, git on up in the garret a few minutes, will ye?"

The dwarf crept to the ladder, and Deforrest let him go. A dozen questions leapt to the lawyer's lips at the same time, but the girl against his breast looked so desperately ill he had no heart to ply them. Tess lifted her lids heavily.

"Ye won't tell nobody he air here?" she gulped.

"How long has he been here?" asked Young, instead of answering her question.

"Ever since spring," sighed Tessibel.

"Was he here that day when Mr. Waldstricker and my sister—"

"Yep." The girl's whisper was very low.

"And when Burnett came too, I suppose?"

"Yep, I hid 'im ... Daddy loved 'im, Daddy did."

She began to cry softly. Her confession had taken her mind back to the huge figure on the bed.

"I wanted to go with Daddy," she sobbed. "I didn't know—I thought I couldn't live without 'im."

Stooping, Deforrest gathered the mourning little one into his arms, and seating himself in the big rocker, pressed his cheek against her hair in sympathy. Patiently he waited, holding her thus while the mercy of her flowing tears dulled the first sharp edge of her grief.

Bye and bye the sobs ceased, and a faint, catchy little voice struggled up through the red curls to the man's ears.

"Ye air awful good to me, you air. Oh, I needed ye so, and I feared—I feared mebbe ye wasn't never comin' again!"

"My dear, my dear," Young soothed, much moved. Then he rose and placed her in the chair. "You sit here and tell me about it."

Bravely she looked into the friendly face, a doleful smile quivering on her lips.

"The first thing I want to know," she asked, "what air ye goin' to do 'bout Andy?"

Professor Young had anticipated this question.

"Until I've had more time to think about it, and until after the funeral anyway, I'll keep your secret," he reassured her kindly.

"An' ye won't say anythin' to nobody 'bout 'im till ye talk with me again?" she queried, fearfully.

"That's what I mean, Tess," Young answered.

"Ye air so good to me, ye air," sighed Tess, satisfied.

"Child," began Young a moment later, "can you bear to tell me about it, now?"

"About Daddy?" asked Tess, "or about the other—"

The lawyer's nod, responsive to the latter half of her question, reawakened the suffering girl's memory of the horror of the church meeting.

"It were so awful," she said after a pregnant pause. "I mean—Mr. Waldstricker—"

"What about it? Tell me," Young interrupted, as the gentle voice hesitated.

"See ... this!" she murmured, turning her head.

Young's eyes caught the red of the wound on her neck.

"He did that!... How?" he ejaculated fiercely.

"He hit me with a piece of—coal!" answered Tess, sinking back, very white.

"No, no; God, no!" he cried desperately. "He couldn't have done that!"

"He said I were ... bad," interrupted Tess, very low. She bowed her head, and the man, stunned, made no move toward her. His muscles seemed powerless, and he had no volition to comfort her. He could not erase from his mind that horrid picture her few direct words had brought before him. "But ... you air trustin' me!" was the way Tess brought him back to himself.

"Then it's true what—what—"

His tongue grew parched.

"Yep, but trust me, please!" cried Tess.

Trust her! Believe in her with her confession ringing in his ears. God, if he did not love her, it wouldn't be so hard to believe, to trust, to help. But with this fierce jealousy stabbing at his heart, he felt he must know more—all. His mind went back to that time when she had come to him with a child in a basket, and her plea had been the same, "Oh, trust me! Please trust me!"

"If you could only ... tell me ... something," he groaned.

"It air true what Mr. Waldstricker hit me fer," bowed Tess, swallowing hard, "but I can't say nothin' 'bout it, I can't! I ain't able to tell nothin' more'n that!"

Young still stood several feet from her.

"I must do something to help you," he implored. "Won't you even tell me when it—it will be, Tessibel?"

Through her tense fingers the girl murmured a stifled "March."

March—scarce three months away! He would have given five years of his life to have had her tell him the truth about this thing that had crushed her. He made a nervous movement with his fingers to his hair.

"You are bound by a promise?" he demanded sharply.

A white, uplifted, pained face was his answer.

"You'll tell me some day, if you can," he said, going swiftly to her.

"Yes," whispered Tess.

And then for a long time nothing was heard in the hut but the winter without, the growls and mutterings of the bulldog in his sleep by the stove, and a sob now and then from the dwarf in the garret.

The healing silence of a common love in the presence of a common grief settled upon the strangely matched couple. The little squatter girl, with her shameful secret, and the great lawyer and teacher, kept solemn vigil over the body of Daddy Skinner.

Daddy Skinner was buried. All the arrangement in connection with the obsequies devolved upon Professor Young. It was he who brought the girl back to the shanty in her simple, clinging, black gown, and after the carriage had delivered them at the hut door, carried her, almost unconscious, into the house and laid her gently upon her bed. Then he closed the door and sat down beside her. It was perhaps an hour later when she lifted her eyes appealingly.

"I air awful glad ye stayed with me," she choked.

"Tess,"—Young's voice shook.... "Will you let me talk to you a little and not feel I'm intruding upon your sorrows or your secrets?"

"Ye wouldn't do anythin' what wasn't right," murmured the girl, under her breath.

For some moments he smoothed her burning forehead. Then he lifted her hand and held it in his.

"Tessibel," he began.

"What?"

"First, tell me about the little man in the garret."

"There ain't nothin' much to tell," she responded, shaking her head. "When he got out of Auburn, he come here and asked me an' Daddy to take care of 'im, an' we done it, that air all."

"I see, dear—and—and you didn't think the law required you to give him up?"

Tess moved her head negatively on the pillow.

"Sure not, or I'd a done it long ago. The law—what do I care 'bout the law?... It air always puttin' innercent men in jail. That air all the law air fer."

"But this man is a murderer," Young tried to explain to her.

But Tessibel's gesture, both hands raised, palms outward, expressed her dissent.

"They said as how Daddy were a murderer, too," she retorted, "but you found out he weren't, didn't ye?"

Young, not able to gainsay this, nodded his head.

"How long are you going to keep him here?" he asked presently.

Tess sent him a glance pathetically sad and discouraged.

"I don't know. The poor little duffer hain't no friends. He ain't no other place to go where old Eb won't git 'im."

Young thought of his brother-in-law. He realized immediately with what joy that stern disciplinarian would snatch the little man back into Auburn prison. Doubtless, too, he would visit his rage on the girl who'd shielded him.

"Ye helped Daddy git out o' jail," Tess whispered. "Couldn't ye keep Andy out?"

126

Deforrest Young turned his face to the ceiling. A pair of gleaming eyes were staring down upon him from the square hole.

"Come down here, you," he said peremptorily.

Andy slid down the ladder and squatted himself beside the cot. Young considered the boyish face some time in silence.

"What made you kill Waldstricker?" he demanded.

Andy shook his head.

"I never done it, mister," he denied positively.

"Tell me how it happened! If I'm going to help you, you must tell me the truth."

This wasn't what Young had intended to say at all.

"Andy ain't a liar," came from Tess.

"Tell me every word," urged Young.

The dwarf curled himself into a little ball and began.

"Well, us was all in a saloon at the Inlet, an' old Waldstricker, he come in with a nuther man, an' they both got a drink an' t'uther man went out. Me an' Owen Bennet were settin' at the table, ... Waldstricker he says somethin' nasty 'bout squatters an' ... Owen went fer 'im. Waldstricker pulled 'is gun. I knocked it out o' his hand an' Owen grabbed it up offen the floor an' sent a bullet right through Waldstricker's heart. Then us uns beat it, I mean me an' Owen, an' when they caught us ... he put the shootin' on me. I didn't do it, an' Owen knows I didn't."

Young was very quiet during this recital. He was considering the eager, boyish, upraised face.

"I hope ye believe me, mister—sir—please do," Andy pleaded.

Deforrest Young crossed his legs, smoothed his hair with one hand, and sat back in his chair.

"I think I do," he nodded presently. "Only I am placed in a very peculiar position. By rights I ought to send you back—then help you afterward if I can."

Tessibel sat up, her eyes wildly frightened.

"Ye couldn't do that!" she cried. "Ye couldn't do that! Don't ye remember a day on the rocks, when I was awful sad, an' you said, 'Tess, if ye ever want me to do anything for ye, come and tell me.' Didn't ye say it?"

Young bowed his head.

"I air askin' it now," said Tess, throwing out her hand. "I air beggin' ye not to send Andy back. Let 'im stay with me. I promised Daddy I'd take care of 'im."

"Lie down again and be quiet, child," urged Deforrest, sadly. "You don't want to make yourself sick.... Hush, you mustn't cry!... Oh, child dear, will you please stop shaking that way?"

He had forgotten that when Tess loved any one, she would battle until her death before she gave him up.

"Then don't send little Andy back, an' I'll be awful good," she pleaded.

Young sat for some time, one hand on Tessibel's, the other beating a tatoo on the arm of Daddy's wooden rocker.

"I suppose," he said at length, as if speaking to himself, "I'll be highly criticized if any one finds out about this irregular proceeding. Nevertheless—"

He turned to Tess. "I'll go quietly to work and see what I can do. In the meantime, dear child, you can't stay here in this house."

"But I promised Daddy I'd take care of Andy here, an' I air goin' to. Him and me can live here all right."

Young sighed. There was the same stubborn tone in her voice she had used in those days when her father was away in prison, and he had argued with her to leave the settlement.

"Well, at any rate," he said after a while, "I'll take time to consider it, and then we'll decide something."

Ten minutes later he was riding slowly up the hill, and as the past panoramied across his mind ... and evolved itself into the present, he shook his head. Tessibel had separated him from his family, had made him a stranger to his best friends. Would she now, by holding to Waldstricker's convicted murderer, deprive him of his honor?

CHAPTER XXX
SANDY COMES TO GRIEF

The Skinner home was resting in its winter calm. Daddy Skinner was gone. Andy still crept about the dark garret, and Tessibel passed her days in study, performing the few duties the small shack required.

When Deforrest Young had gone away a few days after Daddy's funeral, he'd smiled into her eyes and had bidden her to be of good courage. Henceforth, he said, she was to be his charge. She felt a little lighter hearted. It made her happier, too, to think he knew about Andy Bishop and was going to help him.

The only person she feared was Sandy Letts. She'd not seen him since that day in the church when he had tried to draw her nearer the minister. Bitterly angry, she knew he must be. That he had delayed his revenge so long seemed to her rather menacing than comforting.

Her mind was drifting back over all the events of the past few months, when a shadow passed over the curtain at the window. She stole to the door and placed her ear to the latch. From that position she could plainly hear creeping footsteps crawling closer.

With her ear glued to the crack, she listened. There was no sound now of walking. The outsider was listening, too. Suddenly, he knocked heavily. Tess glanced to the garret. The dwarf's face was not in sight. Then the knock came again.

"Who air there?" Tess called, her breath catching.

There was no answer, save another knock.

Tessibel spoke once more. After a pause, Sandy Letts' voice came gruffly to her.

"Open the door, Tess. It air me, Sandy."

"What do ye want?" demanded Tess.

Sandy growled inarticulately, gave a kick to the floor, and rattled the latch.

"I want to come in, I said. I air goin' to talk to ye!"

Tessibel thought of Ben Letts and of how he, too, had demanded entrance to her home in just such a manner as his cousin was doing now. She glanced about for something with which to protect herself if needed. She wished with all her soul the brindle bull were with her then in the shanty.

Sandy gave another rough pull at the latch-string.

"Open the door, Tess," he growled again, "or I'll bust it down."

Tess knew Sandy would carry out his threat, and, if he broke down the door, his temper would be worse than now. She muttered a prayer to quiet the terror in her heart, and slipped up the bar. Sandy, gun in hand, stepped into the kitchen, and Tess closed the door.

"What do ye want, Sandy?" she questioned.

"I want to talk to ye, what do ye 'spose I want?" he flung out, swaggering his shoulders.

"Well, sit down," invited Tess, seeking to propitiate. "Ye knowed Daddy was dead, didn't ye, Sandy?"

"I can set down without bein' asked," grunted the squatter, dropping into a chair. "Sure I knowed yer pa's flew the coop."

"What'd ye want?" Tess asked again after a moment.

"I've come to settle with ye for somethin'," said Letts.

"I ain't done nothin'," replied Tess.

Sandy threw out an angry hand.

"Ye have, too, ye have, too! Didn't I want ye for my woman, and didn't ye go an'—"

"I said ye couldn't have me," interrupted the girl. "Folks ain't havin' everythin' they want in this world, Sandy."

"Then ye turned me down in the church afore Waldstricker," went on Sandy. "Ye might've been glad to marry a decent man after what ye'd done. But ye ups and says, 'I won't!' An' I've come to ask the reason why."

Tess walked across the shanty kitchen and sat on the edge of the cot. Sandy followed her with his eyes, his face growing crimson as he gazed at her.

"I air here for two things," he continued. "To find out the name of that man Waldstricker asked ye 'bout—"

Tessibel's low voice stopped his impudent speech.

"I couldn't tell ye that, Sandy, not even if ye killed me," she murmured. "What was t'uther thing?"

"I air goin' to take ye away with me fer my woman. But ye needn't think I air goin' to marry ye decent like I would in the church t'uther day, fer I won't."

Tessibel, weary and aching, grew cold with fear. She knew the squatter would keep his word, if he could. He would abuse her as Ben had tried to when her father was in Auburn unless help came. Then remembering all the days she had lived and suffered and still'd been saved from Sandy and his like, she breathed a deep sigh.

"I couldn't go with ye, Sandy," she explained.

A cruel expression set Sandy's large, sensuous mouth.

"Ye'll be glad to go with me when I git done with ye." He placed his gun against the chair and stood up. "First, I want to know what made ye act like that in the church fer. Don't ye know me well 'nough to think I'd get ye sooner or later. Ye knowed yer Daddy couldn't always live in the shack. Ye might better took me while ye could. I would jest have beat ye a bit fer yer cussedness, then mebbe after a while I'd fergive ye. But now—"

Tessibel's struggling to her feet broke off the man's volubility. She was so frightened that almost without thought she circled toward the door. Sandy got up and placed himself directly in front of her.

"No, ye don't git out o' here," he sneered, "not till I git through with ye. Jest make up yer mind to that."

Sandy was moving toward her, his eyes gleaming with rage. What could she do? She threw a hasty glance about the shanty. She knew Andy was under the straw tick in the garret and could not hear the low conversation going on in the kitchen.

As if in answer to her agonized prayer, another shadow passed the curtained window. Sandy had not seen it or he would not have thrust forth his great arms and snatched her to him. Tess uttered a scream. In another moment Jake Brewer sprang into the kitchen and was looking from Tessibel to the angry squatter.

Sandy pushed the girl roughly on to the cot—took two steps toward Brewer, his manner threatening.

"What ye sneakin' 'bout here fer?" he growled out.

Jake grinned slowly.

"I allers come in to see Tess," he replied. "What were ye doin', Sandy?"

"I air goin' to take Tessibel to be my woman," muttered Letts.

Jake glanced at the pallid girl.

"Oh, well, I swan! So that air it, eh?"

"Nope," Tess got out through her chattering teeth. Then all the pent-up rage in her body broke loose. "I ain't wantin' to be his woman. I want to be let alone in my shack! Oh, Jake, won't ye make Sandy go away and let me be?"

Sandy laughed evilly.

"It'd take a bigger man'n Jake," he remarked.

Brewer, unruffled, seated himself with the slow manner of a squatter.

"I don't say as how I air very big," replied Jake, crossing his legs, "but I guess no man'll take Tess long's she don't want to go, when I air here, Sandy."

Letts shook a threatening fist.

"Get out o' here, Jake," he growled, going toward the other man. "If ye don't, I'll make it worse fer ye! Git out, I say!"

"Shan't do it. Now, Sandy, I ain't no woman to be 'fraid of you, so just hold yer horses till us uns talk this out. Ye say ye want Tess fer your'n, an' Tess, she don't want ye, now what ye goin' to do?"

"I air a goin' to take her jest the same," snarled Letts.

But thinking better of placing his hands on the other man, he went to his chair and sat down. Tess, too, drew a little sigh of relief. Then the three sat for several quiet seconds looking from one to the other. At length, Tess broke out.

"Sandy said he'd keep away an' wait till he caught Andy Bishop afore he come to git me."

Sandy glared at her.

"But I told ye if ye had a nuther man hangin' round I'd fix both of ye, an' I'm goin' to keep my word," he snapped back.

"Ye can't fix any one but me, Sandy, 'cause ye don't know nobody else to hurt, do ye," she interrupted him.

"It air easy fer a man like me to choke the name out of ye, brat," replied Letts, blinking his eyes at her. "I'd be likin' nothin' better."

Jake moved his big boots back and forth several times.

"I wouldn't try it if I was you, Sandy," he cautioned, "'cause ye know uther folks might be interferin' with ye."

Sandy's throat emitted a deep, doglike growl as he clambered to his feet.

"I'll do it now, dam ye both," he barked back in ugly defiance.

Jake was on his feet before Letts could take a forward step and had placed himself between the big squatter and the girl.

That afternoon when Jake came back to see Tessibel, she threw a quick question at him.

"Air he dead, Jake?"

"Lordy, no, Tess, 'course not! He's tougher'n cow's tripe.... Sit down, brat, an' I'll tell ye about it.... Don't be shakin' so. It were like this! I was stoppin' Sandy from tryin' to git ye an' when I pushed 'im back, he kicked his own gun an' got a bullet in his big, fat leg, that air all."

"It was awful," cried Tess, wiping away her tears.

A slight smile played around Jake's lips, and showed a few of his dark teeth.

"Brat," he chuckled, "Sandy ain't done to his death by no means, an' you didn't have nothin' to do with it, nuther did I. 'Twere his own cussedness that put that bullet in his leg. There air one blessed thing, he won't be comin' round here for a long time yet botherin' you; so cheer up, an' be glad ye air a livin'."

Then Jake went away, leaving the girl and the little man in the garret, comforted and happier than they had been in many a day.

CHAPTER XXXI
WALDSTRICKER'S THREAT

Something had happened in the house of Waldstricker. Since the churching of Tessibel Skinner, everything had been topsy turvy. The criticism heaped on Ebenezer for his part in it had only served to make him more arrogant at home and abroad.

One morning at breakfast, Frederick being absent, Madelene was alone with Ebenezer and his wife.

"Put down your paper a minute, Eb," said Madelene, "will you?"

Scowling, Waldstricker let the paper rattle to the floor.

"What do you want now?... I can't have a minute's peace. What is it?... More money?"

"No, nor nothing to do with it, Ebenezer. I want to ask you something, and do be quite frank with me. Does Fred ever go to see that Skinner girl?"

The man's heavy brows drew into a straight dark line above his eyes.

"He'd better not," he gritted between his teeth.

"That isn't the point," answered Madelene. "Does he?"

"I don't believe I'd give myself much concern about that if I were you," he said presently. "I understand that man Letts, Sandy Letts, who is working for me on the Bishop matter, still wants to marry her."

"Of course she won't as long as Frederick—"

Waldstricker interrupted her.

"If Frederick does go there, he won't long when Letts finds it out."

Madelene's eager glance brought the unmatched lips aslant of each other.

"I don't think he'll go often," he repeated. "I'll see to it myself. She can marry Lysander Letts or—"

"Or what?" Madelene's elbows came to the table, a hand on each cheek. "Oh, Ebbie, do tell me! I'm so miserable about her. I wish she was dead!"

"But, Ebenezer," said Helen, "it seems awful for such a refined girl to marry such a man!"

The elder's uplifted hand came down on the table with a bang, and higher mounted his proud lip. He ignored his wife's pleading speech, but answered his sister's.

"So will Miss Skinner wish she were dead before I'm done with her," said he.

"Why?"

Waldstricker leaned over the table, looking first at his wife, then at Madelene. Helen shuddered. How relentless he looked when his mouth turned down at both corners! She had grown so afraid of him of late.

"I've an effective way to keep him from her," said he.

"Goody!" exclaimed Madelene, and "How, dear?" asked Helen.

The man spoke only two words in a low, husky voice, but each woman heard them.

"Good!" gasped Madelene, standing quickly. "How perfectly glorious!"

"How perfectly awful!" groaned Helen. "Ebenezer, don't do anything so dreadful."

Waldstricker looked across the table with that strange glitter in his eyes.

"Helen, must we go over again the same painful ground that women should not interfere!"

Mrs. Waldstricker rose to her feet.

"No, Ebenezer, no, no! Only I was thinking of Deforrest!"

"Deforrest will not know of it until it's too late," said Waldstricker, rising too.

"Does he know of Letts' trying to force her to marry him?" asked Helen.

"I've never told him. Possibly the girl has."

"I think not," answered Helen, gravely. "He'd have mentioned it to me, I think!"

As her brother passed Madelene, he tweaked her ear.

"Just clear your pretty head of further worry, little kitten ... See?"

Madelene caught his hand affectionately in hers.

"Kiss me, best of good brothers," she smiled. "You've made me perfectly happy! Isn't it dreadful to have to keep tabs on one's husband?"

"You won't have to long," Waldstricker assured her.

Then he kissed her and followed his wife into the library. Mrs. Waldstricker walked to the window and looked out, her eyes full of tears.

"Helen," said Ebenezer, gravely, taking her by the shoulders and turning her face toward him. "You displease me very much."

The drops hanging on the long lashes fell suddenly.

"I'm sorry, dear, but I can't see why you always antagonize Deforrest. You remember how angry he was after that church affair."

"Your brother's anger doesn't affect me in the slightest," returned Ebenezer coldly. "When I see my duty to God, I do it, that's all."

"And you're really determined—Oh, Eb dear, for my sake, please—"

The husband made an impatient movement.

"Helen, how many times have I got to forbid your crying this way. You're always in tears. You'll make yourself sick."

"Lately you've been so cross to me," sobbed Helen, burying her face in her handkerchief.

Waldstricker put his arm about her.

"I don't want to be cross.... There!... Now lie down here on the divan.... I'm going out for an hour or two."

Then he put on his cap, took up his riding whip, and went away to the stables.

A few minutes later Helen Waldstricker sat up straight, and rang the bell. To the servant who appeared, she said,

"Find Mr. Graves and send him to me immediately."

When Frederick received the message, cold chills chased each other up and down his back. Dismayed, he desired to disobey but dared not, besides Helen was the least dangerous of the three. What could she want, he considered queruously. He hadn't had a minute's peace since he came home. Madelene was in a state of tears nearly all the time; his brother-in-law, dictatorial, difficult even in his milder moods, seemed secretive and suspicious. As far as he was concerned, he kept from the house as much as possible, but this only provoked to a greater degree his young wife's tears and complaints. Only this morning, he had been treated to a spell of hysterics the like of which Madelene had never before equalled.

His wife would not believe his oft-repeated assertions that he had not been to the Skinner cabin since the day she had surprised him there. Frederick had spoken truly. His fear of his powerful brother-in-law and his own lack of moral courage allowed the days to drift along until now he felt he could not go into the presence of the girl he had thus neglected.

He watched until his brother-in-law drove from the stables and disappeared. Then he turned and went into the library. Helen beckoned to him to come near her.

"I must tell you something," she breathed.

She pointed to a chair near the divan. For a time she talked in an undertone, telling him something which sent the blood flying from the young man's face, and left him faint and sick at heart.

And later by an hour, Frederick Graves was walking the railroad tracks toward the Skinner shanty.

CHAPTER XXXII
HELEN'S MESSAGE

Tessibel Skinner was sitting in the shanty kitchen. She had a book in her lap but her mind was far from her surroundings. Andy had been quiet so long she'd almost forgotten him. Suddenly, his slight cough brought her back to the present.

"Ye look awful peeked, brat, dear," he said. "I think ye'd ought to see Young's doctor, hadn't ye?"

A vague smile crossed the girl's face, and she shook her head.

"No, Andy," she answered, "I don't need no doctor, yet."

"I wish ye felt better," sighed the dwarf. "An' the days is gettin' awful blizzardy for ye to go outdoors."

"But I got to go out, dear, fer wood an' other things. Hark!" She got up swiftly. "There air some one comin'."

In another instant the little man had crawled away from the ceiling hole and was under the tick. The garret was as silent as the frozen lake and the kitchen below, where Tess stood in anxious expectation. Tessibel, knowing it couldn't be Sandy, put aside her first impulse not to heed the rap. An instant later, she opened the door. That it might be Frederick was farthest from her mind, until she saw him standing there so thin and tired. Surprised and shocked at seeing him, the stress of her feeling found her faint. She would have fallen if he had not suddenly seized her.

"Tessibel!... Tess, darling!" he cried, sharply. Lifting her up, he carried her into the room. She clung to him, crying, her confusion calmed by his caresses. He placed her in a chair and sat down beside her. Suddenly, she sat back in her seat, roused from her revery by mocking memories of her wrongs.

"Couldn't ye let me alone?" she breathed hoarsely, covering her face with her hands. "Ye might a let me be."

"I had to come, dear," Frederick told her. "I want you to do something for both our sakes.... Oh, Tess, what terrible days have passed since I saw you last!"

After a short pause, she dropped both hands and glanced up at him. Then knitting her fingers together, she pressed them hard until they looked like the veined stems of a pale flower. He had come to make another demand of her—and she was so tired—so sick!

"I want you to make me a promise, Tessibel," urged Frederick.

"I said as how I'd help ye all I could," murmured Tess. "Ye're wantin' me to do somethin' awful hard, huh?"

Her soul in her eyes, she looked at him, but his gaze was on the gloves he was twisting back and forth between his fingers.

"Ain't ye goin' to tell me?" groaned Tess.

She dropped her chin into her hands with a touching gesture of pathos. Frederick bent nearer.

"Tess, Mrs. Waldstricker sent me with a message—and you've got to do what I want you to."

His strangely persistent reiteration that she should do his will served only to produce another, "Why don't ye tell me, then?" from Tess.

"You must do something to save yourself!" he cried.

To save herself? What did he mean by saving herself? What did any one intend to do? She'd stayed so alone no one could intrude upon her now. And then, there was Andy, poor forlorn little man!

"Is anyone goin' to hurt me?" she faltered, faint and frightened.

"Yes, dearest, yes, and you must—"

He was on his feet and Tess struggled up, too.

"What've I got to do?" she breathed miserably.

"Tess," he groaned, "can't you understand how much I love you; that I would save you if I could?"

With uplifted hand, he tried to raise her face to his.

"Don't!" she cried, pushing him away. "Tell me what Mrs. Waldstricker said!"

"You've got to do it, dear," urged Frederick, "or they'll take you away."

135

"What do ye mean by takin' me away?" she implored, moving a frightened step backward. "Who's goin' to try to take me any place?"

"Why—why—Mrs. Waldstricker says—"

He paused so long Tess could not bear the suspense.

"Oh, tell me!" she gasped. "Can't ye see ye air killin' me?"

Frederick began again.

"Mr. Ebenezer Waldstricker—"

Tess swayed on her feet.

"What air he goin' to do?" she panted.

Had her enemy discovered she was protecting Andy?

"He's going to take you to a—a—" stammered Frederick.

Tessibel grew faint and dizzy. She uttered a sharp scream.

"A reform school!" she cried.

"Yes."

The blow had fallen at last! She would be dragged from her home, up before the eyes of the world in all her illness and shame. Then she sank to the floor in abandoned misery.

"Oh, Frederick, save me!" she wailed. "Don't let him take me away, and I'll promise never to go outside the shanty. Oh, make him let me stay! Why can't I stay, oh, why can't I?"

"Waldstricker says you've got to go," said Frederick, sadly.

Tess sat up and flung back her curls.

"Well, he don't own the hull world, does he.... Couldn't you, well couldn't you say somethin' to make him let me be?"

"I don't know what to say," the boy mumbled.

"Couldn't ye tell 'em?" entreated Tess. "Please listen. Couldn't ye—couldn't ye tell Mr. Waldstricker 'bout our little baby—our baby, Frederick?"

He refused by a negative gesture of head and hand.

"Oh, don't shake your head, Frederick!" cried Tess, frantically. "Please!... Please!... Me an' the baby won't be any bother to you!... We'll jest love ye always an' forever, me an' the baby will....

"Ye could save us that way! Ye needn't tell 'em anythin' but that!"

Suddenly another thought took possession of her.

"What else did Mrs. Waldstricker say?" she demanded. "What were ye both wantin' me to do?"

"Mr. Waldstricker told his wife and my—I mean Madelene—that you'll either be sent away or must marry—marry Lysander Letts."

Tess stared at him wildly as though he were going mad. Or was she losing her reason! What awful thing had he said. Lysander Letts—surely she had not heard straight.

"Ye weren't tellin' me what were true, Frederick," she whimpered overwhelmed. "Oh, ye scared me so!"

"But I am telling you the truth!" he exclaimed miserably. His voice broke. "I can't save you, Tessibel. Waldstricker can do anything he wants. Why—why—Waldstricker's hands're stronger—are stronger than God's."

She heard his words as if in a dream. "Stronger'n God's," echoed through the recesses of her brain in fearful mockery. She was lost, engulfed in

136

the hatred of Waldstricker. She saw through the mist over her eyes, Lysander Letts leering menacingly at her. She sat very still and held her breath. If she let it go, her heart would break.

"Stronger'n God's," were the only words she remembered. Then, if that were true, and Frederick had said it—then—then, nothing—nobody—could take from her this brimming cup of disgrace and destruction. She struggled to her feet, walked to the door and opened it. Her eyes sought the dejected looking man.

"I air askin' ye to go now, please, right now," she said quietly. "Tell Mrs. Waldstricker, I air much obliged."

"And haven't you something to say to me, Tess?... Oh, God, don't send me away like this!"

She laid one hand on her heart. "Only go," she whispered, "an' never, never come again!"

Frederick stepped over the threshold, and Tess shut the door behind him.

CHAPTER XXXIII
HANDS STRONGER THAN WALDSTRICKER'S

Tess stood with swift-coming breath, her back to the door, waiting. Frederick must leave before she dared speak to Andy. It seemed an eternity ere the sound of the retreating footsteps died away, and she knew he was gone.

Then she started across the room, haltingly. Strange, how difficult it was to walk, and how giddy her head felt! What was it that had happened? What was going to happen a thousand times worse? Frederick's brutality left her bruised and broken. His threats twisted themselves through the tangled tumult of her thoughts and his sinister suggestions stunned and stupefied her.

Frederick had come and gone! She remembered that. Her skin still burned where his hot lips had touched her. He had told her he loved her, had begged her to say she loved him! Love? Yes, she had loved him—she did love him, but her love lay low, its structure, like a squatter's hut, she had seen, shattered on the sand by a storm.

Tess put a stick of wood in the stove, and a second later forgot she'd done it.

Ebenezer Waldstricker came into her mind vaguely ... vindictive and violent. Her hand went suddenly to her face. He was going to send her to a reform school, going to take her from the shanty for years! How powerful he was! Frederick had said Waldstricker's hands were stronger than God's. What strong hands he must have—those hands descending upon her defenseless, desolate life.

Andy was peering through the hole. Tessibel collapsed into Daddy Skinner's chair.

"Brat," he said in a whisper, "I'm comin' down!"

Tess mechanically got up and barred the door.... Then she returned to her seat. The dwarf was already squatted beside it, his eyes fastened on the girl in eloquent silence. His chin sank between his knees. Then the two of them sat.... The crackling of the freshly burning wood and the ticking of the clock were the only sounds in the room.

"I heard what the man said 'bout Waldstricker's hands bein' stronger'n God's," reflected Andy, aloud, presently. Then he raised his body a little from the floor that he might look into the girl's face. "Say, brat, has old Eb got any marks on his hands?"

Tess shook her head, brown eyes sombrous with suffering.

"No," she denied. "His hands are big an' white an' long an' soft."

Andy pondered a minute.

"They ain't no marks of nails on 'em, air there, kid?" he demanded, solemnly.

The pursed, hurt lines around Tessibel's mouth softened a little.

"No," she murmured wearily, again. "No, Andy."

The dwarf reached and took one of the girl's hands. It lay on his own quite limply.

"Look at me, brat, dear."

The red-brown eyes moved toward the upturned face.

"Tessibel, will ye think of this one little thing?

"The Christ's holdin' his hands over the hull world, givin' everybody peace; you an' me, too, brat-kid. Waldstricker's hands ain't dragged me back to Auburn, an' God's hands has kept me here.... You showed me that from the beginnin', eh, brat?... It's sure, ain't it?"

He hunched himself nearer her, his face beautiful with faith.

"Ain't it true, kid?"

"Sure! Sure, it air true!" faltered Tessibel.

"Then if God's hands kept me here in the shanty 'gainst all Waldstricker could do, can't they keep you here, huh?"

Tessibel's head lifted suddenly. What was Andy saying about hands— Waldstricker's and—and—With her free fingers she brushed the dampened curls from her forehead. Waldstricker's hands! Oh, incomparable memory! How could she have forgotten the hands of the Christ! They had brought Daddy Skinner from the shadow of the rope. She had forgotten the power of those hands.... Hands of peace—hands of love! As shadows fade before the majestic advance of the sun, so under the inrush of divine light did the agonized expression fade from Tessibel's eyes. The menacing figure of Waldstricker slipped away like a gliding night-serpent, and Tess got to her feet.

138

"Andy," she breathed, bending over him. "Oh, Andy, darling! Ye're telling me Jesus can keep me from bein' sent to that awful place? Ain't that what ye're tryin' to show me?"

The dwarf scrambled up, reaching forth his hands.

"And he sure can, brat," he made answer. "Waldstricker can't pull ye out of this hut when God's holdin' ye in."

Andy was smiling his rare, boyish smile. A large lump rose in Tessibel's throat.

"I air goin' to ask God to hold me here, Andy," she choked brokenly.

So when night closed the grey eyes of the winter day, and darkness descended on the Skinner shanty, a red-haired squatter girl and a wee dwarf knelt in the glow of the hut lamp and petitioning lips framed in whispers a simple prayer for their protection.

The next day passed, quiet in the shanty and over the shining span of frozen water. Waldstricker had not come. Tess crept into bed sighing with relief. Andy rolled himself in his blankets and slept.

The morning arrived crisply cold, bleakly grey. Tess shivered as she broke the ice for water. Would this day bring Waldstricker? Then, as that harrowing thought flitted through her mind, another exultant, smiling flash took its place. Tessibel's head reared with a proud uplift. No human power could set aside the majestic promise of Heaven that she might stay in the hut. Smilingly, she opened the shanty door and cheerfully answered the dwarf's, "How d'y' do, brat dear?"

But the next few hours were laden with a sense of approaching calamity, that sense which ties the tongue in apprehension. Andy was perched on the ladder while Tess sat just below in the wooden rocker.

Suddenly, from far up the lane, the sound of wheels grating on the snow, could be heard plainly. Both man and girl stared white-faced at each other for perhaps thirty seconds.

"They're comin', but they can't take ye, Brat," muttered Andy. "You'll stay in this shanty the same 's if you was nailed to the floor."

Then, he sought his place under the straw tick, and as nearer and louder came the clatter of the horses hoofs, the more quiet grew the Skinner hut.

Tessibel stood in the middle of the kitchen, her hand pressing down the beatings of her heart. Somebody was approaching! There were footsteps on the dry snow!

Directly the crunching sound ceased, a loud knock fell on the door. Tessibel lifted the bar, and at her faint, "Come in," the door flung back on its hinges and Ebenezer Waldstricker stepped over the threshold. Another man, seemingly by common consent, waited outside. Waldstricker came to a halt at the sight of the squatter girl. Even in her mourning, and ashen pale, she looked glorious. Her burnished, unmanageable hair clung like a golden mantle about her. She had lifted heavy lashes and was looking him straight in the face.

Ebenezer, suddenly, felt a wild desire to strike, but he dared not touch her, nor dared he go forward one step. Her advancing motherhood crowned her with unapproachable dignity, and the man muttered an imprecation under his breath. To have her appear in court so austerely lovely would be to lose his case. He had expected she would plead, cry, perhaps scream. What should he say to break that steady calm? He did not know what a day and night of communion with the Infinite had done for the squatter girl. He did not understand that beneath her were everlasting arms, that her life was held in the hollow of a hand more powerful than his own.

"I believe, my girl," said he, without preliminaries, "I told you when the church took action against you, you'd be sent to some place where girls of your class go, didn't I?"

Tess didn't move by so much as a wink. She seemed simply to have grown deaf and dumb. How could she answer when she had not heard? She was staring back into the man's bold, dark eyes. Her silence was like a spark to his inflammatory temper.

"Aren't you going to answer me, Miss?" His rasping voice aroused Tess from her trance.

"I didn't hear what you said," she told him, still very calm.

"I said," replied Ebenezer, arrogantly, "you're going to be sent to a reform school."

"Today?" asked Tess, breathing deeply, now fully possessed of her senses.

"Yes, today." Then he remembered Madelene.... he had made her a promise. "But I'll help you to get out after a while, if you tell me who—who brought you to this condition." He threw out both hands disdainfully toward her. Waldstricker's white hands, hands stronger than God's! Who had dared say it?

The girl cast her eyes to the rafters. There, the nets hung in strings and mingled their tassled ends with the dry herbs. There, somewhere, were that other pair of hands upholding her. She lowered her eyes again to the man.

"Don't you hear me talkin' to you?" he grated. "I said you were going today—but if you tell me—"

He bit off his words, her apparent helplessness shaming him to silence. Then the import of what he had said flashed over Tessibel and she swayed backward. This small break in that superb calm brought Waldstricker forward the step the girl had yielded.

"Are you going to tell me?" he demanded again.

"Nope," said Tess rigidly, "Air I to go with ye now, this minute?"

He inclined his head with a bitter nod. "Yes," he snarled. He strode to the door, and addressed the officer. "Come in! Come in! She's a hardened huzzy.... Serve the warrant on her."

Tessibel took the paper but dropped it to the floor without glancing at it. She didn't care what it contained, for minute by minute came the sweet assurance from up there among the nets that God had heard and would answer.

The officer was staring at her, askance. He remembered distinctly when she had climbed up the ivy on the county jail to see her father. Then she had been a child. Now she was a woman. Being a good-hearted man, he hated his task, and a moment later hated it worse than ever. She sent him one pleading, heart-rending glance, then dropped her lids.

"Ye couldn't let me stay till after March?" she whispered. "If ye only would—"

It had been an effort to say it; an effort to both inclination and voice. It was as if her throat were filled with ashes ... nor could she finish the appeal.

"You can't stay even one day," thrust in Waldstricker, "I told you long ago what to expect.... Get your things together."

Tess made no move to obey. She was waiting for an answer from out of the dry nets, even from far behind the snow clouds where the blue slept.

"Get your things on," commanded the man, once more.

Oh, yes, she could do that! Putting on her things didn't say she was going. She turned mechanically, took down her coat and scarf. These she put on and went for her rubbers. She stood very near the wall as she bent dizzily to slip them on. All the time her soul was looking upward for the eternal answer, an answer from a power stronger than Waldstricker's.

Then she went slowly to the little box where she kept her hat. After brushing her hair back, she pinned it on in front of the mirror. Today—well, now she was dressed, ready to go. She turned and came forward. The constable stared from Waldstricker back to her. Was this the girl who had stamped and screamed when Daddy Skinner had been taken to Auburn?

"Are you goin' without any fuss, miss?" he asked dully.

"If I go at all," was all Tess said.

At the door she flung back her head, her eyes searching the rafters. Straight as knife cuts hung the broken strings of the unused nets, threaded here and there with wheels of silken cobwebs. Up through these Tessibel stared. Up and up, above the curling of the chimney smoke, up among the stars, up where the hands of love—God's hands, were ever spread in benediction over her own wild, beautiful world. She smiled as if responding to a smile. Waldstricker touching her made her turn suddenly.

The cold wind from the door just opened by the officer, swept her hot face. She flashed her eyes past him to the vast open stretches of winter, and there, standing in the lane, smiling directly back at her, was Deforrest Young. God in his own good time had sent her hands stronger than Waldstricker's.

CHAPTER XXXIV

LOVE AIR EVERYWHERE THE HULL TIME

The moment the red-brown eyes fell upon Professor Young, the pale face of the girl lit with a radiant smile.

"Oh, ye've come!... God sent ye, didn't He?"

141

At the sight of the tall, commanding lawyer, the officer and his powerful principal stepped each to one side of the path in front of the house and left Tess standing in the doorway, with trembling arms outstretched to her approaching friend. Young came directly to her, ignoring his brother-in-law.

"My dear," he murmured, snatching her hands, "you needed me! Poor child, you certainly did!"

"Are you coming in," pausing on the threshold, he spoke to Waldstricker, "or are you going on to Ithaca, Ebenezer?"

A smile passed over the elder's lips. He was secretly much amused at the professor's assumption of authority.

"I'm coming in," said he. "I've something to show you."

Evidently not impressed by his brother-in-law's statement, Deforrest led the passive girl back from the threshold of the shanty into the kitchen.

"Let me take off your wraps, dear child," he said tenderly.

Waldstricker's growing amusement found audible expression in a condescending laugh.

"Wait a minute, Forrie," he commanded, spreading his feet pompously. "She can't take 'em off. She's coming with us."

"And why with you?" Young asked, in simulated surprise.

Waldstricker fairly gloated with joy. Never had he felt so righteous and uplifted. By his brother-in-law's actions, he was assured he did not know of the warrant for Tessibel Skinner. But the girl's attitude amazed him. To the quiet dignity with which she had submitted to arrest, there had succeeded an air of complete detachment as though her responsibility, even her interest in the matter, had wholly ceased. Mutely watching the two strong men, she seemed like some small prey over which fierce forces fought. Young began to remove the hat from her bronze curls.

"We're going to take her away," cut in Waldstricker, putting one hand in his pocket.

"Where to?" demanded Young, laying the hat on the table.

"To a—to a—" Waldstricker hesitated.

The frown on Young's brow deepened. He had paused for the other's explanation, his under lip gathered between his teeth. Then, he laid his hand protectingly on that of the silent, white-faced girl. Tessibel's fingers turned upward and closed over his, and they stood thus a moment, Waldstricker contemplating them through half-closed lids, one corner of his mouth superciliously curled.

"You haven't told me where you were going to take her," Deforrest insisted.

Bitter anger rose in Eb's throat. He had been balked at every turn he'd taken against this red-headed girl, and instead of helping him, Deforrest was aiding her. He did not intend that Madelene should suffer any more, and he imagined his own home life would be more peaceful when Tessibel Skinner was wiped from its horizon.

"If you'll have it plain," he cried triumphantly, "she's going to be sent to a reform school! If ever a girl needed correcting, she does. She's already been served with the warrant."

Young muttered under his breath. Holding out his hand, he said, "Let me see the warrant."

Ebenezer pointed to the paper on the floor where Tess had dropped it. Stooping, he picked it up.

"Look that over!" he said and handed it to the lawyer.

Professor Young took the paper, and before reading it, looked reassuringly at Tess with that wide, white-toothed smile of his that always cheered her heart.

"Sit down," he told her. "You do look tired, child."

With one swift glance at Waldstricker's face, she obeyed him.

Deforrest merely glanced at the paper in his hand.

"Oh, is that all you have?" he asked the constable.

"Yes, sir," the officer replied obsequiously.

"You're sure you haven't anything else?"

"Quite sure, sir," was the answer.

"That being the case," said Deforrest, quietly, "I'll match it with—with this."

He drew from his pocket another paper which he tendered the officer. After the man scanned it, he handed it without a word to Waldstricker. The elder in his turn read it through. It was an order from the court recalling the warrant obtained by Ebenezer Waldstricker for Tessibel Skinner's arrest. The constable grinned sheepishly at Waldstricker.

"I guess that ends my usefulness here," he said, smiling admiringly at Professor Young. "Good afternoon, miss! Goodday, gentlemen!"

Waldstricker, murder in his heart, took one stride toward Young, as the door closed behind the departing man.

"How'd you find out this was to happen today?" he gritted through his teeth. "I insist upon knowing."

"A little bird told me," grinned Professor Young. Then, glancing at Tess, and seeing how white she was, there rose within him a righteous indignation, and he went on, "You might employ your time to better advantage than torturing—"

For a moment he didn't know what to call Tessibel. She was no longer a child, no longer a little girl, although she looked deplorably young and sick as she sat huddled in the chair.

"Tormenting women," he finished, sharply. "And, Ebenezer, unless you want to make an enemy of me, you better let Tess alone. You can't do anything to harm her, for I won't let you. I may as well tell you, too, that the day after her father's death I constituted myself her guardian, and I'll move Heaven and earth to prevent any one harming her. Just remember that when you plot against her next time.... Now go home and forget there are such people as squatters.... You'll be happier, and so will I."

"Deforrest," Waldstricker appealed, changing his belligerent tactics, "if you keep this thing up, you'll rue it! You know very well Bishop is hidden somewhere in this squatter settlement. I can only get him by rooting his people out one by one; if you'll have that court order rescinded and let me send the girl away, I'll make it possible for you to run for Governor next fall."

For one minute, the lawyer surveyed Waldstricker critically. He reached one hand toward Tess. She got to her feet, grasping his fingers with hers.

"Ebenezer," Young said with great deliberation, "if I crawled across this girl's body into the Governor's chair, I'd be the basest cur alive. And furthermore, you promise too much! You can't deliver the goods! What! You name the next Governor! Why you can't even remove this little squatter girl from her lonely hut!"

Waldstricker shrank from the scorn in his brother-in-law's voice, opened the door and strode out.

"Tess," Deforrest said, putting an arm around her, "when are you going to let me take you away from such things as this? I shudder to think what might have happened if I hadn't come today, and I've got to go away again."

Tess smiled up at the big man. Drawing herself erect and lifting her head proudly, she looked into his face, exultantly, full of buoyant joy at the tremendous proof of Love's protecting power in the hour of her great need.

"I jest knowed old Eb couldn't get me," she asserted. "Jesus sent ye jest in the nick of time, didn't he, huh?"

"But, my dear, listen," Young argued, his love making him apprehensive. "It's awful for you to be here alone and unprotected. Let me take you away somewhere."

"I ain't alone," Tess insisted confidently, serene courage resounded in the sweet voice. "Jesus air here an' He keeps me safe all the time. He got Daddy out of Auburn an' kept Andy an' me in the shanty. Why, He sent you today. I know He won't let nothin' bad happen to me."

Untroubled, the brave eyes looked into his, conveying a message of courage and perfect peace that somehow uplifted the man's anxious thought to catch a glimpse of her exalted faith.

"But you know, Tess," he continued, "you are not so well this winter and you ought to have some one here to look after you."

Tess shook her head, the bronze curls twisting and falling over her shoulders and upon the arms embracing her.

"No, siree," she answered. "I can't have any one here, on 'count of Andy. Oh, ye mustn't worry 'bout me. I air all right an' will be every minute."

"At least, dear," Deforrest insisted, "let me get a doctor and nurse when—when—"

The brilliant head suddenly bowed itself forward against Young's rough coat. For a moment, her high courage faltered, but not for long. Surely, the same power that had cared for her today would see her through this other trial.

"Nope, not any doctor or nurse," she refused. "I'll have Mother Moll. She knows what to do an' she air safe."

Withdrawing herself from Young's arms, she took his hand and kissed it.

"God sure air good to Tessibel," she murmured.

A moment they stood there. Then the lawyer took up his hat and turned to the door.

"You know, Tess, I love you and want to help you always."

In the doorway, he paused and with bared head heard the girl's parting speech.

"Sure, ye're lovin' me an' I air lovin' you, too. I know Mr. Young, love air here an' everywhere the hull time."

CHAPTER XXXV
BOY SKINNER

A pale winter moon nestled among the snow clouds in the storm country. The shacks of the squatter settlement were dark and silent, save for a slender little light glimmering from the side of the curtains of the Skinner shanty. Inside, all was quiet. The squatter girl had been in the valley of shadows, and had struggled back from its depths, bringing with her that miracle of miracles, a son, a little son not much bigger than the hand of a man; and, now, pillowed on her arm, very near her heart, lay a small head, a baby's head, covered with soft, damp curls.

Mother Moll had come and gone. When the old, old woman had looked down upon the girl, she'd smiled that senile smile of age that split her lips like a knife cut.

"Ha! So it air another brat comin' to the shanty," she shrilled. "Holy Mary! It air the way of the world, the way of woman."

And now she'd gone, leaving the boy baby under the coverlet with Tessibel.

A weary apathy had settled over the young mother. Strange dreams filled the small room with haunting, tangible things which she could reach out and touch if she dared. The rafters, too, were peopled with faces partly hidden in the dry nets. But she seemed to be staring at something out and beyond—as Daddy Skinner, too, had stared that never-to-be-forgotten night.

The past months, where the grey days and sun days had all been the same, moved vaguely in silent procession before her. She had lived through them like a pale ghost indifferent alike to sunshine or shadow, and this night she had drained to the last drop the bitter cup Frederick Graves had given her to drink. Frederick, her husband, her beloved! She thought of him indifferently. Even his babe at her breast seemed unimportant. She considered them without emotion. But the ghostly faces, hovering among the nets, interested her.

Then, distinctly from among them advanced a figure, a dear, familiar figure. Daddy Skinner ... the same old adorable daddy—his shaggy, thready beard hanging over his chest. For one single instant he bent over her, lovingly laid his hand upon the bronze curls and smiled in the way he had of doing before he had gone away with mummy. Tess flung up her hands.

"Daddy! Daddy Skinner!" she cried.

The movement startled the babe from his sleep. The dwarf, roused by the cries scrambled to the open hole.

"Tessibel—Tess," he called brokenly.

The girl lifted heavy lids.

"Daddy was here, Andy," she wailed in misery. "My own Daddy Skinner. I want to go with him.... I can't live any longer without him."

"Can I come down, brat?" begged the dwarf, huskily.

"Yep," whispered Tess. "Mother Moll air gone."

"I heard 'er when she went," said Andy, and he slipped down the ladder. The babe's shrill cry continued as the dwarf went to the bed.

"Yer daddy don't need ye as much as me an' the little feller. Let me take 'im—I ain't seen 'im yet, ye know."

Andy bent over the cot. Gently he lifted the infant and carried him nearer the lamp's dim rays. He stood gazing intently into the rosy face. Then, he raised a tiny hand and spread first one finger, then each baby fellow out in his own palm.

"Why he's real handsome," he decided at last. "Brat, he air the most beautifulest in the world!"

At the last words he turned shining eyes toward Tessibel. She lay gazing, not at Andy or the babe in his arms, but up into and beyond the nets in the rafters, seeking another glimpse of her father's dear face. Alarmed by her strange silence, the little man bore his precious burden back to the cot and knelt beside the passive figure. Holding the baby close, he breathed,

"Don't, brat, dear! Look at me. I been feelin' yer daddy round all day, too. He'll always be near to help you an' the little kid."

A pathetic trembling of her lips hushed the flow of his words.

"It seems's if I couldn't live, Andy. I dunno how I can, I dunno how!"

Her voice trailed away into a plaintive moan.

"Let me take hold of yer hand, brat," murmured Andy. "I want to tell ye somethin'."

He clasped one of her hands in his, while her free fingers shaded her eyes.

"You got three folks standin' by you, kid," continued Andy, earnestly. "Me, Young an' Jesus. While I been alone in the garret, all this time, I been readin' an' a reasonin' out things. Don't ye remember when Mr. Young come that night how he said he didn't blame ye fer nothin' ye'd done?"

Beneath the tense fingers, she breathed a simple, "Yes."

"An' me—why me—I know yer heart's if I'd made it, honey, an' Jesus—Air ye listening Tess?"

"Sure," assented Tess.

"Then I'll tell ye a story. Once a woman loved a man awful much, an' she loved 'im like all women love men folks. An' a hull lot of righteous ones

146

dragged 'er right up to Jesus an' says, 'She air a sinner, sir, what'll we do with 'er?' An' he says, 'Go away an' leave 'er with me.'"

Tessibel's hand clutched at the fingers holding hers.

"An' when he were alone with 'er," went on the dwarf, "an' she were a kneelin' at 'is feet, he jest touched her lovin' like, an' says—"

"Don't, Andy, you—you hurt me ..." moaned Tess. "Don't!"

"An' I wanted to help ye, sweet," insisted Andy. "But still, I air askin' ye to listen to the rest. Will ye?"

Tess acquiesced silently, her hand falling away from her white, drawn face.

"An' Jesus says to the woman in baby trouble like yours, he says, 'Poor soul, I ain't blamin' ye this day, I ain't!'"

The little man's eyes shone with the sublimity of the truth he was imparting, and an uplifted expression of faith settled on his features. The baby whimpered in his arms, and loosening his hold upon the girl's hand, he rose to his feet carefully. Tessibel was crying now, in low caught breaths that wrenched and tore at Andy's heart cruelly.

To soothe the child, he pattered to and fro upon the shanty floor; and when he began to chant in a low, sweet voice that old, old precious hymn, "Rescue the Perishin';" Tess cried out again. Andy Bishop, the dwarf, was impressing upon Tessibel Skinner's heart that mysterious faith she'd known so long, that same sense of God's love which she'd taught him in those days when the dark doors of Auburn Prison yawned wide for him.

The state had branded him a murderer, but here, with glistening eyes, he preached the Christ and Him crucified. In the solitude of the garret, he had learned his lesson well ... by the dim attic light, he had studied the story of the forgiveness of sin. Suddenly, he ceased his song, and as he trotted back and forth, swaying the little child in his arms, Tessibel caught murmured words, "'Nuther do I condemn thee," said Jesus. "Nuther do I condemn thee," said he.

And in that next pulsing minute through the eyes of her soul, the watching girl saw above the squat dwarf the shadowy image of the smiling Christ, and unspeakable peace descended upon her like a benediction. The lines of suffering vanished from about her pursed mouth. The hurt within her heart gave way to the "still waters."

"'Nuther do I condemn thee,' said Jesus Christ," whispered Andy over the boy's face, and "neither do I condemn thee" sank into the very being of the squatter girl as warm rain sinks to the heart of a parched flower.

She followed the waddling figure, a gleam of gratitude beaming in her eyes. Surely, the bread Tessibel Skinner had cast upon the waters of Andy Bishop's stormy life was returning after many weary days!

"Andy," she called. "Andy, dear, bring me my baby."

The dwarf laid the sleeping child within its mother's arms.

"The man on the cross, your man an' mine, brat," he whispered, "said, 'If ye have burdens, come an' I'll rest ye.' Didn't he say it, kid?"

"Yes, yes, Andy," whispered Tessibel. "Everything'll be all right fer—you an' me an' the baby," and she ended, ... "Get back in the garret an' pray for my brat's daddy, too, Andy. He air needin' it worser'n me an' you."

Then the squatter girl turned her face to the wall, drew the baby under the coverlet, and the dwarf scuttled up the ladder.

CHAPTER XXXVI
DEFORREST DECIDES

Deforrest Young sat alone in his bachelor apartments, which he'd obtained after the quarrel with Waldstricker over the churching of Tessibel Skinner. He was in Ithaca in response to a letter from Mrs. Waldstricker, stating that she would meet him in his rooms this afternoon.

His mind was busily at work with many problems. For the past week he had had no word from Tessibel Skinner. Her silence was significant. Mischief-making anxiety, which always pictures the worst side of a situation, tormented him cruelly. He hoped Helen might have news from the shanty by the lakeside.

When Mrs. Waldstricker finally appeared, his first impulse was to ask about the squatter girl, but the troubled expression of his sister's face checked the question on his lips. He drew her tenderly into his arms, and attempted to comfort her with reassuring pats and caresses.

"You shouldn't have ventured out, dear," he chided. "Sit down here!... There! Now tell me what's the matter."

"I'm so miserable, Forrie," she wept. "I can't do a thing with Ebenezer.... He's in such a state of temper all the time!"

"Don't try to talk for a moment, dearest," soothed the lawyer, much moved.

"But I must—I want to! It seems as if my whole life has been upset in some unaccountable manner. And it isn't any better since Frederick and Madelene went away. I was in hopes after they'd gone, I might have some peace."

"Is it still—" Young's inquiry was broken off by his auditor's exclamation.

"Yes, it's Tessibel Skinner! He seems perfectly possessed about her. I can't understand why, either. I always tell him she's nothing to us. He has even gone so far—Oh, Forrie, dear, tell me it isn't so!"

"What isn't so?" asked Deforrest, puzzled.

"Ebenezer says—he says you'd marry—" The inquisitor's courage oozed away before she finished her sentence. Her brother turned and strode up and down the room, while Mrs. Waldstricker's eyes, full of questioning anguish, followed his tall figure.

"I suppose he said I'd marry Tessibel Skinner. Is that it?" His voice was low, deep and intense. Wheeling about he looked across at his sister.

She got up from her chair and went to him. Her desire to placate her brother supported her determination to know his precise attitude toward her husband. She placed her hand on his arm and replied hurriedly,

"Yes, that's what he said. I told him it was no such thing; that you did what you could for the lonely child without a thought—"

Deforrest's hand closed over the speaker's.

"You were mistaken, then," he asserted quietly. "I'd have married Tessibel Skinner long ago, if she'd consented."

"Forrie, dear, you wouldn't! You couldn't! Especially now! Oh, darling, you're all I've got in the world.... Can't you see it would break my heart?"

"You needn't worry about it, sister mine." A sad shake of his head emphasized his reply. "Tess won't marry me. She knows I love her and want to care for her, but she won't let me. She sticks there in that wretched shanty, alone with her trouble and refuses every offer I make. Her courage is splendid. I love her for it, although I'm torn to pieces with anxiety."

"And I never knew," Helen mused. "I thought—I thought it was—just you were charitable and kind."

"No, it wasn't that. I've loved her since the first, but she couldn't love me, that's all. Then this awful thing happened." The deepening lines in his face and his twitching lips revealed the intensity of his solicitude. "Have you heard anything about her?"

"Yes. A man by the name of Brewer, one of the squatters, brought me a message."

"Yes, yes!" interrupted the man, very impatiently.

Helen pressed her face against his arm. She divined the pain he was suffering. How was she to soften the hurt her answer would inflict, even her loving heart couldn't imagine.

"She has a baby boy," she whispered.

"God!" groaned Deforrest.

"The baby was born a few days ago, and every day the squatter's been at our house, ostensibly to sell something, but really to tell me about her.... I saw him this morning, and he says they are both doing nicely. Forrie, don't you think—" There was something in her brother's stricken face that broke off her question.

"Don't I think what, dear?" He got up and resumed his restless pacing up and down.

"Oh, I want you to be happy. Couldn't you possibly—forget you've loved her?"

"No, I can't," and he came to a standstill in front of her. "I might as well be truthful, dear, as long as you know this much.... If Tessibel will marry me, I'll take her and the boy—" he choked, paused a few seconds and went on. "I'll take them both away from Ithaca. It's the only happiness in store for me, and I believe I could make her happy, too."

"I can't bear the thought of it," cried Helen, desperately. "Please don't think I'm meddling, but has she told you anything?"

"No. Some one has mistreated the child shamefully, but she won't tell anything about it."

"Poor little girl!" sighed Mrs. Waldstricker. "How I wish now I'd done more for her! I might have, you know."

The lawyer raised his hand deprecatingly.

"What's past, is done with," he answered gloomily. "I don't know how much she'll let me do, but I am going to help her in spite of herself. That shack by the lake is an awful place. I swear I'll give her decent surroundings and a chance to live.... I'm going down today."

"But, Forrie," his sister objected, "I want you to come home with me to dinner. You haven't been to our house in a long time, not since the night you came from Binghamton and went off to Skinner's in the storm."

"Helen, dear," Young explained, apologetically, "I can't come to your house as long as Ebenezer feels toward me the way he does. You see, don't you?"

"Oh, I suppose I do, but I just can't stand it. Eb has acted badly and tried to shoulder it all off on you. But can't you overlook it, honey?"

"Why, Helen, how can I? I don't feel any too pleasant toward him, and he doesn't want to be friends, either. He pays no attention to my wishes but tries to ride rough shod over me. He regards my interest in Tess as a personal affront. He persecutes her because he thinks he's annoying me. But there, don't cry any more. You'll only make yourself ill! I think you ought to go home and lie down. You've some one else besides yourself and Eb to think of, dear girl."

"I know it," she sobbed, "and I've tried to show Ebenezer how happy we'd be if he'd forget those people down the lake and let you do what you want to. Sometimes I think he's lost his mind. I really don't know what to do."

Helen rose from her chair.

"Nor do I," replied Young.

"But, Deforrest, don't you think if you talked to Ebenezer, he'd see things differently?"

"I'm afraid not," said he, adjusting Mrs. Waldstricker's furs. "You see, Eb's always had his own way in most things, and I can't take any other position about Tess, and I won't."

"I wish you would come home with me," sighed Mrs. Waldstricker, when her brother was tucking the sleigh robe about her.

"I'm sorry I can't, Helen. You'll hear from me soon," he promised, as the sleigh moved away.

Half an hour later found the lawyer astride his horse, his fine face clouded in sorrowful thought.

He cantered along the hard packed road. Here he noted the shimmering veil of ice over some brooklet waterfall in a cleft of the hill side. There the precise punctures of a rabbit track dotted the level snow of the woods. Beyond a herd of cattle standing placidly around a straw-stack blew clouds of vapor from their steaming nostrils. The silent beauty of the hills, glistening in their frosty covering, set off to advantage the silvery sheen of the ice-laden lake. Through the trees, he caught occasional glimpses of East Hill winter-wrapped in its white mantle. Just north of the city shone the resplendence of the ice-cloaked rocks and waterfalls of Fall Creek Gorge, like a massive garniture emblazoned on the mantle's skirt. The unbroken calm of the quiet winter afternoon touched the rider's overwrought heart and awoke in him a sense of the peace and the dignity of the visible creation. The untroubled serenity and repose which all nature presented, soothed his troubled spirit. Something of the unruffled confidence expressed by Tessibel, when he'd last left her, penetrated his revery. Her words, "I know Love's everywhere the hull time," had comforted him many times, and now they came again upon their healing mission.

Tessibel's baby was one week old. This afternoon she lay partially dressed on the cot while Andy was plying his noiseless way about the kitchen. He stopped a moment on the journey to the stove and smiled at the young mother.

"I bet he comes today," said he. "You'd better be gettin' that sorrow offen yer face, brat."

"I ain't right sorryful, Andy," she answered. "I was jest thinkin' of all the good things Mr. Young air done for me, an' hopin' he'd get you free, too. Mebbe when Spring comes, Andy, you can run in the woods with me!"

"I air prayin' for it every day, kid."

"When you ain't afeered of Auburn any more," said the girl, after a moment's silence, "we'll go away from this shanty, an' mebbe we can both work. That'd be nice, eh, Andy?"

"Anything'd be nice if I air with you, an' the baby, brat," he choked.

"Oh, you'll stay with us all right," smiled Tessibel. "Daddy left me to take care of you an' I air goin' to do it!"

Conversation lagged for a time. The dwarf poured out a cup of tea, and placed a large slice of bread on a plate with some potatoes and meat. These he took to the bedside.

"I don't know what we'd a done without Jake," he observed, drawing his chair to the table.

Tess was beginning to eat a late dinner. Between bites she smilingly assented.

"Jake air a awful good man.... Andy, ain't the baby stirrin' on the chair?"

The dwarf went to the improvised cradle and carefully drew away the blanket.

"He wants turnin' on 'is other side, that air all." With deft fingers he rolled the baby boy over, placed the sugar rag between the twisting lips, and went back to his dinner.

"Jake was tellin' me this morning," she continued, "Sandy Letts got three years and a half in Auburn."

"That'll be dreadful for him," the little man responded, thinking of his lonely years in prison. "But body-snatchin' air an awful thing. Reckon he won't try it again when he gets out.... Eh, kid?"

"At any rate, he won't be after us for a while," she replied, sighing contentedly.

"Well, I must slick up a bit," Andy announced presently. "I want to get the shanty fixed. Young'd think I weren't doin' right by ye, if 'tain't red up, brat."

"When I tell him all ye've done," she smiled affectionately, "I bet he'll be praisin' ye."

Then they were silent until the little man'd gathered and washed the few dishes.

CHAPTER XXXVII
THE NEW HOME

WHEN Professor Young arrived at the end of the lane near the Skinner's shack, he dismounted, blanketed the horse and hitched him to the fence. The approach to the hut had been shovelled recently and the snow was banked high on either side. He hurried along the path and knocked at the door.

A stir in the shanty told the lawyer the dwarf was seeking the attic. After an instant of quiet, he heard Tessibel's voice.

"Who air there?"

The man's nerves throbbed quick response to the clear young tones that came sure and strong through the shack boards.

"It's I, Tessibel," he answered.

And at his answer the bar raised from its holder and Young opened the door and stepped in. The change from the brilliant glare of the almost horizontal beams of the declining sun on the sparkling snow to the half-light of the closely curtained room, obscured his vision for a moment. But by the time he'd removed his cap and rebarred the door, he could discern the familiar outlines of the shanty kitchen. He saw Tess, half-risen on the cot. She rested on one elbow and stretched the other arm out to him. Her face, wreathed in smiles, shone a cordial welcome. When he'd gone to her and snatched the extended hand in both his own, she bent moist lips and touched the back of the fingers.

Her spontaneous joy brought him a sudden hope that tingled through his blood and warmed it. To see her so well, so sparkling and joyous, lifted his burden of anxiety and warmed in him a glow of profound thanksgiving.

"Tessibel!" he greeted her, relief and yearning compressed into the one word.

It was some time before either spoke. In Tessibel's heart swelled an affection such as she held for no other person. In Young's, in spite of his self-communion on the way, surged the insistent call of the man for his mate, a hopeless longing which might never be satisfied.

"I'm glad it's over, child," he said softly. "My sister told me—"

"I got my baby!" she broke in. "He air over there. Take a peep at 'im."

There was no embarrassment in the bright smile she sent him, no sense of shame in showing her friend the dear little being who had come to her out of the Infinite to be worked for and loved. Young smothered a groan but he turned obediently and went to the chair in which the baby was cradled.

Folding back the blanket, he gazed at the sleeping infant. Manlike, he was experiencing the passionate wish that this small boy were his own. Jealousy, sudden and violent, assailed him. Hardly could he restrain the words of interrogation and denunciation that demanded utterance.

The mother's question brought him back to the cot.

"He air beautiful, ain't he?" she breathed, a misty gleam on her lashes.

"Yes," said Young, and he sat down in Daddy Skinner's big rocker.

"Wouldn't ye like to hold him?" Tess hoped he would.

"Not yet," replied the lawyer. "I want to know more about him. You must tell me now whose son he is, and let me help you decide what to do about it.... Won't you trust me a little, Tess, dear?"

He hitched his chair nearer the cot and looked earnestly into the dear, brown eyes she turned fearlessly and unashamed up to his own.

"He air mine," Tessibel told him, and a tender smile played about her lips, "but I can't tell ye any more.... There ain't nothin' to do about it. It air all right—huh?"

"Oh, my dear," sighed the man. "I hoped you'd relieve my mind a little. But—but I'll not speak about it again till you come of your own accord and tell me.... I've been thinking about something else, though—"

"Air it about Andy?" interrupted Tessibel.

Young looked up and discovered a boyish face smiling down upon him from the attic.

"Come down," he said to the dwarf.

Andy descended the ladder and trudged across the floor.

The lawyer stood up and extended his hand. "How are you, Andy?" he enquired pleasantly. "Pretty well, I hope?"

Andy shook hands gravely.

"Yep, thank ye, professor, I air that," he assented. "Hope ye're the same."

"Andy's been more'n good to me," Tess confided. "Please sit down again, Mr. Young.... Set on the floor, Andy!"

Obediently the dwarf curled up on the floor and turned eagerly to Young who had resumed his chair.

"Ain't Tess got the fine baby?" he queried, and as though not expecting an answer, added, "And she air awful happy."

A fugitive smile trembled on Young's face.

Awful happy! Awful happy! Was it possible? He looked into Tessibel's joyous eyes and pondered. Yes, she was happy. He could see that! Happy in a squatter's hut! Happy in the companionship of a condemned murderer, and happy with a nameless child! His eyes went to the little one on the chair. Yes, the three of them were happy. Tessibel's love was bound up in Andy and the baby, and the dwarf had forgotten his own danger to serve the other two. To help in the same loyal and unselfish way would be his future work. At that moment Deforrest Young buried deep in his heart the passion which hurt like nothing else hurts on earth, and something very like happiness took its place.

He leaned back and crossed his legs. Then he reached into his coat pocket and produced his cigar case. He bent forward and offered it to Andy.

"Smoke, Andy?" he queried.

"Nope, thank ye, sir. Hain't smoked since Pal Skinner got sick. Couldn't smell up the shanty with a pipe, ye see, eh?"

When the cigar was glowing and the fragrant smoke drifted in eddying clouds through the kitchen, the smoker rocked a few minutes contemplatively.

"I've seen Owen Bennet," he began presently. "He sticks to the story that you did the shooting, Bishop, but I knew all the time he was lying."

"Yep, he lied," interpolated Andy, bobbing his head.

"But as long as he won't tell the truth," Young stated "you're liable to be taken back to Auburn."

The dwarf cringed as from a blow. Fear of going back to prison killed the joy in his face instantly, but the speaker's quick assurance straightened the bent shoulders.

"But no one knows where you are, and perhaps something can be done to bring a confession from Bennet. Just at this time, though," looking from the little man to the girl on the cot, "I'm more concerned about your futures."

Tess didn't speak. She knew wherein her confidence lay and was willing to await her friend's suggestion. She sat up, punched the pillow, turned it over, and lay down again.

"It's perfectly evident you can't stay here, either one of you," said Young, after a pause, "and if you'll be guided by me—"

"We'll do what ye want," murmured Tess, "if ye'll let us stay together an' keep the baby."

"Yes, that is my plan," he replied.

Andy folded his short legs under him nervously.

"We want to stay together, me an' Tess does," he echoed, "an' the baby's awful glad to live with us."

Young's lips curled an instant into a smile responsive to the quaint statement.

"You remember, Tess," he resumed, "I have a lease of the house where Graves used to live."

She answered only by a little forward bend of her head.

"My idea is this: I'll open the house, and you, Tess, can come there with the baby. You can keep house in a little way for us all."

"Ye said Andy could live with—"

"Wait," interrupted the lawyer. "There're two nice rooms on the top floor. You can arrange them for Bishop and he will be as snug as a bug in a rug."

A sharp cry of joy broke from the young mother. She sat up straight. She threw back the tangled curls, and leaning forward grasped the hand the speaker thrust out to support her.

"Oh, what a good, good man!" she rejoiced. "An' me an' the baby'll love ye forever, me an' the baby will."

Tessibel didn't remember she'd made the same promise to another man when she'd begged him in vain to help her. She only knew that Deforrest Young was offering herself and her little child a home, and a safe refuge for Andy Bishop.

"It won't be all for you, you understand, child," said Deforrest. "Think! I'll have a home, too, and you can study and work."

"An' some day when I'm earnin' money, and Andy's free, we'll pay you all back," the girl interjected.

"Well, we won't worry about that now!... As soon as you're well enough, I'll move you all up to the house. Tomorrow I'll see that coal and things're sent down from town!"

The reply to his offer was a tighter squeeze from the squatter girl's hand, and a sob from the dwarf. Unable to restrain his joy, the wee man bounded from the floor and fled up the ladder into the garret. For a time the man and girl in the room below sat silent, and all was quiet in the shanty save the voice of Andy Bishop giving forth a thanksgiving such as he had never expressed before.

Two weeks later a light filtered through the closed shutters of Young's residence on the hill. The old Graves house creaked in the blustery March gale. The hurtling snow-particles rattled upon the blinds and against the clapboards like small shot. Deforrest Young came out of the house and fought his way against the blizzard's buffeting down the hill to the Skinner shack.

Stumbling, he fell against the door.

"It's I, Tess," he shouted.

The girl lifted the bar and admitted him. Dressed in her outer wraps, she stood in the kitchen, anxious and expectant. This minute to Tess was the changing point of her life. Young as she was, she understood what it would mean to the three of them to leave the shanty, to take up their abode in a real home.

"Ye said we was to take the baby first," she greeted him, reaching for the shawl on a peg in the door post.

"Yes, but it's so bad I'll have to take you first, child," the lawyer replied. "Come down, Andy, and after we're gone, bar the door and stand by the boy.... I'll come back after you in a few minutes."

Then he flung an arm about Tess and drew her into the winter night. Wind-blown and snow-covered, Young almost carried the shivering girl up the steps into her new home. How luxurious the comfortable furnishings seemed compared to the poverty of the shack! Young helped her off with her coat and rubbers.

"Get the baby and Andy, quick," she panted.

Left alone her imagination followed her champion out under the frost-

155

laden trees into the drifted lane. She knew his call would raise the bar and let him into the shanty. She could see the dwarf's beautiful face smiling his welcome. The thought that Deforrest would wrap up her baby, protect him from the keen blasts, thrilled her.

She went to the window in the north room and pressed her face to the pane. Ah, yes, there in the little path were two figures, one little and one big, struggling through the drifts. Her two friends! Presently, in the arms of the tall figure, she could discern a bundle, a small bundle. She watched them until she heard their steps on the porch. When Deforrest placed the baby in her arms, and she noted Andy's happy face, Tessibel's joy was complete.

CHAPTER XXXVIII
DINNER AT WALDSTRICKER'S

Three years and a half had passed since the birth of Tessibel's baby, a period of growth and security for the squatter girl and Andy Bishop.

Just before Boy Skinner's birth, Frederick and Madelene had gone to San Francisco. A place had been made for him in Waldstricker's office there and Madelene felt the continent none too wide to put between her husband and the Skinner girl, but her efforts to win his affection had been a complete failure.

Lysander Letts, convicted of grave robbing, had been sentenced to prison and was still confined at Auburn.

During the weeks after Frederick's departure, Ebenezer Waldstricker had been unusually busy. In May, just as the tardy promises of the Storm Country spring, were beginning to be fulfilled by the full leaved glories of early summer, little Elsie Waldstricker was born. A few weeks later, the three of them had left Ithaca for a long period of travel. Mr. Waldstricker had visited all his business friends and correspondents and established many new connections. Proceeding leisurely around the world, they'd returned to Ithaca not long after Elsie's third birthday.

During their absence abroad, except for the caretaker, the great house above Hayt's had been closed. Affairs at the lake side had run along in their usual way. Tessibel had been able to ameliorate the conditions of her squatter neighbors and was regarded by the inhabitants of that end of the Silent City, as their lady bountiful. They put her in a niche by herself. None prouder than they of the evidences of culture and refinement she showed, while with characteristic independence, they called her "Brat" just as in the days, when she ran bare-legged and dirty on the lake side.

Andy Bishop had occupied the room on the top floor of Young's home. He'd devoted himself to the same studies Tess pursued and by greater application had been able to overcome the handicap of the girl's quickness and greater natural ability. Not so readily had he learned to speak correctly. The idioms of his boyhood days still slipped out of his mouth. But no suspicion of uncouth English marred the girl's speech.

Forlorn and abandoned, the Skinner shanty lay moldering under the weeping willows. Summer heat and winter storms had worked their will upon it. Thick grasses and tall weeds had driven out the squatter girl's flowers and the hedge had grown into a tangled thicket.

The brilliant sun of a hot June morning found no more home-like place than the old Graves house, where Deforrest Young lived with his squatter friends. On the porch stood Tessibel Skinner. The girl's ruddy curls fell in the same profusion as of old and shrouded a smiling, happy face. Professor Young had caught her one day doing up the red hair in a great ball on her head.

"Tess, it's a sacrilege," he protested sharply, "like wadding up the petals of a rose or the leaves of a fern. Keep the curls, won't you?"

Below, from the pear orchard, came a joyous shout, the free, careless, laughing response to the girl's call.

"I'm coming mummy," cried a child's voice.

Tess leaned forward, the better to watch the small boy lightly climb the terrace. Her face evinced the joy which she found in her baby, and in the quiet, happy life under Professor Young's care. She held out her hand to the little one. He danced to her side and she bent and kissed him.

"Mummy's boy, oh, mummy's little boy! Didn't I tell you, darling, not to soil your blouse? Uncle Deforrest'll be here soon."

"Boy rolled down the hill," pouted the child. "Boy loves to roll down the hill, mummy."

His mother kissed him again, diverted by his words, which recalled her own girlhood frolics. Hadn't she many times tumbled the length of the lane, while Daddy Skinner had stood and watched her indulgently? Her arms about the boy, she allowed her eyes to rest for a moment on the hut at the lake side. Tessibel loved the shanty and always would love it, but more did she love the home in which she now lived. Her fingers played idly with the child's dark curls. All that Deforrest Young had done for her in the past years swept before her mind like a panorama.

How safe he'd made it for Andy! How the little man had improved! How delightful their studies together! They constantly looked forward to that day when they should be able to return to their friend some of the generosity he had shown them.

Now he was coming home after an absence of many weeks, and the three were awaiting his arrival.

"Run up to Andy, darling," Tess said to the child, "and let him wash your face and hands, and put on another blouse, my pet. Oh, there 're grass stains on this one, too."

A trembling, rosy mouth turned up to the speaker. She kissed it quickly and passionately.

"Never mind, honey, just run along. Mummy doesn't care.... There, kiss me again."

Two loving arms went quickly around the mother's neck.

"Boy loves his pretty mummy," was whispered in her ear.

"And mummy loves her pretty boy. There! Run along to Andy. I want to gather some flowers for Uncle Forrie."

Andy was studying at a table, when the door opened and the dark-faced boy popped into the room.

"Mummy says wash Boy's face and put on clean blouse," said he. "Please, Andy. I forgot to say 'please'!"

Andy pushed back his chair and waddled to the child. The dwarf was the same ungainly figure that had moved about the hut four years before. His face had lost all its tightly strung misery and his expression was more thoughtful and he seemed more manly.

Boy was a continual joy to him. The little fellow supplied an outlet for his overflowing love. True, he adored Tessibel, but his care of the little one had drawn them together so intimately that he and the baby boy thoroughly understood each other.

He'd have liked to romp with the child under the trees and to row him up and down the quiet span of blue water, but grateful for the love and protection he'd found in Young's home, he seldom permitted his mind to dwell upon the hardships necessarily incident to his secluded life. Just now a little sense of discouragement touched his thought and clouded his face. While he was washing Boy's chubby fingers, the little one observed him closely.

"There's tears in your eyes," he burst out suddenly. "What for, Andy?"

"I was just thinkin,' pet."

The child thrust his feet apart and flung up an entreating face.

"I don't want you to think if it makes you cry."

"All right, sir!" Andy replied promptly, tickling the youngster till he laughed and shouted, "I won't think any more if you don't like it."

When Deforrest Young came around the corner of the house, Tessibel was standing on the lower step of the porch, her hands full of flowers. To his adoring eyes, the girl typified the unfolding life of the spring. Strong was she, like the sturdy trees, dainty as the flowers she held in her hands. To his passionate desire as unresponsive as the sullen lake on dark days, yet grateful for his kindness as the field flowers to the sun after a hard rain. She was a child with a woman's heart, but the woman's heart closed to him by the secret of Boy's paternity. Her smiling lips greeted him. She dropped the flowers and two arms stole around his neck. Young drew her very close. How dear, how very dear, she had grown in these last studious years!

"It seems ages since you went away," she said, and pointing to the flowers, "I hoped to get these all on the table."

"My dear," interjected Young, "you're the rarest blossom of them all."

Tess was used to his compliments, and she loved them, as she loved the birds and the friendly sunshine.

"For that, sir," she laughed, "you'll have to help me pick 'em up."

While they were gathering together the scattered bouquet, they heard a stamping down the stairs.

"Boy couldn't hardly stand it till you came," smiled Tess, opening the hall door.

A small avalanche of concentrated eagerness piled out of the house.

"Uncle Forrie! Uncle Forrie!" cried Boy, swarming upon him. "I'm awful glad you're home."

"Now, then," said the lawyer after dinner, "I think our little mister here ought to crawl into bed.... Well, one more romp, then bye-bye. Eh?"

"One more romp!" screamed the child.

His mother carried him away half an hour later, and when she went to Andy's room, she found Young there talking to the dwarf.

"I've such a lot to tell you two," said he. "Now we're all comfy, I'll begin."

"Will it please Andy?" asked Tess.

Deforrest shook his head.

"I'm afraid not!... Bennet won't have to stay long in prison and he still insists he didn't do the shooting and that Andy did."

The latter groaned, and a shadow fell over Tessibel's face.

"I wish something could be done," said she.

The lawyer considered the end of his cigar.

"Well, I can't think of anything right now," he sighed.... "I suppose you've heard Lysander Letts is out of prison?"

Young asked the question as though it amounted to little, but he knew by the sharp cry from the girl and the upward lift of the dwarf's head that they both dreaded Sandy's return to Ithaca.

"But I don't want you to worry. I'll send him back if he comes around here."

Tess shook her head despondently.

"Oh, I hope he'll let me alone!"

"I'll see that he does," said the professor, rising and straightening up. "Well, I'm going down to write some letters. Cheer up, Andy! Maybe something'll turn up."

"Kid," began Andy, when the lawyer had gone. "I been thinking, we don't have to worry 'bout Sandy Letts. Ye know the lots of times when we didn't have Boy's Uncle Forrie to do things for us, how we prayed for a helpin' hand and got it?"

"Yes, Andy dear," Tess answered, thoughtfully.

"Then let's do it now. Let's get busy prayin' so Sandy can't hurt ye an' I get out of my pickle.... Huh?"

CHAPTER XXXIX
FATHER AND SON

After an absence from his native city of three years and a half, Frederick Graves was returning to Ithaca, a very sick man. He had learned from Helen's letters to Madelene that Tessibel Skinner had a small son. His brother-in-law's exasperation at Young for giving the squatter girl and her little son a home at the lake had also been reflected in the correspondence. He had been able to glean but the bare outlines of the story, because Ebenezer and Helen had been abroad most of the time, and his impatient spirit chafed to know the intimate particulars of Tessibel's life. Jealousy of Young tormented him. Hopeless brooding over his situation, and Madelene's continual nagging had made him a neurasthenic wreck. Worn by insomnia and almost starved by a nervous dyspepsia, he could no longer maintain even a pretense of usefulness in the business. Madelene, thoroughly disillusioned, herself worn out by his sullen and savage temper, had brought him back to Ithaca, hoping the familiar sights and sounds of the home-land might help him.

They arrived one rainy night at the station, where Ebenezer met them with the carriage. He greeted both effusively, and his manner perhaps was more cordial because of his brother-in-law's death-stricken face.

"You'll buck up now you're home, Fred," he said, after he had kissed his sister and helped them into the carriage.

"Maybe, but I doubt it," the invalid replied wearily.

"Nonsense, Fred," his wife broke out. "You make me tired. You're always whining. Of course, you're going to get well."

Too fatigued to argue, Frederick leaned back upon the cushions. Except for an occasional word, they were silent during the long drive through the rain.

Home at last, they found Helen waiting in the great hall. To Madelene, who preceded the men into the house, she looked much older, more dignified. Lines of worry around her eyes and mouth told the girl that her sister-in-law's life with Ebenezer had not been entirely easy.

After kissing Madelene, Helen extended her hand to Frederick.

"I hope you'll be better soon, Fred," she encouraged. "Our country fare'll put some flesh on your bones.... You look after the invalid, Ebenezer, and I'll take Madelene upstairs."

The two women walked upstairs together. Waldstricker gazed after them, pride and joy in his eyes. His wife and his sister reunited brought him a feeling of content. Frederick, fussing with his coat and rubbers, seemed hardly aware of their going.

"I'm glad to have you back, Fred," began Waldstricker, anxious to express the gratification he felt.

"We're glad to get back, of course," Frederick responded coldly. He followed the elder into the library and threw himself on a lounge to rest until dinner.

In the room above, Helen helped Madelene off with her things and listened to her chatter about the journey. She could detect a sullen dissatisfaction with Frederick running like a dark thread through the current of her talk. It was clear to Helen that Madelene had lost her regard for her husband. Apparently, she cared so little that she didn't feel it necessary to hide or explain her feelings.

"And, now I want to see little Elsie," gushed Madelene. "I've been crazy to see her ever since she was born."

"She's such a darling," smiled Helen, "and is the very joy of her father's heart.... Come on in the nursery."

For a few seconds Madelene leaned over the sleeping child, a rosy child with thick blonde curls. A keen sense of the emptiness of her own arms stirred in her an envy of the complacent young matron standing at the foot of the little white bed. Perhaps Fred would've been different if they'd had a little one.

"I'd love to have a baby," she breathed discontentedly. "But—"

During the significant pause, Helen linked her arm through the speaker's.

"Let's go down to dinner," she suggested. "You must be famished after your long ride."

At the table, the conversation touched many matters relating to the happenings in the lives of the long separated families. Madelene plied her knife and fork industriously, and jumped from topic to topic, expressing a lively interest in all the events in Ithaca.

"And your brother, dear?" she asked her hostess. "Is he still at the lake place?"

Helen threw a quick glance at her husband, whose lips sank at the corners, his face coloring to a deep red.

When his sister asked the question, the glass from which the elder had been drinking struck the table sharply, as though he wished to emphasize his displeasure.

"Yes, he lives there," he broke in. "In your father's old place, Fred. His lease is not up for almost a year."

"Helen wrote me he had the Skinner girl and her baby with him," said Mrs. Graves. "Wasn't that a funny thing for him to do, Ebbie?"

Waldstricker pushed back angrily.

"Funny! Funny!" he ejaculated. "It isn't decent, and I've told him so, too."

Frederick's face flushed, and he toyed nervously with the silver at the side of his plate.

"But, Ebenezer, you don't mean she's living with him, do you?" he faltered, leaning forward.

"They live there together, Young and the girl and her—" Ebenezer's anger almost made him forget the conventional respect he owed his wife and sister, "—her son," he concluded lamely. "That's all I know, and it's enough. He's had the best houses in Ithaca closed to him on her account."

Indignation at her husband's injustice burnt a red spot in Helen's cheeks and kindled a flame of unusual animation in her placid blue eyes.

161

"You know better, Ebenezer," she retorted. "Forrie's given her a father's care, and every one worth while honors him for it."

Frederick, kept in his attitude of tense attention by a sudden revival of his jealousy of Young, sighed audibly and settled back in his chair.

"I'm glad to hear you say that, Helen," he said earnestly.

"Oh, are you, Fred?" cried Madelene. "So your old interest in that girl isn't dead, yet? Well, all I can say is, I am sorry she didn't get you, but I'll bet she's glad, now, she didn't."

Waldstricker looked keenly from the speaker to her husband. But Frederick had again put on his mask of apathetic indifference and answered his wife's gibe only by a shrug of his shoulders. Noting her brother's scowling face, she went on maliciously.

"You'd better keep away from the lake place, my dear husband, or you'll have both Ebbie and Forrie after you."

"Will you have your tea now, Madelene?" Helen was alarmed at the threatened tempest, and hoped to change the subject.

"Yes, thanks, dear," and to her brother, "After all, Ebbie, Forrie probably knows his own business best. You know he's quite partial to the squatters and always did things for 'em."

Mrs. Waldstricker summoned the servant, and while the dishes were being removed, Ebenezer sat and glowered from Frederick, white and distrait, to his wife, who was explaining to Madelene the way she'd made the salad dressing. When the servant had gone, Waldstricker began again.

"I'm out of patience with Deforrest! If he'd let me alone, I'd had all the squatters off the lake side before this and probably would have located Bishop."

"You've heard nothing of him, Ebbie, I suppose?" asked Madelene. "It does seem queer a dwarf could disappear like that and not a word about him from any part of the world."

Waldstricker's powerful hand clenched the teaspoon in his fingers so violently as to bend the handle.

"No, I haven't," he growled. "I've a notion he's being harbored by some of the squatters. But I want Deforrest to understand this—"

"Oh, let's talk of something else besides squatters," cried Madelene. "Helen, your salad was divine.... Tell me, Ebbie, how you enjoy little Elsie. I think she's lovely."

"Lovely!" he repeated in a very different tone. "Lovely is no word for that child. She's an angel, isn't she, Helen?"

Helen smiled dubiously.

"An angel, very much spoiled, I fear."

"No such thing," argued Waldstricker, glad of an opportunity to air his favorite theory. "Now Helen thinks the child's spoiled because she drops on the floor and kicks and cries until she gets what she wants. I tell her it's human nature, and perfectly right for my child to have her own way. Thank God, there's nothing in the world she can't have."

Then looking from Frederick to his sister, he made a heavy attempt to be humorous.

"What's the matter of you two? You've been married longer than Helen and I. When are you going to start your family?"

Frederick maintained his pose of bored unconcern and an angry flush mounted to Madelene's face.

"You think you're smart, Eb," she retorted. "Fred's all the baby I can look after, and goodness knows he's trouble enough!"

"But, now, you're here, dear," Mrs. Waldstricker extended the olive branch again, "we'll help you look after him.... I do hope the weather'll clear so we can get out. The lake's been simply beautiful this summer."

"Just after I returned from Europe, I tried to dispossess Deforrest," Ebenezer told Fred, "but he beat me in court. I wanted to clean up the scandalous mess. I felt he was breaking God's law in harboring a woman of that kind. But I'm only biding my time." His voice sank as he cast his eyes slowly from one to another, at last, fixing them ominously upon his wife. "Biding my time," he growled deeply, laying his napkin on the table.

The gloom of his manner spread over the diners like a cloud. Helen's face expressed consternation; Frederick's discouragement, and Madelene's impatience.

"I must say this is pleasant," snapped Mrs. Graves. "Ebbie, I forbid you to speak of those people again tonight."

Helen made a little move as though to rise. In her capacity as peacemaker, it seemed advisable to change the scene of hostilities.

"Let's go to the drawing room," she invited.... "Fred, don't you think you'd better go to bed?"

"Yes, I'm all tired out. I think I will."

At the drawing room door, he turned to the stairs.

"Good-night, all," he added, and went slowly up to his room.

Reclining in a big chair, Frederick recalled the talk at the supper table and let his fancy rove in dreams of Tessibel and his son.

What a cruel persecutor Ebenezer was! How Helen had suffered during his outrageous harangue! The young man ground his teeth. So Ebenezer was but biding his time to do some terrible harm to Tessibel and her little boy, his boy! Frederick breathed deeply, and pressed his hand upon his heart. Would the thing never stop beating that way! Would it never in this world quit that awful hurt when he thought of the squatter country! He undressed hastily and went to bed, nor did he speak when Madelene crept softly in beside him.

CHAPTER XL
HUSBAND AND WIFE

The next morning found Frederick Graves more nervous than ever. The weather had cleared. The air, washed by yesterday's downpour, came through the open window sweet to his nostrils. The countryside sparkled in the morning sun and the greens of the woods and fields were deeper and richer; but the beauty of the landscape touched him not. He'd scarcely slept, and when weariness had at last overcome him, his dreams had been filled with visions of a red haired girl, and a sturdy, handsome boy playing about upon the ragged rocks. When he came down to breakfast, Ebenezer told him he'd better see the doctor that day.

"You might go while Madelene and I are out this morning," suggested Helen. "Ah," hearing a child's voice in the hall, "here comes my baby!"

When the door opened, a little girl of three bounded in. Ebenezer held out his arms and Elsie sprang into them.

"Listen to Mrs. Waldstricker," he laughed. "She said, 'my baby,' and I say, she's mine.... Aren't you my baby, pet?"

Helen smiled indulgently. This wee bit of femininity was the one creature who could keep her father amiable from one end of the day to the other.

"My girlie wants to eat with daddy?" Ebenezer went on, his face buried in the flaxen hair. "Then she shall."

"Elsie wants to eat with daddy," parroted the child.

"That's why I say she's spoiled," offered Helen, shrugging her shoulders. "Now her place is in the nursery, but what can I do?"

"Her place is right here on her father's knee," replied Waldstricker, "where I always want her, bless her."

During the discussion about the child, Frederick got up from the table and went out of doors.

As he left the dining room, he had no definite plan; but no sooner had he walked across the front lawn and taken a view of the long road—the way that led to Tessibel and his boy—than his feet, seemingly of their own volition, led him along the grassy path up the hill. If he could only see the two of them without his family knowing! One kiss from his boy, one loving look from Tess, and he felt he could start again to live!

To the sick man the distance was considerable, but minute by minute he grew stronger, restored by revivifying hope. An hour, only a short hour, only a little distance further and he would be at the lake; in sight of the willow trees around the shack. He went down the hill to the top of the lane. Here Tess had come to him that long ago night he'd married her. Every familiar spot stung him with bitter memories of the squatter girl.

He went slowly down and stopped under a great tree opposite the house where he'd formerly lived. Young had the place now, and Tess lived there and his boy. Ebenezer's insinuations hurt him. His jealousy of Deforrest revived. Remorse for his criminal selfishness burned him, an unquenchable fire.

Shaken by conflicting emotions, he went on by the deserted hut under the willows to the lake shore. He'd go out to the ragged rocks and rest, and then he'd try to see Tessibel and the boy.

He came to the great gray slab where he'd left Tess the night he told her of Madelene, and sank down in the shade of the overhanging rocks. Screened from the blazing sun, his hot skin rejoiced in the coolness of the damp grotto.

With unseeing eyes, he glanced out over the glassy mirror of the placid water. Unheeding, he heard none of the bird-calls, and paid no attention to the intimate little sounds of the lake side.

What should he do when at last he saw Tess and the boy? Would he dare claim them?

Suddenly, something made him sit up straight and listen. It was a child's laugh. He got up and stepped behind the hanging shoulder of the rock and waited. He looked cautiously around the jutting-rock, and there, racing toward him through the brilliant sunshine, was a little boy, a handsome, sturdy boy, and bounding along beside him, Kennedy's bulldog.

Then, instinctively, Frederick knew this was his son. He would speak, he must speak! He stepped from his hiding place and came face to face with the little fellow and his companion. The dog, uttering a great growl, crouched on his hind quarters in rage. A stranger had ventured upon ground belonging to his dear ones, and Pete was demanding, in his doglike way, the reason thereof.

"Pete, Pete," called Frederick, soothingly, and Pete dropped his head and came forward, as if to a friend. The boy stood, feet wide-spread, staring fixedly at this man whom Pete knew and he had never seen before.

Frederick patted the dog and smiled ingratiatingly at the boy. He was looking down into a pair of dark eyes, eyes like his own, into the grave face of a child asking why he was there.

The dog nuzzled the man's hand and fawned upon him, making in his throat little noises of welcome.

Frederick held out his other hand.

"Won't you come, too, little boy?"

"I can't!... Mummy wouldn't like it. I don't know you."

"She won't mind, I'm sure," replied Frederick, his heart beating so hard he could hear it. "Pete knows me, and I know your mother. Her name is—is Tessibel.... Isn't it?"

The man could scarcely get that beloved name from between his lips.

"Yes, Tessibel is my mummy," said the boy. "You know my mummy, and my Uncle Forrie?"

"Yes," assented Frederick, sitting down. "Come here and let me tell you all about your mother's beautiful curls."

Boy hitched nearer the tall stranger. He was drawn in some unknown way toward this man whose arms were out-held to him. Then, suddenly, he walked straight into them, his eyes still very grave, still very questioning.

The moment Frederick touched the little one he felt the world was his. He forgot Waldstricker, forgot Madelene, forgot everything, but his elf-like son within his cuddling grasp. He touched his lips to the little face.

"Oh, I've wanted to see you so," he murmured.

"Why didn't you come, then?" demanded Boy.

"I was away," said Frederick.

"My Uncle Forrie goes away, too. When he came home yesterday, he brought me a beautiful engine—it goes on wheels. I love my Uncle Forrie."

"Could you love me, dear?" breathed Frederick.

"Yes, oh, yes. I love everybody. God, too. So does Mummy. And Deacon, he's my owl, and An—"

Boy's lips closed on the nearly spoken word. He suddenly remembered the daily lessons he'd had from his mother never to mention Andy's name to any one; that, if he did, a big man would come and take his darling Andy away. No, Boy couldn't stand that. He wouldn't say anything about Andy, not even to this strangely attractive man.

"What were you going to say, boy?" petitioned Frederick.

"Nothin'. Just nothin'."

And the father was satisfied, satisfied not to talk, glad to have his son so heavenly close. The long years of his exile were slipping away. The nerve-racking yearning of tedious days and yet more tedious, sleepless nights was partially quieted. His son, so long, merely, the pulseless image of his dreams, had become a breathing reality, and the child was the living link between its mother and himself. The longer he held the little one, the more intense grew his desire for Tess. At length this demand urged him to ask,

"Where's your mother?"

"She's home, just up there in that house. She's working."

"You haven't any father?" the man queried at last. A lump rose in his throat and choked him. What had the child been told about him, he wondered.

"Oh, yes, I have somewhere's, but I got another up in the sky, away back in the clouds, Mummy says. And he's awful glad when I'm good, and he cries like anything, when I'm bad. So I try to be good, and sometimes I'm gooder'n gold."

To hear a name from the child's lips, the name he had dreamed of, was the one thought filling his mind.

"Let me be your father?" he said, his voice breaking.

"Sure I will," he answered. "There's my mummy, now!"

Around the jutting rocks came Tess. The red curls hung about her shoulders like a vivid velvet mantle, just as Frederick always dreamed of them. But her figure, in her simple morning dress, was fuller and more womanly. Upon her face was an expression of serenity and peace. Ah! The woman was even more lovely than the girl he'd married, and to the love-hungry man, on the great, gray slab of rock, she was infinitely desirable.

"Mummy," shouted the child, joyfully, "I've found a daddy for us. Petey and me found him."

Tess stared at the man, undisguised horror and dismay written in her eyes. She'd not seen Frederick since that day he'd urged her to marry Sandy Letts to escape Waldstricker, whose hands, he'd described, as stronger'n God's. She'd hardly heard of him after he and Madelene had gone West. She had long ago ceased to feel any desire for him. Indeed, she scarcely thought of him. During the full happy years since she left the shanty, under the loving tuition of Deforrest Young, the disgrace this man on the rocks had heaped upon her had covered its claws and lacerated her no more. But, at the sight of him, visions of the past reared themselves in her imaginative mind. Memory, suddenly, flung all the cruelties of his treatment of her into a kaleidoscopic jumble, and meddlesome fear presented numerous suggestions of calamity. A moment she stood as if turned to stone.

"Come on, come," Boy cried, tugging at her dress.

Frederick struggled to his feet, and held out his arms.

"Tessibel, oh, my Tess, be kind," he supplicated.

But she'd taken the child's hand and without answering, was making her way swiftly backward to the rock-path.

CHAPTER XLI
TESSIBEL'S DISCOVERY

Frederick stood for one tense minute watching Tessibel hurry over the rocks. Many times he had pictured this interview, ... even framed the sentences in which he would express his remorse and win her forgiveness. It had never occurred to his brooding thought that the years of absence which had increased his own ardor, might have lessened the squatter girl's regard for him. But the meeting wasn't working out as he'd planned. He'd been almost paralyzed at her coming, speechless except for the few halting words of entreaty. Now, it dawned upon him that she was going away without a word, that she was taking the child with her, and that he might never see either of them again.

"Tessibel," he called hoarsely. "Stop, or ... I'll tell Waldstricker."

His words brought Tess to a standstill. The threat filled her with fear, for well she knew the elder's power. Still keeping hold of Boy's hand, she retraced her steps.

"Why did you come here?" she asked, fear and distaste making her voice cold and hard.

"To see you and ... him." Frederick pointed to the child, who was now hiding behind his mother's skirts.

"Well, now you've seen us."

Frederick stared at the speaker, his lips pursed with surprise. Was this Tess Skinner, the squatter girl? The voice was hers, but its tones were resonant with contempt! Face and form he recognized, but not the new poise, the dignity of her motherhood. The brown eyes he remembered as lighted by love, now expressed unutterable abhorrence.

"Tess, dear Tess," he pleaded, "let me talk to you."

Tess stooped over the child, rearranged his little waist, and pushed back the curly hair.

"Boy go home now, and mother'll come directly."

She kissed the bewildered upturned face. The baby couldn't understand what was going on.... Mummy seemed sad, and the nice man, who was so white and sick looking, had spoken angrily to his beautiful mother.

"I'd rather stay wif you," he lisped.

"But Mummy asks Boy to go," said Tess, and to the dog, "Here, Petey, go home with Boy."

Placing his hand on the dog's collar, the child turned slowly and unwillingly toward the house. He'd taken but a few halting steps along the rocks before Frederick's voice rang out.

"Tess, Tessibel, let me hold him ... kiss him once more. Don't shake your head! Don't say no! I've wanted him so all these years. Oh, Tessibel!"

His pitiful pleading touched the listening girl. At last, face to face with the man whose cowardice and selfishness had brought her so much trouble, her one desire was to escape ... to run away. But he was begging for her to be kind, to allow him to hold her baby!... What right had he to kiss him?... To be sure, the child was his, too, but—but—

"Oh, No! No! I don't want you to!" she cried, protesting. "You can never be anything in his life. Why don't you let us alone?"

Frederick had walked very close to her side by this time, his white face twitching.

"I must kiss him once more," he persisted.

Tess turned to the loitering child. She could see that at a word of assent from her, Boy would rush into the outstretched arms Frederick held toward him. The mother, with a twist at her heart, recognized the tie which drew together this man and her son. A dreadful fear clutched her. Would Frederick do as he had threatened, hoping that he might thus come in contact with his son? Her mind flew to Deforrest Young.... He must never know the name of Boy's father. She could feel the blood coursing madly through her temples, and her head ached dully.

Nevertheless, she went back and took hold of the child's hand.

"You may kiss the gentleman ... good-bye," she said in a constrained voice.

"The pretty man was goin' to be my faver," said the child, pleadingly. "I want a daddy awful bad."

"Yes, yes, I know," Tess returned tremulously. "Now hurry, dear, and then run home."

Only too gladly did the child jump away and bound into his father's extended arms.

"Mummy says I has to go home," he whispered.

While the tall man silently caressed the dark curls of her boy, Tess of the Storm Country endured such pain as she'd never known before. The mutual attraction between the two, so differently related to her, seemed anomalous and impossible.

Frederick unwillingly allowed the child to slip to the rocks and after Tess'd started Boy and the dog on their homeward way, she stood before him, her lips quivering. She knew he, too, suffered, and she waited quietly as he dried his eyes and recovered his choking breath.

She was sorry he'd come. She'd hoped never to see him again. But, now, she must be assured that he would continue the deception in regard to the past. As anxious as she had once been to have him claim her as his own, to tell the world she belonged to him, she, now, wanted to keep silent.

"It was useless for you to come," she chided presently.

Frederick made an impetuous movement with his hand.

"Oh, no, it wasn't.... Won't you let me atone, let me make up for all the things I've done ... and haven't done? I want—oh, how I want—"

"It's too late," interrupted the girl. "Much too late."

"But, Tessibel, I know you love me. You can't have forgotten. And I'll make the boy love me. He does now! Didn't you hear him call me father?"

"He has no father," she responded coldly. "And I—I haven't any love left for you."

The words were low but distinctly spoken.

"I don't believe it!... I won't!... You shall love me!... I won't have you with Young. ... He can see my boy every day ... be with you hour after hour.... I hate him!"

"You hate him!" Tessibel's eyes burned and flashed with indignation. "When you should be grateful, because he's done everything you should've done.... You've said all you can. You can't make up to us ... the baby and me.... Won't you please go?"

Frederick felt he was losing his reason. The love he'd nursed in secret, the passion that had wasted him away, shook his frail frame. He wouldn't be denied!

"God help me, I won't go!" he gritted, the words carrying on his thought.

With one sweep of his arms, he encircled Tess in a close embrace. She made frantic efforts to free herself, but Frederick, strong under the emotion consuming him, only hugged her closer.

"Let me go!" Tess almost screamed the words. Then, her voice changed to a tense whisper, hoarse with loathing. "How can ... oh, how dare you!"

But she could not protect her face from the searching mouth. Violently, Frederick twisted her around and for one moment his lips fell upon hers. Deep groans came between the kisses he thrust upon her.

A moment later the sound of advancing steps lifted Frederick's face from hers. Muttering an oath, he threw Tess forcibly from him, for there in the path was Ebenezer Waldstricker, about whose sagging lips played a supercilious smile.

"So I was not mistaken," he sneered, looking his brother-in-law full in the face. "If Madelene doesn't care, I do."

"Well?" growled Frederick. "You've found me here, now do what you cursed want to, I don't care."

"Perhaps you'll care before I finish," said the elder grimly, and he included the girl in his baleful glare. "I think you both will."

Tessibel's mind flew to Boy. What could these two men do to her darling?

She went forward toward Waldstricker, her eyes raised appealingly to his.

"Won't you make Mr.... Mr. Graves keep away?" she petitioned. "I don't want him here."

"Yes, it looked, when I came around the corner, as if you didn't want him, miss," scoffed the elder. Then he laughed, and the laugh cut the throbbing girl to the quick. "Very much as if you wanted him to go.... Now, then, sir, what's this girl to you?"

"I'm nothing to him, Mr. Waldstricker," she asserted, without giving Frederick a chance to speak.

Graves still felt that maddening passion, that demand for his own.

"She lies," he said in low tones.

Tess turned to him passionately.

"You know what I say is true. You came here without my desiring it! I don't want anything to do with you.... Haven't you both harmed me enough?... Do I ever come around and hurt you?... Why don't you tell the truth?"

"All right," he shouted, his irritation at her resistance overcoming his fear of the elder. "If you want the truth, here it is. I'm——"

"Don't! Don't!" screamed Tess.

"Ah!" hissed Waldstricker's lips like a jet of steam.

He'd caught within his powerful net the girl he wanted. He'd bring to light the secret that'd preyed upon his sister's spirits so long. For the squatter girl he felt no pity, for Frederick only contempt. They were both weaklings that he'd sweep away in his pursuit of Young and the squatters.

"He's sick," said Tessibel, trying to discount Frederick's confession. "Your brother-in-law's sick. You can see that!... He thinks ... why, he's mad!"

"I'm not mad!" Frederick turned upon her fiercely, then back to the big man whose eagerness bent him forward. "I'm the father of her boy."

The blood left Waldstricker's face, so that it looked like carved marble.

"So 'tis so," he got out, "and you admit it, you cur, and you dared to marry my sister? Now, as God lets me live, you'll both suffer for this, and as for you, Tessibel Skinner, look out for that bastard of yours!"

The squatter girl uttered a heart-broken cry, and turning, fled around the rocks into the lane and up the hill.

CHAPTER XLII
A MAN'S ARM AT THE WINDOW

It seemed to Tess that her feet were leaden, as if she could never traverse the distance between the ragged rocks and the house. The interview with Frederick had been a terrible ordeal, and she was sick with disgust from his odious kisses. Waldstricker's untimely appearance and his stinging taunts hurt and frightened her. She knew he would do his worst and that Frederick wouldn't or couldn't help it. The desire to get Boy into her arms, to keep him from the men below urged her on. Wildly, she fled through the orchard, crying as she went.

"Boy! Mummy's Boy! Where's Mummy's Boy?"

Gasping for breath, her voice ejected the words explosively. Exhausted, she sank upon the top step of the porch. The long run up the hill had been almost too much, but in a moment, she lifted herself, still calling and panting, and stumbled into the house.

"He's upstairs with Andy," said Young, looking up from his book. Then, alarmed by her appearance, he jumped up and hurried to her. "What's the matter, Tess? Tell me."

"Where's the baby?" she demanded hysterically, clinging to him.... "Tell me where my baby is."

Drawing her into an easy chair, Deforrest attempted to quiet her.

"Boy's upstairs with Andy. Hush, hush, child! Don't cry like that!... Oh, my little girl!... What is it?... What's happened? Tell me ... quick!"

But Tess couldn't speak. She only clung to his arms, trying to stifle her gasping cries.

Just then Boy's clear laugh came pealing down the stairway, a conclusive comfort to his mother's heart. When her extreme agitation had subsided. Professor Young sat down and called her to him. As of old, when first he had heard her lessons in his home, she dropped at his feet, resting her curly head against his knee.

"Now I want to know what's frightened you," said he, softly.

The girl made a gesture of refusal. "I can't tell it," she replied, under her breath. "It's too terrible! It's too awful!"

"There's nothing too terrible for me to know," answered Young. "What happened while you were out?"

"Don't ask me to tell you, Uncle Forrie," pleaded Tess. "I can't! I can't!"

"Tessibel," demanded the lawyer, "was it Sandy Letts?"

"Oh, no, no, not him!"

The man pondered a moment.

"Was it—"

"Please don't ask me any more questions." She lifted a crimson face. "I was foolish, I suppose, but I thought, I thought the baby—"

"Some one threatened Boy! Was that it, Tessibel?" he cross-questioned.

"Yes." The murmured answer was scarcely audible.

"One of the squatters, then?"

The red head sank again. This time a decided shake of the shining curls made the denial.

Hoping to avoid further examination, the girl tried to rise to her feet, but the questioner's hand pressed her back.

"Don't ask me," she entreated. "I'm better now."

She tried to smile, but the sweet lips trembled. Young hadn't seen her so stirred in all the years of her residence in his house. He'd been able to hold his love in check while he saw her happy and content, but her present pitiful state broke down the barriers he'd erected and hardly conscious of the change in his attitude, he kissed her.

Tess drew away sharply. The strange new quality in his caress aroused an answering thrill the length of her body. In that moment she discovered how deeply she loved Deforrest Young.

"Don't ... don't kiss me! Never, never kiss me again."

What was it she had said? The man felt his heart contract with a shooting pain.

"Why, child, I've kissed you since you were a little girl.... Why shouldn't I?"

"I don't know, I don't know," she faltered. "Somehow it's different, now."

Something in her tones, some dejection in the bowed head brought the man's hand from the shrouding curls. His heart began to live again, to come forth from beneath his stern will and make known its own desire.

"Tess," his voice tense with emotion, "will you marry me?... Will you, Tess?"

The girl got to her feet, swaying. Marry him? Her fingers twisted together as her eyes dropped before the expression of his. He, too, was on his feet, holding out his arms.

"I'd ... marry you," she confessed haltingly, "but I can't."

"Is it Boy?" demanded Young. "Why, child, don't you know I love him almost as if he were my own?"

"I can't," wailed Tess, again. "How I wish I could!"

"You saw some one today, didn't you, Tessibel?"

She nodded affirmatively, but volunteered nothing further.

"I must know," cried the man. "Don't you see, child, you've just told me—Tess, look at me."

The drooping lids raised slowly.

"Tess, when you said you desired to marry me, did you mean—oh, you meant you love me, child dear, didn't you?"

"Yes," she breathed.

"Then, can't you see your love for me and mine for you makes it necessary I should know everything? Some one today—tell me, dear."

"Waldstricker came down—" Tess paused, but trembled on. "I was talking to—"

"Who?" ejaculated Young, fiercely. "Who?"

"The baby's father."

Shocked by her unexpected answer, he dropped into his chair and covered his face with his hands.

"Don't feel that way," she whispered. "Listen, I'll tell you about it.... Boy ran to the rocks with Pete, and I went after him. I found him there with—with—"

"Oh, Tess," groaned Young.

"His father's been away a long time," the girl went on, "and now he's

172

back, and he wanted to see the baby, and then I sent Boy home and Waldstricker came—"

"My God! won't you ever tell me who was there with you?"

Boy's mother bowed her head, and through the red hair came two trembling words, just one whispered name that seared the man's heart like flames.

"Frederick Graves."

Only one long shudder showed the listener's agony. Tess, too, remained quiet, her veins bursting with pulsing blood. She could not tell him the rest, Frederick hadn't told, neither could she. Her promise on the rocks, so many years ago, still bound her.

The lawyer lowered his hands, and the whiteness of his face drew Tessibel to her knees beside him.

"I've always made you sad," she murmured. "I'm sorry, forgive me."

"Just tell me ... all," he insisted.

Then she began at the beginning and told him over again how Boy had gone to the rocks with Pete and she went after him. At the part where Frederick had taken her in his arms, she faltered. In the light of the wonderful, new love for Deforrest, she couldn't go on!

"Won't you let me ... keep the rest?" she implored.

"No, I will not!" groaned the man. "I will not!"

"Then, let me stand up."

She got up slowly and stood looking out of the window.

"He kissed and kissed me," she said, choking, "and just then Waldstricker came and ... saw."

"Oh, God help me!" the heavy voice pleaded.

Tess knelt again. His supplicating cry aroused her faith to vivid activity. Deforrest had prayed, "God help me!" and, oh, so differently than the same words used by Frederick a short time previous. He was bearing pain for her. Hadn't she suffered, too, and time and again called into the heart of the Infinite for help? And always at the times needed, it had come. God would surely help her friend. Tess forgot herself in her ardent desire to comfort him.

"He will help you, dear," she whispered. "He'll always help when you ask Him. Didn't He get Daddy Skinner out of Auburn and He kept Andy with me in the shanty till we came to you? Oh, I know He'll help you and me, Uncle Forrie."

The loving appellation, taught Boy when first he could lisp, roused the man as perhaps nothing else would have done. The three of them still needed him, needed him more than ever. He was there at their sides like a wall of stone, to defend, to love and protect. And whatever happened, Tess loved him!

He drew her to her feet and smiled a twisted smile into the lovely face. This day had started another epoch in their lives. She had said God would help, and he had learned many lessons from the squatter girl. For the first time in his life he understood something of the overwhelming faith of Tessibel Skinner. Yes, he would be helped!

The girl's next words cut off his thought.

"Waldstricker said he'd hurt Boy," she said, flushing, "but, but—"

"But you have faith he can't, haven't you, Tess?"

"Of course!" she nodded. "I know he can't! You remember the day Waldstricker tried to get me and you came and stopped him, how I told you I knew he couldn't," and more softly, "do you remember what I said when you went away that day?"

"Yes, indeed, I do, dear! I've often thought of it. 'Love is everywhere, the hull time,'" and, he smiled.

Radiantly she told him, "And, now, somehow, I know that Love will let me be all yours some day."

Young turned swiftly, and going to the door, swung out without another word, and Tess hurried upstairs to Boy.

CHAPTER XLIII
SANDY'S JOB

Tessibel Skinner's flight left Ebenezer Waldstricker and Graves together on the ragged rocks. The bigger man turned and surveyed the other, scorn, anger and disgust struggling for expression in his face. The latter, paying no apparent attention to the enraged elder, leaned against an outcropping gray rock and fixed his gaze on the lake, noting mechanically the play of sunshine and shadow upon its dazzling bosom.

Through the elder's seething mind thoughts tumbled tumultuously. Could this moody, pale-faced man be the same nice young fellow that had married Madelene? How had he dared to marry her, and having done so, what had compelled him, after all this time, to acknowledge the Skinner brat?

He walked forward a step or two, coughed and began to speak. Frederick seemed not to hear him.

"I said," repeated Waldstricker, "I've discovered what I've suspected for four years."

Frederick allowed his eyes to rest an instant on his brother-in-law's dark, passionate face. Then, again, he turned his attention to the lake.

"And I don't intend to allow my sister to suffer by this," went on the elder.

"I suppose you'll tell her, won't you?" questioned the other, foreseeing unpleasant complications and already regretting the rashness that'd betrayed him.

"She won't learn it from me," promised Ebenezer.

"Nor from me," agreed Frederick. "I've no wish to have a whining woman hanging to my neck."

Waldstricker muttered an oath under his breath.

"Well, of all the contemptible pups in the world!" he snorted. "Talk of ingratitude! Here's a girl, a good girl, too, and Madelene's that—"

"No one said she wasn't," snapped Graves. "But her goodness doesn't keep her from nagging, my dear Ebenezer."

"Shut up!" snarled his opponent, the last atom of his patience exhausted by the speaker's flippant criticism. "You cur, you deserve a good thrashing, and I'm going to give it to you, now!"

Jumping for him, he lifted his arm to strike, but before the mighty fist descended, Frederick, outworn by his long walk and the excitement of the morning, slumped upon the rocks, a limp form at his assailant's feet. Stunned, the tall man gazed down at the crumpled figure, and mechanically lowered his arm. Then, he stooped, examined his fallen foe and stretched him out upon the rocks. Leaving him there, Waldstricker hurried to the lake and filled his hat with water, and returning, bathed the stricken man's face and neck. In a few moments, the faintness passed, and Frederick drew himself to a sitting posture against the rocks.

"You great brute! It's like you to strike a sick man," the white lips taunted, as soon as their owner could speak.

The slurring words brought a hot blush of shame to Ebenezer's face.

"I'm sorry, Fred," he stammered at length. "I was so angry I must've forgotten you're not well. I'm glad I didn't strike you. But what are we going to do, now?... If we don't tell Madelene, how about the Skinner girl?... Won't she make trouble for us?"

"No, she won't say anything, I'm sure!" Frederick's voice was low, but positive. "She doesn't want to have anything more to do with me. What she said about not wanting me was true. She wouldn't stop to speak to me, even, until I threatened to tell you.... I suppose Young's made her so happy she's glad to forget me."

"What gets me is how you and Young, decent fellows, got mixed up with such a girl," Ebenezer growled meditatively.

"If you knew Tess as I do, ... you'd understand," wailed Frederick. "She's the dearest, bravest, sweetest girl in the world."

"Bosh!... Now, the question is about getting you home. My buggy's up in the road. Do you think you can walk there?"

"I guess so."

With his brother-in-law's help, Frederick got to his feet. Slowly, leaning on the big man's supporting arm, he made his way, with many pauses for rest, to the waiting vehicle.

Waldstricker put his companion into the carriage and unhitched the horse. Instead of getting in beside him, he handed him the reins, saying as he did so,

"You can drive all right, can't you? Old Ned knows the way back and will go home if you let him alone. I want to see Young."

Before turning away, the speaker chirruped to the horse, which started

175

obediently up the hill toward Ithaca, drawing after him what cowardly selfishness had left of Frederick Graves.

The elder walked slowly up the path to Young's house, turning over in his mind to what advantage he could best use his newly acquired knowledge.

Coming out of the door hurriedly, Deforrest Young met his brother-in-law face to face as the latter rounded the corner of the house. At the sight of this pompous person, whose meddling threatened so much trouble to his dear ones, the indignation which Tessibel's words had in a measure quieted, flared up anew. He wanted to fight, to pound, and if possible to kill with his hands the man in front of him.

"You'd better come no farther," he said between set teeth. "Just stay where you are!... I shan't be responsible for my acts if you don't."

"So she's told you," said Waldstricker, laughing loudly. "And it hurts, eh? Now, you know what you're keeping?"

Trembling with suppressed passion, the lawyer walked deliberately to the steps, his face waxen-white.

"I told you to come no nearer. I'd advise you to go away," said he. His low voice, contrasting sharply with his flushed cheeks and blazing eyes, testified eloquently of the tremendous curb imposed upon his temper.

"Yes, she told me, ..." he continued in the same tone, "and the more she told me, the more heartily I pitied her. She told me of your threats, too, but I want you to understand, the moment you turn your hands against her, I'll fix you."

"Don't forget my wife's your sister. I'll see our family's honor upheld even if you've forgotten it." Waldstricker simulated a confidence he didn't quite feel.

Young's fists knotted.

"You mind your business, Ebenezer, and let my house alone."

Waldstricker, kicking uneasily at a stone in his path, thought a moment. At last he looked up.

"I'll let your house alone all right, if you'll get rid of that girl, and that—"

He didn't use the word he'd intended. Deforrest didn't give him time.

"My house is my own," he interjected. "If you watch yours, you'll have all you can 'tend to."

"I'll go," said the big man, hoarsely, "but I don't say I won't come again, and I warn you, as I warned that squatter girl, when the time comes—"

"Get out!" snarled Deforrest, starting down the steps, "and get quick."

And the elder, not daring to stay, turned and went toward the pear orchard. It was then, that he glanced up and saw Tessibel and her little one at an upper window, watching with startled eyes for his departure. The baby turned from the window and raised his arms to some one within, and a hand below a man's rough coat sleeve clasped the boy and lifted him up out of Waldstricker's sight.

Walking along the road to Ithaca, he reviewed the exciting events of the morning and tried to consider and determine the complications they involved. He was unable to find a motive for Frederick's dramatic announcement, although he did not for a moment doubt its truth. It was queer though that, after having kept still so long, he should blurt out his secret in that fashion. He considered his promise not to tell Madelene and concluded he'd been wise. Probably Frederick wouldn't live long anyway, and in the natural course of things, Madelene would soon be free and the Graves chapter ended. He wondered what had kept Tess silent all these years. How had she withstood his persecution even in her betrayer's presence and made no sign? He was glad she had, but he couldn't understand why. Evidently the girl's disclosure to Young wasn't going to make any difference in his brother-in-law's conduct. Suddenly, like a bolt shot into the midst of his revery, rose the question. Whose arm was that? Young was on the porch, the girl and the baby in plain sight at the window. But there was some one else, a man. He had seen his arm and coat sleeve.

"That's certainly peculiar," he ruminated. "I didn't know Young had any one else there. It may be all right, of course, but it seems mighty suspicious."

All the way home and all the evening, the thing bothered him. In every way imaginable he tried to account for that other man in Young's house. He canvassed the neighborhood. A chance visitor wouldn't be upstairs, and anyhow he'd have looked out to see the row with Young. But this man kept away from the window. He'd only shown his hand and arm. Whoever he was, he was hiding in Young's home.

Was his brother-in-law a party to it? A man couldn't be kept for any length of time in the house without his knowing it. Young and Tess were hiding someone! At bed time he decided that the next day he would find out who was the other man in Young's house. It might give him a hold on his obstreperous brother-in-law and the hateful squatter girl.

CHAPTER XLIV
SANDY'S VISIT

The next day, Ebenezer Waldstricker met Lysander Letts, just back from Auburn, loitering along Buffalo Street near the Lehigh Valley station. The prison-pallor of the squatter's face and hands and the ill-fitting, cheap prison clothes on his big body made him conspicuous among the men on the street. Waldstricker pulled up his team.

"Sandy," he called, "come to the office when you're uptown. I want to see you."

An hour or so later, the squatter slouched into Waldstricker's private room.

The elder rose and greeted him.

"So you're out again?" The question was really a statement.

"Yes," assented Letts, sitting down on the edge of the chair, "an' I wouldn't a been if I hadn't been let out on good behavior. I made up my mind I wouldn't stay a minute longer'n I had to."

"I guess after this you won't be stealing dead bodies, will you?" asked the rich man.

"Nope, you bet I won't! I've enough of Auburn. It ain't like the Ithaca jail!... Heard anythin' of Tess Skinner?"

"Yes, she's got a boy over three years old."

Lysander nodded his head slowly, as if he'd received confirmation of a conclusion previously formed.

"Thought likely," he muttered. "Where air she livin'? I met Jake Brewer on the street an' he says she air left the shack."

"So she has, but not very far away.... Letts, I want you to do something for me. Are—or I might put it—do you still want to make up to the Skinner girl?"

Sandy's face grew dark with uncontrollable anger.

"I want to rip the skin offen her inch by inch," he snarled.

The other man gave a low, mirthless laugh. The picture of the girl he disliked so intensely, writhing in the great hands of the brute opposite him, appealed to the elder's sardonic humor.

"That wouldn't be a bad idea," he averred. "But she's got some one who won't see her hurt."

Letts jumped up and stepped close to the desk where the other was sitting. Here was a complication he hadn't anticipated. He moistened his dry lips with a tobacco stained tongue and demanded,

"Who air he?... Air she married?"

"No, she's living in Graves' old place, the house I, now, own, with Deforrest Young."

"Ye mean, your wife's brother, the lawyer?"

Waldstricker nodded.

"An' ye say she air livin' with him?"

"Well not exactly that, I suppose, but she's keeping house for him. She's got her child there, too."

"Has, eh?" said Sandy, dryly.

A wicked look came over his face and he slouched back into his chair. Ebenezer went to his office window and looked into the street.

"Want to earn some money, Letts?" he demanded, without turning around.

"You bet! Ye bet I do!"

Ebenezer returned to his desk and sat down again facing his visitor.

"You'll have to go about this business carefully."

"Trust me," promised the squatter.

"I am. There's a mystery about Young's house—I mean, there's some one in it beside my brother-in-law, the Skinner girl, and the boy."

178

"Who air it?" The question was no perfunctory expression of interest. Anything relating to Tess was vitally important.

"That's what I want you to find out. It's a man!"

"Mebbe it's the brat's pa," offered the other.

"No, it isn't, and by the way, you let up trying to find out about that."

"What do ye mean?" interjected Sandy, sullenly.

"I mean I want that matter dropped."

Letts merely grunted, for to acquire that information was one of the first things he intended to do, but there was no use telling the elder so.

"What ye want?" he muttered.

"I'll give you a hundred dollars to find out the name of the other man living at Young's."

"Done!" cried the squatter. "Do I get any of the dough, now?"

"Part of it, if you like," replied Waldstricker, slipping his hand into his pocket. "But listen to me. You're to come directly back here and tell me, when you find out. Discover his name, if you don't know the man. Do you understand?"

"I does that. You leave it to me. Then, I'll settle with Tess Skinner."

"As you please about her," consented Waldstricker. "Go along now. I'm busy."

CHAPTER XLV
ANDY VINDICATED

Lysander Letts left Waldstricker's office highly pleased. He was going to see Tess, and he had twenty-five dollars in his pocket. In the long hours of silent meditation in prison, he'd tried to outline that meeting, and to figure out how he could work Waldstricker. His errand provided for both contingencies.

He swaggered along the street, bumped into people roughly, and for his rudeness gave them oaths instead of apologies. At an inlet saloon, he displayed his money ostentatiously, and bought many drinks for himself and the "setters." The squatter's capacity for the Rhine whiskey had been impaired by his imprisonment, and it was not long before he began to feel the effects of his liquor. A full pint in his hip pocket, Sandy, finally, broke away from his companions and started up the railroad tracks for the Silent City. Staggering a little, he meditated with drunken seriousness what he had done and was going to do.

179

Famished by his detention in prison, he hungered for the sight of Tess. All the fierce passion of his undisciplined nature clamored for her. And when he had her, he'd carry out all the brutalities conceived in the long nights in his cell. He'd find out the father of her boy. If that duffer, Waldstricker, could discover it, he could. He'd make Tess tell. He'd show Young, too. He'd get even with the lawyer for helping send him to Auburn. His grievance grew more active every step he carried his load of liquor through the broiling sun, the long four miles from Ithaca.

"Wait till I get 'em," he muttered over and over, "I'll show 'em what's what."

Before he reached the lane leading past Young's place to the Skinner shack, he left the tracks and climbed the fence. Throwing his legs over the top, he sat down to enjoy the breeze which blew from the green lake, and, vibrating the leaves and bowing the shrubs and grasses, swept up and over the hill into the illimitable space beyond. Sandy wanted another drink, and reached back to his hip for it. The bottle stuck in the pocket and he jerked at it savagely. He pulled it out, but he, also, lost his balance, and in his efforts to save himself from falling, smashed the bottle on the top rail of the fence. The whiskey ran down to the ground and the thirsty moss drank it up.

Letts gazed at the jagged-edged glass in his hand, stupefied by the magnitude of his calamity. Then he drew a long breath and cursed his luck. He cursed the bottle, the fence, the whiskey, Waldstricker, who'd sent him, and Tess and the unknown man, on whose account he'd been sent. His maledictions included everything except his own drunken clumsiness.

Bye and bye, he got down from the fence, muttering and grumbling to himself. Cautiously, in spite of his inflamed temper, he worked his way through the trees. There was no sign of life about the house, but large hammocks swung in the breeze on the porch. The squatter walked around and around, keeping far enough away so his movements could not be noticed. He stopped under a large tree to look up at the windows Waldstricker had described.

Attracted by a sound to his right, he wheeled about and saw Tessibel coming down the hill. His breath came sharply through his dark teeth. Never had the girl been so desirable, and for the instant, he felt possessed to rush upon her, to take her in his arms, to hold her close. Then, Waldstricker came into his mind. Before he worked his will on the squatter girl, he must find out the name of the unknown man. He had to please the elder to get the rest of the money. But to speak to her would be all right. He might discover something. He walked stealthily through the trees and placed himself so that when the girl turned toward the house, she would meet him face to face.

Tess was humming happily. When her eyes rested upon Lysander Letts, she stopped.

"Hello, brat!" grinned Sandy.

The girl didn't answer. His prison pallor fascinated her. It contrasted so sharply with the wind-tanned brown of the swarthy skin she remembered. All the accumulated horror of him, which had been forgotten while he was safely restrained at Auburn, swept over her.

"I said hello!" sniggered the other, once more. "Ain't ye glad to see me?"

Ignoring his question, the frightened girl assumed a haughtiness quite unusual, and in her turn questioned coldly,

"What do you want?"

"What do I want?" mocked Letts, not a whit disturbed by her manner. "I want you!"

Tessibel stepped to one side, but the squatter put himself in front of her, again.

"Now none of yer foolin'," he growled, and he added to his remarks a collection of sulphurous epithets.

"Sandy," commanded the young woman, still in her grand manner, "step out of my way! Right now! Do you hear?"

Unmoved, her drunken tormentor flung up his arms, hands open in assumed disgust.

"Well, hark to the way the squatter girl's talkin', will ye?" he sneered. "I'll take that outten ye, kid, afore I've had ye long. Where air yer brat?"

The brown eyes, responsive to his suggestion, glanced toward the house. There was Boy coming slowly up the little path toward her. He dearly enjoyed the rare occasions when visitors came, and his face lighted up when he saw the man talking to his mother.

"Boy, run back home," she called.

Sandy made a dash down the hill toward the child, shouting curses and commands to him.

"Wait, kid! Don't ye move! I want ye."

The young mother instantly flew after him. Her swift feet took her on and on, up to and past the squatter whose speed was impaired by his years of confinement and the whiskey he'd swallowed. Then, she flung herself in front of the child and held out her arms.

"Stop, Sandy! Wait!" she panted. "I'll talk to you. Let the baby go home."

The race which had flushed the girl's cheeks and deepened her breathing, left the fat squatter wind-broken and exhausted.

"Let 'im go, then," gasped Sandy.

"Go back, Boy dear," urged Tess.

Boy didn't move. He seemed mesmerized by the strangely white face of the drunken man.

"Mummy, come home, too," he hesitated.

"Yer mummy can't. Git out, ye beggar, afore I kick ye!" threatened Sandy.

His breathing was easier but the discomfort he felt aggravated his ugly mood. He reached forth one of his great arms and, seizing the child by the shoulder, threw him roughly to the ground. The little one, more frightened than hurt, cried loudly. His shrill shriek of terror reached the ears of the dwarf. Alarmed, Andy sprang to the window and looked out.

The scene on the lawn below petrified him. Tess was picking up the child, and standing over her, fists doubled menacingly, was—Lysander Letts.

181

Andy thought the enraged squatter was going to kill her and Boy. Wholly forgetful of his own danger, he continued to watch.

His small boyish face was still at the pane, when Lysander looked up. Andy saw the upturned glance and flung himself back out of sight. Had Letts seen him? Impelled to look out again, he drew a long breath of relief. Tess and the child were slowly coming, hand in hand, toward the house, and the man they feared was making his way through the orchard.

"I saw Sandy," was the dwarf's greeting. "What was he a botherin' you about, honey?"

"I thought he was going to kill Boy. But suddenly he said good-bye and went away. Were you at the window, Andy?"

"For just a minute, kid. I don't think he saw me. I heard Boy cry, an' that's why I went."

A frightened feeling took possession of the girl.

"I hope he didn't see you. Did he, Andy?"

"Sure not. I was watching him all the time. I dodged back before he looked up."

Tess considered the little man a minute.

"If you saw him look up," she argued, "maybe he saw you looking down. Oh, I hope he didn't, but I'm afraid he did," and she sighed.

Sandy Letts had recognized the dwarf. The shock of the discovery sobered him. He couldn't bother with Tess and her brat any longer. He had business in Ithaca! Waldstricker's five thousand dollars, so long sought and so eagerly desired, summoned him. All the way to town, he built castles in Spain with the money. Through every dream, like a thread of hate, ran the purpose to get Tess, and when he had the girl, to torture her through her child.

When he arrived at Waldstricker's office, he found the elder absent. An evil leer on his face, he swaggered up and down the street, his hands thrust deep into his pockets.

He had made the great discovery of his life. He had lined his pockets with gold, and more than that, he had made a lifelong friend of one of the powerful men in Ithaca.

He saw Waldstricker when he turned the corner from State and made his way down Tioga. The squatter turned into the large building, slunk in an alcove, and waited. He heard the heavy tread of the elder on the stairs, heard him pass and go higher up. A few minutes later, he followed.

When he opened the door, Waldstricker greeted him.

"Back again?"

"Yep," chuckled Letts.

"With news, I hope," stated the other.

"Sure," replied Sandy.

"Then tell me," answered Waldstricker, peremptorily. "I'm busy today."

"Did ye ever hear anything of Bishop?" asked the squatter.

"No, I never did."

"Want to?"

"Yes."

"Air that reward up, yet?"

"Certainly. But why all this talk? If you know anything speak out!"

Sandy walked very near the rich man, lowered his voice, and said,

"I found 'im, mister."

Ebenezer's nose was offended by the rank odor of liquor Sandy exuded.

"You're not telling me the truth," he asserted. "You've been drinking. You're drunk now."

"Yep, I air drunk some, but I air tellin' ye what's so," insisted Letts. "Andy Bishop air the man ye saw t'other day."

"In my brother-in-law's house!" gasped Waldstricker, beginning to comprehend all that Sandy's discovery meant.

"Yep, that air it," replied Sandy.

"My God, oh, I thank thee!" ejaculated the elder, falling into his chair.

"How long he air been there, I don't know," continued Sandy.

"And that doesn't matter.... Now, then, to get him back to Auburn. I want it fixed to hustle him there quick, so Young can't put a stay on the proceedings."

Breathing hard, he took out his watch.

"It's half past four. Do those people have the least idea you saw Bishop?"

"Nope, but I saw 'im all right," said Letts, an expression of satisfied malice animating his ugly white face. "Maybe we can't make it hot for that dum lawyer who air got my girl, now."

Towering over Waldstricker's desire to lock up his father's murderer, was the wish to get even with Deforrest Young and Tessibel Skinner. If they'd had the dwarf all this time, they were all in his power. Now, he would wring their hearts! He'd show them no mercy.

"We'll even up some old scores, eh, Sandy?" he agreed.... "You get sober and be here tomorrow morning at nine o'clock, sober—cold sober, understand?"

"Sure, Mr. Waldstricker, sure, I get ye. I ain't tight now, not real soused."

Moving to the door, he stopped. "But I air not goin' to swig any more booze till we gets Andy Bishop an' I finger that reward."

More intoxicated by his dreams of affluence than by the liquor he'd had, the pale-faced graduate of Auburn swung out of the room and clattered down the stairs.

After Waldstricker'd written and despatched a letter and a telegram, he closed the office and went home.

Helen met him smilingly.

"Elsie's asleep," she announced, taking his hat.

He snatched it from her slender fingers, and his wife moved back. She looked more closely into his face and the exaltation shining in his eyes frightened her.

She followed him into the drawing room and closed the door. Patiently, she waited until her husband had thrown himself into a chair and was looking at her.

"What is it, dear?" she murmured.

"I have your brother just where I want him," fell from his lips.

"Now, what's Deforrest done to displease you?"

"I've found Andy Bishop in his house!"

The woman couldn't believe her ears. It could not be! She mustn't take him seriously.

"Oh, how perfectly ridiculous!" she said, relieved.

"It's true enough," replied Ebenezer, getting up. "There's no doubt about it, and the prison yawns for him and for that Skinner girl, too.... No! no!... You needn't beg for 'em. I won't hear it!... They've done enough to me.... Now, it's my turn!"

"Ebenezer," gasped Helen, "don't do anything you'll be sorry for. If Forrie has had the dwarf there, let him tell you why. If you put him in prison for it, I couldn't—I couldn't live with you!... Can't you understand that?"

"As you please, madam. I shall do my duty, even if the criminal is your brother."

"But you couldn't get along without Elsie and me."

She was very near him now, having taken little steps while she was speaking.

"Without Elsie!" he mocked. "I don't have to live without Elsie. You can do as you please, but my daughter stays with me, and your brother, my dear, and the woman he's living with—go to jail."

CHAPTER XLVI
SANDY'S COURTING

Sitting on the porch late that afternoon, Professor Young heard from Tess of the coming of Sandy Letts.

"And, Uncle Forrie," she continued. "I can't understand why he went away so quickly."

"Perhaps he thought I was around somewhere."

"Perhaps," meditated Tess. "But I don't think so. You see, Andy was looking out of the window. Oh, dear, I've told him not to, but he's always trying to see what Boy's doing. You don't think Sandy saw him, do you?"

The unpleasant consequences of Andy's discovery rushed through the lawyer's mind. To be sure, he'd lived with this possibility ever since he'd brought the squatters from the shack, but the lapse of time had developed a sense of security which the girl's question rudely shattered.

184

"I hope not. What time did you say that Letts was here?"

"About dinner time," said Tess.

"Well, now it's after five. If he'd seen him, they'd have been back before this. What does Bishop think about it?"

"Oh, Andy's quite sure Sandy didn't see him, ..." Tess explained, shaking her head.

"Anyhow, it's no use to worry, honey," smiled Young.

The next morning three men in a wagon passed the Kennedy farm. Ebenezer Waldstricker was driving and beside him sat Lysander Letts. Alone on the back seat sprawled the big sheriff, a half-smoked cigar between his teeth.

When they reached Young's barn, they left their rig and walked quietly toward the house.

"You don't want to give 'em any chance to get the dwarf out of the way, sir," said the sheriff. "We'd better get in without their knowing we're here."

"Yes," agreed Waldstricker.

They'd rounded the porch and were in the living room before Deforrest Young and Tessibel Skinner were aware of their coming. The officer held a revolver in his hand. Leering triumphantly, Waldstricker spoke to Young.

"We want Andy Bishop."

The lawyer turned to the sheriff.

"Put up your gun, Brown, you won't need it," he ejaculated. "Here, child," to Tessibel, who had risen from her chair and started for the stairs. "Wait a minute. Sit down."

Tess sank into a chair, white-lipped and silent.

"I suppose there's no use trying to hide him any longer?" continued Deforrest, turning back to the officer.

"No, I reckon not, Mr. Young.... Where's the dwarf, Professor?"

"Upstairs. I'll call him," replied the lawyer.... Then glancing at the girl, "You go and get him, Tess."

"Let me git 'im, sheriff," Sandy thrust in. "I'd like the job, sir. Eh?"

"Mebbe I better myself. It's my duty to take him."

Tess smiled at the speaker and getting up moved a step toward him.

"Let me bring 'im, sir," she entreated. "I'll get 'im. Please let me!"

Charmed by her beauty and the sweetness of her voice, the sheriff glanced doubtfully from the frowning elder to the lawyer.

"Mebbe it isn't quite regular, but if Mr. Young says it'll be alright, I'm willing," he decided finally.

Young nodded, and Tess rose and started toward the stairs. Passing Sandy and Waldstricker, she had to draw aside her skirts to avoid touching them.

The dwarf, seated on the floor beside Boy, was mending a train of cars when Tessibel's white face appeared at the door.

"Andy," she said, trying to speak calmly. "Remember about the hands stronger'n Waldstricker's? Nobody can hurt you. But—but—"

At her hesitation the little man scrambled to his feet. He'd heard men's voices from the room below but had paid no particular attention. Now, he knew the long-dreaded calamity'd happened. He looked pitifully up at the speaker.

"They've come for me?" he gasped.

"Yes, dear, and you must go. But remember all the time, God's hands're stronger'n Waldstricker's," repeated Tess. "Nothing can hurt you.... Come, dear."

A few moments later, the three of them entered the living room, but stopped short at the sound of the elder's angry voice.

"I'll send you and your squatter woman to Auburn with him, if you don't look out," he said.

"Do what you please," snapped the lawyer.

Holding the dwarf's hand, Tess went directly to the sheriff.

"Here's Andy, sir," she faltered. "Be awful kind to him, please, sir. He's so little!"

Still dry-eyed and showing a quiet dignity, she stepped to Young's side while the sheriff adjusted the handcuffs to himself and to Andy and led him out into the sunshine.

At the door, Waldstricker allowed Letts to precede him, then turned.

Shaking his fist, he threatened, "I'll get you two, next."

"Very well," Young answered. "Do anything you like, only get out ... now."

The sound of retreating footsteps had hardly died away when Tess dropped into a chair and began to cry, the baby wailing in sympathy. Deforrest put his hands on her shoulders.

"There, there, Tess, you musn't do that! Dress yourself and Boy quickly. We're going to Auburn, too."

The gates of Auburn Prison swung slowly back and admitted a party of six people and, clanging, closed together again. Large-eyed with wonder, Boy clung to Professor Young's right hand, at whose other side walked Tessibel Skinner. In front of them between two officers was little Andy. Once, Tess caught his eyes and smiled at him. Both were certain that somewhere up and beyond were the hands stronger'n Waldstricker's, but they'd hoped those pitying hands would have lifted them up before this. Still they clung to their faith and all the long ride from Ithaca had bolstered each other up with wan smiles and comforting promises.

The business in the warden's office was simple and quickly dispatched. Once in the room, Andy was permitted to stand with his friends. The officers made their report and the clerk wrote some entries in his books and gave them a receipt. Then, he rang a bell.

Professor Young was talking to the warden when a guard came through the iron door from the interior of the prison.

"Take Bishop in," the clerk directed briefly, without looking up from his books.

Andy turned to Professor Young, took his hand and tried to stammer out some words of gratitude.

"There, there, old man, brace up!" said the lawyer, patting him on the shoulder. "Hope it won't be for long!... Here, Boy, say good-bye to Andy."

Troubled, the baby clung to his friend.

"I don't want Andy to go. I want 'im to come home," insisted the child.

Kissing the little fellow passionately, the dwarf gave him to Deforrest and turned to Tessibel. She took his hands firmly in her strong ones and looked earnestly into his face.

"Remember the hands stronger'n Waldstricker's," she whispered. "They'll bring you right back home, dear. They did Daddy Skinner, Andy, darling."

Shaken by suppressed emotion, the little man sank to the floor.

"Oh, God help me to come back to ye!" he moaned dully.... "God help me!"

A moment, Tess fought the uprushing tears.

"You are coming back, Andy, remember that," she said quickly. Then, she lifted her friend to his feet and kissed him.

"Here, sir," she said to the officer, "take him!"

Infected by Tessibel's faith, Andy ceased to weep. He flashed a last loving glance at her and the boy, and preceded the guard through the iron door into the prison.

Some time later, after what seemed an eternity of waiting, the warden came to Professor Young.

"The lady can see Bennet now," he said.

Silently, an attendant conducted Tessibel through the long stone corridors to the prison hospital.

As she passed, eager eyes watched her from the rows of cots against the wall. She was piloted to a bed near the end of the room.

"Here's your company, Bennet," said the officer.

The figure on the bed turned and pain-ridden eyes peered up. Tess felt her throat throb with sympathy.

"What do ye want, miss?" growled a weak voice.

Tess smiled and bent over the bed. "I want to talk to you," she said. "May I?"

Bennet's face softened immediately. He thought a beautiful angel had dropped from Heaven to the side of his prison bed.

"Yep," he whispered, blinking at her. "There air somethin' under the bed to set on, ma'am."

Drawing forth a stool, Tess raised the lowered back and sat down.

In the presence of such misery, she had almost forgotten her little friend in the cell outside. Just then, she wanted to comfort Owen Bennet, to say something which would take away that writhing expression of suffering.

"You're very sick," she murmured. "Poor man, I'm sorry!"

Bennet kept his watery eyes on the pleading young face.

"Yep, I'm sick enough," he muttered.

"What can I do for you?" asked Tess. "Can't I do anything to make you feel easier?"

"Nope," was the answer. "I'll be dead, soon. Mebbe, I'll get out time nuff to die."

Then, Tessibel did forget Andy. And, even, Deforrest and the baby left her mind. She stretched forth her hand and touched the man's arm.

"Would you like me to sing to you, a little?"

Bennet bobbed his head.

"I like singin'," he mumbled.

In a low voice, Tessibel began to sing; nor did she take her hand from the thin arm lying inertly on the sheet.

 "Rescue the Perishin';
 Care for the Dyin'."

came forth like the chanting of the chimes.

When the words, "Jesus is merciful," followed, Bennet put up his hand and touched the girl's fingers. Tessibel closed her own over his. There was no thought then of her errand, no remembrance that the man before her was a murderer and had sworn his crime on little Andy.

"Jesus is merciful, Jesus is kind," sang Tess, and Bennet began to cry in low sobs that made the singer finish her song in tears.

"Oh, He is kind," she whispered. "He is merciful. Won't you believe that?"

"Sing it again," entreated Bennet, huskily.... "Sing it again, will ye?"

Tess scarcely heard the words they were so low, so sobbingly spoken. She cleared the tears from her voice, and "Rescue the Perishin'," and "Jesus is kind," echoed once more through the long room. From here and there, suppressed weeping came to the girl's ear; but she did not turn to look at the weepers. Here, before her, was a man who was watching as Daddy Skinner had watched the slowly opening gates of eternal life, through which he must pass, alone and afraid. Ah, if she could make him less so! If she could give him a little faith to grope on and on and up and up into the freedom of the life beyond.

Bennet's hand was clasped in Tessibel's; the other covered his eyes.

Suddenly, he dropped his fingers.

"Ye say he's kind?" he gasped. "Jesus air kind, ye say?"

"Yes, yes," breathed Tess.

"But I air such a wicked man, awful wicked. I've done things God'll never forgive."

"But he will," murmured Tess. "Don't you remember what I sang?" and again,

"Jesus is merciful," brought a fresh rush of tears from the dying squatter.

A hoarse rattle sounded, suddenly, in his throat.

"Be ye knowin' Andy Bishop, missy?" he muttered, when he could speak.

"Yes," said Tessibel, aghast. She'd forgotten Andy!

"Yes!" she said again, almost in a query.

"He were up here five years ... innercent," wailed Bennet, "an' they just telled me he air been brought back again for shootin' Waldstricker. I were glad at first, but, now, I—"

He coughed spasmodically, and Tessibel closed her fingers more tightly over the thin hand.

"Tell me about it," she implored. "Don't you want to?"

"Yep, an' I air wantin' to write it.... Bring a paper." Bennet gave the last order to the silent attendant. The latter left the room but almost immediately returned with the warden. Tess relinquished the stool and stood near the head of the bed. In silence the officer wrote the story Bennet told them.

"It were like this," he stumbled. "Andy didn't have nothin' to do with shootin' Waldstricker. He were a tryin' to stop me from doin' it.... I done it!... Let Andy go!... Don't keep him in the coop."

The sunken eyes closed wearily.

"Sing about Him bein' kind, miss," he whispered.

Low, solemn and beautiful, the sweet soprano brought him back from the brink of the grave.

Leaning over him, Tess whispered, "Jesus is always kind."

"I done the murder," repeated Bennet. "Let Andy go, and tell 'im I'm sorry.... Here, let me write my name to the paper."

It took many efforts for the cramped fingers to scrawl the words, but "Owen Bennet" was legibly written when the man dropped back, exhausted.

The warden folded the paper and, smiling, put it into his pocket.

"I've always believed he did it, Miss Skinner," he confided to Tess. "Now, come away."

Bennet's ears caught the last words. In dying effort, he lifted an imploring hand.

"Don't go, lady!" he mourned. "Stay a minute!... I air a needin' ye.... I air afraid, so awful alone!"

Tess spoke to the warden.

"Tell Mr. Young I'm staying for a while," said she, "and will you please let Andy know about it?" And she sat down again.

Through the rest of the afternoon, until the long shadows of Auburn Prison were lost in the gathering gloom, Tessibel sat beside the dying man. Sometimes, she whispered to him, sometimes, she sang very softly, and, when Deforrest Young and the warden came through the hospital ward to her side, Tessibel had piloted Owen Bennet through the darkness into a marvelous light.

CHAPTER XLVII
WALDSTRICKER'S ANGER

Lysander Letts wanted to get married and settle down in a home of his own. He had received and banked the five thousand dollars for discovering the dwarf, and was, now, looking forward confidently to his marriage with

Tessibel Skinner. He was quite sure his wealth would overcome the objections the squatter girl had hitherto opposed to his suit.

He grew quite sentimental thinking of her. He'd buy a real house, and put some fancy furniture in it, plush sofas in the parlor and lace curtains at the windows,—not any squatter's shack or pecking-box hut on the Rhine for him. His face darkened at a disturbing thought. He'd make the girl give up that kid! He wouldn't tolerate another man's brat in his home. But Lysander had a wholesome fear of Deforrest Young, and he didn't venture down the lake until the second day after he'd heard Tess had returned from Auburn.

On his way along the railroad tracks, he concluded he'd better go to Brewer's and find out just how the land lay. The talk in the Rhine saloons, the night before, had been that the dwarf'd returned from Auburn, pardoned. He wanted to know the details, and was sure Jake Brewer would be able to tell him. He passed through the woods and scrambled down the steps the fisherman had cut roughly in the cliff side. Mrs. Brewer answered his knock and invited him into the house. Recognizing Sandy's voice, Jake shouted from the back room:

"Heard about Andy Bishop gettin' free?"

When Brewer came into the kitchen a moment later, Letts had taken a seat. Beside him on the floor lay a large tissue-wrapped package and in his hands he held a shiny new hat.

"Sure, I've heard he's back," he grinned, brushing a little flower-pollen from a very loud trouser leg. "How'd it happen?"

Sandy handed Brewer a cigar and stuck one, jauntily, in his own mouth.

"Smoke that, while ye're tellin' me 'bout Andy," he suggested. "It air the best money'd buy."

When the cigars were burning satisfactorily, Brewer sat down on the doorstep and cleared his throat loudly. His news was the biggest thing that'd happened in the Silent City since Orn Skinner escaped the rope. Glad of another opportunity to recount the story of the dwarf's liberation, he began:

"Well, ye see, Sandy, in the first place, yer tellin' old Eb, an' gettin' the little feller sent back to Auburn air the best thing ever happened to the kid. Tess and the Professor went with 'im. When they got to the prison, Owen Bennet were dyin' in the horspitle. The brat seen 'im, an' sung to 'im an' talked to 'im, an' he confessed; said Andy didn't do the shootin' but was tryin' to stop it, just as the kid allers claimed."

"Yep," interrupted Letts, earnestly. "That air the way it were."

Jake nodded and continued:

"Sure, Sandy, us-uns all knowed ye swore false on the trial.... Well, next day, Young an' the brat went to Albany to see the guvener."

The ex-convict's eyes widened at the thought of the squatter girl in such august company.

"He were fine to Tess. Seemed kind a stuck on her, the Professor says. The brat told 'im all about how she'd looked after Andy, an' how he were in prison five years innercent, an' then, he give 'er a free pardon for 'im. Day before yesterday, they brought 'im home. Some happy they air, I tell ye!"

"Well," commented Sandy, "I air glad he's out. I never did feel jest right 'bout his bein' shet up, but I were needin' the money."

Jake rose, and coming into the room, took up a broken fishing tackle and sat down again.

"That ain't all the news, nuther, Sandy. While the Professor was to Auburn, some skunks tore down old Moll's shack. She come down here in the rain madder'n a settin' hen. The old woman's going to stay with us-uns."

"It air a fine thing fer old Moll," added Mrs. Brewer. "I been thinkin' fer a long time as how she were too far 'long in years to be alone in the shanty."

"Well," said Sandy. "I'm glad to hear it."

"What air ye doin' down here, Sandy?" inquired Mrs. Brewer.

"Me? oh, me!" He paused to choose his words. "I got some news for you folks. I air goin' to get married."

"Air that why ye're all togged up?" Jake queried. "Gosh, but ye air some beau, Sandy.... Ain't he, ma?"

"Yep, I air on my way to get my girl. I been waitin' over three years for this here day, an' now—I air got flowers in this bundle."

"Who ye goin' to marry, Sandy?" demanded Mrs. Brewer.

Letts grinned again, straightened his shoulders pompously, and lined his feet together on a crack in the floor.

"Tess Skinner," he answered, looking from the man to the woman.

Mrs. Brewer dropped on a stool, and her husband's jaws fell apart in astonishment.

"Tess Skinner?" he repeated dully. "Pretty little Tess Skinner?"

"Well, I swan!" gasped the squatter woman. "Did she say she'd have ye, Sandy?"

"Well, it air like this. I been askin' 'er to marry me ever since she were sixteen year old, but she wouldn't while her daddy were alive. Then once she says to me, 'Sandy, you go git Andy Bishop an' git that five thousand, an' come back here.' Now I got the cash. I air a goin' to git the girl."

"Mebbe she's foolin' ye," suggested Brewer. "Ye see, she had the dwarf the hull time! Looks to me as if she'd put one over on ye."

"She'd better not try anythin' on me," returned Letts, snapping his teeth.

"I heard 'er tell ye once," put in Brewer, "she wouldn't marry ye ... the day ye shot yer leg up."

Sandy cocked the new hat on the side of his head, picked up his bundle, and went to the open door.

"I'd a had 'er afore now if ye'd kept yer hands to hum, Jake," he stated. "But I ain't holdin' up anythin' against ye for what ye done. Now I got money, Tess'll be all the gladder. I air goin' to take 'er over to Seneca Lake. I got a job on there. Good-bye, folks. Mebbe me an' my woman'll drop in an' see ye some day."

The husband and wife watched the big squatter going down the rock path, the tissue-wrapped flowers in his hand, then looked at each other and laughed in perfect comprehension.

"I wonder if he gets 'er," chuckled Mrs. Brewer.

191

"I'll bet a bullhead he don't," grinned Jake.

Sandy Letts wasn't anxious to meet Deforrest Young, but just how to avoid it he hadn't figured out. It took him a long time to consider just what was best to do. Perhaps the lawyer had gone to Ithaca. He hoped so. At any rate, he could go to the house and if the professor were there he'd give the flowers to Tess, and if he had to, come another day when she was alone.

Strutting along, supported by his fine clothes, and the consciousness of doing the right thing in the right way, the newly-rich man walked up the path to Young's house and ascended the steps quietly. The door stood open. Without knocking, he stepped across the threshold into the sitting room.

Tessibel was working at a little table, cutting out a blouse for Boy. She looked up, and recognizing her visitor, got quickly to her feet.

"Hello, Tess," said Sandy, coming forward a little. "Nice day, ain't it?"

Tessibel's fear of him since his roughness to Boy was very active. She had suffered in anticipation, for he'd threatened to come again, and she knew he would. Now he was here she didn't know what to do. Deforrest wasn't home and Andy was out with Boy.

"Yes, it's a nice day," she assented.

"Ain't ye goin' to ask me to set down?" demanded Sandy, at the same time helping himself to a rocking chair. "I brought ye somethin', brat." He unwrapped the bundle and took out a huge bunch of flowers.

"Ye want to nurse 'em a long time, 'cause they cost money, them flowers did. They ain't no wild posies!"

"They're awful pretty," she thanked him. "I'll put them in water right away."

While she was arranging the flowers, Sandy got up.

"How do ye like my new togs, kid?" he asked, pivoting around and around on one heel.

"You look very nice," replied Tessibel, gathering courage from his good nature.

"Ye bet I do," grinned Letts. "I air some guy when I air all flashed out in new things. Got all this with Waldstricker's money. Lord, brat—" Here the man reseated himself. "Ye ought to hear that bloke bluster when he found out ye'd got Andy back. Now for me—I were glad, for I knowed all along the dwarf didn't kill Eb's daddy. But in this world I find ye got to look out for yerself first. That air how I got the five thousand."

"I see!" flared Tess, her disapproval of his spying getting the better of her fear. "But your blood money won't do you any good."

"Won't do me no good? My five thousand won't do me no good? What do ye mean, brat? 'Course it'll do me lots of good. I air a rich man, I air. It's goin' to buy us a real home, kid, frame house with plastered walls an' shingled roof, painted red an' yeller. All what I want now air my woman, an' I've come fer ye, Tess."

The girl's heart sank. She glanced about helplessly. What could she say or do? There was no other human being within call. In hasty retrospection, her mind swept back to Ben Letts. She shuddered as she remembered the many times he'd made the same demand upon her. And then, she as suddenly remembered how, during those days, she had been saved from men like Ben and Sandy, and courage came again in response to her silent call for help.

"Ye heard what I said, brat, didn't ye?" demanded Sandy, leaning back and throwing one leg over the other. "I air here fer ye."

"Yes, I heard."

"An' ye're comin', ain't ye, kid?" ... His voice was deep and persuasive by reason of the passion that surged through him.... "I air a little sorry fer bein' mean to ye afore, brat, an' now I air rich ye can forgive it, can't ye?"

He bent forward and held out his heavy hands, palms up, ingratiatingly.

"Yes, I forgive you, Sandy, certainly. But—but—"

"Now, there ain't no 'buts' in this matter, kid! Ye said as how ye'd marry me when I got Andy's reward money. Now I got it ye got to keep yer word."

Tessibel shook her head.

"I didn't say I'd marry you," she answered. "I said, away back there, when I was only a little kid, you could come back and ask me again. But I'm a woman, now, and I'm never going to marry anyone."

The squatter leaned his elbows on his knees, cupped his white face in his hands, and glared at the girl steadily.

"Ye're goin' to git married to me today," he growled. "Ye can't play fast and loose with me, kid, an' don't ye think ye can, uther. Get on yer togs. I air goin' to give ye the time of yer life."

Tessibel stood very still. She could hear plainly, through the silence, the lap of the waves on the shore below, and the soft chug-chug of a lake steamer. A bee flew in at the door, lighted on the lace curtain and clung there, making sprawly motions with his thread-like legs. She remembered without effort the day the squatter alluded to—remembered also Daddy Skinner's telling him to go. Perhaps he had thought she meant to marry him if he were rich.

"Sandy," she said, dragging her eyes to the man's face. "When I tell you I can't marry you, I mean it. Please don't ask me any more.... Would you like a piece of cake?"

"Cake?..." snarled Letts. "Hell! What do I want with cake? No, ma'am, I don't want no cake nor nothin' but you, an' I air goin' to have ye, too!"

He got up slowly, as if to make more effective his menacing words.

"If ye put on yer things like I says," he continued, "there won't be no trouble, brat. But if ye don't—" he moved toward her, "ye'll wish ye had."

To this Tessibel couldn't reply. Insistent, in her panting heart, was a constant call for rescue. She looked steadily at Lysander and he glared back at her.

"Tess," he threatened, "ye know me well 'nough not to come any monkey shines on me. I says again, get yer hat, fer I'm goin' to take ye one way or t'other."

"I told you I couldn't," she answered. "I'm not any longer a little girl. I've got to work. I want to learn things and take care of my baby."

She couldn't have said anything that would have fired the squatter's rage any quicker. Her baby! What did he care about the brat?

"Ye don't have to work no more fer Young," he retorted. "I ain't goin' to have my woman keepin' house fer no professor, an' ye can make up yer mind to it 'out no further clack." In one bound, Sandy rounded the table. "If ye won't do what I tell ye, then, I'll make ye wish ye had. Ye throwed up at me once, ye brat, ye, I never had no kisses from ye! After today ye won't be able to say that."

A strong hand shot out, guided by a powerful arm. Fingers clutched for her, but Tess, eluding them, slipped to the window.

"Sandy!" she implored. "Sandy, don't touch me, don't! Wait!"

"I won't wait," snarled Letts. "I air waited years an' years, an' I won't wait no longer."

At that moment there seemed no escape for the girl, who was holding out her hands to keep off the brute facing her. The very quiet of the day, the singing of the birds, and the shrill chirping of the crickets, only added to her sense of isolation. She glanced hopelessly from the huge squatter out into the summer air.

"Ye can't get no help," said Sandy. "Ye might's well give up!... God, ye're all the sweeter fer havin' to fight like I been doin'!"

By a motion, extraordinarily quick for so big a man, he clutched her bodily, and dragged her to him. She lowered her face against his chest and buried it under her curls.

"I air goin' to kiss ye, my pretty wench," muttered Letts. "Gimme yer lips, gimme—"

In the scuffle neither heard the step on the porch and neither saw the tall form loom in the doorway. Sandy wrenched at the red hair, drawing Tessibel's face upward. Then Deforrest Young grappled with him, and in the one blow he landed under the squatter's chin, the angry lawyer concentrated the vim of years of exasperated waiting. Sandy slumped to the floor. Kneeling beside him, Young's leg pressed against something round and hard in Letts' pocket.

A quick investigation brought forth a small revolver.

"Are you hurt, child?" he inquired, getting up. "Did he hurt you?"

"Not a bit, Uncle Forrie, but he scared me awful."

The prostrate man groaned, moved his limbs and sat up, slowly. He glanced around as though trying to figure out what'd happened. The sight of Young, holding the gun Waldstricker's money bought, told Sandy the whole story of his downfall.

"Get up, Letts, and get out of here quick!" Young ordered, prodding him with his foot.

Sandy scrambled to his feet unsteadily.

"Now, take your hat and get out," said Young, "and don't stay in Ithaca, or I'll have you locked up again."

Sandy didn't wait for any further advice. He grabbed his hat and flung out of the door. Deforrest followed him down through the pear orchard to the lane, and there he stood for a long time watching the ex-convict struggle up the hill to the railroad tracks.

When he returned to Tess he found her leaning on the table, her face

194

buried in her hands. She did not lift her head, nor make a move at Deforrest's entrance.

"Child," he said, taking a chair at her side, "Letts won't bother you any more. If he doesn't go away, I shall have him arrested tomorrow.... I won't have you insulted like this.... And, dear, I believe I'd better send you and the boy away for a spell. A change will do you both good."

"Yes, yes, do!" pleaded Tess. She snatched his hand and pressed it to her cheek hysterically. "Let me go somewhere, please!"

CHAPTER XLVIII
THE SINS OF THE PARENTS

A few days after Sandy's tempestuous courting, Tessibel Skinner and her son left Ithaca to spend the remaining part of the summer in the North Woods. In September Young joined them for a few days and then brought them back to the hillside above Cayuga Lake.

Later in the fall, when the cold winds and driving rains of the lake began to find out the cracks in the shanties, Tessibel asked, and the lawyer consented, that old Mother Moll come from Brewer's to them. Tess gave her one of Andy's rooms. The dwarf had entered a school on College Hill and lived in the city most of the time, but was home now for the Christmas vacation.

The day after his return dawned bright and cold—one of those beautiful winter days occasionally seen in the Storm Country. Heavy snows had already fallen and made certain a white Christmas. Andy was helping Tessibel in order that she might have time to complete her Yuletide preparations. She'd filled her son's heart with delightful anticipations of the holiday, now but a few days distant, and he was eagerly looking forward to the Santa Claus who came to visit good little boys and fill their stockings with goodies.

At the north of the house Deforrest had made a little snow-hill for Boy. Many a happy hour the little fellow spent upon it with his sled. Oftimes his mother joined him in the sport, and the joyous laughter of the two children of nature rose high and clear in the winter air.

The morning's work finished, Tessibel wrapped up Boy and sent him out to play. She stood for some moments on the porch watching the sturdy little figure arrange the sled at the top of the hill.

How she loved him, and how good he was! Never since the day of his birth had he given her one sorrowful moment. She turned her eyes from Boy to the lake, and allowed them to rest upon the shanty near the shore. A disturbing thought pressed into her mind. They would not be long there now.

Deforrest had told her that his lease of the house expired the first of January, and Waldstricker had refused to renew it. If they moved away, she'd be lonely for the sight of her old friends and all the dear, familiar things that had met her eyes every day since she could remember.

She hoped her new home might be in the Storm Country. She loved the lake in its every mood. Dark and sullen, visitors had called it. But she'd seen it on summer days, a band of burnished blue cementing the harmonies of greens and browns into a picture of perfect beauty. She knew its deep, brooding peace when the light was fading and the evening breeze gently ruffled its surface. She'd skated over its shining bosom in the blinding glare of the unclouded sun and in the soft radiance of the shadow-filled moonlight. She knew the soft spots in the ice caused by flowing springs in the lake-bottom and had drunk their pure, cold water. Her lifelong intimacy had wooed from rockbound lake its inmost secrets. Today the water lay a gleaming jewel, huge by contrast to the myriad sparkles the sunbeams pricked out of the snow. She looked across to East Hill at the frosty veil of a ravine waterfall and sighed.

At a shout from Boy, she went to the far edge of the porch to watch him slide swiftly through the pear orchard toward the lane. Glancing along the line of his flight, she saw Waldstricker on his horse directly in Boy's path. Fear and horror held her dumb and motionless. Evidently the rider hadn't seen the swift-coming sled—but the horse had.

He reared and attempted to turn. At that point the ditches were deep and the rounded crown of the road covered with ice. The animal slipped and fell. At the proper moment the horseman jumped off and pulled the bridle rein over his mount's head.

Her muscles taut with fright, Tess jumped from the porch and ran down the hill to the scene of the accident. When she arrived Waldstricker was jerking his steed savagely.

"Get out of the way you little imp," he shouted, in the midst of his struggles with the animal. "What do you mean by riding in a public road scaring horses this way?"

"Mummy said Boy could ride down hill," answered the child, holding his ground staunchly.

"I'll mummy you!" The man's exasperation was increased by the child's resistance. "Get out of the way!"

"Boy, come straight here to me," Tess called, trying to pass the excited animal.

The child picked up the rope fastened to his sled, gave it a jerk and started toward his mother. Frightened by the flash of the sled in the snow, the horse reared and plunged anew.

"Drop that sled and get out of here!" Ebenezer thundered. "How many times must I tell you? Get out!"

Tess called again, but Boy flung up a red, angry face to the elder.

"Mummy said I could slide," he repeated stubbornly.

"I'll teach you to argue with me," snapped Waldstricker, and before

Tess could reach him, he'd raised his arm and given the child a sharp cut with his riding whip. "Get out, I tell you!"

"Mover!" screamed Boy, jumping back and falling over the sled. "Oh, Mover! Mover!"

Like an enraged tigress, Tess threw herself upon Waldstricker, and tore at the upraised whip in his hand. The frantic horse, fairly beside himself with fear and excitement, pulled them both down the hill through the snow. By a strenuous effort Ebenezer threw off the girl's grip, and when he finally conquered the steed he was below the top of the lane near the Skinner hut.

Before Waldstricker could mount and ride back up the lane, Tess had picked up the boy from the snow where he had fallen. Without waiting an instant, she fled frantically toward the house.

"Andy! Andy!" she screamed.

Andy came downstairs as fast as his little legs could carry him.

"Waldstricker's killed Boy!" gasped Tess. "Andy, get something.... Tell Mother Moll.... Some water!"

She laid the baby on the divan in the sitting room and stood over him until old Moll came.

"He air got a spasm," croaked the old woman. "Poor little brat! Get some hot water."

For hours the child passed from one convulsion into another. When Deforrest came home, Tess was in a state of frantic despair.

"Waldstricker struck him," she explained. "He's going to die."

In response to his questions, the girl gave him the details, and hotter and hotter grew the listener's anger. He attempted to quiet Tessibel's fears while he got ready to go for the doctor, but she persisted in her claim that Boy wouldn't recover.

On his way home, the elder tried to make peace with himself. He was rather sorry he'd struck the boy; that he'd hurt the little imp, he poofed at. Anyway, he had taught Tess Skinner to keep her brat out of his way. His efforts to discipline her had resulted in an open breach with his brother-in-law and caused discord between himself and his wife. His disputes with Deforrest about the squatters had not turned out to his satisfaction. His efforts to drive the old witch off his lake-land by tearing down her shack had opened to her the house that he himself owned. He had had to pay Sandy Letts the $5,000 reward for the capture of Andy Bishop, and the whole city had laughed at the price paid for the little man's short imprisonment. He'd tried every way he knew to put an end to the situation. Helen ought to be able to do something with her brother. She should have saved her husband from the gossip Forrie was causing.

When he entered his home, Helen perceived that he'd acquired a new grievance and discreetly remained silent while he was preparing himself for dinner.

After a quiet meal, when they had seated themselves by the log fire in the library, Mrs. Waldstricker took up a doll's dress she was finishing for Elsie's Christmas. Her husband, stretched in an easy chair, glowered sullenly into the grate flames. The meditations of husband and wife were quite different. Helen wondered what was bothering Ebenezer now. She wished they were more companionable; that things were pleasanter, more as it used to be when they were abroad. Since their return, he'd sit for hours in gloomy meditation. His fits of complete abstraction filled her with dread.

She brought back in sequenced retrospection the happy years of travel—how proud she'd always been of her handsome husband and of his courtly deference to her. She had never ceased to be grateful that Heaven had given her this man to love and cherish her. She couldn't tell how or when the change had come, but somehow they weren't happy together any more. He was so moody and quarrelsome lately. She missed her brother, too. Why those two men should get by the ears over the inhabitants of the Silent City she couldn't understand. But her thoughts were soon concentrated upon the work at hand and contemplating the joy she would have in Elsie's pleasure, she began to hum to herself.

Two or three times she peered at Ebenezer through her lashes. How moodily quiet he was! She wished Elsie were awake—the little girl always succeeded in dissipating the frown from her father's brows.

Suddenly, she held up the doll in all its newly-adjusted festive attire.

"There, now, dear, isn't the doll baby pretty?" she smiled.

Ebenezer didn't take his gaze from the burning logs.

"I'm not interested in dolls tonight." His tone was harsh and his manner studiously rude. Then, as though he'd finally determined to say something else, he looked around at her.

"I taught Tess Skinner a lesson today I don't believe she'll forget," he burst forth savagely.

The doll dropped from Helen's hands, its head striking sharply against the arm of her chair.

"What do you mean?" she gasped.

"You needn't get that expression on your face, my lady—"

"Oh, Ebenezer!" interjected Helen, drearily. "What makes you act so? One would think you spent your whole time trying to get even with somebody."

"I got even with my lady Skinner," smiled Waldstricker. "I gave her brat a whipping." The words came slowly, and the man watched their effect.

Helen was not able to sense the full meaning of his statement at first. Mechanically, she rescued the doll and laid it on the table. Beginning to see the picture he'd suggested, she opened her mouth, closed it again and at the next attempt spoke.

"Why, Ebenezer, Tessibel's baby is only a month or so older than Elsie!"

"Well, what of it! He's an impudent little whelp. Takes after his mother, I suppose."

"But you don't really mean you whipped him!" Helen exclaimed, still incredulous.

"That's just what I do. With my riding whip. What do you think of that?"

His words brought to Helen's recollection that other time he'd used his riding whip. Then it had been upon Mother Moll, and the old woman had screamed at him, "It air like ye to hit the awful young and the awful old." She recalled, too, the other mysterious words the witch woman had uttered. "Curls'll bring yer to yer knees—the little man air a settin' on yer chest!" The prophecy addressed to herself, that he'd make her life unhappy and that she'd leave him, she'd never before taken seriously. But the question hammered at her consciousness. Could it be that Moll had a second sight or something of the sort? Ebenezer's trouble about the squatters centered about Andy Bishop and the Skinner girl; the dwarf was certainly a little man and Tessibel had wonderful red curls. Her husband had made her life unhappy and his mood tonight was unusually ugly. She was touched with a superstitious half-conviction that the old woman's words would be fulfilled.

"I asked you a question, Mrs. Waldstricker," the wrathful voice interrupted her meditations. "Answer me, if you please."

Perhaps it was the recollection of Mother Moll's sibylline utterance; perhaps merely that her husband's hostile attitude aroused a corresponding feeling of animosity. At any rate, she sat erect in her chair and fixed her eyes upon his scowling face. Never had he seen her rounded chin so squarely set; never the red lips drawn into such determined lines.

"I think you're a brute, that's what I think!" she responded deliberately, as though stating a conclusion arrived at after due consideration. "Yes, worse than a brute!" The answer was as unexpected to the elder as though a lump of ice had suddenly boiled over. A quick fury took possession of him.

"Think I'm a brute, do you?... What's the matter with you? Are you getting soft on the squatters, too?"

Helen made a hasty gesture, indicative of denial.

"Well, you better not!" warned Ebenezer, angrily. "Your brother's conduct is disgraceful enough. I'm sick and tired of having my own townsfolk winking at each other every time his name's mentioned. Lawyer Young and his squatter women! Sounds nice, doesn't it?"

To be loyal to herself and Deforrest, she could not help but disagree with him.

"Now, Ebenezer, you oughtn't to say such a thing," she expostulated.

A flame of anger shot into the elder's steady stare.

"Don't you 'Now Ebenezer' me!" he snorted. "Young's making my lake property a disorderly house. It's positively indecent! I won't stand it any longer. I won't have those squatters there, and your brother can make up his mind to that!"

Helen tried to interrupt but her husband waved her to silence.

"Mother Moll and Andy Bishop!" he mocked. "An old witch and a jail-bird! Wouldn't it make a man tired?"

Helen leaned forward. An angry red spot burned on either cheek and her eyes flashed. Her gentle temper didn't take fire easily, but even to her endurance there were limits.

"You seem to forget, Mr. Waldstricker," she retorted sharply, "that your men tore down the old woman's home and your money procured the perjury that sent the dwarf to Auburn. It strikes me you'd better not throw stones at Forrie."

Waldstricker jumped to his feet and rushed to his wife's side.

"What!" he roared. "You dare that to my face! Some more of Deforrest's influence, I suppose. Nice family I married into, I must say."

Helen got up from her chair. The one thing that stirred her quickest was an attack upon her brother.

"Ebenezer Waldstricker, you ought to be ashamed of yourself. Forrie minds his own business and you should mind yours." An hysterical sob brought her to a pause, but she struggled on. "I don't know how I've stood your temper so long. You must have lost your mind."

In view of the grievances he'd been nursing, his wife's sudden rebellion seemed almost too unreasonable to be credited. She'd joined his enemies! She was making common cause with her notorious brother and the squatters! Very well, he'd use her the same as he would them.

"You think rather well of me, don't you Mrs. Waldstricker?" he rasped. "Nice names you call me. Brute! Home destroyer! Procurer of perjury! Liar! Crazy!" His voice grew louder as he hurled the epithets at her and broke into a shriek upon the last one. "Get out of here before I teach you the same lesson I taught Tess Skinner!" He lifted his arm above his head; the great fist was clenched, and the cruel mouth was drawn at both corners. "Get out of here before I hit you!"

Helen stood petrified. The blow had fallen. Mother Moll was right! She retreated before his menacing gestures, but stopped near the door and held up her hand in entreaty. She'd make one more effort.

"But, Ebenezer," she began, "where shall I go?"

Advancing toward her, he fairly shouted:

"I don't know and I don't care. Go down and help your brother take care of his squatter baggage!"

He seemed fairly beside himself. Helen realized the hopelessness of further resistance.

"Then I'll go and take my baby," she cried. "Perhaps when we're gone—"

Her words only added fuel to the flame of his wrath.

"You'll not touch my daughter," he interrupted. "She'll stay with me."

He rushed at her, pushed her rudely aside, and hurried up the stairs to the nursery.

His wife followed as quickly as possible. At the nursery door Ebenezer met her and blocked her way.

"You needn't wake her up," he hissed. "Go on! Get out of here! You're worse than the Skinner woman!"

She could not go into the nursery. The angry man on the threshold effectually prevented her. Mrs. Waldstricker turned down the hall and went to her own room. She could hardly comprehend the untoward disaster that had destroyed the whole fabric of her life at one stroke. The blood was throbbing at her temples and pounding through her body. Her ears rang; her face burned and she was trembling all over. Mechanically, she fumbled for the matches on a nearby table, found one and struck it. She attempted to light the lamp but dropped the chimney and it rolled away under the bed.

Drearily, she tried to consider her course. Ebenezer had ordered her to go. Then she must go. She'd always done as he directed. But where? Her cheeks burned more fiercely as she recalled the brutal answer he'd given that question. No, she wouldn't go to Forrie! It would only make Ebenezer more angry and make more trouble for her brother. It didn't make much difference where she went anyway. Life without her husband and her baby wouldn't be life at all. She couldn't visualize her days without Elsie, the little one they'd both longed for and prayed over. Slowly, because each little act required a separate effort of volition, she dressed herself. Prepared at last to depart, she took a long look through the rooms. Past events went in giddy rapidity across her vision. How she'd loved and still loved Ebenezer! They'd been so happy together. She sighed and went through the hall to the nursery. Her movements had evidently been heard. When she approached the door, her husband stepped out and pulled the door to behind him. For a moment their eyes met. In his she saw the dull smoldering coals of hate. She bowed her head and silently went through the baleful glare he cast upon her down the stairs and out of the mansion to which she had been brought a happy bride.

CHAPTER XLIX
TESSIBEL AND ELSIE

Gloom lay over the Silent City. Bitter hatred burned in the simple heart of every squatter. Waldstricker's open enmity had expressed itself in a series of injuries, calculated to enrage them. The shanty folk resented his cruelty to Mother Moll. The destruction of her shack promised a similar fate to their homes. When the story of Waldstricker's attack upon Boy Skinner spread among them, fierce threats were muttered at the fishing holes and by the firesides. The wintry winds of the Storm Country, shrieking over the desolate masses of ice and snow, were not more fierce and cruel than the squatters' demand for vengeance. The daily bulletins of the little one's illness kept the interest alive and added to the growing excitement and indignation.

Day after day, the doctor had come to the Young home, each time shaking his head more gravely. To Deforrest, the helpless witness of the unfolding tragedy, the days and nights were but a continuing torture. Andy Bishop stole about the house like a small white ghost, waiting upon Tessibel and Mother Moll. One morning, a few days before Christmas, the doctor told

Deforrest Young he considered Boy beyond earthly help. And now it devolved upon the lawyer to tell Tessibel she must lose her baby.

He went softly to the sick room. Whiter than the pillow upon which his cheek rested, Boy lay relaxed, breathing rapidly. Tess stood at the foot of the bed, her hands clasped loosely in front of her. Anxious eyes turned to greet Young. At the bedside the man stopped a moment and looked down upon the little figure. Shocked by the imminent signs of approaching dissolution, he went over and placed an arm around the girl.

"He's awful sick," Tess whispered. "What'd the doctor say?"

"I'm afraid, Tess—I'm afraid," he answered, unable to frame the medical man's decision.

Dawning comprehension and dismay struggled in the young mother's eyes, for the agonized tones of the well-loved voice and the tender solicitude of the supporting arms had put into Young's halting words the dread import of his message.

"You mean—you mean—?" she questioned.

"Tess, darling; my pretty child," Young murmured helplessly.

The red head dropped upon his chest and for a moment Tess clung to him as though to find protection from the menacing horror. Then she freed herself, dropped on her knees by the bedside, and rested her head on Boy's little hand. During the hours of watching she had striven to steel herself against this possibility. But she couldn't understand. Boy, her cherished bit of living joy and sunshine! What would become of him? Separation? Yes, but where was he going? She didn't know. She couldn't think. A sudden shudder, a kind of voiceless sob shook her.

Young stood quietly by the bedside, watching and waiting. His love for mother and son centered all his thoughts in them. He shared his darling's grief and desired above everything to console her; but the very depth of his sympathy prevented him. Hopeless himself, in this grim crisis, every human effort seemed futile.

Placing a tender hand on her shaking shoulder, he bent down.

"My poor little girl!" he breathed. "I wish I could help you some way."

"Nobody ... can." The hopeless despair of her voice made vocal the utter desolation she felt.

A gentle movement of the little hand against her face commanded Tessibel's immediate attention. She smoothed the pillow the while she whispered softly little words of love to Boy. Then she looked around at Young.

"Please tell Andy to fix the kitchen fire," she said, even at this time mindful of her domestic duties.

"I'll see to it myself," and he went out softly and down the stairs.

He found Andy in the sitting room.

"The doctor—what'd the doctor say?" the dwarf demanded.

"Go to 'er," trembled Young. "Brace her up all you can."

The little man went slowly upstairs and entered the sick chamber. Through the tears in his eyes, he saw the dying babe in the white bed and the young mother kneeling on the floor, the flaming red of the clustering curls an incongruous note of brilliant color.

202

Andy waddled across the room and knelt down beside Tessibel. Lifting his arm he let it fall across the girl's shoulders. His silent sympathy, always unselfish, never intruded. Tess stared at Andy a moment, and then buried her face in her hands upon the coverlet.

"He's going away," she got out through her fingers. "Andy, I can't let 'im go!"

"I've been prayin' for 'im, Tess," choked the dwarf.

The girl made no response, but to show her friend she'd heard, one of her hands sought and held his.

"If it air right for 'im to stay, dear," murmured Andy, "the good God'll help 'im.... Don't ye think so, Tess?"

"I don't know, Andy.... I'm afraid!... It's too awful!"

"Kid, ye know it air true. You've only to ask him," Andy insisted.

A hopeless shake of the bowed head accompanied the whispered answer.

"I can't, Andy! I can't!... I'm so afraid!"

"What you 'fraid of, brat, dear? Jesus air loving you same's He did in the shack. He got Daddy Skinner out of prison, an' he took care of me, didn't he, huh?"

Maddened by suffering, she drew herself impatiently, away from the dwarf.

"Don't, Andy! I don't want to hear! He let Waldstricker whip my baby."

Although the young mother could hear the muttered prayers of the dwarf, no answering faith came into her soul. Hot hatred of the man who'd struck her son surged through her. Never again would she think of him without the raging cry within her for revenge. Her anger barbed the shafts of his rancor and dulled her own understanding of Life and Love. Resentment inhibited every constructive effort. The courage, even the desire to fight against death's coming, was wanting.

"I hate 'im worse than anything in the world," she muttered.

"Yes, darlin'," soothed the dwarf.

"I'd like to kill him. Oh, I must do something—" She tried to get to her feet, but Andy held her tightly.

"Stay here!" was all he said, and Tess ceased to resist.

At midnight Boy died. He went away very quietly, without a cry or struggle. At the very last, he turned upon his side, looked into his mother's face, his eyes unshadowed and joyous. He smiled a little, sighed with the passing breath, "Mummy," and sank to sleep. So dazed was Tessibel that without protest she allowed Deforrest to pick her from her knees and carry her out of the room.

Mother Moll and Andy performed the necessary services to the mortal clay that'd been their darling. Loving fingers, tenderly touching the delicate body, made Boy ready for the grave. Through the stillness of the night, the sighing of the ceaseless wind of the Storm Country, soughing of death and desolation, called to their minds the weird superstitions of squatter lore. The old witch mumbled of signs, portends and warnings, and uttered dire prophecies in which her wrath at Waldstricker found expression.

203

While Tess and her squatter friends were carrying Boy through the sullen cold to God's wind-swept half-acre, Ebenezer Waldstricker sat before the glowing hickory logs in his sumptuous library. Several letters in his morning mail required his presence in the city. On the table before him lay a list of things he intended to buy for little Elsie's Christmas.

Since the day he'd whipped Tessibel's son and forced his wife from his home he'd devoted himself to the little girl. In spite of his best efforts, the child's grief for her mother had driven him almost to his wits' end. He'd made up his mind to spare no expense to bring joy back to his darling.

Whenever his mind reverted to the scene at the lake he tried to justify his act in striking the little fellow, but the news of Boy's death had, for a moment, given him an uncomfortable turn. He hadn't intended anything like that. He wasn't to blame! Probably the little imp would have died anyway!

Helen had sent every day to ask after Elsie, and the thought of his wife's anxiety pleased the elder. Perhaps, after a while, the squatters, as well as the members of his own household, would learn his word was law; that he would not allow any of them to go against his will. Again and again the corner curl of his lips showed his satisfaction.

Hearing the jingle of sleigh bells at the door, he rose from his chair and slipped on his great coat and cap.

"Daddy, bring mover back," quivered Elsie, when he kissed her good-bye.

Waldstricker stooped and gathered her into his arms.

"Daddy'll bring Elsie lots of pretty things, and so will Santa Claus. He's coming down the chimney tonight—"

"Elsie wants mover," sobbed the little one.

Ebenezer surrendered her to the nurse.

"Get her mind off crying," he said morosely. "Give her everything she asks for."

"I can't," muttered the woman, and when the door had closed, "There, there, child, don't cry! Your mother'll be comin' back some of these days."

In the early afternoon Waldstricker bought and packed into the sleigh all kinds of presents for his daughter. His spirits rose when he thought that her demands for her mother would be quieted on Christmas Day.

It was quite dark when his powerful team fought their way through the storm up to the porch of the house. While the man was coming for the horses he took the bundles from the sleigh. At the door he met several white-faced servants.

"What's the matter?" he queried, relieving his arms of their load.

"The baby!... We can't find her.... She's gone," said a voice.

"Gone! Gone where?" roared Waldstricker.

"Nobody knows, sir," gasped the nurse. "She was in the library looking at the pictures—"

Waldstricker brushed past the speaker. He rushed through the house calling his child frantically. In his wife's sitting room he stopped, arrested by an illuminating thought.

Helen had stolen the baby! He drew a long breath that hissed through his teeth. Of course, that was what had happened. Instant anger filled his mind. He'd show her. He wouldn't stand it. He went below and called the servants into his presence.

"Who was here this morning?" he questioned.

"Nobody." Not one of them had seen a person.

"Mrs. Waldstricker was here, wasn't she?" he insisted.

"No, Mrs. Waldstricker hasn't been home today."

The elder set his grim lips and went out again. Elsie was with her mother! That Helen hadn't been to the house didn't prove anything. She'd sent some one. Elsie wouldn't have gone away of her own accord.

When Ebenezer appeared at Madelene's home he was fuming with fury. His sister greeted him cordially and ushered him into the drawing room.

"I'm glad you've come, Ebenezer. Helen's been crying ever since she's been here."

"I'll make her cry more before I'm done with her," gritted Waldstricker.

"But, Ebenezer, she's sick. And you were so cruel to send her away like that."

Waldstricker turned savagely upon the speaker, hands working convulsively and face and eyes ugly from fear and anger.

"Never mind about that now—Where's Elsie?" he demanded. "I want her and I want her right away."

Madelene fell back a step, wax-white.

"Elsie!" she echoed. "Isn't she home?"

"Madelene," Ebenezer began in a deadening voice, "you know me well enough not to play with me like this. Where's my daughter?"

Madelene's hands came together.

"She's not here!... She's home, Ebbie, dear, she must be!"

"She's not!" fell from Waldstricker. "Call Helen!"

"Helen can't come down, Ebbie, she's in bed!"

"I'll see her." Low thunder rolled in his tones. His sister grasped his arm.

"Be kind to her, Ebbie, dear—"

"I'll see her," repeated Ebenezer, not changing the tone of his voice.

Without another word, Madelene whirled and went toward the stairs, the church elder following his sister with slow tread.

Helen turned her tired, white face to the visitors. At the sight of her husband she sat up straight.

"Where's Elsie?" the man shouted harshly from the door.

Something had happened to her little girl! Her husband was asking for the child! Mrs. Waldstricker jumped out of bed quickly.

"I haven't seen her," she answered. "Isn't she home?"

Then Waldstricker believed. Elsie had disappeared. She was not with her mother!

"She's gone," was all he said, and, wheeling, went out.

Not one of the servants could tell Madelene or the distracted mother any more than they had told the father.

The search began without the slightest clue of the child's whereabouts. Elsie had disappeared, as if she had been snatched into the sky. The storm, already very severe, had thickened the early twilight into dense darkness. The light snow that had fallen earlier in the day to the depth of several inches drove in swirling clouds before the wind and piled in deep drifts, while the congealed air pelted icy particles of frozen moisture into the confused uproar upon forest and field. Fear that the child had started out to find her mother and had been overtaken by the blizzard obsessed Waldstricker. He sent messengers in all directions, and himself rode furiously through the snow inquiring everywhere. Finding no trace of her at the neighboring houses, he instituted a systematic search of the locality.

All the afternoon Young had sat with Tessibel, most of the time in silence. She showed no desire to talk, and he knew not what to say. Watching from the sitting room window, Tess seemed to find diversion in the wind-driven snow, as though the blizzard's riot met and matched the aching bewilderment in her own breast.

Nor did she pay any attention to a knock which resounded above the beating of the storm. Deforrest went to the door and carried on an undertoned conversation with some one outside. Then after dispatching the caller, he went back to the girl.

"Tess," he hesitated, but his voice broke and he was unable to complete his sentence. In responsive inquiry, she turned from the window and looked up at him. The deep dejection of her attitude depicted her despondency and despair. The brown eyes, dull and lustreless, staring out of the drawn white face, expressed the hopeless wonderment the man had seen in the glazing orbs of a stricken deer. A great wave of pity welled up in him. How could he break this frozen composure and bring to the overwrought heart the healing blessing of flowing tears?

"Tessibel," he continued, sitting down, "what were you thinking about?"

"I was wondering what I could do to ... hurt Waldstricker," she replied, gripping the arms of her chair. Then she rose suddenly, throwing up her head. The intensity of her emotion fanned the dull coals of hate in her eyes to a hard brilliance and touched her white cheeks with vermilion. Vivid, active, her beautiful face, passion-drawn and cruel, red curls writhing and twisting upon her shoulders, Tess seemed a veritable fury crying for vengeance. She lifted clenched hands.

"I'll hurt Waldstricker," she vowed. "God help me to do it!"

Springing to his feet, Young ejaculated:

"Don't, Tess! You mustn't!"

Turning away, she paced up and down the room, muttering imprecations. Her companion stood silent, unable to assuage her agony or rebuke her vindictive words.

At length Tess stopped directly in front of him.

"I know you don't like me to feel that way about Waldstricker, but I can't help it. I hate him so!"

Then she went to the window and stared out into the storm again.

After a moment's hesitation, Young touched her. Drawing her back, he held her in his arms, attempting to soothe and quiet her by murmured endearments.

"I'm awfully sorry, dear," he explained. "I must go to town. Helen's sent for me."

Tess nodded indifferently. It was all one to her now. She'd lost Boy, and she was willing to be alone to plan how she could punish his murderer.

"I'll send Andy to you," said Young, leading her to a chair.

He went in search of the dwarf and found the little man in his room huddled on the bed.

"Andy," said Deforrest, "come here."

Without a word the dwarf went to the lawyer.

"I'm going to Ithaca. Go down and stay with Tess until I get back."

He turned and went out, and Andy, silent and sick at heart, followed him down the stairs.

Andy was not able to persuade Tess to talk with him, but obeying Professor Young, he stayed very near her. The blizzard howled and banged outside, adding by its noisy commotion an element of dread to the grief within.

About nine in the evening footsteps sounded on the porch; the dwarf got up and went to the door. Jake Brewer entered and closed the door against the storm. The squatter took off his hat and shook the snow from the top of it. He looked, alternately, from the girl in the chair near the window to the little man staring up at him.

"I come to speak to the brat," he said.

"She ain't very well," answered Andy.

Tessibel looked around.

"Sit down, Jake," she invited. "The night's dreadful, isn't it?"

Brewer coughed and remained silent.

"Can I do anything, Jake?" inquired the dwarf, softly.

"Nope, it air only Tess can do it," replied the squatter.

Tessibel heard but remained in the same position.

"Tess air the only one can help," repeated Brewer.

The girl sank back in her chair, allowing her hands to drop in her lap.

"What is it?" she asked listlessly.

"Ma Brewer air sick," said the squatter. "She air knowin' ye air in trouble, but—but—"

It seemed to the girl as if this Christmas-tide had brought sorrow to everyone.

She rose to her feet, stiff from sitting in the same position for so long a time.

"I'll get her something, Jake," she said quickly.

"Ma an' me know ye got a lot of sorrow, brat," choked the man, "but Ma were a wonderin' if ye'd run to the shack fer a minute." Noticing the girl's hesitation, "She's awful sick an' mebbe if ye'd come, she'd feel better.'"

"I'll get your wraps, brat," Andy offered.

207

Both men helped Tessibel into her things. She stood very quiet until Andy held out her mittens.

"I'll only be gone a few minutes," she promised the dwarf. "Come on, Jake!"

And together they went out into the storm.

CHAPTER L
TESSIBEL'S VISION

Tessibel and Jake Brewer made their way through the bleak, dark, pear orchard to the lane. The night held no terrors for the girl. All her winters, she'd battled with the cold and winds of the Storm Country. Now, through the lane to the lake, they struggled, heads bent against the blinding blizzard. Under the weeping willow trees stood the empty shanty which had housed her childhood days, and, mechanically, she turned her eyes toward it. She recalled, dully, the strange sequence of events that had transformed her from a squatter's brat and lifted her out of the bleak barrenness of life in the shack. She'd escaped the squalor, the horrid cold and the hardships, common to the women of the Silent City. She lived more comfortably and decently than the fishermen's wives. She'd learned many things, but all her efforts to improve herself had been centered in her ambitions for Boy. Now it was all wasted! She'd won for him nothing but Waldstricker's enmity. Her aspirations for him and for herself were buried in the little grave on the storm-swept hillside by Daddy Skinner. Like a borrowed mantle, the culture she'd gained under Professor Young's loving tuition slipped from her and the elemental passions of the primitive people that produced her assumed their sway. Subconsciously, the squatter's standards re-established themselves, and she hugged to her heart the hate she'd been cherishing.

On the ice-covered rocks, where they were sheltered from the wind, Jake began to talk.

"I wouldn't have asked ye to come, Tess," he apologized, "if we hadn't needed ye bad."

"I wasn't doing anything at home," the girl answered tonelessly.

"Mr. Young weren't there, were he?" asked Brewer.

"No," replied Tess. "His sister's sick and sent for him."

"I guess she air sick, all right," commented Jake, ominously.

If Tess heard, she didn't heed the sinister suggestion in the squatter's speech. She was busy, her whole attention devoted to plans for revenge upon Waldstricker.

The light from Brewer's hut, which was set back a little from the lake shore, in a frost-riven and water-worn niche in the precipitous cliff, shone mistily through the storm. Cut by slanting lines of driving snow-crystals, its milky radiance obscured rather than defined the drifted path. Breathless, from the blizzard's buffeting, they gained, at last, the hut door.

The fisherman lifted the latch and they stepped into the hut. Seated in chairs around the bare little room were several men, squatter friends of the neighborhood. Near the stove stood Ma Brewer, white-faced and anxious. As soon as she recognized the girl, she began to weep and gesticulate hysterically. Tess went to her and seized her hands.

"Why! Ma Brewer, what's the matter? What'd you want of me?"

Before she could answer, a rough voice broke the silence.

"We all wanted ye, Tess."

She wheeled about and looked from one to the other.

Jake was still standing near the door. The triumphant leer on his face was reflected in the several expressions of the other men.

"Then, Ma Brewer wasn't sick?" Tess demanded slowly.

"Nope," said Jake, "but I'll bet someone else air."

Tessibel allowed her eyes to rove about the shack. A slight movement in the corner attracted her attention. There, like a forlorn little lamb, a tight rag about her mouth, her curls matted and damp, crouched Elsie Waldstricker. Instantly, Tess recognized her and her heart pumped with joy. Surely, her prayer had been answered! Here was her opportunity! The child was suffering, she could see that, but the very extremity of torture could hardly repay for the pain Boy'd endured. While Tess was pondering the penalties she'd inflict, a smile touched her lips. The frightened blue eyes searched the hard brown ones, but the child found no comfort or encouragement in the frowning face of the squatter girl.

"It's Waldstricker's brat," declared Jake, exultantly. "I were a snoopin' 'round Eb's place an' run on 'er down near the road by that there bunch of tamaracks. I says, 'What air the matter, Kid,' an' she says, 'I want my ma.' I says, 'Come along an' I'll git 'er fer ye,' an' the kid come jest like a lamb goes to the slaughterhouse." And Jake threw back his head and roared.

The other men joined in the grim laughter. After a minute, another voice sounded above the last ugly chuckles.

"Now, we got 'er, Tess, ye air to do anythin' ye want to with 'er."

Still, the blue eyes looked into the brown, and, still, Tessibel's heart raged its satisfaction. What were the squatters going to do with Waldstricker's daughter? The girl turned her head slowly and glanced at the row of dark men in their chairs against the wall. She cared nothing for the child on the floor, except that she was the one thing that Waldstricker loved best. Surely, to injure her would injure him! The little feet were tied and so were the small hands. This pleased Tess, too, for she remembered how they'd held Boy when he was imploring them to keep the big man away.

Waldstricker! Ungodly, wicked Waldstricker! His time had come! She'd go and leave the little girl with the squatters. Well she knew that a word from her and the baby would be seen no more.

"I guess when old Eb found out his kid were gone," grated Jake Brewer, "he got a wrench or two hisself."

The heavy voice brought Tess about.

"What'll we do with her?" She flung her hand toward the child in the corner.

"Yer say'll go, brat," put in Longman. "That rich duffer air had his way too long. Us squatters're a goin' to show 'im 'tain't so safe to ride rough shod over everybody."

"You're going to kill her?" asked Tessibel, dully.

"Yep," flung in Brewer, "if ye say so."

Mrs. Brewer was crying softly. Her husband turned fiercely upon her.

"Ma, here," said he, "air makin' some awful fuss over nothin'. She wants the kid took out of the state an' put some'ers. Us men says it air got to die."

"It air too awful, Tessie," sobbed Mrs. Brewer. "The baby ain't done nothin'."

Tessibel refrained from looking at the speaker. Her heart bled afresh at the woman's words. Boy hadn't done anything, either, but Waldstricker'd killed him. It was just, he should give his daughter for her son. It wouldn't bring Boy back, but surely he'd rest easier if Elsie joined him. The thought that her enemy would know the ache that tore her heart, was balm to her own heart. Yet something within her tugged her eyes to the baby on the floor. How Boy'd cried when the convulsive pain had tied his little limbs into cruel knots! She wanted to hear Elsie cry, too. The wails of her enemy's child might drive the shrieks of her own little one from memory.

"Take the rag off her mouth," said she, quickly.

"She'll cry like a sick cat, if ye do," warned a man.

Tess crossed the room to the corner where Elsie lay and kneeling by her, unfastened the cloth about her mouth. The baby held up her bound hands, blue and swollen from the tight ligature, and whimpered,

"Elsie's hands hurt."

The squatter girl had never voluntarily hurt a living thing. All her life quick sympathy had responded instinctively to helplessness and misery. Even the toads and bats knew her tender care. Waldstricker's child was to her, then, the most loathsome of breathing creatures. She might let the squatters kill her; she might even do it herself. But this was another thing! Face to face with the concrete case of pinching a baby's wrists, her instinct sent her fingers to the tight cords about the uplifted hands. Without conscious purpose, she, also, loosened the plump ankles. Elsie rolled in a whimpering, little heap on the floor.

"I want my Daddy," she whined.

"You can't have your Daddy," answered Tess. Lifting the child to her feet, she noted how like to Deforrest Young's were the little one's eyes.

"Your daddy air a dirty duffer," said Jake. "Give 'er a whack in the face, Tess."

He came forward from his place by the door and stopped near the two girls. The fisherman raised his own fist, and Tessibel moved a little aside. She regretted, now, that she'd loosened the little one's bonds or had done anything to relieve her suffering. She didn't care what they did to Waldstricker's girl. If they wanted to strike her, what affair was it of hers?

She turned her eyes upward, and, there, from among the rafters, she seemed to see Boy's face smiling down upon her. Love, shining from the dear eyes, radiated bliss and joy. How very sweet and peaceful he appeared! Then, Brewer's voice penetrated her consciousness. He was leaning over the rigid little girl.

"Brat," he was saying, "you air goin' to get the lickin' of yer life, an' don't ye ferget it."

"Pretty lady, help baby," mourned Elsie.

Tessibel shoved the squatter aside.

"Don't touch 'er yet," she said in low, distinct tones.

Jake took something from his pockets and thrust it into the girl's hands. It was a small, wiry, riding whip.

"It air the one her pa used on Boy," he muttered. "I stole it from 'is stable."

Tessibel uttered a cry and dropped the whip. The terrible scene in the lane, invoked by the speaker's words and the sight of the whip, poured into her mind a new flood of hate.

Yes! Elsie should be treated as her father had treated Boy! She stooped and picked up the whip. The men leaned forward, watching intently. Their heavy breathing and Ma Brewer's sobs mingled with the ticking of the clock and the storm's racket against the hut sides.

She studied the whip and tested its hissing pliability. That tip had stung Boy beyond endurance. The length of it had put him in his grave. Waldstricker's hands had tortured her son. She would make his daughter pay the reckoning. She drew a deep breath and raised her arm.

Elsie had crept unnoticed to her side, and as Tess glanced down, the child touched her hand with little fingers, marble-cold. The girl drew away from the suppliant touch, then, lowered the whip and stood considering the baby face.

"I hate you worse'n anyone in the whole world," she spat out.

"Then, lick 'er," growled Longman, and the other squatters muttered their approval.

Elsie dropped her head against Tessibel, and clung to her skirt.

"I want my—mover," she burst out, crying.

"Get even with Waldstricker, brat," said another voice.

Tess raised her arm and glancing along the uplifted whip, again, she looked into Boy's eyes, and, as she gazed, the little face in the rafters receded, grew dimmer.

She dropped the whip, and unmindful of the squatters, lifted her hands.

"Mummy's baby boy!" she called. The happy eyes faded last from her sight and it seemed to her they summoned her thence. A moment more, she stood shivering, staring into the shadows, and, then, she turned upon the dark-browed men.

"You said I could do anything I wanted to with 'er, eh?"

"Yep," Brewer assented. "Beat 'er, kill 'er, the more the better for us-uns."

"Then give me a blanket to wrap her in. I'll take her home where—where—Boy—died."

Brewer's lips fell apart and he laughed evilly.

"Good idee, brat," he said. "Ye can make it a thousand times worser for the kid if ye do.... Get a blanket, Ma."

Carefully, the girl wrapped the blanket around and around the little one. Elsie whimpered disconsolately but made no objection. Anything was better than being left with the men who tied her up. Lifting the bulky bundle, Tess started for the door, Jake picked up the whip from the floor, handed it to her.

"Ye're forgettin' somethin' ain't ye, brat? Ye'll be wantin' this, I'm thinkin'," he chuckled.

"I can't ever thank you all enough," she flung back hoarsely, tucking the whip into her coat pocket, "for giving me this chance at Waldstricker."

Longman got up and opened the door and Tess stepped out into the storm, carrying Waldstricker's daughter.

Deforrest Young was trying to calm his sister. Her frantic cries for her baby contrasted strangely with the icy despair of the other mother he'd tried to comfort. His heart, still sore from Boy's loss, bled in ready sympathy to his sister's mourning. He grasped Helen's hands which were tearing her hair.

"Don't!" he said. "We'll find her soon. By morning she'll be back home again. Ebenezer has nearly every man around looking for her, ... searching every barn and asking at every house.... Darling, do you think you could stay here with Madelene and let me go out, too?"

"Yes, yes, go, but Oh, God, I shall die if you don't find her!"

Hour after hour men on horseback and men on foot hunted through the hills and gullies for little Elsie Waldstricker.

It was almost twelve, when one by one Ebenezer's friends rode sorrowfully home after a useless search.

CHAPTER LI
THE CHRISTMAS GUEST

When Tessibel carried Elsie into the living room, she looked furtively about to assure herself that Professor Young had not returned during her absence. Only Andy should know! He would help her—he, too, loved Boy with all his soul. The little girl still in her arms, she hurried up the stairs to her own room, and after removing the blanket, placed her in a chair. Elsie stared about, too frightened and tired even to whimper. The whip fell to the floor and Tess picked it up. For a long time, she held it in her hand, meditatively trying its strength and suppleness while she glared at the child. Then she slipped quietly into the hall, still carrying the riding crop at her side.

"Andy," she called softly. "Is Mother Moll asleep?"

Andy came out of his own room.

"Yes, she's asleep. I been singin' to her most ever since you been gone. The old woman sure does like my singin', Tess." He waddled toward the girl and when he noticed the expression on her face,

"Somethin's happened," he ejaculated, "Anything the matter with Ma Brewer?"

Tessibel backed into her room and beckoned the dwarf onward by a movement of her head. After she'd shut the door, she pointed to the child with a hissing swish of the whip.

"Waldstricker's," she announced briefly. "The squatters stole her and gave her to me."

The sight of the little girl stopped Andy near the door. Instantly his alert mind pictured Waldstricker's present anxiety and the awful retribution he'd exact when he learned of her abduction. He had no idea as yet what Tess intended to do and her attitude revealed no hint. Personally, he was powerless because, to his physical weakness, the storm presented an unsurmountable obstacle. Except for Mother Moll, he was alone in the house with Tess and the Waldstricker child. Here was a terrible predicament. He'd already lost many years of his life, because he was present when Waldstricker's father was killed. He'd done what he could to avert that crime and paid a heavy penalty, for his interference. What to do, now, he didn't know. How to save the little one and protect Tess he couldn't guess. Casting frightened eyes first on the girl, then on the silent child, he crouched against the wall.

"What ye goin' to do with 'er?" he mumbled at last.... "What's the whip for?"

"I don't know yet," replied Tess, and she balanced the raw-hide in her hand. "This is the whip Waldstricker used.... Jake says to beat 'er like he beat Boy."

The cruel look on her face and the fire in her eyes frightened the dwarf. To him, she seemed almost insane.

"What'd ye tell 'em you'd do, Tess? Air you goin' to lick 'er?"

"I guess so. I didn't tell 'em for sure what I'd do."

She dropped the whip on a table and walked across the room to the window where she stood looking out into the night with unseeing eyes. Then, whirling on Andy, she clenched her fists and burst forth.

"She's the only thing Waldstricker loves! If I hurt her, don't I hurt him?"

"Sure, dear," the little man acquiesced. "Sure, it'd make 'im ... think a bit ... mebbe."

Elsie stirred uneasily, making the chair rock back and forth.

"Baby's hungry," she whimpered.

Tess threw off her wraps and flung out of the room. In the kitchen she stirred the fire and heated some milk and broke bread into it.

While she was gone, the dwarf made up his mind that now, if ever, he must prove the power of the faith Tess'd taught him. Motionless, but watching the baby, he reviewed the proofs he'd had in the shack and during his years with Tessibel on the hill. Surely, the hands stronger'n Waldstricker's had lost none of their protective power! So absorbed did he become, he hardly noticed when the girl came back, but he heard her say to Elsie,

"Here, cat! I hate you so, I could strangle you with it!"

Tess was kneeling beside the chair and he noted that her fingers fed the child carefully, and when a few warm drops of milk ran down the shaking baby chin, Tess took out her handkerchief and wiped the little face gently.

"Uncle Forrie won't be back tonight," he observed, after a while.

"Don't talk about him," gasped Tess. "I don't want to think of 'im."

"I don't see what we're goin' to do, brat," returned Andy miserably.

"I'll never give her back to Waldstricker, that's certain," Tess gritted. "I'll throw her out in the snow first. Let 'im find her, then, if he can."

Hunger satisfied, warm and snug, the tired baby smiled her thanks and fell asleep. After placing the bowl on the table, Tess drew the blankets about the little figure and stood up.

"Don't tell me not to do it," she said fiercely.

"I weren't going to, brat, dear," sighed the little man.

Then, the girl went to the window again. For what seemed hours to the dwarf, she stared silently into the winter night.

In her mind's eye she could see the high waves of the lake rolling and tumbling from hill to hill, and could outline the forest opposing its rugged weight to the tempest. Under the successive attacks of the gale, the loosened old joints of the house creaked their protests at the blizzard's roughness. The shrieking of the wind, the sharp rattle of the storm-driven snow against the glass, everything in the wild night without, responded to the conflict in her own breast.

She felt sorry, now, she hadn't left Elsie to the mercy of the squatters; but the thought of what they would have done to the child made her shudder.

"No, not that!" she groaned aloud.

"What'd ye say, brat?" asked Andy, without moving.

"Nothing," muttered the girl, and she maintained her position at the window. It was as though she were waiting for something she knew not what. In a sudden hush of the storm, she heard, faintly, the chimes in the library tower on College Hill.

Ah, yes, it was Christmas Eve! How Boy had looked forward to Santa Claus! How many little things she'd made for his stocking! She drew a long, sobbing breath. Boy wouldn't want any of her love-things any more.

She knew the chimes were playing,

"Peace on earth, good will to men."

Every Christmas Eve, at midnight, the bells rang out the sacred chorus. For many years, the music had completed her Christmas preparations. The annual message had always brought her inspiration and spiritual uplift. A brick, torn from its place in the chimney, tumbled down the roof. Its clatter rudely broke in upon the joyous refrain. So had Waldstricker destroyed her peace. No peace for her, no peace for him! She tried to fit the words to the chiming notes but without success.

"Peace on earth, good will to men."

Straining her eyes into the darkness, while the angels' message tugged at her heart strings, the overwrought girl saw another vision. Boy smiled upon her out of the storm. Ineffable happiness shone in the lovely face and steady eyes. Freed from mortal chance and change, she beheld him safe and secure in the everlasting now of eternity. The apprehension of Life's unalterable continuity—unfolding to her uplifted thought—destroyed the hopeless sense of separation and banished hate and anger from her heart. The compelling light of reawakened Love penetrated the inmost recesses of her spirit, and dissipated the shadows of discord and resentment. Peace possessed her. While the wonder of her healing held her motionless a little longer, the song she'd often sung to Boy at twilight came bubbling to her lips.

"In heavenly love abiding,
No change my heart shall fear."

Amazed, Andy stepped to her side. Gratitude for his darling's deliverance filled his heart. Turning to him, she put one arm around his shoulders. His throaty tenor joined the caroling soprano.

"The storm may roar without me,
My heart may low be laid,"

Above the raging of the wind, they lifted the triumphant refrain,

"But God is round about me,
How can I be dismayed?"

Moving into the brighter light of the shaded lamp, she seemed transfigured. All the strained hurt look was gone. The brown eyes expressed a deep brooding content and the bright face glowed with love.

"Tess, dear Tess," cried Andy, "you found 'im, didn't ye, Tess? It air wonderful."

"Boy lives forever!" the smiling lips ejaculated.

A tiny snore directed their attention to the little girl in the big rocking chair.

"Wrap her up, Andy," Tess directed. "I'm going to take her home."

Andy's shaking hands could hardly do the girl's bidding.

"It's an awful night, brat. Can you do it?"

"I'll get her back, all right," promised Tess, and she went out and down the stairs.

When she came back, Andy viewed her with amazement. She stood tall and slender before him, dressed like a stripling youth in one of Deforrest Young's riding suits, boots on her feet and a cap in her hand.

"I couldn't walk in a dress," she explained simply. "Help me wrap up my hair. I've got to go cross-lots."

Quickly, Andy fastened the shining curls under the big cap. Elsie was still asleep in the blankets. Tess picked her up and went out into the hall and down the stairs. When the dwarf opened the outside door, the stinging gale slashed at the open portal.

"God help my brat!" prayed Andy. Tess looked into his face a moment, and then strode away with her burden.

The lane was even harder to reach than it had been when she came from Brewer's. She labored to the tracks, and struck off across the fields. The wind stung her face with particles of ice, that cut like needles. A snow owl dropped from the gloom of a tree, poised a moment on wing, and stared at her with glittering, hungry eyes. Then, he fluttered upward and was gone. To force her way along took all her skill and experience with snow and storm. Unable to wade through the deep drifts by the fences, she had to roll over and over the tops of them. At such times, she put down the warmly wrapped baby and as she rolled, jerked her along through the snow. The bitter gale contested every inch of the way. The wind blew with such tremendous power in the cleared spaces that she could not face the biting blast, but again and again was compelled to creep over the icy crust, and pull the blanketed baby behind her.

When she reached the Trumansburg road, she could hardly breathe. The icy winds froze the sweat upon her toiling body and chilled the very marrow of her aching bones. The little one lay a dead weight in her arms. The ceaseless attacks of the cruel wind sapped her strength. She wanted to rest, but she remembered it wouldn't do to stop. Every step was a nightmare of impossible effort.

Suddenly down the road but a little way, a white light spread before her like a beckoning hand. Gathering her remaining strength for a final effort, she staggered toward it.

CHAPTER LII
THE STORM

The blizzard that raged in the Storm Country, the day before Christmas, was general through the East. Frederick Graves, on his way home for the Yuletide festivities, had been hampered and delayed by the storm. Indeed, the Lehigh train almost lost its way among the drifts, and instead of arriving about supper time, it came limping in late in the evening. When the much married man stepped off the train at the Ithaca depot, he moved slowly down the long platform toward the carriage stand. Waldstricker's coachman met him near the end of the station and relieved him of his suit case. One glance at

216

the newcomer's emaciated face, bearing the tell-tale spots of hectic red, told the man why Graves had been in the mountains.

"Mr. Waldstricker sent me down to meet you, sir," the servant told Frederick. "Your wife is up to our house and I'm to take you there. It's a bad night, but I'll get you through all right."

Frederick hesitated a moment before getting into the covered sleigh. He hadn't calculated to go to Waldstricker's. But the servant's next words decided him.

"You see, sir, Miss Elsie's lost. She went out this afternoon and hasn't been seen since; at least, hadn't been found when I left there about seven o'clock. Mr. Waldstricker's tearing around through the snow like a wild man and every one at Hayt's is out hunting for her."

Warmly wrapped, Frederick leaned back in the sleigh. While the horses plodded slowly against the storm up the long hill, he renewed his meditations and reviewed the course of action he'd determined to follow. His unsatisfied passion for Tess had grown more insistent during the months spent alone in the mountains. He'd written her many letters which had not been answered or returned to him. Indeed, he hadn't heard of or from her, directly or indirectly, for many weeks. Her failure to reply to his letters, as well as her hostile attitude, the last time he'd seen her, he ascribed to Young's influence. That Tessibel had become actually indifferent to him, he couldn't comprehend at all. Surely, the love she'd shown him couldn't die! The separation had only made his passion the greater. It might be that, through his neglect, her love had grown dormant, but nothing could destroy it. Freed from the lawyer's control, and in new surroundings, the well remembered sweetness of their short honeymoon would become a present experience.

He'd been able to secrete, when he'd been in charge of the California office, considerable sums of money. By careful management, he had increased his takings to an amount that would be a comfortable fortune for himself and the squatter girl. There had been no break between him and Madelene, but he had persuaded himself she would be glad to separate from him. It was too late to do anything about it tonight, though. Tomorrow, or the next day, he'd take his dear ones away.

As soon as they were settled in some distant city and were secure from the elder's wrath, he'd write Madelene. He chuckled grimly to himself at the thought of their rage when they learned of her anomalous position as his unmarried wife.

Then, his fancy played about the home he'd have. He pictured Tess moving through the rooms in the intimacies of domestic life. Almost, so vivid the picture his passion painted, he held her in his arms. He'd do wonderful things for the boy. He should have the best education possible! Lost in his dreams, the time slipped rapidly away, and he found himself, all at once, in front of his brother-in-law's brilliantly lighted home.

When he came into the great hall, Madelene hurried out of the library to meet him. She presented a cool cheek for the customary kiss of greeting and helped him out of his extra wraps.

"Take off your coat, dear, and come into the library," she urged. "The man told you about Elsie? But Eb's sure to find her. I'll see about something to eat while you're getting thawed out."

She bustled off to the kitchen and her husband went into the library and dropped into a chair before the grate.

When Madelene came back, she stopped by the table impressed, suddenly, by the pathetic weariness of his appearance. The change in him startled her and reawakened all the love she'd ever felt for him. In addition, there was, in her affection for the sick man, an element of maternal devotion, as though the unsatisfied desires of her empty arms demanded him. She crossed the room and seated herself on the arm of his chair.

"Fred, dear," she said, "you must have had an awful trip. Now, that I have you home again, I'm going to look after you, myself."

One after another, she noted the symptoms of decay and dissolution presented. His clothes no longer fitted but hung, bag-like, upon his emaciated frame. His shoulders were stooped and his chest sunken. The high linen collar he'd always been so particular about, no longer set close to a shapely neck, but sagged away from the taut cords below his bony jaw and chin. She lifted one of his hands and stared, through the tears that welled into her eyes, at the claw-like fingers resting in hers. Her husband's pitiful plight completely softened her heart and wiped away the memory of her jealousy and dissatisfaction with him. He needed her, now, and everything that love could do for him, she'd give him.

Lifting his fingers to her lips, they sat, thus, in silence, before the log fire until Frederick withdrew his hand and let it fall into his lap. Madelene shifted her position a little and slipped one arm around his neck. Although somewhat amazed at the demonstration, Frederick submitted to the caresses and found in them something of peace.

"I'm awfully sorry, Fred," she whispered, after the lapse of a few moments. "Let's begin again and do better. I do love you, so. Put your arms around me and tell me you'll forgive and forget."

Convinced that it was easier to humor his wife's soft mood than to risk the strain of repulsing her, Frederick slipped his arms around her and held her close.

"There's nothing to forgive, Madie," he muttered. "I've been awful selfish and I'm paying the penalty, that's all. You better let me go and forget me."

Supposing he referred to his approaching death, Madelene cried out sharply, in protest.

"No, no, Fred, you mustn't say such things. You make me feel like a murderess."

She wound her arms tightly around him and kissed him stormily.

"I love you and you love me," she continued. "That's all there is to it. We'll be happy, yet!"

For a few moments, she rested in his embrace, happier than she'd been in many a long day. Then, she disengaged herself and stood up.

"Come, dear," she smiled, "your supper is ready."

218

After he was seated at the table, she told him of the quarrel between her brother and his wife, of the loss of Elsie and the search then going on.

"Helen's most crazy," she concluded. "She's lying down, now. I gave her a powder and I think she's sleeping."

Frederick toyed with the food before him. He made occasional monosyllabic comments that kept the running fire of his wife's chatter going. Unable to pretend to eat more, he leaned back in his chair.

"I'm not much of an eater," he smiled, "but I've enjoyed your lunch very much."

The sound of steps on the stairs interrupted him.

"Hark, Fred!" his wife exclaimed. "That's Helen, now."

Together they left the dining room and went to the library, where Mrs. Waldstricker had preceded them.

Helen's distraught manner prevented anything like a conventional welcome to her brother-in-law. After Frederick had expressed his sympathy for her anxiety about Elsie and tried to quiet her fears, Madelene carried him off to his room. When she had seen to the details for his comfort, she returned to the library to share Mrs. Waldstricker's vigil.

Frederick found, when he was left alone, that he was in no mood for bed. He was too tired to sleep, too nervous to be quiet anywhere. It seemed to him as though there were some unusual quality in the air, some mysterious whispering to his inner consciousness. He felt vaguely excited. He tried to read but the words conveyed to him no meaning. To an extent never before experienced, possibly because he was again in the Storm Country, he wanted Tess. After a time, he heard the banging of the front door downstairs and confused cries in the hall, but paid little attention to them. In the silence that succeeded, the narrow walls of the bedroom became unbearably close. He'd go downstairs to the library. It might be he'd be able to rest in a chair before the log fire.

CHAPTER LIII
THE HAPPY DAY

Like the kindly eyes of a welcoming friend, the two great lights upon the posts of Waldstricker's gateway met Tessibel Skinner as she struggled between the tall stone pillars to the private driveway. In sheer fatigue, she allowed Elsie to slip to the snow and sank down beside her. Her heart sang with joy and thanksgiving. She was going to give Helen her dear, golden-haired baby. There was no thought, now, of her hatred for Ebenezer, only wondrous anticipation of his joy at receiving his little girl out of the storm. Through the white light, Tess could outline the rounded figure in the snow. Rhythmical breathing assured her the little one slept in security. Once more, Tess got to her feet and, once more, she gathered up the living bundle. She was almost at the end of her journey. The short rest had given her new strength, and when she got to the stone porch she was able to mount the steps, and move laboriously, almost breathlessly, to the door. Memories keenly bitter-sweet rushed over her. The last time she was on that spot she was going to sing for the master's friends. What numberless happenings loomed before her mental vision, happenings to her and to Waldstricker. She was too dazed, too cold, to consider them in sequence. In the confusion of her soul, only two things stood out distinctly. Her marriage to Frederick Graves and Boy's shining face when the assurance had come to her that he lived and would ever live. Then Deforrest Young—Ah, yes, she had forgotten him! In a little while she would see him, and he would take her back to Mother Moll and Andy.

She was directly in front of the heavy portal, now, and with one stiff set of fingers she laid hold of the handle and twisted the knob. The door opened under her pressure and displayed the long reception hall. A rush of warm air welcomed her, and she uttered one little cry and staggered across the threshold.

Helen Waldstricker and Madelene Graves were waiting wearily for some message from the searching party. Hours had passed that seemed like centuries strung into eternities, hours that had brought no word of the lost baby. Suddenly, Helen sat up as an unusual sound came to her ear.

"Did I hear something?" she asked. "I thought it was a voice."

"Only the wind," answered Madelene, drowsily.

The girl was thinking of Frederick and dreaming what their life might be, now that they were beginning again. Of course, he was ill—very ill, but she'd take him away and nurse him back to health again.

Then, another hoarse little sound forced its way through the closed door, and Helen got up and opened it. In that moment, when she looked the length of her spacious hall, the whole world took on a gladness unsurpassed. True, the door was open and the blizzard battled in and flung its snowflakes to her very feet; but across the doorway was a human body—Tessibel Skinner, and at her side, a rosebud face from which the blanket had fallen. Mrs. Waldstricker gave a glad cry and sprang forward. Tess tried to get up but failed. All she could do was to whisper,

"I've brought you back your baby." Then, she crumpled forward over Elsie Waldstricker in a forlorn, snow-covered heap.

By that time, Madelene was in the hall. She recognized Tessibel, and felt a keen thrill of biting pain. She had suffered much from this beautiful squatter girl, but she, also, realized that Tess had brought the child back to her distracted parents. Between them, the two women managed to carry the girl and baby into the library. Both were crying, and Elsie, too, now awake, was insisting that her mother "Rock baby."

To answer their hysterical questions, when her throat was so hoarse, was impossible for Tessibel.

"Let her rest right here, then," said Helen. "Mercy me! If the child hasn't some of Deforrest's clothes on. Let's take the baby upstairs, and, Madelene, you bring down some dry things for Tess.... Here, Tess, dear, let me wrap you in this for a few minutes."

Tessibel sank into the warm woolen robe Mrs. Waldstricker placed about her. Then, the two women went upstairs with wee Elsie. Tessibel felt the warmth from the fire permeate her whole being. She had suddenly grown so sleepy! It was delightful to be able to close her eyes and watch in perfect peace the figures of her dreams! Memories, deep and entrancing, engulfed her. Many forms passed to and fro across her vision. There were the dark faces of her squatter friends, then Ebenezer Waldstricker. Her lids lifted heavily, her eyes centering upon another face—a face which made her cry out and struggle to her feet with trembling desire to get away. Frederick Graves closed the door behind him softly and the girl noted how thin and sick he looked and that his twitching lips tried to smile her a welcome.

"Tessibel," was all he said. She sank back into the great chair, white and weak, her face strung with terror.

Frederick didn't pause to ask why she was there. It was enough to know she was near him, and he forgot all else; his recent promises to Madelene,—Ebenezer and his mother. Only, did he remember that his young squatter wife, the mother of his baby son, was near enough for him to take her in his arms. Ah, yes, he'd take her away, right then, just as he had planned to do so many, many times. He bent over her, his breath coming in labored, explosive gusts.

"Tess, darling," he murmured, much moved. "How wonderful you should be here tonight. Say something to me, sweetheart."

Tess attempted to push him from her. The touch of her hand thrilled him to his toes. How he would care for her—take her away from her squatter world, that stormy world filled with sorrow and pain! His world should know of her goodness, her loyalty and strength.

"I'll tell Ebenezer I'm your husband, Tessibel," he breathed in her ear. "Oh, my darling, what joy there is in store for us, what wonderful happiness—"

"No, no," cried Tess.

Then, again, he seized her hand, murmuring,

"Yes, yes, my love! I know it's hard to forgive me, but I've never loved any one but you. I didn't even try to care for Madelene. I couldn't. And, now, my precious—"

"Please, don't say such things," cried Tess. "I only came—"

She wrenched her fingers loose from his and through her own interruption, he went on quickly.

"Oh, my dearest, be a little kind to me. Forgive all I've done. No, I shan't let you go until you promise me something—you must listen!"

Driven on by the passion dominating his weak body, Frederick dragged her to him. Deforrest Young came into the girl's mind. How she loved him! She would not tolerate Graves' hateful embrace. She made a frantic struggle against the arms holding her.

"Frederick, Frederick!" she gasped.

"No, I won't listen, Tess," he cried. "I'm sorry enough for all I've done and I won't go away from you any more."

He crushed his mouth against her cheek. She should not baffle him thus. Now, that she was in his arms, his hot breath mingling with the warmth of hers, he was sure she could not resist him. Suddenly, she ceased to struggle—Limply, she lay against his breast. How he loved her! Frederick remembered with a thrilling, cutting desire that in those dear, olden days, she had been the sweeter and better part of himself. He had come back to fight for her, to take her and the boy away. Between passionate kisses, new resolves raced through his fevered mind. He told himself no barrier was strong enough to keep him from her. But he had forgotten Ebenezer Waldstricker. It was not until he heard a short, sharp ejaculation that he turned partly around. His brother-in-law was standing in the open door, clad in a long fur garment, his handsome face dark with terrible anger. Frederick dropped one arm, but tightened the other about the squatter girl.

Waldstricker could feel himself growing hot to the edge of his collar. At the sight of the girl he hated, a sudden fury took possession of him.

Tess became aware that the crimson churchman was looking her over from head to foot. She flushed painfully as she realized her masculine attire and thrust one hand behind her to loosen Frederick's arm, while with the other she steadied herself against a chair. She could not force herself to speak.

Waldstricker cleared his throat.

"How long has it been considered good taste, Mr. Graves," he demanded icily, "for a man to bring his mistress into his wife's home?"

Every word was perfectly articulated. Frederick grew deathly sick and sat down quickly, making a violent gesture with his hand. He wanted to deny Waldstricker's deadly insult, but he, suddenly, had no strength. How Tess came into the house he did not know. But he did know she was not there at his instigation. He could see that Waldstricker had hurt her beyond expression, too. She was staring at his brother-in-law, silent, as if frozen by his cold contempt.

Looking from one to the other, Ebenezer went on.

"It is my painful duty to ask Miss Skinner to leave this house ... now," said he.

Frederick managed to stand up and fling one protecting arm about the pale girl.

"Not in this terrible storm, Ebbie," he got out hoarsely.

"She came in the storm," returned the elder, "and I see no reason why she can't go back in it. She seems nicely dressed for such weather."

He went forward and seized her arm and quickly swung the slender form from Frederick's embrace. The girl was so dazed and weary she made no resistance. The powerful elder snatched up her coat and cap and roughly put them on her. Then, he pushed her ahead of him through the long reception hall. Tessibel had not spoken a word, nor did she speak when Waldstricker pulled open the door and, with a low growl, shoved her out into the darkness. When he returned to the library, he found Frederick stretched out upon the divan. A look of death had spread over his face, and the appeal in his eyes brought the elder forward quickly.

"Fred, what possessed you to bring that girl here?"

"I didn't. I found her here," murmured Frederick. "She'll die in the storm. Call her back, Eb, she'll die—"

"No, she won't," replied Waldstricker, gruffly, "and what's more I won't have her here. How she had a nerve to come at all, I can't see.... Where's Helen?"

"Upstairs with Madie, I guess," sighed Frederick.

"Poor Helen," groaned Ebenezer, moodily. "If I could only give her some news of Elsie. But I feel sure we'll have her home by morning."

"I hope so!" answered Frederick. Then, he raised on one elbow and spoke with difficulty. "Eb,—Ebenezer, I've something to tell you." The effort made him gasp for breath, and fall back.

"I guess I'm done for," he muttered.

"I'll call Madelene," said Waldstricker, turning quickly.

"No, no, Ebenezer. Come here. There, now, let me tell it. I—I—married Tessibel Skinner before I married Madelene."

Waldstricker staggered back. He was appalled at the death-stricken face opposite. He knew Frederick was dying, and had no doubt he was telling the simple truth. The world seemed turned upside down. Now, in the light of this new knowledge, he could see many things. He shuddered when he thought of Tessibel. He and his were in the squatter girl's power. What mercy could he or Madelene expect at her hands? The shame and disgrace would kill his sister. Had the Skinner girl come to his house to claim her husband?

At that moment, he heard Mrs. Graves' step on the stairs. He turned, intending to ask Frederick not to tell Madelene of his secret marriage, but quickly changed his mind. Frederick was too ill; the first thing was to relieve his suffering.

"Get some water," the elder commanded when she appeared in the doorway. "Fred's sick."

Madelene dropped the armful of clothes she held and fled to obey. When she came back, the young wife tenderly ministered to the dying man. Never before had he seemed so dear!

"I think we'd better call a doctor," said Ebenezer, and he went out.

For a moment, he felt impelled to go to his wife, to tell her how sorry he was for all his ugly moods. He blamed himself bitterly for Elsie's disappearance. If her mother had been home, the little girl would not have gone away.

In the servant's quarters, he gave orders that a doctor should be sent for. As he came back to the reception hall, he saw Helen looking down up him,—and she was smiling. How could she smile when the world was no longer glad, no longer beautiful? But a few hours before he had left her in tears, almost insane. Now she stood quietly, happily, as if joy unlimited were hers.

Mrs. Waldstricker placed her fingers on her lips.

"Come up, dear heart," she whispered.

223

Ebenezer mounted the stairs.

"I'm so miserable, Helen," he said. "I don't know what to say."

Helen stood on tiptoe and put one arm around his neck. She drew the massive head down and pressed her face to her husband's cheek.

"I don't think there's anything much to say," she said softly, "but to thank her for bringing her back."

Waldstricker straightened himself impatiently.

"Brought who back?" he demanded. "What do you mean? My God, Helen, the whole house has gone mad."

"Didn't you see Tessibel in the library?" Helen asked. "She—"

"Well, I should say I did," Ebenezer snorted, "and I cleared her out of there. How dare the impudent huzzy come to my house?"

"Great Heavens! Ebenezer!" exclaimed Helen. "She carried Elsie all the way from the lake!"

When these words fell upon Waldstricker's ears, he couldn't comprehend their import entirely. Elsie was found! But—Then, the full horror of his impetuous action burst upon him. The squatter girl had brought her back! Oh! Brute and fool that he was! He groaned and started to speak but his wife's voice interrupted him.

"Elsie's in here. Come see her! Won't you come, dear?"

The husband followed his wife through the nursery door, and as he centered his eyes upon the little bed in which his baby lay, life turned over for Ebenezer Waldstricker. He bent down and placed a reverent kiss upon the flushed, sleeping face. Then, he turned to Helen.

"I'm going to find Tessibel Skinner," he said, and, abruptly turning, went out.

Deforrest Young forced his foaming horse into Waldstricker's gateway and galloped up to the porch. It took him but one brief moment to fling himself to the ground, and up the steps into the house. Andy had told him Tess had gone to Ebenezer's with little Elsie. To know his darling was out in such a night nearly drove him mad. It hadn't taken him long to decide to go after her.

Meeting Ebenezer coming down the stairs, the lawyer's first demand was,

"Where's Tessibel—" and Waldstricker's reply came low and self-accusing.

"I sent her home, but, Deforrest, I didn't know about her bringing Elsie, then."

The lawyer didn't wait to ask anything more. Sick at heart and apprehensive, he went from the mansion and into his saddle and once more out between the great stone gate posts.

When the church elder pushed her through the doorway, into the winter night, Tessibel stood one moment swaying, back and forth, in an effort to steady her mind enough to plan her next action. She knew the long, wintry road to the lake must again be traversed before she could lie down and rest. A

224

sob came to her lips. She was so tired, so wearily unable to think. She had wanted to stay where it was warm, to wait until Deforrest came after her; but Mr. Waldstricker had almost thrown her into the snow. He had told her she couldn't stay, so, of course, she couldn't go back. How cruel he had looked and how strong his hands were! Once, some one had said Waldstricker's hands were stronger than God's. But, no, that wasn't true! She and Andy had proved it false. It was just that Waldstricker didn't like her; he didn't like any of the squatters, that's why he made her go away. Probably, he wasn't as glad as she thought he'd be to get his baby back. She drew her coat closer about her shoulders and stepped from the porch. The snow had ceased to fall, and the wind had quieted its turbulent raging. Very cold and quiet, the whole white night-world seemed. Of a sudden, the solitude was pierced by a hoarse sound from a sleepy fowl in the great barn below in the meadows. A night bird uttered a shrill, belligerent cry and sank to silence in his tree top. Tess turned her head sharply. These life-sounds out of the dusky beyond came from her friends. She wasn't afraid, only cold and chilled to her body's depths. Slowly, she went down the drifted driveway to the Trumansburg road and turned lakeward. She wondered if it was safe to return home cross-lots when she was so tired. It was shorter through the fields, but her legs seemed almost unable to bear up her weight in the deep snow.

At the top of the hill, opposite the Stebbins' homestead, she crouched down to rest a moment. Once, she thought she heard a horse. It might have been, but if so, the animal had passed, for no longer could she hear the thud of hoofs upon the snow road. Then, something touched her, and she turned her eyes upward. There, in the sky, was a moon—Was it her moon, that pale riding thing, taking its way through the white clouds? How cold it looked, and how cold it was! She shivered, settled a little in her coat and closed her eyes. A moment later, something brushed her hand. Slowly, the long red-brown lashes lifted and the red-brown eyes settled upon a figure bending over her, a figure, white like one of Mother Moll's conjured ghosts. Tessibel wanted to go to sleep. Why had the night stranger touched her, just then? Oh, she was out in the snow. A person ought never to lie down in the snow. Daddy Skinner had told her so many times. She mustn't sleep. She must get up instantly—but— her legs were too stiff, too difficult to move. Then, the figure faded slowly from her vision. How heavy her chest felt. A moonbeam lay slant-wise across it. That couldn't be so heavy, just a bit of the moonlight. Why, of course, something else was cradled in the white beam. Tess looked closer. A babe, as fair as an unblemished rose leaf, lay straight across her breast and considered her with unfathomable, interested eyes.... It was Boy—her Boy—she had him back again. Then, he hadn't been put in a little box in the ground beside Daddy Skinner. She managed to raise one arm and drop it across the small body. How lovely he was, this moonbeam babe, so white, so gentle and dark-haired.

Tessibel was warmer since he had come to her; her arms no longer trembled, but her legs seemed to have lost their desire to walk. She felt glad of that, too, because she was too tired to walk, anyway, and the baby was very sweet. Then, once more, a long shadow came between her and the moon and someone bent over her. Ah, 'twas Daddy Skinner, the same beloved, heavy humped-shoulders—the same precious face, and he was fondling the moon baby, and twice kissed her with tender, twitching lips. She smiled happily and moved a little in the snow. She tried to catch Daddy's hand, tried to call his dear name, but only a little sound came from her tightened, frozen throat. Then, smiling, Daddy Skinner went back to the moon, and Tess, drowsily, cuddled the white babbling closer, and went to sleep.

Deforrest Young brought his horse to an abrupt standstill. Had he heard a faint sound off there in the path? With a sudden spring, he dismounted. Over near the fence, he thought he had seen through the streak of light a human hand move upward and then sink into the snow. He paused a moment and shuddered. Had he lost his senses through the suffering the week had brought him? He shook himself and turned to his horse again. No silly vision should drag him across a snowdrift on such a night. He was going home to Tessibel. In hesitant quandary, he still stood staring west to the rail fence. Then, something impelled him to do the very thing he had decided would be fruitless.

One bound took him through the piles of snow at the side of the road. The lawyer bent down, his heart tightening with fear. A human being lay close to the fence. Young quickly pulled the face into the moonlight. The quiet, death-like form was Tessibel Skinner.

A huge sob tore its way from the lawyer's throat, and burst fiercely through his teeth. Was she dead, his dearest who had received evil, perhaps death, for the good she had done?

Above his head the limbs of a great tree sang their song of winter to the night. Deforrest remembered Tess had always loved the whispering of the wind. A low cry followed by words fell from his lips.

"Love air everywhere the hull time," he sobbed. "Oh, Love, Divine, merciful Love, protect my pretty child!"

In another sixty seconds he was pounding through the snow road toward the lake with a sleeping red-haired girl in his arms.

It was broad day when Tessibel opened her eyes. She lay for some time looking at the ceiling, then around her. She was alone in the room, yes, in her own room at the lake. Something had hurt her dreadfully, for even her arms ached so she couldn't move them. She wondered where Andy was, and Mother Moll, and if Deforrest were home.

She tried to sit up, but the pains shooting through her body made her content to be quiet.

Later, by a few moments, when Deforrest Young opened the door and stole in, she smiled wanly at him.

"My little girl's had a good sleep," he said softly, coming forward. Then, he took her hand and stood looking down upon her, his whole soul in his eyes.

"Tessibel," he hesitated, "do you remember what happened last night?"

Tess stared at him, a little pucker between her eyes. Last night? What about last night?

226

Oh, yes, she did remember. Elsie Waldstricker at the squatters; her own struggle through the snow to the mansion on the hill; how Waldstricker had turned her away.

"Yes, I remember," she whispered. "Did you find me, Uncle Forrie?"

Sudden tears swept away Young's vision. He nodded his head.

"And my brother-in-law's downstairs and wants to speak to you, Tessibel," said he.

Tess made a negative shake with her head, and a look of fear crept into her eyes.

Through Waldstricker's baby she had measured the height of God's love and forgiveness, and through his own unrighteous arrogancy she had plumbed the depths of human woe. She thrilled at the thought of little Elsie, of Helen's joy this birthday of Jesus, the tender teacher of her youth. She would have welcomed them, but she didn't want to see Waldstricker. By the crack of his whip, he had destroyed her love-life, as a bubble from a child's pipe is broken by a gust of wind. But before she could frame her refusal, Ebenezer Waldstricker appeared in the doorway. He came forward to the bed and held out his hand.

"Tessibel," he said huskily, "I'm bowed with shame before you. Child, I cannot tell you how sorry I am."

Tess took his hand without the slightest show of hesitation.

"I'm glad you've got your baby home," she murmured brokenly, and that was all.

A great emotion shook Ebenezer's soul as a giant oak is shaken in a mighty wind.

"Last night when I sent you away," he explained tensely, "I didn't know about your bringing her back. I appreciate, child, that's no excuse for me. Nor did I know, then, that you were married—"

He stopped, the bitter pain in his throat aching his voice into silence.

"Mr. Graves is dead," he whispered, "and my sister—"

"Oh, I'm so sorry for her, Mr. Waldstricker," cried Tess, struggling up.

Deforrest stepped forward to Ebenezer's side and supported her.

"Yes, you would be," the elder asserted. "Your heart is so tender.... My poor little Madelene—I fear the shock will kill her. She doesn't know yet that she really had no husband."

Tessibel's eyes grew large with astonishment. Then, Frederick had exonerated her to Waldstricker. Her eyes sought Deforrest Young's.

"Mr. Waldstricker told me downstairs about it, my darling," he said tenderly. "My brave little girl!"

Tess flashed a sudden look at Ebenezer.

"Mr. Waldstricker, I never want your sister to know she wasn't Fred—I mean Mr. Graves' wife," she told him. "It won't do any good and I'd rather you wouldn't tell her."

Then, surely, did Tess win from her proud enemy all the respect and reverence he could bestow on any human being. Ebenezer Waldstricker lowered his lips and pressed them to the slender hand he held.

"My dear, my dear," he moaned. "If I could only undo some of it."

227

Oh, how Tessibel wanted some of it undone, too. Her red head bowed slowly over his strong white hand.

"Oh, Mr. Waldstricker," she burst forth with sobs, "I want my little baby so bad, so awful bad."

Ebenezer uttered a groan and wheeling quickly went from the room.

Later in the day, when they were alone together, Deforrest sat down beside Tessibel.

"Now, you can tell me all about it, child," he said.

"Yes," whispered Tess; and she did. It was difficult to go back to those long, terrible years through which she had stumbled in shame and disgrace, but Deforrest Young upheld her by sympathy and encouragement. When the pitiful tale was finished, he bent forward and drew her into his arms.

"This Christmas is the happiest of my life," he murmured.

Hearing Andy on the stairs, they'd just taken more conventional attitudes when he burst into the room.

"Mother Moll's been havin' a seance all to herself," he grinned, "an' she says, there's a wedding ring hanging over the brat's head, an' she said to tell you, Uncle Forrie—" He paused, giggled a little and ended—"Red curls'll twist around your heart so close ye won't ever get away."

Then the dwarf toddled back upstairs, chuckling to himself.

"Mother Moll's right," whispered Deforrest into the small ear. "I'm the happiest man in all the world, Tessibel."